I0579506

Wild Thing

L. J. Kendall

The Leeth Dossier Vol. 1

**For my wife, Stella, who encouraged
me and helped me, through all the
happy years we had.**

National Library of Australia Cataloguing-in-Publication entry (pbk 2)

Creator: Kendall, L. J., author.

Title: Wild thing / L.J. Kendall.

ISBN: 9781925430004 (paperback)

Series: Kendall, L. J. Leeth dossier ; v. 1.

Subjects: Magic--Fiction.

 Science fiction.

Dewey Number: A823.4

Copyright © L. J. Kendall, 2015
Cover image copyright © Mirella de Santana

Girl image copyright © Pindyurin Vasily / Dollar Photo Club

Background image: https://depositphotos.com/49042221/
stock-photo-destroyed-tenement-house.html

Debris, dust: https://www.deviantart.com/roen911
Fire and effects: https://www.textures.com/

All characters and corporations in this story are fictional, and
any resemblance to real people or institutions is accidental.

Story length: 130,000 words
Typeface: Georgia 9pt

This book is available as an A or B-format paperback, and in ebook formats.

Original publication: A-format Oct 2017. (B-format, Jan 2016; ebook, Dec 2015)
Release version: 16. Aug 2022. (Removed one repeated word.)

ACKNOWLEDGMENTS

I want to thank my wife, Dr Stella St. Clair-Kendall, from her generous use of red ink in the first editing of this story, to putting up with the chagrin which followed, and for all her ongoing support and encouragement.

An especially deep thanks to Jon Marshall for his insight, support, and help in shaping Leeth over two decades.

Sincere thanks also to Dave at *www.thEditors.com* for his extraordinarily valuable insights and advice, and particularly for pushing me to tell more of Sara's time at the Institute: this book would not have existed on its own if not for that. If you see a problem, you've probably found a spot where I ignored his advice.

Another special thank you to Mirella de Santana, the artist who designed my cover. You can see more of her wonderful art at: *www.mirellasantana.com.br*

And last but not least, I wish to thank the Online Writing Workshop for Science Fiction, Fantasy and Horror site, *sf-f.onlinewritingworkshop.com*, and all the writers who reviewed chapters, there – more than a few years ago.

Thank you, all.

I should add: a special thanks to Louise Harris, who gifted me with a free proofreading; but any errors remaining are my own work, not the fault of anyone who has helped me.

Note: there's a special offer if you're 1st to inform me of errors in the text – see *Publishing, 2015* for details.

Novels by L. J. Kendall

The Leeth Dossier:

Wild Thing

Harsh Lessons

Shadow Hunt

Violent Causes

Leeth Ascending:
Lost Girl

(Cold Heart)

...

Contents

PROLOGUE

Chief High Cloud crouched, silent, hands still trembling in shock. Trying to understand it all: the vision; the bonfire's snuffing; the hungering cold.

One small ember struggled in the frozen ashes, and blowing gently he nursed the fire back to life, taking comfort from the simple act. Firelight breathed traces of warmth and hope back into the shocked faces around him. Their desperate expressions pressed on him like the hopes of distressed children, eager to believe a parent could somehow make everything all right.

There would be no way to make this right, he knew.

Behind him, beyond the gathering of mis-matched people, the sun's last light crowned their geodesic domes in a glow of burnt orange. Even as he watched, the tallest slid into darkness. *Not an omen,* he told himself, as the flame took tentative hold.

But he could delay no longer. Old bones, weakened from too many zero-gravity months in years long past, protested as he stood to speak into the wretched stillness.

"Let us talk. We can not accept one whose Way is murder. Human Beings should kill only for food, respecting our brother creatures for the gift of their life. We cannot open our hearts to the woman in the vision we have just seen.

"The rules of the Sky Corn community are clear. The child must be sent from us. She must leave her name. She must take nothing. Let her go to a people for whom killing and destruction is a part of their culture: she will go to the *Wasichus.* Let her killings happen there, just as we saw, rather than among the People. If one day she sees the evil of her actions; if the Great Spirit moves her, and she proves herself worthy, then perhaps may she rejoin our community." He stopped and waited, letting any other speak who wished to.

Abruptly, the girl's mother rose to her feet. Black hair cascaded down her back like liquid, one hand briefly brushing the gentle curve of her belly for reassurance, yet something – the way she stood, the expression on her face – made her seem dangerous. Her husband flowed swiftly upright behind her, placing large steadying hands on her shoulders. His touch seemed to calm her; allowed words to come. "I would speak."

The chief looked from her to the shaman who still stood leaden with sadness. The wise-woman slowly lifted her head and nodded. He turned back to the child's mother. "The Sky Corn community will hear Shining Hair."

Her words leaped forth. "My daughter would never do these things! She is a good child. Good, and brave. The young woman in the vision was not Happy Mouth." She looked around at the doubting faces. "You all know my daughter: she is loving, not cruel.

"My husband and I follow your ways. We teach them to our child. We *know* that violence is wrong. Deeply. It's why we came to you – not just for your vision for the future, or your honoring of the past. We are teaching her to respect life, to reject violence. You know this is true." She stopped, meeting the eyes of each of the solemn faces, hating the note of desperation which had crept into her voice.

Her voice sank, against her will, fighting fear for her daughter and shame for herself. "Aunt White-Eyes' vision was not of the future, but the past. She saw me, from my bad days. You have all mistaken my daughter for me."

A mutter ran through the patchwork tribe. Her husband's head was bent, now, his face impossible to read. But his hands, still resting on his wife's shoulders, tightened involuntarily at her words.

The wise-woman shook her head sadly. "No. All saw. It was not you, Shining Hair. You speak with love, but not with truth."

The vision was too fresh for denial. Raw, red meat, *pulsing* bloody in a delicate hand. Then flames, one girl dancing like a scythe through panicked leather-clad bikers while another fed....

Finally, the twisted scene with its inhuman cold. Cold

which had, terrifyingly, reached for them all *through* the flames, scrabbling for purchase in the watchers until the wise-woman broke the link. Leaving a circle of stunned faces around a bonfire suddenly black, cold, and dead.

All had thought their hearts equal to the reluctantly-shared vision. But that vision had been far worse than they had feared.

The child's mother pushed herself away from her husband. "In the vision, her killing was in a city. Perhaps if we keep her amongst us, the vision can be broken."

"Our shaman's visions have always revealed truth," the chief answered, "even for those who tried to change the future foreseen. Keeping your daughter would be to nurture one who will be a murderer. Should she stay here, maybe she would bring her killings here, to our small community.

"But worse: might not such attention reveal your presence to those who hunt you?"

At those words, all present stiffened.

"But now we know this future we can raise our daughter so it won't happen!"

"How? You do not know what will make Happy Mouth that way, so you can not know what to change," the Chief said. "We have seen the natural future for your child. Would you seek to change her true nature? To bend her?"

"So you're saying it's natural for her to kill? That it's *all right*? That goes against everything the Sky Corn community is supposed to stand for!"

"Shining Hair, you have much to learn." He looked sad. "Though a Way is wrong, we do not try to force others to our path. That Way is wrong too, and most treacherous. A coyote is not a coyote without its teeth. But we will not have her here, now we know her Way." He stopped again and waited, watching all the faces.

Only silence answered him this time.

"Then it is so." He looked back to the parents, troubled. "And you, Shining Hair and Crazy Bee, will you hold to your vows and stay? Or will you go with your daughter, and join in her killings?"

The mother glared back. "We will go with our daughter and *prevent* her killings."

"But if you leave, and they find you – what then? When you sought refuge here, did you not say his vengeance would be terrible, on both you and all who had harbored you? Did you not both give your word to do nothing to draw that vengeance down on any here?"

The woman said nothing. Simply stood, with fists clenched.

The Chief turned to the tired shaman. "White-Eyes Woman, will you seek their future, should they leave with their daughter?"

The shaman nodded, slowly. Nothing could be worse than the future she'd already seen tonight. She and the Chief looked back at the fire-pit – once warm and welcoming, now cold and somehow hostile, the new flame still struggling.

The Chief beckoned. "Come, we will use my tepee."

In ones and twos, then, the council disbanded. Shining Hair stalked behind the Chief, hardly aware of Crazy Bee's larger hand gripping hers as they followed the chieftain to his hide-lined, geodesic 'tepee.'

The wise-woman, crouching before the fire pit and remembering the hungering cold, struggled still to understand. A chilling awfulness lay beneath the impossible quenching of the bonfire. *What* had killed the blaze?

Finally, heavily, age aching in every joint, she rose to follow the girl's parents.

-

The semi-permanent structure used traditionally-tanned hide, bonded to interlocking Bucky-struts earned from the community's expertise in sustainable orbital technologies. Inside, the four sat while the Chief kindled a small ritual flame.

The shaman was surprised by how easily the new vision flowed; and as the monstrous scene smashed through her, *ended* it just as quickly, amidst horrified cries.

All four reeled from the image now scorching their retinas: the community's holding, a wasteland scoured black. Nothing but drifting ash, mile after mile. Recognizably the same trees and buildings, but reduced to charcoal spars and triangular charred skeletons. *In the same positions they were today.*

"Fuel-air bomb." Crazy Bee's analysis was reflex; his tone, hushed disbelief. "Maybe a tac nuke."

Still the woman denied. "No. Once we leave... even if

they found us, we would never tell them of your aid. This can't be-"

The shaman interrupted. "These people who seek you: what would you *not* do, should they threaten your daughter?"

The man and the woman flinched.

The wise-woman did not relent, though she took no pleasure from her words; her voice sinking to a whisper. "Or, might they not even seek to force the truth from your four-year-old child herself?"

The parents froze in horror, knowing the answer. Imagining what he would *enjoy* doing to their daughter.

"Which future do you choose, Shining Hair?" the Chief asked. "Which future for your daughter, and for us all?"

The two stood motionless for a long time, the man's arms close around his wife's shoulders. At last his head bowed forward.

Shining Hair stared across the small fire into the milky eyes of the wise-woman. "No. It's not true." The woman's long black hair whipped in angry denial. "You can't see the future. No one can. I reject this prophecy. Either you let my daughter stay, or we take her and leave."

The Chief shook his head. "We cannot let your daughter stay. If we are not true to ourselves, our community poisons itself. She must leave. And if you leave with her...." His head moved left, right, refusing that fate. "We have just *seen* the doom which that choice would bring to all who remain here."

She made a cutting gesture with her hand, chopping off the Chief's words. "No. Aunt White-Eyes is mistaken. Or deceived. Come on, Crazy Bee, we're going."

"Shining Hair- *'Lita*- wait, let's think this through. Maybe...."

Crazy Bee faltered to a stop at the look his wife turned on him. She stared at him as if he had just transformed into a complete stranger. Somehow, that expression unlocked his voice, and he spoke from the heart. "I love you, 'Lita. I love our daughter. But I know we've seen the truth tonight, in these visions. I don't understand – not the how, not the why – but I *believe*. You do too, I know you do."

Her lips thinned into familiar stubborn lines, and he found his fists clenching helplessly. Still he tried. "'Lita, we gave our words when we came here; when the Sky Corn took us in despite the danger we brought to them all. Remember that night: every member agreed. *Every member.* And in return we made them a vow. You can't break that vow."

His wife stared at him, her shoulders hunched. "So... what: you'll *stay* here, 'B? What about your *marriage* vows?"

Her jaw set grimly. "Right-"

"No, 'Lita. No. I will stay here, and so will you. Only Happy Mouth will leave."

She looked at him as if he'd gone mad. Or she had. She shook her head, words briefly failing her. Took one step back. "No," she whispered, before her voice strengthened. "No, 'B, I'm leaving, and I'm taking Happy Mouth with me. With or without you."

"No, 'Lita. You're not."

She stiffened at those words. Then, strangely, *relaxed.* Her posture subtly shifted. Loosened. An air of danger suddenly draped her once again, like a dark shroud hovering at her shoulders. "You won't stop me."

The man's face looked carved from the Earth itself. "But I'm the only one here who can. So I must. Please, 'Lita, I'm begging, don't do this! Don't risk the safety of our unborn child. *I love you.* You think I *want* to abandon her? That's crazy! But our other choices are *wrong!* And I'll be betraying you, and me – all we have and all we hope for – if I let you do this!" His eyes locked on hers, *willing* her to see what he could. "As deep as my soul, I know if you ignore this vision, you doom us and everyone here."

Her slim hands moved across her belly, instinctively protective, and for those seconds, as her gaze turned inward, he dared to hope his words had reached her.

Then her hands fell away, her expression darkened, and she turned sideways to him, rolling her shoulders as she took a defensive stance. "Never."

From behind, he heard the shaman mutter – he recognized the beginnings of a spell – and he spoke without looking around. "Aunt, even if you *do* succeed in putting her to sleep, you will lose her trust forever. It must be me who stops her. Who makes her see."

His wife was abruptly in motion, flashing forwards, lit

by the warm light of the fire in the enclosed space. He rocked his head to one side to avoid her palm strike, right hand rising to deflect her left, anticipating the simultaneous knee strike, sliding his thigh forward and into it, diverting the force a moment before it could blossom. Her left leg flashed up... to those watching, it seemed the two danced: a strangely-accelerated series of moves and powerful countermoves choreographed in fury and love.

The Chief's heart ached in his chest as he watched Shining Hair, for the first time in over four years, forsake her vow of non-violence; the mother in her literally fighting against the impossible choice suddenly confronting her.

Husband and wife contested their daughter's fate with frightening intensity, feet weaving intimately in and around each other, body jolting body, limbs blurring and meeting, the impact of flesh on flesh jarring the man time after time, rocking him.

As they fought, the Chieftain felt a chill run through him. He was no expert in combat; was very far from a martial artist; and the two *had* been frank about their past. But perhaps in their brevity, he had underestimated the depths of their capabilities. The fight stopped making sense to him as the pace increased, the two bodies locking together in a series of blows, grips, twisting moves and blindingly-fast strikes from hands, fists, knees, elbows, which he simply could not follow. Dirt flew from the floor as the two spun and wove together. He felt he watched two tigers fighting, inches from him. Skin prickling, he had to stiffen his spine.

Time and again, Crazy Bee jerked or flinched, often only the ugly sound of a hammer blow on meat signaling a successful stroke. One of 'Bee's eyes was swelling, his cheek already darkening with a livid bruise. A *crack* of bone and a sharp gasp from the male warrior, and Shining Hair spun away, rebounding from the powerful impact of her elbow into his ribs. For a moment, Crazy Bee paused, stunned, while Shining Hair completed her spin. This time the Chief saw her right leg flash out against her husband's left knee, an audible snap as ligaments broke. The man buckled.

Instead of moving away, though, the woman flowed instantly forward again, sobbing as if she were the one who'd been injured. The man *had to* collapse; but instead, somehow he turned, sliding behind her as if he'd expected the maneuver. Or as if she had deliberately left herself open. One massive forearm suddenly clamped across her throat while his other curved lower, above her waist, pulling her against him to trap her there, and for just a moment, she sagged into him as if relieved. He murmured soft words even as his forearm tightened against her throat.

No one moved.

But then she snarled, in denial: *still* refusing the truth. One tautly-muscled leg flashed vertically upward to smash against Crazy Bee's face with the impact of a club, rocking his head backward as blood gushed from his now-broken nose.

But his hold did not falter, his grip did not shift. Tipping himself backwards, he fell heavily to the floor, absorbing the impact as best he could.

Shining Hair smashed her head back into her husband's chest, each impact sounding like a mallet blow, screaming her defiance and desperation. He withstood each strike, murmuring still in her ear, tears running from his craggy face as he carefully tightened his grip across her neck, silencing her cries even as those cries changed to panicked attempts to draw breath. She struggled harder, the fury of her smaller body arching his own much larger form forward into a bow.

But still his grip did not ease, and slowly her movements weakened even as the desperation in her cries grew, and his tears flowed harder, as if his soul broke.

Long seconds passed as her struggles faltered; and, finally, ceased. She fell still. For a few seconds more he held his grip, eyes closed, panting but alert even now for a trick: he knew his wife. But at last he released his arm from her neck and awkwardly slid her gently to the ground, eyes now imploring the shaman. "Please. Aunt White-Eyes. Check my wife. Check our unborn child."

The blind woman moved forward, the strangely beautiful dance of terror and love that she had sensed, now settled into an awful pool of peace – and of terrible fear. The blood dripping from his nose to the floor shone in her Sight like flares of molten fire.

Tears flowed freely down her own face as she moved forward to sink beside the man, her hands moving surely over the woman, dreading what she would find – but soon amazed at how little injury Shining Hair had suffered in the furious melee. She sensed the small life within, shaken and frightened, and sent it soothing waves of reassurance, of calm.

"She is well. *Both* are well. She will wake, soon. But what then, Crazy Bee?"

"Then: I *hope*."

-

She swam up into consciousness with a strange reluctance, as if not wanting–

Remembering, ashamed, she gasped, leaping to full awareness, lurching upward, her eyes darting.

She lay in their own tepee-dome, while her husband sat calmly across from her, sketch-pad in his lap, head down as he drew. One leg stretched out awkwardly before him as if his kneecap ached, and one of his eyes was swollen shut. His whole face was bruised and purpled. Her eyes widened in shock. *I did all that!* she suddenly remembered.

One hand flashed to her belly, and the relief that flooded through her almost made her groan. But her – other? – daughter?

They've taken Happy Mouth!

She lunged forward, grabbing the pad from her husband's lap; furious with herself, furious that *he* could be sketching–

Oh.

A long dark line now scored his drawing, but the scene struck her with the same force, the same sickening blow to the belly as when the shaman had shared it earlier.

His pencil sketch showed the once-green lands of the Sky Corn community as the burned and charred wasteland of the second vision: charcoal spears that had once been pines, now sharp black bones extruded from the earth; blackened triangular spars, the skeletons of scorched geodesic tepees. He'd been partway through drawing a carbonized skeleton. A very small carbonized skeleton. Her breath caught in her throat, and she flung the sketch pad away and rose, stalking to the entry-way.

She paused. "Where is-?"

"When I asked you to marry me," his quiet words from behind her somehow stopped her own. He continued in that same gentle voice. The same love in the tone as when he had fought her, when he'd been forced to risk their unborn child's safety by rendering her unconscious. "I promised to respect your wishes. Today, for the first time in our lives together I could not do that. If you wish me to leave, to find a different tent, then... then I will." He pulled angrily at his hair, like he wanted to tear it out. "Just *think*. That's all I ask.

"*Think*. I swear, 'Lita, in my bones: I know if we do as your heart begs you to do – as mine begs me! – within two weeks the Sky Corn will be a sea of ash blowing in the wind, and Fate alone knows what sick vengeance he'll visit on us. And on Happy Mouth, to hurt us best. *He won't kill us*, 'Lita. He has people surgically altered for his amusement! Remember his own *daughter*?"

"Have you finished, 'B?" She refused the truth, turning away. "Good. Then I'm going to find where they've sent our daughter, and get her back. With or without your help. I'll-"

"She's not gone, yet. They're waiting for your okay."
"*What?*"

"I stand by my vows to you, Shining Hair. I always have, and I always will. If you go, I will go too."

"Then what are we waiting for?" Refusing the doubts; refusing to even acknowledge them.

Her husband unfolded without his normal fluid grace as he stood, then limped across the small living space to his splayed-open artist's pad. Picking it up, favoring his left side, he limped back to his wife still standing at the doorway. A part of her, an old and well-trained part, realized he must have had some healing already, or he would not have been able to use his knee at all.

Flipping to the nearly-completed sketch, he held it up before her as he moved behind her, pulling her into his embrace. It was a measure of the depth of their understanding that she knew this was no ploy. There would be no more choke holds.

"Just look. And listen to me.

"The Chief told the second vision to the whole tribe. And they understood. Yet they also understood your reaction. And they decided. They have already risked all their lives, all their dreams for the future, to aid us once. And they spoke again, and decided to entrust all they have and all they strive for, to us, again. To *you*. To your decision.

"It's your decision, Shining Hair. Let Happy Mouth be taken away. Or take her, and go.

"They leave it in your hands.

"They ask *only* that you to take time to think, and feel, before you decide."

Neither spoke, and abruptly, he felt the tension in her shatter. She collapsed into his arms, an awful keening wrenched from deep within her. Like she were dying. Or their daughter was.

He made the call.

Outside their tepee, the wise-woman waited for them both. As the mother moved to step angrily past, the blind shaman spoke. Softly. "Stay. Do not say goodbye to her."

"What? That's crazy! She's only *four years old*."

"Will she suffer more knowing her parents gave her away, or if she can tell herself she was taken against their will?"

Shining Hair's fists clenched till the knuckles glowed white. Then slowly, she nodded.

"Shining Hair. Crazy Bee."

Their desperate gazes snapped from each other, to the wise-woman's sad, blind eyes.

"Our Way is not violence. We do not believe that death and bloodshed is ever a solution."

They simply stared grimly back, growing still more angry at her, she Saw. "Yet my second vision speaks of a powerful evil that moves unopposed. Perhaps there is yet a reason for your daughter's terrible Way, a reason we are not wise enough to see."

By their auras, the shaman saw her tiny seed of hope take root. And at that moment, also sensed the child's painting clutched in the woman's hand, wisps of love curled through the paper: the sense of a child standing between her father and mother, the adult female figure gently swelling with the promise of life.

-

"Why are we going this way? Where's mama?"

Not answering, the woman continued leading the child to the edge of the village. A land skiff sat rigged and ready in the moon's clear light, the young warrior chosen to remove the child scowling beside it.

"Oh! Look there, a land boat. And the Chief! Will *he* give me my growed-up name?"

The shaman had already been and gone, summoning a wind spirit to fill the sails of the small land yacht. The woman and the girl reached the Chief, and the child risked a smile when they stopped.

He did not smile in return. "Remember these words, child: a Human Being kills only for food."

Confused, she repeated them solemnly. She'd seen other naming ceremonies, for her older friends, and knew this was different. More serious somehow.

She waited, a little bit scared. Maybe she wasn't going to get a Bear name after all?

The Chief's large hand clasped around hers, leading her to the land skiff where Aunt High Mirror and one of the young hunters, Walks Straight, stood. The adults didn't smile. She looked around. Where were her parents?

When they stopped, the Chief turned her to each of the four directions, then to the sky, and finally to the earth. To each he spoke the words that took away her Child name, giving it into the care of those Powers. When she had no name, he turned the girl child to him. He looked tired. Old.

The girl put one small hand to his cheek, trying to cheer him up. But the gesture only seemed to make him sadder.

"You are no longer Happy Mouth." The ritual words fell heavily from his lips. "You are no longer alive to the Sky Corn community. Your parents are dead to you."

Her eyes widened, and her hand fell away.

"You go now to the white man's lands, so you will take a name for the white man. You will take the name *Sara*."

She shook her head once, slowly, then stood stunned, shocked into immobility, trying to absorb the meaning of the Chief's words.

He handed the young hunter a folded white paper and reminded him what to do when they reached the lands of the *Wasichus*. Walks Straight nodded curtly, then circled the skiff, checking the brakes and squeezing its tires in a final inspection before leaping up and over the side. Swinging past the rigging lines, he hoisted the mainsail while the Chief lifted the girl and placed her on a seat.

"Where's mama?"

"Your mother is dead to you now, Sara. We can not have killers here."

She struggled to understand.

Walks Straight checked the reef in the sails. Releasing the brakes as he eased out the boom, cloth billowed taut as it caught the wind and the skiff pulled away, jolting over the rough ground and quickly gathering speed.

"I didn't kill anything, grandfather!" Sara screamed back, her small face straining over the lip of the hull.

Drops of moonlit silver glistened on suddenly-pale cheeks, sparkling faintly as Night swallowed the land yacht.

"But you will, Sara. You will," he whispered sadly into the wind.

PART I

(Four years later)

CHAPTER 1

Enough, thought Dr Alex Harmon, and draped the spell delicately over the Mother Superior's mind. Paging through student records in the grim office of the orphanage, he watched from the corner of his eye, amused, as she forced her teeth to unclench – again. But now, he heard her outraged thoughts as though they echoed in his own mind: «*Browsing through my children's files like they're items in a shopping catalog!*»

Dust motes glimmered in the watery sunlight, drifting through the room's still air. Seated at the other side of her heavy oaken desk, he felt the weight of the nun's stare.

He looked up, unable to keep the hint of a smile from his lips. "Really, sister, this would have been so much easier for us both if you kept your records online."

"My first concern is caring for my children, Dr Harmon," she snapped. With his spell still running, he also picked up the following thought: «*Not in making it easy for corporations to examine them.*»

He raised one eyebrow, puzzled by her mis-identification. But all he said aloud was "None of your charges seem to have tested positive for any sign of Unfolding. Statistically, I would-"

"You won't find anyone with magical potential in the orphanage records."

He was no longer amused. "Sister, I did ask to see the records of *all* the children here. If you recheck the papers I presented, you'll see that I have permission-"

"You won't find anyone with magical potential because there *are* none, doctor. Any that test positive are auctioned off to corporations like Asgard or Medigene by the government. Or taken by the government itself."

"Really: *auctioned* off?"

"That's what the 'normal procedure' amounts to, yes," she snapped.

About to reply, a sudden thought made him pause: was *this* why his research request had been granted – they thought there was nothing *to* grant? Still, if his theories were correct, he only needed to find a child with just a bud of potential, to be able to Unfold them into full magical ability. Calmly, he returned to studying the orphanage records.

He noted the nun slide the second form in front of her

again, and heard the echo of her thoughts as she re-read the paragraph which had disturbed her so much. *«The adoption of (blank) by Dr Alexander Harmon has been duly investigated and approved... custody being granted herewith.»*

When he'd presented her with his documentation he'd watched, at first appalled by the certainty with which she had challenged its validity with Govnet; but soon delighted by her dismay when that challenge had been rejected.

Even then, though, she had refused to accept the validity of the automated response. "After all, 'Doctor,' you could have hacked the government site," she had stated, then insisted on making a direct link to someone in Child Affairs. So they had both had to suffer through a period of mind-numbing '20's German 'neurock' hold-music interspersed with jarring reminders that 'a service representative will be available shortly.' A period during which she refused to allow him to begin examining her records. Eventually, however, she spoke to a pleasant young woman who assured her that, no, everything was perfectly in order. One minute later Mother Superior Mary Provïc had disconnected, and reluctantly handed over her *paper* records.

Apparently, a bureaucratic bungle of enormous proportions had occurred. But it would be all for naught unless—

Ah-ha! Extracting some papers from the file, he leaned back in his chair. For a moment he met the nun's gaze, keeping the triumph from his face as he settled back to examine his find.

He kept part of his attention on her thoughts – highly illegal, but such an advantage in negotiations. *«Sara,»* she was thinking. *«Of course. Full of energy, always in trouble – yet beyond that, something somehow odd about her. Yes, of course it would be Sara.»*

Harmon looked up, calmly meeting the Mother Superior's cold stare, and began prodding. "Well, sister, I think I may have found... who I came for. I'm sure you won't mind having Sara sent for?"

He searched the folder he held for a surname, but found none. "Just 'Sara,' sister? Isn't that a little unorthodox?"

"It was clearly indicated on the paperwork provided by her people that 'Sara' was her full and complete name."

Her annoyance at that unorthodoxy was clear in both her body language and her thoughts.

Without shifting her glare from him she stabbed a button on her ancient intercom. "Sister Augustine: please have someone bring Sara to me as soon as possible."

A brief electrical crackle accompanied the response. "Umm. I'll see what I can do."

Harmon raised one eyebrow at the doubt in Sister Augustine's voice, but the mother superior pointedly ignored him, swinging her chair around and shifting her gaze to the decayed dockyard outside the window. Harmon saw her shoulders relax as she turned. *«Let's see how* you *deal with our attic-haunting little eight-year-old demon.»*

A few minutes passed.

"Of course, I *will* need some time alone with Sara, before I can make my final decision," he said.

The mother superior swung back round to him, taking a great deal of satisfaction in her reply. "*Not* while the young lady is in *my* care you won't. Out of the question, Dr Harmon."

Sensing she wanted a fight, Harmon simply inclined his head and smiled. "As you wish, sister." Steepling his fingers he settled back into his chair, while she glared at him once more before turning her back to look out the window.

Silence descended. It hung heavily in the room as uncomfortable minutes inched past.

Ten minutes passed; fifteen. At last he could no longer contain his impatience. "Sister, I am a very busy man. Is there a problem? Do you not know where your charges are?"

The nun spun her chair back to face him. "Please don't let us keep you here, doctor. I'm sure there are other orphanages in which to do your *shopping*."

Needled, but hiding the fact, he sat back in his chair. "I can wait. I was simply expressing surprise that you are having such difficulty in locating one of your charges."

"As I said, please don't let us detain you."

He shook his head, not deigning to answer. He would be doing the girl a favor, removing her from such ineptitude.

Silence descended again. The nun made a show of taking back her records and re-filing them. Harmon hardly needed the telepathy spell to tell she disliked being in a position of weakness, and her thoughts confirmed his assessment. *«Really, the girl is impossible! Perhaps this is for the best, after all.»*

Harmon began tapping a slow beat on the arm of his chair, pretending to be unaware of just how much it irritated her.

At last there was a gentle rap on the door, before it burst open an instant later. A small, colorfully dressed girl arrowed into the room, flapping her arms and startling him backward in his chair.

"AAAARK! AARK!" She raced once around him before coming to a halt and folding her hands under her armpits. She glared at him, then cocked her head to one side: "Aaark." Long black hair, a round face. Alert amber-flecked eyes, brown skin, freshly-grubby pink jeans.

The mother superior's open mouth closed, and she collected herself with a visible effort. "Sara! If you don't start behaving like a young lady rather than some crazy thing, *at once,* it will be six of the best!"

Sara pouted. "But I'm an eagle." After a moment, though, she added a final, almost-polite "aark" of compliance.

Sister Rowena had cautiously followed the girl in. "I'm sorry for the delay, Mother, but Sara had climbed to the top of the old elm again."

"Because eagles like trees," Sara whispered.

"Oh Sara," Harmon began, before the nun could reprimand her further. "An eagle is *just* what I've been looking for."

An hour later, Sara slumped deep in the back seat of the cab, neither looking back nor waving farewell to the two nuns who had followed them out. Harmon entered the cab too and gave their destination to the driver, who met his eyes in the mirror with a worried expression. Only fares deemed commercially risky – or high status – warranted a human driver. Harmon simply frowned at the man, then settled back.

The nuns had of course been aware that he had cast spells on the girl, and also that he had been satisfied with the results. But he had been careful to do nothing overt enough to allow them to file a complaint, and they had clearly had no idea he had begun the initial mental adjustments – the erasures – right under their noses. Especially after he had slowed his pace to avoid any suspicions. Sara, too, had settled down, rather to his surprise. He had expected her to become fractious, but instead she had rapidly tired.

The cab pulled out from the curb and headed down the shabby street. In the gutter, two grubby children continued their game of 'rock death-match,' while a tramp yawned, spat, and staggered up from the pile of refuse he'd been nesting in. But as their gazes locked, the intensity in the man's eyes surprised Harmon. The impression of more-than-casual interest was so strong he considered probing the hobo's mind, but there simply wasn't time.

For some reason, though, the 'encounter' made the oddity of his pre-approved adoption spring to mind. He shook his head, annoyed at the transparent fears of his subconscious.

Don't be ridiculous, he told himself. *What am I suspecting: a government conspiracy assisting my research? How would they even* know *of it?* Never assume conspiracy when stupidity was sufficient explanation. No doubt some programming or other human error had worked in his favor in acquiring his test subject.

Ward, rather. He had better become accustomed to referring to the girl as his *ward*. Human experimentation was highly illegal, especially since '38.

Passing the empty lot at the corner of the street, the cab turned, the nuns and the old brown-brick orphanage – and the tramp – disappearing from sight.

CHAPTER 2

They reached the Golden Gate Bridge, Sara still struggling against her exhaustion. Finally she sat up with an obvious effort, then simply clonked her forehead against the window and rested it there. He wanted to ask her what she remembered of her life before the orphanage, but didn't dare do so at this early stage, while the erasures were still fresh.

He continued observing her. For a long period she didn't move, though in the reflection he could see her eyes tracking back and forth as she took in the changing scenery.

By the time they'd left the 101 behind and entered the rolling Sonoma hills, though, she seemed a little revived. Once or twice she summoned enough energy to point out the occasional horse, even exclaiming in surprise at the cows.

It *was* good to see the herds again, though the grapevines still struggled. Compared to his childhood memories, the hills appeared blasted. He sighed and eased back in his seat, ignoring the girl's occasional childish remark while he planned ahead.

At last, in the distance, the wall encircling the Institute signaled the end of their journey. The high, pale stone barrier hugged the gentle curves of the extensive grounds. Every meter, of course, magically warded and electronically monitored. The cabbie's eyes met his again in the rear view mirror, the usual fearful expression a mere irritant after so many years. At least the annoyance factor was balanced by the knowledge that with a human cab driver he could take control should he ever need to.

Still, Harmon cut him off before the fellow could speak. "It is perfectly safe, I assure you. Just stop outside the gates to let the security drone scan us and we'll be allowed in. Nor will you have any trouble in leaving, provided you do so directly. You *will* be monitored while inside: do not do anything foolish, like accepting an unusual fare on your way out."

The cabbie laughed, nervously.

Not that any inmates were allowed outside without supervision. Close supervision. He shouldn't needle the cabbies, he knew, but their knee-jerk fear always annoyed.

"Are we here?" Sara piped up. "What will the drone look-?"

A low hum announced the arrival of the mottled-green device. The optics mounted in its insect-like fuselage locked on the cabin as it quickly swung around to Harmon's window. Turning toward it to simplify its job, he let it scan and ID him, then waited while it circled the vehicle, looking down into the floor spaces and under the vehicle. It zoomed off, and the heavy iron gates swung wide: access approved. The cabbie accelerated smoothly up the winding road through the wooded acreage then finally out into the cleared area surrounding the Institute proper, eventually halting on the gravel courtyard by the wide sandstone steps of the main entrance.

Sara sighed and clambered out while he settled the account. The fellow wasted no time in removing her meager belongings from the trunk and jumping back in to drive off – escorted, Harmon saw, by one of Shanahan's less-obtrusive security drones.

Sara was staring up at the building, and though her eyes drooped with tiredness he could see she was intrigued. *Still not recovered. Probably a good thing I disengaged the mental probe when I did.* Though he suspected it was more a reaction to the *adjustments* he'd made rather than to the simple mindmeld. Still, he frowned. It could indicate a problem ahead.

A little later he stood with two of her small suitcases of clothing while she clutched the third herself, struggling with its size and weight but determined to manage it on her own.

A heavier-duty drone emerged from a window-port and swooped to a halt in front of them. "Evening, Dr Harmon." Shanahan's voice came from the drone. "So you were successful, were you? Or do we have a baby villain here?"

"I'm *not* a devil girl. I'm *good*."

Harmon blinked, and the drone's silence suggested equal surprise from the security officer.

"Thank you, Sara, we know that. Mr Shanahan was just making a rather foolish joke."

She frowned up at the drone. "I'm not gonna kill people."

This time, even Harmon was lost for words. Several long seconds passed before Shanahan's softly-accented voice spoke again. "Uh, that's good, darlin", that's real good. Maybe Dr Harmon could show you into Admissions and imprint you on the security systems." The drone pivoted its lens toward Harmon. "Her room's ready, Doc. The bots've cleaned up the empty office next to yours just fine, and I've had a bed and all set up.

"Surprised everyone, Doc, when we heard you were adopting. Never figured you for the parenting kind. No offense."

"None taken. Appearances can be deceptive. Is Professor Sanders expecting us?"

"He said he thought you'd both be tired, and you could see him tomorrow afternoon."

That was not unexpected – Sanders ran the Institute with too gentle a hand – but it was quite welcome news, nonetheless. "Very well. Thank you, Shanahan."

"You want me to come out and help you with that luggage?" came the voice from the drone. "Sara looks-"

"I can carry it. I'm very strong," she said, frowning up at the hovering drone.

It wiggled in response. "Right. Okay. Good. I look forward to meeting you in person, young lady." The drone swept off, disappearing around the outside of the building. Harmon turned to Sara, surprised to see tears in her eyes.

"I didn't do anything wrong! Why did he say that!"

"Say what, Sara? Call you a baby villain? He was just-"

"Not *that*. 'Young lady.' But I was just *standing* here! Why does everyone always think I'm bad?" Her lips trembled, but she stood her ground, staring at him as they faced one another, there at the bottom of the pale stone steps leading up to the front entrance, demanding her answer.

"'Young lady' is merely a polite way of referring to a girl of your age, Sara. Why would you assume it was... Ah. Sister Provïc referred to you that way, didn't she? When you were in trouble. I see."

She stared up at him doubtfully. "I'm *not* in trouble?"

"No. You're not."

"Oh." She continued watching him, and an odd expression crossed her face. "Are you going to be my father?"

He choked, flinching back. "Good god, no! Certainly not!"

"Then what *will* you be? Didn't you adopt me?"

"Yes.   That makes you my ward, and me your

guardian."

"I don't need guarding."

"It doesn't mean- Never mind. Consider me your Uncle."

"Uncle."

"Yes: *Uncle*. Do you have a problem with that?"

It was clearly less than she'd hoped for, he suddenly saw. But in the end, she nodded her acceptance, as though consenting to a deal.

"I'm not a devil girl."

"Did the nuns call you that?"

"Sometimes. When they got cross with me. Then they'd get all funny and hush each other. But that's what they really thought. That's why they gave me away." She looked away. "That's why they always give me away."

"Those people didn't understand you, Sara. They were afraid of you. But I see your potential, and it doesn't frighten me."

She looked back at him, blinking watery eyes, her expression slowly changing. He saw a faint hope dawning, the defensive lines melting away. *This could be a critical moment.* Quickly re-casting the mindmeld he settled it lightly over her. Illegal, and an invasion of privacy, yet necessary for his research.

But the tsunami of warmth that flooded in almost undid him. *«He understands me! Maybe he will-»*

He dropped the spell, retreating from the wall of affection as if it were a cliff's edge seductively calling him forward. It took effort to pull himself together. *Too close.* He'd ended the spell just in time: the force of her longing had been... immense.

But it would not do to become emotionally attached to his test subject. Not with what he would have to put her through.

Forcing a smile, he indicated their suitcases. "Come along, Sara. I'll introduce you to the security system, then show you to your room."

Still shaken, he led the way up the wide steps, both doors swinging open at his approach. He strode inside, Sara struggling like a small boat in his wake, hauling her suitcase in both hands.

With the correct authority level, introducing Sara to the

security systems was merely a matter of a few scans and some non-invasive bio-sampling. The whole procedure took little time, and they soon left the small booth and headed to the main staircase, then up four flights to the second level. He had to pause at the top as she struggled up with her single case. Then down the long corridor to his office.

"This is the door to my work area and rooms, Sara. Your room is this next one."

He put her cases down, opening her door and turning back to see her still eyeing the ceramic-copper plaque on his office, clearly struggling with his research area, 'Meta-magical Resonance.'

But when she saw him studying her, all she asked was if his first name was 'Alex.'

He narrowed his eyes. "I think it best you call me 'Uncle,' Sara."

At the way she shrank back into herself he felt a pang of guilt. It was for her own good, though. "Come along. I'll show you your room."

She didn't move. "But...?"

"Yes?"

"You're a doctor?"

"Yes. Surely you can read well enough to–"

"And you help the people here."

"Yes. But I doubt you would understand my work."

"Am I *sick*? Is *that* why you adopted me?"

His mind went blank. How did he respond to *that*?

"You don't really want *me*."

"I most certainly do, Sara. You are very important to me." He almost added: *I think you will be of enormous value to my research*, but stopped himself in time. It could be very awkward if she came to realize that.

"But rest assured, you are not sick."

"Then why *did* you want me?"

"Because I see great potential in you, and could not bear to see it wasted by having you raised by a group of withered religious fanatics."

That drew a smile, and she covered her mouth with one hand. "Sister *Rowena* wasn't withered," she giggled.

Afterward, in the cafeteria, Harmon showed her how to operate the dinner machine. She selected ham carbonara with fried eggs, he opted for a synth-steak and vegetables, and then they chose their drinks. He'd half expected to have to stop her from ordering a Coke, but to his surprise she hadn't even considered the soft drinks. Perhaps the nuns hadn't been totally inept in raising her? Instead, she had copied his drink order, opting for the same glass of sparkling mineral water and a Japanese green tea. At the table, her nose wrinkled as she sipped the hot drink suspiciously, all the while watching him carefully but saying nothing. They sat in silence, studying one another, while he struggled to think of a suitable topic of conversation for an eight-year-old girl.

The arrival of the two attendants for this wing was a relief. A small blonde woman, and that black fellow who looked like he'd been a quarter-back. What were their names? Monica? Miranda? And the man – it was Martin, wasn't it? M-something, anyway. The two stopped by their table, the woman crouching down to Sara's eye level.

"Hi, sweetie, I'm Nerida, and this is Dwayne. You must be Sara."

"Um, yeah. I just got here today."

"I know, sweetheart, you're already in the system. And not as an inmate, either," she winked. "So our Dr Harmon has adopted you, has he?" Her eyes swung to his, a definite challenge in her glance. "A little odd, bringing up a child here of all places," she said to him, before looking back to his ward. "What happened to your parents, dear? If you don't mind me asking?"

Sara looked down at the table, her jaw set stubbornly. "They sent me away 'coz they thought I was bad." She looked up defiantly. "But I'm not, I'm good. And I'm *not* going to do the devil's work, nuh-uh." She shook her head.

Silence reigned until Sara helpfully filled it. "I'm not going to kill anybody, either. *People* kill only for food."

The silence stretched even longer. Before Sara could explain further, Nerida stood, and both attendants, smiles now frozen to their faces, took a step back. "Uh, that's good. That's good to know. But, ah, we just dropped by to say hi, and Dwayne is taking me out to dinner."

Dwayne's mouth opened. "I-?"

"*Come on*, Dwayne, we don't want to be late. Bye, Sara.

G'night Dr Harmon. I'm sure you and Sara will get along *just fine.* You two seem a nice match." Tugging Dwayne's hand, she backed away and left the cafeteria.

"*They* were a bit strange, weren't they, um, Uncle?"

Someone at this table certainly is, he thought.

After dinner he'd taken her back to her room and left her to unpack. Instead, she went straight back into her bath-room – *her* bathroom! – and hugged herself. Her own bathroom! She-, uh...

She frowned. It seemed real nice to have her own bath-room, but all of a sudden, she wasn't quite sure why.

Anyway.

She looked around, checked out the cupboard under the sink – spare toilet paper, tubes of cream, shampoo and more – stood on tiptoe to eye herself in the mirror, tried the taps for the bath, flushed the toilet, and then froze, staring at the ceiling.

Oh, wow!

It had a secret trap door up there, just like back at, back at, the... oh, yeah, how could she have forgotten? Back at the orphanage! But instead of being down the end of a cor-ridor, out in the open and tricky to get to, it was right here *inside her own room!* She looked around, biting her lip, wondering how she could get up to it.

But without warning, the tiredness washed back through her. Besides, she didn't want to explore every-thing all at once. She should save stuff up for later.

She smiled, sleepily.

It sure looked like she had lots of exploring ahead of her!

A knocking sound from outside made her start, and she tiptoed back into the main room – *her* main room! - to in-vestigate. It came again, from the door, and she realized someone *was knocking on her door!* With a delighted smile, she crossed the room and opened it, to find her new uncle standing there. What were you supposed to say...?

"Can I help you?" she asked.

He blinked several times before shutting his mouth and frowning slightly. He held a bunch of smartsheets at his side. *For me?* "Would you like to come in?"

He looked at her sideways, still frowning a little, but

stepped into her room. What was she supposed to do next? "May I get you a glass of water?"

Still frowning, he transferred the 'sheets from his right hand to his left and stretched and wriggled his fingers in a funny little dance, like he'd done back... before, then looked at her. Really deeply, actually. It made her a little uncomfortable, like he could see inside.

This wasn't how things worked in the vids, and she looked around, trying to remember any stories where the guest behaved weird. Suddenly, though, her uncle laughed, ruffled the hair on her head, and started acting like visitors were supposed to.

"Thank you, Sara. Yes, a glass of water would be wonderful."

She smiled, relieved that she was doing it right after all, and dashed back into the bathroom where she'd seen a mug standing on the basin. She filled it to the brim and carried it back carefully with both hands so as not to spill a drop, and handed it to him. She felt strangely grown-up as he smiled and took it, despite the tricky business of getting it from her hands to his while both hers were still wrapped around it.

But then he just stood there, and she had to ask him if the water was nice before he even took a drink.

After that, though, he seemed to settle down, and together they browsed the net for books and vids to download to the 'sheets. Mostly he steered her to really old stuff, ages before the Unfolding, just like at the, the... just like she was used to. They found lots of stuff on African animals, as well as one that sounded 'specially good, about a king of the lions. He also loaded a map of the Institute like he'd promised, and then spent some time pointing out stuff like where she could put her dirty clothes for the 'bots to launder; and zooming around the grounds. There were also a couple of smaller buildings quite close by. One of them was Mr Shanahan's, he said – the security man who'd spoken to her from the drone.

A lot of the map of the Institute building itself was kind of sketchy, though, and marked as unused. She thought her uncle looked a little sad when she asked why, but he just said it was complicated. Which was what grown-ups said when they didn't want to tell you stuff.

There were a whole bunch of 'interview' and 'treatment' rooms, mostly on the levels below and above this one. She noticed there were two basement levels, too, which he tried to distract her from. Which probably meant they'd be especially good to explore. But she was extra careful not to look *too* interested in them.

Finally, he helped her unpack her clothes and craft stuff. By that time, though, her tiredness had come back and she could hardly keep her eyes open. At last he said goodnight and left her to clean her teeth. She clambered onto her bed and fell straight to sleep.

From his office, Harmon activated the holovid he himself had concealed in Sara's room.

She lay on her bed, surrounded by a scattering of the smartsheets to which they had 'printed' all the pre-Unfolding and copyright-expired children's vids and books they had downloaded. And the free superhero trids and movies she had been so keen on. He focused his trideo camera upon her little form, until her small face floated in the air before him, just within arm's reach. She seemed tired still, and slightly confused. The more he considered that fact, the more it indicated a problem.

Deep in thought, he tapped a stylus against his teeth. The conclusion, unfortunately, appeared quite clear. She still suffered from the effects of his magical adjustments in the nun's office. Although... perhaps that was as interesting as it was annoying? The spark he sought to fan to life, though unquenchable by normal means, seemed in some ways delicate when shaped by the currents of magic. It *could* be interpreted as striking confirmation he was on the right track: that the human spirit itself was akin to the paranormal patterning of magic. Perhaps even, was constituted of the same stuff.

He stared at the girl, tapping his stylus. Shutting his eyes, he mulled the possibilities.

And gently, slowly, drifted into sleep....

He stood in an American forest – old, undisturbed. Searching. Searching for something he had trained, some animal. Down dark trails he traveled, following faint scents. Gradually, though, he grew aware of another presence; and sensed that it, too, felt *him*. Searched for him:

hunting. His pulse quickened as he realized he had come too far, that he needed to leave. He turned, retreating.

It followed.

He ran, knowing it drew closer, gaining ground.

Running, bushes tearing at him, he burst from the forest, heart pounding in fear. Turning to look back he saw it emerge from the trees: a mountain lion. With feline grace it padded closer, jaws a little open. He met its eyes. And saw Death.

It gathered speed, padding faster, accelerating, but now he stood transfixed: the eyes were not a cat's: the eyes were amber-flecked – Sara's. A growl escaped its throat as muscles bunched for the attack.

The noise broke his paralysis. Suddenly free, he wrenched himself around, leapt-

And sat up straight in his office chair, panting.

A dream!

His heart still raced. He also realized he felt strangely disturbed, and had the beginnings of an erection.

Dismissing the physical reaction and shrugging off an odd feeling of unease, his fingers drummed as he contemplated the rest of it. Perhaps... could his dream have taken him through the strange layers of the Imaginal? Had he in reality tapped into the great Unconscious?

On his video feed Sara, asleep, moaned as if in frustration.

CHAPTER 3

At breakfast the next day, eating her second bowl of muesli, the girl seemed fully recovered. Harmon tried to mull all the various possibilities, but thoughts of the upcoming session with his most challenging patient kept distracting him. His wristcomm chimed, and he took the call from the Director.

"Just checking that you'd seen your patient's latest missive, Dr Harmon."

He didn't need to ask which patient Professor Sanders referred to: ninety percent of his attention went to the Institute's most troublesome case. "You mean last night's one, where he wrote of sensing a 'disturbance in the Force?' Rather mixing his metaphors. You are aware, Director, that it's a quote from a very old Hollywood movie?"

"Really? Odd timing, though – matches your arrival last night. The Synchronicity Effect, you think? We know he can't sense beyond his cell. Not through *those* Wards."

"I agree, Director. I really don't see that it would be possible. I'll check their integrity however, as always, when I see him."

"Good, good. Do take care, though." The Director disconnected.

Sara looked ready to burst with questions, but he waved her off. "Just my work." He ignored her pout, easing back in his chair as he recalled 'Godsson's' arrival.

Not that he would ever forget it.

Five years ago Godsson had been brought in, not by ambulance, nor police escort, nor even by FBI helicopter. No, Godsson had been carried in, unconscious, in the arms of a Chinese man. A man whose arrival had made all the Barriers at the Institute's boundaries flare into alert, clawing at the pair as if they were spirits rather than corporeal beings.

The magical Barriers were only there to counter arcane intrusions. At the time, they had assumed the trespasser was attended by unseen entities, now held at bay beyond the walls. Otherwise, he could not have entered....

No one who had raced out to confront the intruders had had the slightest idea how they'd arrived: there had been no vehicle of any kind. Just the front gates wrenching open and the powerfully-built oriental man stalking up the long winding road to the main entrance, somehow traversing the half kilometer in under a minute.

It had been Harmon and the previous Director – and at that time, the more-numerous orderlies – who had faced the fellow, then, on the graveled path.

The sheer force of will radiating from the man had been disconcerting, even as Harmon had noted the strange injuries to them both – not burns, or cuts, or bruises, but stranger *alterations* – patches of skin with a glassy sheen, the flesh itself a sheath over something black underneath. Twitches and movements where there were no muscles or tendons; disturbing ridges....

He still didn't like to think too deeply about that.

There was something strange about the man's eyes, too: as if tiny chips of gold gleamed in the near-black irises. A cosmetic alteration?

"It is done. Melisande d'Artelle is dead. We won."

It was only then that they realized who he was. Who *they* were. Harmon remembered how Director French had gasped beside him, as they all belatedly recognized Lord Lao Pi Shen, the New Emperor of China and self-proclaimed dragon. He and his small team – the second team to make the attempt – had been missing, presumed lost or dead now for three months.

"This is... Benson?" the Director had asked. "But what of your third member? The monk?"

The golden motes in the man's dark eyes glittered as he stared at them, considering.

"Victory, as ever, came with a cost. My companions fought bravely, but...."

The powerful voice shivered, almost cracking. Hearing *that* had been strangely disturbing; seeing a fissure in the indomitable certainty that wreathed him. In the sudden silence, Harmon had found himself wishing the man would hold back the words on his lips, as if he expected a curse.

"She had chosen to retreat to a place where no... person... should ever stand. A place that casts long shadows. Where every action has consequences. It was well for us all that she reached it only shortly before we did."

No one spoke.

"And there we slew her."

He had gazed at Harmon then; and as if the man had spoken, the young magical researcher sensed that there had been some *other* price for that death; a price as yet unpaid. Those dark eyes had held his before tracking very deliberately down to the young man held casually in his bronzed arms. Harmon felt his own eyes dragged down to the unconscious, innocuous-looking man cradled there. Held out now to him.

Your problem now. The words sounded inside his head as the man, or dragon, stepped forward and Harmon found his own arms lifting without conscious thought to accept the burden. Which suddenly lightened, though Harmon had seen just the sketchiest motion of spell-casting.

"What- what's wrong with Benson? I thought, that is, his reputation, surely...?"

Some had said Benson was perhaps as powerful as Shen; perhaps as powerful as d'Artelle herself. Harmon struggled to marshal his thoughts. "Why did you bring him *here*, to us?"

"Because here is where he needs to be." The *satisfaction* in the accompanying smile made Harmon's hackles rise. "Unfortunately, his mind has broken and he now represents a great danger to us all."

"But why not keep him in your own country? Surely, you are better placed..."

There was the slightest twitch to the eyebrows, the faintest gleam of malicious pleasure in the strange gold-and-black eyes, and he stopped, sensing that every word he spoke somehow made him appear more naïve in the eyes of the dragon. Who, somewhat to his surprise, answered his question. In a fashion.

"Well, since the Fey-born declined to help, she can hardly object to hosting her replacement during his... convalescence."

Again, the faintest emphasis on the final word made Harmon feel he was missing something important. And who did he mean by 'the Fey-born?' Surely not the trillionaire, Morag Feyborn – she'd been dead a decade. And what did he mean by 'her replacement?' Was he claiming the deceased Feyborn had been one of the two strangely-anonymous companions who'd made the first attempt, with him, to track down the Enemy of Mankind?

Shen's statement raised more questions than it answered. Before Harmon could ask more, however, the man was moving.

"Come. We will need to strengthen and improve your Barriers. I will show you how: I will do that much, at least, to ease your burden."

And with regal self-assuredness despite his tattered silk clothing, he swept past them and up the wide steps as if the building were his own.

Which was how, minutes later, Dr Alex Harmon, 36, had found himself assisting the man who was now very likely the most powerful mage on the planet as he constructed a series of towering, interleaved magical workings Harmon scarcely understood.

Lao Pi Shen had also worked with Harmon to mend the younger man's disturbing injuries. Or perhaps *alterations?* A second working of magic, even subtler this time, and Harmon felt uncharacteristically humbled as he saw it wasn't only the strength of the man's magical power, but his knowledge and skills which clearly exceeded his own by at least an order of magnitude.

It had been humbling, yet also enlightening. It made him the only person still alive, as far as he knew – with the probable exception of their newest inmate – who had worked magic with the sorcerer who had recently come to rule China.

Harmon had dared to ask, then, how the third member of their team had died. The dragon lord had remained silent so long he had decided there would be no answer, when their visitor finally responded.

"There are some humans whose spirit make even one such as I, humble. We would not have succeeded without his sacrifice."

But after that, the dragon had spoken no more. Except, as he left – surrounded, to his apparent amusement, by a hastily-assembled group of State Department officials and FBI agents – to wryly observe that he thought their government would be wise, in the circumstance, not to hold him to task over his lack of a passport.

Harmon had half expected the man to depart as mysteriously as he had arrived, but instead, the Emperor of China had simply bent his frame elegantly to enter the provided limousine.

Harmon snapped out of his reverie, blinking, as Sara's insistent tone ended his introspection.

"What is this place, anyway? Are we under the ground?"

"This is the Institute of Paranormal Dysfunction. I study magic, Sara, and what it means when it goes wrong inside people. Indeed, at the Institute we have one of the most skilled and powerful mages of our times. Unfortunately, something damaged his mind and he is here now to *be* studied: not to study *with* us.

"And no, we are not underground at present – although this building is such a maze of corridors it would be easy to imagine you were. Would you like to go outside into the fresh air?"

"Yeah!" She pushed her chair back and jumped up, ready to leave at once.

"*After* you have finished your breakfast, little one."

She cocked her head to one side, staring at him. *Her eagle look*, he recalled with a smile. Structuring his will and thought, he gestured, and her chair returned, turning round a little toward her. Her eyes widened at the casual display of magic. Impressed and showing it, she returned to the table. "Do some *more* magic!" she demanded.

He cocked *his* head to one side. "Say *please*."

She considered the command, pouting. He looked away, twirling his fingers idly, and had to conceal his satisfaction when at last she broke. "Please."

"Very well." He gestured again, frowning slightly in concentration. She dropped her spoon as it suddenly twisted in her hand, then gazed at it wide-eyed as it drifted down into her cereal bowl. Her eyes followed it avidly as it dipped to ladle up a mouthful and then float up to her mouth, which she opened with a delighted grin.

He almost jumped when she unexpectedly snapped forward, trapping the spoon. Then slowly, gently, drew back to slide it from her mouth, her eyes locked on his all the while. A spark seemed to leap between them.

Harmon felt quite... strange.

CHAPTER 4

She kept an eye on her new uncle, just in case he did more magic, while eating her cereal as fast as she could. But it still took *ages* to get outside.

Blinking in the bright sunlight she pushed open the too-slowly opening door, pausing on the top step and drawing in great big breaths of the air. It smelled weird but good, all kinds of rich scents that were nicer than those back in the city. They were somehow familiar though, and she frowned as she tried to remember where from.

Jumping down the steps two at a time, she raced across the gravel and onto the grassy area beyond, stretching her arms out in eagle wings to swoop in a wide banking turn, a single "Aaark!" escaping from her, that she just couldn't hold inside. She paused then to look back at the building and the strange man who'd adopted her. As his hooded eyes watched her intently, she wondered what he'd be like, as... as an uncle. Would he get married one day? Give her a... uh, an *aunt*?

She watched him standing there all stern and serious, in his white coat like a proper doctor, or maybe a scientist. She tilted her head sideways, considering him. Could he be a *mad* scientist? That'd be pretty cool.

Except mad scientists didn't get married.

She stared up at the building. It sure was big! It even had those up and down steppy-things running all along the edge of the roof. She wondered what it would be like to run along them. It did look a little bit dangerous, though. Maybe when her legs were longer, she decided.

He was *still* making his way toward her, so she ran back to him. "It looks like a castle!"

He turned and actually looked at it, which was nice. Most grown ups just ignored what you said, except to tell you you were wrong.

"It was Victorian, originally, but there *has* been a mish-mash of later extensions. I suppose... it *is* reasonably old."

From the corner of her eye, she saw something run across the lawn between two trees, and grabbed his hand. "Look, look!" she squealed, but he just stood there like a lump. She darted off toward it, but it disappeared before she'd gone more than a few steps. She turned back to him, wondering if he'd seen it too. "What was it?"

"A squirrel, Sara. There are many small animals in the

grounds."

A squirrel. So *that* was a squirrel. She wondered how hard it would be to catch one? What would they be like to hold? Could you pet them? It'd be nice to have something to cuddle. Quietly, she stalked toward the tree it had run up, then stood at the bottom, checking out the hand-holds. It didn't look like it'd be too hard to climb.

She looked back at her, uh, her uncle, and he had an odd expression on his face, like he was studying her, maybe deciding something. But he looked interested, too. Which was kinda nice.

The sky was blue, the smells so nice. It was like she'd moved to live in a castle in the middle of a forest. She wondered if maybe there'd be a wicked witch lurking somewhere? She turned in a big circle, taking it all in, amazed by just how clear and sharp everything was, right to the horizon.

She stopped, at the sound of steps coming around the side of the building behind them. Only a man, but by his side....

"Oh, wow, who's *that*?"

"Hmm? Brian Shanahan, our security-"

But she was already in motion, racing toward the sleek and powerfully-muscled dog. Its glowing red eyes had locked on hers with such interest, and its tail had already thumped once in hopeful anticipation.... She could tell straight away the robo-dog needed someone to play with: its eyes – *her* eyes – said how alone she was, and how happy she was to see Sara.

"Sara, stop, don't-!"

Her uncle was shouting dumb stuff, as if he couldn't see how much the girl dog looked like HyperGirl's companion, Argon. She had the same sleekly bulging weapon pods at her shoulders, but without the rocket thrusters at her hips. Probably he didn't watch *Heroes, Inc*. She wondered if she had unfolding wings like Argon, too.

The man ahead of her was also shouting at her to stop. She had to dodge as he reached down and tried to grab her while barking orders at 'Faith' to 'stand down' – but he was too slow. 'Faith's' lips curled back in delight-

And then she was past the grasping hands, her own arms wrapping around Faith's furry neck to hug her tight while she inhaled the rich doggy smells. With her head pressed into the hard muscles, from the corner of her eye she could see the tail thumping madly. Her arms couldn't quite reach around the large chest. "Oh, Faith, we'll have *such* adventures, just wait and see! Come on, I'll race you to the building!"

She broke away, pausing to slap her thigh for Faith to follow, then took off at a sprint. Behind her, she heard the whine of turbines spinning up, then Faith appeared at her side, head cocked briefly to see what *she* was doing, before the turbines whined higher and Faith bounded ahead.

She couldn't help but squeal in delight, laughing as she put her head down to chase the dog even harder. "No fair!" she called out, "You've got robo legs!" Then saved her breath for running.

Behind her, the men's shouting had finally stopped. She'd showed *them!* As if Faith was going to hurt *her*. Grown ups could be so dumb, sometimes.

When she and her faithful companion finished their first ever patrol circuit of the building together and loped back up to the two men, of course the two grown ups blahed and blahed for a while. She rolled her eyes at Faith. As if Faith would shoot *her*. Good grief! While the men complained, she and Faith secretly agreed to meet up later – that was obvious by the thumping of her tail and the way her long tongue lolled out happily over her steely teeth.

Eventually the men stopped talking. After a while she guessed they were probably waiting for her to say something.

"Uh. Sorry? I won't do it again?"

After a little more blah, Faith and her man headed off, while her uncle stared down at her.

He didn't say much, but she got the impression he was secretly pleased. Which was kinda surprising, but nice. The nuns would have been telling her not to run around like a crazy girl, or worse. Maybe he really was nicer than he looked? It was just his heavy eyebrows and how they made his eyes look like dark caves that made him look so fierce. But *she* could look fierce, too!

She wanted to stay outside and explore, but he pointed out that the building inside was quite interesting in its own right, and even had a display that would give her an overview of the Institute for Parra Normal Dis Numpton's – or whatever it was called – 'considerable acreage.' Which just meant 'a lot of land,' he explained. *And*, he'd added, it'd be a good idea to get a tour of the building itself so she could learn which areas were safe, and which to avoid.

Safe? Now *that* sounded interesting, but she was extra careful not to let her interest show. Was it the *wrong* people that were the danger, or was it because they did mad-scientist experiments here? Or maybe it was both? They could have secret labra-tories or underground lairs, or any-thing, here! She had to hug herself to convince herself it was all real. *I'm so lucky!*

Looking back as she followed her uncle inside, she saw Faith turn at the same moment. Their eyes met before Faith turned back to concentrate on her duties. But her tail was wagging!

And the woods beyond! Sara gazed out at the forested area inside the walls of the Institute, and had to hug herself again. So many new places to explore!

At lunch-time, much later, sweaty and grubby from her explorations, she ran back into the cafeteria, suddenly stopping at the sight of a long, gift-wrapped parcel lying just beyond her place-setting. *Ohhh! He got me a present!* Her new uncle had a smile on his face, though it was a bit funny-looking.

She looked at the parcel. It was wrapped in colorful pa-per, and quite long – longer than her arm. She ran up to the dining table. "Is that a present for *me*?"

"Yes, Sara."

She reached over for it.

"No, Sara. *After* lunch you may open it."

She looked at him. *Maybe if I just grab it...?*

His smile disappeared and he looked very big all of a sudden. And mean. She shivered and sat down. She didn't want to look at him as she ate, and kept her eyes on her food – though whenever he wasn't watching she sneaked a look at the gift. It was wrapped in gay paper which molded over a tantalizingly curved shape. Fairytale castles crouched amidst bright green rolling hills and darker forests, under vivid blue skies with cotton-wool clouds.

She didn't get many presents. Even at, even at...? She

struggled to remember. Oh, yeah. At the orphanage. Maybe uncles gave lots of presents? That'd be nice.

But she'd rather have hugs.

She tried again to guess what was inside from its shape. Her fingers twitched, desperate to open it. She checked him again.

Rats.

She stared down at her cereal, deciding what to do. All right. But if he was going to be a meanie and stop her opening it straight away, she wouldn't talk to him at all.

It was silent then, apart from the clink of her spoon and the quiet crunching as she chewed her muesli. While she ate, she looked up at him from time to time through her fringe. He had a stupid expression like he was laughing at her but thinking she couldn't tell. Annoyed, she concentrated on the bowl in front of her.

At last she finished her cereal.

"You may open it now, little one."

Huh. He couldn't tell *her* what to do. Instead, she poured herself another helping.

"Another bowl of muesli, Sara?"

"I'm hungry."

"It seems you have a good appetite."

"That's cause *I* do stuff."

Silence again, then. She didn't speak, and he didn't, either. She wouldn't even look at the gift. Finally, though, she finished the second bowl.

Cross with him, she nevertheless pulled the parcel toward herself and carefully started to open it, mentally daring him to try to go back on his promise. She looked up, and he had this really annoying look on his face, like '*Oh, yes,* now *you have my permission*' and stuff, but suddenly, a squeal somehow escaped despite herself when she saw what it was. She tore into the paper.

Ohhh. "A bow and arrows!"

She ripped the last piece of paper off and pulled it all out – bow, arrows, even a quiver. And a large, folded-up piece of paper. There was a string, too, with loops already made at each end. She slipped one end on and tried looping the other over the notch at the other end of the bow, but it sprang straight out of her hands, jabbing her between the eyes.

"Ow!"

She tried again, and *this* time the bow twisted and stabbed into her shoulder! Biting down on a cry, she tried again.

"Would you like me to do that for you, little one? I don't think you're strong enough, yet."

"I am too!" *Does he think I'm a baby?* She didn't need *his* help! She'd do it by herself even if it took days.

In the end, it took five minutes plus getting cross with it for the last bit.

She then turned her attention to the arrows.

At the end where the plastic feathers fitted, each arrow had a slot for the bowstring. That made sense. But a flexible black cup was attached to the other end where the point should be. She poked her tongue thoughtfully into her cheek, trying to puzzle it out. Tried to twist the rubber cap off, only to find she couldn't.

Finally, she flung herself back in her chair and stared crossly at her uncle, waving the dumb arrow at him. "What are these bits for?"

"They make the arrows stick when they hit a smooth surface," he explained, picking one up and stamping it down on the table where it stood, quivering. He bent it over and let it spring back upright. "You see."

She just stared at him. Was he serious? "What good is that? Animals don't *have* smooth bits."

He looked at her oddly, and for a moment she thought he might be doing some more magic – but nothing happened. Then he leaned forward, his voice lowering. "Nor does the thing that you can use these arrows on."

Ohhh.

She leaned forward.

CHAPTER 5

"Still, the arrows will work," he added.

He had been observing her carefully, a lightly-cast mindmeld feathering against her thoughts, pleased at her responses so far. Now to begin preparing her. Hopefully, it would suffice to set her own imagination to work for his purposes, assisting him.

"Work on what? What thing? How?"

He looked around, as if checking for observers. "I was waiting before I told you this. Before I warned you." He leaned toward her and lowered his voice further. She scooted closer still in her chair. "In here, we are safe: but outside, something dangerous hunts in the grounds."

Her eyes grew round. "What is it?"

"No one knows. No one has seen it. Some say it is invisible, and moves in the wind."

"Wow. What does it do?"

His voice sank. "It sinks claws inside the mind, and changes people. Sends them mad."

"Oh! Did it make the *wrong* people here?"

"Yes," he lied, though mildly surprised she had remembered his mention of the inmates.

He had his own suspicions as to what – or rather, who – was warping their patients.

"And you want me to help you investigate it? We can be a team!" She chewed her lip. "What's it called?"

His voice lowered further. "It is nameless. If it had a name, speaking it would attract it. Even talking about it as we are now is dangerous: could bring it sniffing around the magical Wards around the Institute."

"Ohhh!" she breathed, eyes alight. He had to hide a smile. "But I can hunt it with the bow, can't I? You put magic on it."

Hmm. He'd expected more fear. He *needed* her under stress. Still, if she had enough imagination for that, she should have enough to imagine her own extra dangers, too. "Yes. But while my magic will let you hurt it, I have no spells to protect *you*. You will have to do that yourself: if you can."

"But if it's unvisible, how will I know where to shoot?"

"*Invisible*. You will have to sharpen your other senses. Train them."

She nodded, wide-eyed.

"Now, knowing all that – do you still want to venture outside?"

"Yeah!"

"Very well – let's go."

Outside, together, they worked out how to fire the arrow.

"Do you think *it's* nearby?" she whispered, standing close beside him, her voice lowered.

He frowned, then pretended to look around nervously. "That's not a safe topic. Don't even think about it."

For a few seconds, she looked annoyed, before a sudden rustle of leaves caught her attention. *«He said it hunts in the wind»* he heard her think, before she moved quietly off into the trees in the direction of the sound, not looking back.

He left her stalking cautiously through the gardens, hunting a figment of her imagination.

If his theory was correct, stress and pain were essential for anyone to unfold magically. So this way he could use her own mind – and a little judicious magic – to apply some of the necessary pressure. He walked back inside, well satisfied.

Standing at a third-floor window of one of the unused offices, he watched her stalk through the woods. *Now to cement its reality in her mind.*

He cast the telekinesis spell and began very subtly helping her imagination along. She immediately noticed the unusual movements of the branches, the slight disturbances of the fallen leaves. Expecting her to fire at the twitching foliage, instead she merely stilled, then crept closer.

He spent five minutes – far longer than he had intended – leading her a merry chase through the edges of the woodlands that surrounded the main building. It was surprisingly difficult to induce her to shoot, he discovered, unless he provided *sets* of movements. To do so he himself had to imagine a suitable creature moving through the vegetation, and telekinese multiple objects at the same time. The concentration required was very like juggling. It was with considerable relief that he sent her deeper into the trees and out of his sight, forcing him to drop his spell.

Back downstairs, in the now-empty cafeteria, he unfolded the colorful circles of the shiny target that had come with the toy bow – and which she had completely ignored. He tossed it into the recycler with a smile.

\-

Later that afternoon, with his new young ward reluctantly in tow, he knocked on the Director's door. At the jovial "Enter!" he opened it and ushered Sara inside ahead of him.

"Ah, Dr Harmon, come in!" The Director gestured them inside. "And this young lady must be Sara, yes? Please, come in, have a seat. I have cookies."

Harmon turned, catching the way her shoulders hunched defensively, and wished Sanders had chosen a different phrase. "Sara, you are not in trouble." He turned back to the older man. "I gather the nuns referred to Sara as 'young lady' when they disciplined her, Professor."

Sanders looked distressed, which stretched the deep laughter lines of his face in odd directions. "Dear me, young- uh, my dear girl, quite right, I meant it in a purely complimentary way. Come, sit down, have a cookie. The oatmeal and raisin are particularly good – my niece makes them."

He held the plate out, and Sara took one before sitting down. After a moment, still watching the older man uncertainly, especially his explosively unruly white hair, she carefully bit into it and began nibbling. Harmon watched her watching Sanders, wishing he could use the mindmeld spell but knowing he probably should not do so in front of the other mage, weak though his talents were.

"I must say, Alex, I was most surprised when I heard you'd applied to adopt a young girl. Most surprised. You've never expressed any desire to raise children before."

"I realized I was becoming too insular. That it would be good for me to have to care for someone other than myself. And Sara is eight years old – hardly an infant, Director."

He glanced at Sara, who was following the conversation so intently she'd stopped eating. Indeed, she appeared quite tense, though clearly she had appreciated his recognition of her mature age.

"But is the Institute really a suitable place to raise a

child?" the Director asked. "Have you fully considered the risks?"

"Professor Sanders, with all due respect, Sara was being raised in an environment designed to foster an outmoded belief system and *twentieth century* patterns of behavior; was being raised in a part of New Francisco rife with gangs and drug abuse. She will be much safer here, where I will certainly not be filling her head with religious nonsense."

"But what of the demands on your own time? Wasn't there a line of research you wished to start-"

Sara jumped up from her seat and clung to her uncle's arm. "Why do you want to make me go away? Uncle and me are a team. He's got papers, 'n you can't split us up! Why are you tryin'a split us up? I don't like you!"

Tossing her half-eaten cookie back onto the plate she ran from the room.

Harmon stood. "Ah, I think I had best go and care for my young ward, Director. You know how easily children can take things the wrong way. If you'll excuse me...?"

That went rather well, he thought as he left the room and caught her up. She turned toward him, tears on her face, and he felt a strange internal tug.

She clutched his arm. "You won't let him split us up, will you, Uncle?"

She stared up at him, alert to his smallest expression. He was once again surprised by the protectiveness her trust awoke. The fervor with which she'd allied herself with him against the Director was satisfying, too. He smiled down at her.

"No, Sara. I won't let the Director split us up. Don't worry. I won't let anyone take you away from me. Not anyone.'

"Not even the Director?"

"Not even the Director. I'll let you in on a secret: I'm better at magic than he is."

"But isn't he your boss?"

"Only up to a point. He can't split us up."

"Even if... even if I'm bad?"

"Even then. I may have to punish you, but I will never abandon you."

"Promise?"

"I promise. Other people may not understand you, Sara, or appreciate you, yet I assure you that I do. You are important to me. Very important."

She smiled, shyly, still a little doubtful. He wiped the tears from her cheeks with his thumb, surprised by the feeling of intimacy that flowed from her innocent acceptance of the gesture. "We are a team, Sara. The whole world won't be enough to split us up, I promise."

She smiled, and for a moment he almost felt like hugging her.

"Come, no doubt you'd like dinner?"

"Yeah!" she agreed, tugging at his arm now to hurry him up, her fears forgotten.

The encounter with Sanders had definitely improved their slightly rocky relationship, he mused. Really, Sanders couldn't have chosen a more helpful line of questioning if he'd tried.

At the end of the day, he entered her room to find her sitting up in her bed, frowning. "How come I don't have any network?" she said. "How am I s'posed to do my lessons?"

He looked surprised. "That's a good point. I'd better get you access. What are you accustomed to?"

"Huh?"

"What apps are you used to?"

"Dumb ones. *Lots* of Scripture ones, and we weren't allowed out into the proper net. Even the games were dumb. Who wants to stack spinning blocks?"

"Well, I'm sure I can arrange better apps, although I don't approve of netgames. They shrink children rather than grow them. But you needn't worry about all that superstition they've been filling your head with. No. I think I'll have you forget all that, too."

Sara looked at him sharply, scanning his face, but from her puzzled expression he could see she had read nothing further there.

Her expression cleared. "When can I get access? I wanna play a game *now*."

"Don't say 'wanna'. 'Want to'," he enunciated. "But there will be no netgames for you, Sara. Would you like me to read you a story, instead?"

She frowned, pursing her lips as she considered his offer. "Okay."

"Which one would you like?"

"This one," she said. "'Where the Wild Things Are'."

How appropriate, he thought.

"Would you like to sit up here with me, Uncle? I could lean back against you to see the pictures better."

He considered the idea, uncomfortably. But it would help bind her affections to him. He himself would not so easily form an emotional attachment, of course.

"Very well. But if you fall asleep, I will put you to bed and you are not to grumble if that wakes you up."

She beamed, bouncing on the bed. "Okay!"

As he read, she gave a running commentary, so he hardly needed the mindmeld he had cast, after she settled into his lap: "I'm not *that* naughty," and "Can *I* get a wolf suit?" and "I'd eat *him* up!" By the time young Max had arrived on the island of monsters, though, her eyes, against her will, were drooping down.

He riffled through her memories, pushing aside a moment of guilt at the invasion. Annoyingly, a link to her freshest memories, the orphanage set, had re-formed. Surprisingly, although those memories were strongest, they were only loosely bonded to her own self-image. As he lifted her up and slid her beneath her blanket, she grumbled gently, but a nudge of her thoughts was sufficient to settle her down again as he took his seat by the bed once more.

Shifting his 'viewpoint' in her memory complex, he saw where a few cuts would break the linkages to most of her last four years. Delicately, he pinched off those links and watched the structure shift and settle, now disconnected. The new linkages would stabilize over time.

With those pushed aside, the deeper and stronger linkages became more apparent. But it would be inadvisable to work on them again, without the patient conscious: the risk of accidental alterations was too high. He limited himself to tagging some bundles of connections, and choking the access down a little to the more obvious sets. There was no rush. Besides, it would be better to proceed in small steps so he could check each change. Especially as he noted her energy levels dropping with each of his new corrections.

Deciding he had done enough for her second night, he gently withdrew his magical probes, ended the spell, and turned off the light as he left her room.

In his office once more, he leaned back in his chair and let his gaze wander over his physical bookshelves. A mere fraction of his digital library, but sometimes, physicality mattered.

Volumes on metaphysics, theology, philosophy, psychology, magic – his own bound research papers – physiology, and neurochemistry. All related to his driving interest: isolating the magical makeup of Man.

His eyes unfocused as he considered his new problem. Sara.

Word about his 'disturbed' ward had already filtered through the thin ranks of the largely-automated Institute. Hopefully, his more delicate adjustments tonight would prevent her asking again why *she* was here, or why he had adopted her. For a moment, he recalled that first occasion and her desperate longing.

His mind shied away from the remembered up-welling of warmth and hunger that had flooded out. Even the memory alone threatened to undermine his resolve. He would need to watch himself. For an instant he considered making defensive adjustments to his own emotional state, before recoiling in horror at the enormous potential for disaster. That route would be not a *slippery* slope, but frictionless.

He put the unnerving idea aside with a shudder and returned to the subject of his ward and her hunger for love....

Certainly that *neediness* would help reinforce his own work. And given what he'd seen of her nature, if she showed no further curiosity about her adoption it would only be the result of his latest alterations to her memories. Some of the initial 'adjustments' he had made under the very nose of the nun in her office had not lasted that first day. Although clearly, from her severe response to them on that occasion, and each time since, he needed to proceed much more cautiously. Even tonight, she had once again tired rapidly.

So. She was now his to mold as he saw fit, to create a key to probe the nature of magic, and to test his own theories.

The question was, into *what* should he mold her?

He remembered her hunting of his imaginary creature earlier today: how very gracefully she had moved as she stalked across the lawn, the way she had so quickly noticed the unnatural movements around her; how thoroughly she had *interpreted* those movements. An idea slowly crystallized. Perhaps not a warrior, but... a Huntress?

Bonsai, he thought. So many creative processes cannot be hurried without thereby destroying the creation. Instead, just a little pressure, often. Constant, gentle shaping.

He frowned. He had planned to investigate up to six Archetypes; testing his theory by unlocking the potential within each subject, forcing each to Unfold. Yet now it seemed the process would take far longer than he had imagined. He ran one hand through his hair – once thick and dark, now starting to gray. The frown deepened. This would likely take years.

Should he go directly for the grand experiment and create a new Archetype? If he did, he should pick something compatible with her personality. The closer the match, the less pressure needed, and the less chance of breaking her. The less chance of pruning off an unwanted aspect of her psyche that might prove to be a critical amputation.

Equally significantly, it might be wise to draw on those parts of the collective unconscious tied to Native American culture.

His mind drifted. Odd that her ethnic background had not been recorded in her files, that he had only learned of it by scanning the Mother Superior's mind. He considered what little he knew of Native American mythology, and the 'Sky Corn Community.' He had discovered they were more a hippie commune who'd adopted Native American culture than a genuine tribe; they made money from a general expertise in zero-gravity technologies. He had found no information about the girl's parents, however.

In the end, he decided to trust his own insights. Sara seemed wild, energetic, willful. He pictured films he had seen of primitive peoples, placed her into the scenes he imagined.

Yes, he decided. *Yes, a Huntress.*

CHAPTER 6

Sara woke quite early the next morning, puzzled about where she was. Why was it so quiet? Where were the other... the thought slipped away as she recognized her new room – which she had all to herself!

In *her* bathroom, she eyed the secret trap door high up in the ceiling. Cleaning her teeth, she wondered if the desk from her other room would fit through the door? Or maybe she could stack the chairs on top of each other....

A little later, three chairs sticky-taped together and her flashlight wedged into her jeans, she wriggled through the opening. It was so tight she wondered if it'd been designed for an arthrobot. Tugging her torch free, she shone it round, disappointed it didn't reveal the cavernous space she'd imagined. She put the flashlight down, hesitating at the hollow sound it made, and rapped the dusty ceiling. It sounded awfully thin. Carefully, then, she pulled herself fully up into the dark space and tested the 'floor'.

It bent, with a cracking noise.

Biting her lip, she sat up, her head brushing yet another ceiling. She picked her light back up and shone it around, flashing on wooden beams that criss-crossed the floor into the distance. At least the beams looked very strong.

She crawled deeper in, exploring, careful to keep her weight on the solid timbers. Her hands got very dirty very quickly.

It was *so* dusty up here. She should have... have... have...

She wriggled and scrinched her upper lip, but no matter how she tried she couldn't hold back the sneeze. Despite pinching her nose shut she exploded.

Crack.

Oh, no! Dismayed, she pulled her foot back from where she'd accidentally shoved it straight through the ceiling, then froze, cringing as she waited for someone below to shout up at her.

After a while, though, when nothing happened, she looked down through the hole she'd made into the room underneath her. Most of the pieces of ceiling tile, she was able to fold back into place from up here; but on the floor directly beneath her lay one large and irregular section of plastic. The space below her seemed to be just an empty, dusty office – though not as dusty as the space around her.

She chewed her lip. Sooner or later, someone would go in there, find the broken piece, look up, and realise she had a secret way of moving around inside the building. And stop her.

She sighed. She was sure Miss X, in *The eXtro Agency,* didn't have these kinds of problems. Now she'd have to crawl all the way back, find out which office it was – maybe even break in – then get the broken piece, clean up around it, then climb back up here and glue it back into place.

Her shoulders rose and fell in a heavy sigh. Sometimes, exploring could be a lot of work. Turning around, very carefully, she made her way back to the opening. Her chair-tower swayed excitingly as she climbed down, but she'd done such a good job of taping it together that it hardly came apart at all.

Later, eyeing the partly-mended hole with satisfaction by torchlight, she considered how her painting and craft stuff was really coming in handy. Maybe there was other stuff she could get her new Uncle to get her, too? That way, she could gradually make up her own spy kit. She'd need mirrors, and glue, and paperclips for picking locks, and matches, and....

She continued happily drawing up her mental list of what she'd need as she crawled painstakingly back the way she'd come.

Her shin was stinging, too. She must've cut it when her foot went through the roof. She should probably get some anti septic cream – 'coz septics were bad. She could add it to her spy kit. And band-aids, too: then she could do her own first aid.

She sneezed again, just as violently, as she hummed her way back.

And maybe get some face-masks, too. She could tell Uncle she wanted them so she could play doctor, or something.

In the end, it took her three weeks to get into the dusty office. It was *much* harder to pick a lock than in the movies, no matter how many vids she watched on the net that claimed to show how to do it. She finally gave up and found some rope, and went in through the ceiling instead.

But she kept practicing on the old padlock she'd found, refusing to give up her dream of lock-picking entirely.

CHAPTER 7

Almost every day, Sara went out hunting alone, alert to every sound. On gloomy days, sometimes, she sensed it; very occasionally, fired an arrow at it. Once, deep in the woods, she'd felt it sneaking up behind her and spun and fired, driving it away.

With a shiver, she remembered the best time: she'd been hearing something with heavy quiet footsteps moving in the forest, somehow always moving away from her no matter how silently she crept toward it. And finally, when it attacked – invisibly grabbing and twisting her, pushing against her mind, trying to force a way in.... In the end, she'd lashed out at it somehow and felt a contact, then a sort of shocked stillness and sensed it retreat. That had been juicy.

When she'd told her uncle about it, though, he'd gotten the strangest look on his face. Like she'd scared him; or like he'd been scared *for* her. He did that nervous finger-dance he sometimes did, and asked her to tell him more, and for a while he'd seemed to get even more worried.

"I must congratulate you on your active, ah, *investigation*. But keep in mind that there must be simple nature spirits within the Institute's grounds. Don't confuse them with *It*."

He'd actually looked quite pleased with her, though; and she had to admit, just to herself, that she hadn't thought about nature spirits. In the end, even though she knew he was wrong, she just nodded like she agreed. After all, she didn't want him to worry about her. Maybe even try to stop her Hunting.

But normally there was nothing, and she simply roamed, breathing in the earthy woods smell as she stole through warm sun-dappled groves, placing her feet ever so carefully so as to make no sound, nor break any fronds from the delicate bracken to reveal where she'd passed.

On days when Faith was busy, she liked to climb the dark rocky hills to the west. Cooled by the wind's chill, it was nice to look down over the Institute from the very edge of its grounds. Or sometimes, down in the Forest, she'd sit with her back pressed up against the tall, mossy wall. She liked the stone wall. For some reason, it felt friendly. It was easy to imagine it was cupping her, holding her safe. Best was when Faith was there with her, though, so she could snuggle up beside her.

It was fun to build dams in the stream that led to the small lake, too. It was hard to wait while the water level slowly grew to bursting point. Sometimes, though, she'd pile on extra earth just to prolong the build-up, to create a bigger climax. Other times she couldn't wait, and she'd poke a small hole, watching in fascination as the whole structure tore itself apart.

She wished she had another girl, or even a boy, to play with though. Faith couldn't build dams or climb trees. Luckily, she mentioned that to her uncle: and after he'd pointed out how she didn't really need anyone else; how Faith was more than enough companionship; and how a Huntress didn't need other people, she'd felt much better. Most of the time.

But as a Huntress, of course, she kept her bow and arrows close at hand. Just in case.

One day to her great delight, she even managed to hit an animal. Unimpressed, the bruised squirrel chittered angrily at her from a safe distance up its tree while she crowed and did a victory dance below. But then she'd wasted the whole afternoon trying to improve the deadliness of her weapon. No matter how she tried, though, she simply couldn't break off the rubbery cup at the end of the arrows. She'd even tried sneaking a sharp knife from the manual kitchen, but it just wouldn't cut through the tough, stretchy black cap.

Nerida had got real upset when she'd found her with the knife. She'd been all, like, 'Sara, put the knife down, there's a good girl,' as if she thought she was gonna attack somebody with it, or something!

Nerida was super-weird. Her boyfriend, Dwayne, was also always looking at her sneakily, whenever he thought she wasn't looking, like he expected her to creep into his room one night and do something scary.

Actually, she hadn't decided yet if that'd be a good idea or a bad one.

But today, since it was rainy, she decided she'd hunt inside, prowling down the cold stone passages with their high ceilings and thick layer of off-yellow paint. Given how many rooms were empty and disused it was surprising how few people there actually were, here. Only a few of the heavy wooden doors had a sign on them, and even then, most of those just had numbers painted on in black. A few locked ones had nameplates, like hers and her uncle's. But they were all boring.

Today's hunting went well, though. Right up until she shot her first victim.

Normally, she just hunted in the grounds – for It or for small animals – but she'd been sitting in the cafeteria, bored, when Dr Ramsin came in. Ignoring her completely, he'd gotten a drink from the machine and then left, still ignoring her completely. Which had given her the brilliant idea.

But when Dr Ramsin complained to the Director, she discovered the tiny problem in her genius idea. With bow and arrows taken away, she'd had to wait a whole week before being allowed to use them again. But she took her punishment like a grown up: she hadn't even complained about her prey cheating, by telling on her.

And Uncle had been real nice, too. At first she thought he might be angry; but if she had to guess, she'd say he actually thought it was funny. All he'd said, in private, was that perhaps it would be better to hunt *It*, rather than his co-workers. His voice had been all whispery, and he'd looked around to make sure no one else could hear – even though there was no one else around.

It was cool having a big secret. She wondered what the others would think if they knew she was hunting *It*. Probably excited, or scared. Pro'lly, they'd tell her to stop.

Thinking about it in her room, afterward, she realized she *had* learned a lot from the experience, though. F'r'instance, her uncle had explained how people made up rules – like not shooting each other – to try to keep themselves safe. As if that would stop a real hunter!

If she'd had *proper* arrows he couldn't've cheated by telling on her.

Oh.

She thought about that.

If she'd used a real arrow, they would have worked out what killed him. Sure, she'd picked a stretch of corridor not covered by cameras for the hunt. But since she was the only one at the Institute who *had* arrows, the Director still would have known it was her.

Wow. Hunting people was tricky.

The week after she *finally* got her weapon back saw the emptying of her quiver as one by one she lost her arrows. She'd solved the problem of the rubber caps by first melting them with real fire – she'd been careful not to burn the Forest down, and to put the fire out properly, after – and then cutting them off quickly with the sharp knife, while the ends were still kind of melty.

Later, she'd sharpened the ends. But then they didn't fly properly, wobbling horribly through the air. By the time she'd worked out that she needed extra weight near the tips, she was down to just two arrows, each with paper clips unfolded and wound round and round the shaft, near the tip.

Then for three days she hunted deep in the Forest with her last, now brightly-painted arrow. Wondering if *It* might come, finally.

Or would it wait until she had *none* left?

CHAPTER 8

In Harmon's office, only the regular tapping of his Tik Tek MetaStylus punctuated the silence as he sat, oblivious to the decades of engineering that had made the combination computer and net access tool immune to such treatment. Deep in thought, he dragged representations of Imaginal structure components into the complex diagram he was building, occasionally murmuring and dragging annotations as he went. Harmon didn't notice the door opening, nor the sad little figure trudging into his room carrying just a bow.

"Uncle?"

Frowning, Harmon adjusted the pressor-chain's handle-patterns from an absolute to a relative emotional index range. That would provide excellent connective strength for a new stress source.

"Uncle!"

Harmon nodded to himself, tapped the search button, and held the end of the stylus near his lips, still unaware of Sara's presence. "Perichoresis near concept acquisition."

Sara stomped right up to the desk and slapped her hand down onto the slightly-raised dome of the holo projector, interrupting the stylus's communications. "Uncle!"

Harmon looked up, startled and annoyed. *Couldn't the girl look after herself for five minutes?* "What is it?" he snapped, moving her hand off the display node and triggering a redraw to refresh it.

"My last arrow got lost up a tree."

"So? What do you expect me to do about it?"

"Can't you magic it down?"

"I'm busy. You may be surprised to learn that I have more important things to do with my time than telekinese toy arrows out of trees where they were shot by careless little girls!"

She just stood there. "But I'm hunting *It*."

"There is no-" Harmon stopped himself. "No need to use the arrows. It is in fact better if you fight it with your bare hands." *Which would be true, were it a genuine inorganic being or spirit.* After her account of battling what sounded like a spirit in the woods, he had given her a simple 'panic button' to use if it happened again. Indeed, two weeks later she had triggered it. Quickly leaving his rooms, he had tracked her via a simple Sending and shadowed her at a distance, mindmeld linked. Of course, as expected, there had been nothing – apart from an odd backlash she'd somehow induced at the end. So convincing had been her charade as she'd stalked the creature, though, so deeply involved in her imaginative play, that for a time he himself had thought he sensed something near her, *invisible even on the Imaginal plane*. Impossible, of course. The Imaginal was the dimension of magic that overlapped the mundane world, perceptible to mages. The magic itself was what was perceived. The idea of a magic that was invisible made as little sense as a silent noise.

Beginning to regret the whole 'invisible creature' stressor, he drew his mind back to the present, where Sara looked back at him doubtfully.

"Play something else for a change. Now go away, I'm busy."

With a sigh, he picked up his interrupted thought and returned to work. He didn't see her stubborn expression as she stomped out.

Harmon was studying his revisions with a satisfaction bordering on smugness when the sound of a wailing child broke into his train of thought. *Dammit, what now*, he thought?

The wailing grew louder before fading out. But less than a minute later there came another knock at the door. This time, it was the head of his irritating colleague Simmons that appeared in the gap.

"Your girl's had a bad fall. Probably broken a leg, that's my guess."

Harmon swore and got up, following Simmons into Sara's room where she lay crying on her bed.

"I hurt my leg!" she wailed.

"Let me see."

His probing fingers provoked a scream of pain. He stopped, looked at her coldly. "Try to be a little less *cowardly*, Sara. Tears are for weaklings."

A light went on in Harmon's mind. *How obvious!* Slipping into the Imaginal, he tapped into her pain channel, carefully adding it as another input to the original stress Source he had first constructed back in the orphanage. Returning his perception to the physical, he spoke to the now-silently shuddering girl. "This is going to hurt for a moment. But you must lie still."

He turned to his co-worker. "Simmons, come here." Simmons approached, looking a little ill. "It's a simple break. I'm going to set it back in position, then I want you to hold it firmly while I heal it. Remember: hold it firmly. And Sara: don't move, or it will heal crookedly and you'll be a *cripple*," he said, distaste dripping from the word. "Are we all ready?"

The other two nodded, shakily. "Very well. Remember, Sara: lie still now." Harmon pulled steadily; there was a most unpleasant sound, and Sara screamed in pain.

"Simmons! Here."

Simmons, eyes a bit glazed, grasped the leg gently, Sara crying out at the touch.

"Firmly!"

Simmons gulped but gripped the small, tanned leg more firmly, and Sara screamed again. But although her upper body writhed in slow agony and tears flooded from her eyes, she kept her hips and left leg still. Harmon's senses shifted back to the Imaginal and *reached* as he grasped the angry break in the pattern of the bone and began altering it, accelerating the in-built regenerative mechanisms. He was a little surprised at how easily the healing flowed; and at how quickly the girl's cries stopped.

Simmons was quite gray. "I say, shouldn't you have... you know, used an anesthetic or something?"

"No. This was faster, and safer. Besides, a little pain is good for the soul. As well as being a reminder not to do foolish things," he declared, staring at the girl as she wiped her face.

Soon, though, she was engrossed in her magically-healed leg, scarcely believing the pain was gone. Harmon watched her feel the limb gingerly.

"Wow!" She grabbed a tissue and noisily blew her runny nose. Swinging both legs off her bed she stood up, carefully. Put her weight on the left.

Her sudden whoop of joy took both men by surprise, as did her leap as she impacted into Harmon with a hard hug around his abdomen before breathing a short 'Thanks!' and running back out to play.

Harmon smiled. She truly was remarkable. He ignored both Simmons' disturbed expression and the way the fellow shook his head as they left her room.

After she left, Harmon went to a window overlooking the front entrance to watch her. He was pleased to see her stalk straight across the lawn, heading determinedly back into the woods. Smiling, he returned to his office.

That night he visited Sara in her room. Harmon noted the brightly-painted toy arrow on her bookcase, though neither of them mentioned it. Sitting on the edge of her bed, he surreptitiously cast his usual mindmeld.

"Do you remember your parents, Sara?"

Harmon's question took Sara by surprise, but the girl nodded. She smiled at her most precious possession – her one and only memory of the woman she knew must be her mother. Closing her eyes, she remembered, unaware of his intruding spell: «*A close, warm room; very small; where one wall, of meshed triangles, somehow moved. The smell of wood smoke. Firelight flickering on a woman's face bending over her: dark, twinkling eyes. The smile. The beautiful, fierce smile. Long, black hair hanging straight down, caught in her own small fist. The sound of men's voices outside, singing deep.*»

Sara, eyes still closed, smiled. Her mind drifted toward «*another night, a cold campfire, darkness-. No.*» She forced her mind away from the pain. Back to the warm embrace of the woman with the long, silky black hair.

"Yes," she whispered, smiling.

She did not see Harmon frown, annoyed and surprised, then shake his head.

CHAPTER 9

"Who are *they*, Mr Shanahan?"

Sara was visiting the security officer before heading off with Faith on a patrol. "We're gonna check the lake shore," she'd told him, "because there could be tracks from invisible monsters."

"That sounds like a good idea, but *please* keep Faith out of the mud this time."

She hid a giggle at the way he said 'mud' – rhyming with 'wood' – but then noticed that one of the screens he was watching showed views of people in separate little rooms.

There were only five pictures, but for some reason, it looked like one person, a grown-up man, was in four of them, in different positions. He was pacing. In the only other window with a picture in it, a woman was scratching her arm.

Down the side of the screen, there was a list of words that looked like codes, and places. Places like 'CorrWB1, CorrNSB1, CorrWB2'; and eleven two-letter codes. There were also, she saw, codes G1, G2, G3, and G4, all in green. One of the other two-letter codes was also in green and said AS. She wondered if the four Gs matched the man in the four windows, and if the AS matched the woman.

She knew that the windows only showed stuff where unusual things were happening. The computer did a lot of automatic watching for Mr Shanahan, he'd explained one day. Though if he wanted to, he could choose to look at any of them at any time. He'd shown her some of the views from cameras that watched the outside of the buildings from high up on the walls, sweeping back and forth across the grounds. She'd noticed each sweep took exactly one minute. She was always careful to notice as much as she could. Like how each window showed its own time, even though the time was always the same for all the windows, of course.

"Those are the inmates. The system keeps an eye on them and alerts me if they do anything dangerous to themselves."

"Oh. Do you have windows for Uncle, and me? And the Director?"

Mr Shanahan laughed. "No, only for the inmates. The patients."

"Who's that one?" she asked, pointing to the man who was in the four pictures. She noticed that whatever he did in one, he did in the others, just from a different angle. He must have four cameras in his room. She wondered why.

At her question, the man looked around, like he'd actually heard her. He looked a bit worried all of a sudden, she thought.

"Ah, best if you don't know, Sara. He's very dangerous. A very powerful mage, and completely loopy."

At her sideways-tilted look, he added, "He's mad."

"Where are they? I haven't seen them. Are they in some of the empty rooms?"

He blinked. "Oh, you mean the unused offices? No. And I don't want you to go looking for them, either, you understand? Stay away from them. They're dangerous."

But she knew the in-mates were all locked up. So how could they be dangerous? Aloud, all she said was, "Uh huh, I get it. You don't want me to look for them."

"Good. I don't want your uncle tearing strips off me."

Mr Shanahan often said weird stuff like that, so she just smiled, and told him she and Faith were going to patrol the lake now.

She wondered where the *in-mates* were?

She figured B2 probably meant basement level 2, and maybe the W, E, and NS meant compass directions. So probably the in-mates were kept in the basement. That seemed a bit mean. They wouldn't have any windows to look out of.

She wondered how she could visit the man with four cameras, without the computer thinking it was *unusual*? That was a problem.

In the afternoon, as she tracked muddy footprints across the polished floors, from the corner of her eye she noticed the door onto the stairs leading down, and remembered the man in the basement. Taking off her shoes she tiptoed over, then noticed another problem: the door was locked. But it had a 'lectronic pad of numbers beside the lock, and she smiled as she thought of a sneaky solution. It shouldn't be too hard to convince Uncle to buy her a small telescope, not if she explained she needed it to help hunt the unvisible monster.

The next day, waiting for the delivery drone, she considered shooting its propellers to get the telescope sooner. She and Faith discussed the idea as they paced back and forth at the front steps, but in the end they decided it'd probably be better not to. But the instant the drone docked with the delivery box and deposited its package inside, she raced up to her uncle's office so he could go and get it for her.

It had been kind of fun playing with the telescope, but having to lurk around inside, out of sight while she waited for her uncle to visit the basement, almost drove her mad! Luckily, she had her 'unsurprising training' for the computer to do, so every now and then when it got just too boring to take, she'd sneak off to the cupboard where she had all her equipment hidden.

She'd chosen the upper level – deserted and unimportant – for the training. Each session was exactly the same: she'd stop at the end of one of the upper corridors, carrying the very old and broken cleaning bot. Then, with a long stick she'd taped to it, she'd push the bot down the corridor till she figured it was clearly in view of the security camera. Then she'd wait forever, to be sure it'd been seen. *Then* she'd walk up, all serious, with a big frown, and put her suitcase down beside it. She'd painted the suitcase red, glad she'd brought her paints and drawing stuff with her from, from..., well, anyway, she was glad she'd kept her stuff from when she was little.

Then she'd push and poke the disk-shaped robot, and turn it over, and say 'hmm,' in a very serious voice, too – not because the cameras listened, just because it helped her Pretend properly. Then she'd open her case and get out a screwdriver and one of her coloring pencils, since that kind of looked like a 'lectronic fixing-gadget too. She'd poke at the bot like a repairman would. After a while, in full view of the camera, she'd 'Humph' – with both shoulders – and put her tools back in her toolbox, fasten it shut and then look down at the bot like she was real cross, hands on her hips like she thought it was misbehaving, before finally picking it up and stomping off.

She did that several times each day for the whole next week, and no one said anything, not even Mr Shanahan. So she figured the computer had decided it was seeing a cleaning bot break down, and had also worked out that she was a repair girl who fixed broken cleaning bots. So the next day, she'd visit the basement. She bet the G man was in B2, since B2 was deeper under the ground.

At the door to the basement levels, she stretched up and entered the code that she'd watched – through her small telescope – her uncle enter. It hadn't been too hard to sneak up behind him, and peep round the corners to watch what he used at the first door leading down. And it got specially-easy when she saw that he'd just changed the last number of his code to a '1' when he got to the 'B1' door. The trouble after that, though, had been that by the time she'd done all her repair-girl stuff, Uncle was gone from sight, so she didn't get to see the code he used for B2. She'd chewed her lip, but decided to try changing the last code number to a '2' and see if that worked – and it did! She wished she and Faith could've gone on the adventure together – that'd be so much better – but Mr Shanahan always knew where Faith was, and it'd be pretty hard to explain how *Faith* could've been opening the security doors.

She pushed the loneliness down. At least she could tell her all about it, after.

She sneaked down the stairs and into another corridor. From not far ahead, maybe just around the next turn, she could hear her uncle's voice, and also someone else replying.

She itched to creep up and just take a teensy-weensy peek around the corner. It was the hardest thing she'd ever done, *not* doing that, and instead sneaking away to try the secret entry codes on her own, later. But Miss X was always patient, and it wouldn't kill her to wait till her uncle had left. Probably.

She'd retreated all the way back up to the ground floor and then hid down the corridor to wait for him to come out.

It took for*ever!*

In the end, her uncle did eventually leave – and didn't see her. He just went straight up the stairs to his office instead. And so she snuck straight back down to the basement, all her equipment ready and all the secret door codes memorized. But when she stepped round the corner of basement level 2 and into the corridor with the cell doors –

her cleaning bot under one arm and long stick and toolbox in her other hand – she straightaway saw a big problem. Each room had just one small window, and it looked like the *bottom* of each was just about the same height as the top of her head!

At the far end of the corridor, where it ended in a 'T', there was a chair that looked just the right height for her. But she was sure the grown ups didn't stand on chairs to look inside, so the dumb computer'd probably tell Mr Shanahan someone was doing something unusual.

For a long time she just stood there, breathing hard, before finally turning and stalking away. Eyes narrowed, she stomped off down the corridor, remembering everything that Mr Shanahan had said about how his computer worked out what was unusual. It helped him do his job more easily, he'd explained when she'd asked why there were so few windows on his screens. She knew there were lots more security cameras than that, from the number she'd counted in the game she'd made of finding and counting them all.

So three days later – three days of dragging chairs down corridors to closed office doors, then picking up her bot – which she'd named 'Bork' – and holding it up to the window for no reason at all except to get the stupid dumb computer used to seeing repair-girl step up to windows on a chair – she was back in corridor CorrEB2 and pushing Bork down toward the first window. She left it for a good long time, then walked up to it with her toolbox and did her cross-at-the-bot fixing-examination. No alarms or anything went off, which she took as a good sign. She tromped down the corridor thinking serious and grumpy repair-girl thoughts, before dragging the chair back down the corridor to the first window.

The chair was almost broken, the thick navy-blue padding squashed flat, like a *really* fat person had sat in it for a *really* long time. One back leg was bent and had a crack, but she reckoned it would be good enough. And if it did break, she'd bring her own stupid chair next time!

Placing the chair by the first door, she picked up Bork and stepped onto the chair, holding him up next to the window and excitedly looking inside-

And the stupid room was empty!

Grinding her teeth, she kept 'examining' Bork, then got down, dragged the chair down to the next room, and repeated her charade.

This room had the woman who'd been scratching her arm, though now she was just lying on her bunk, asleep.

So, she examined Bork some more for the pesky computer, then dragged her chair along to the *next* door.

She almost dropped Bork when she looked inside, because she'd found the G man! He was standing in the middle of his cell and slowly moving his hands in sweeping patterns, facing away from her. She stared, wishing he'd turn around, and suddenly he stilled, and very slowly, did just that.

She smiled, and waved.

And he *freaked out!* His eyes went *huge* and his mouth dropped open, and he instantly did some weird thing with his hands and fingers, and suddenly he was encased in a glowing dome, so bright it hurt her eyes. He'd just made a magical protection circle! And it was *much* brighter, and much thicker than any circle she'd seen on the trids! She could see his mouth move, and peered forward, squinting, trying super hard to hear what he said, or read his lips. 'Meh'-something 'S'-something-short. Merry sand?

She smiled again, and waved again, and he paled – she could actually see his face go even whiter, which was pretty cool: she thought that only happened in books. And he kind of staggered back, like his legs could barely hold him up.

Then her own eyes went wide at a sudden awful thought, and she twisted around on the chair in case something was sneaking up behind her.

But the corridor was empty. It was just *her* there, and she looked back round into the small room. She waved again, trying a smaller smile and just wiggling her fingers, and said "Hi, my name's Sara."

He said something, and did another wriggly thing with *his* fingers, and suddenly a huge bolt of flame shot straight toward the window! She almost fell backwards off the chair in shock.

But nothing happened: in fact the flames stopped like there was a sharp wall a hand's width in front of the window inside the room. All the space between the thick glass and his glowing dome blazed, on and on, until suddenly the flames just winked out.

Inside the cell, the man simply stared at her, blinking, while she stared back. Suddenly she realized, even if *she* hadn't done anything unusual, probably *he* just had, so she quickly hopped off the chair, dragged it back to the T junction, and hurried off, Bork under one arm and her red toolbox in the other.

Wincing the whole way, since she was sure she was going to get into *so* much trouble, she was already trying to think up some excuses.

But by the end of the day, when no one had said anything – not Mr Shanahan, not even her uncle – she began to think that no one had noticed after all. Which was pretty strange. It must of meant that Mr G often made super protection spells and cast fireballs right there in his cell.

But then, Mr Shanahan had said Mr G was mad. *Loopy.* She'd giggled, thinking about it at dinner time, and almost choked on her orange juice. Her uncle had looked at her strangely, but she just said she'd remembered a funny cartoon. She knew he was bored by cartoons and if she wanted to avoid a whole series of weird questions, it was best to keep Uncle bored.

But she could hardly wait till the next day!

-

This time when she stepped up on the chair, Mr G flashed around almost straight away, and again the huge glowy magic circle went up. But this time he didn't look so scared. In fact he looked pretty cool. He'd wrapped a sort of ghost-fire around his hands, though this time he didn't actually shoot it at her.

Which was *probably* good. She smiled, and waved, and this time his eyes just narrowed. His lips moved, and she was sure he was saying M-something. 'Many sap?' But she couldn't hear even a whisper, through the thick glass.

She wondered if she could open the door, but it had a metal plate with buttons with numbers on them, and she figured you needed a code. She pointed down at the lock and very clearly and slowly said "Do you know the unlocking code number?"

His mouth fell open, but after a second he made a sort

of sweeping gesture and the too-bright magic dome vanished like he'd switched it off. He walked right up to the door, then, but kind of on his toes, like he thought she might be about to trick him.

She considered lunging forward and shouting 'Boo', but thought maybe that wasn't a real good idea.

He made more funny wriggly motions with his fingers like Uncle sometimes did when he did magic, and the man's lips moved, and suddenly she could hear him.

"Who are you?"

"I'm Sara. Who did you think I was, yesterday? You were real scared."

"I- never mind. How did you get here? How did you get past the walls? Why are you here?"

She tilted her head to one side. "Uh, I didn't see any walls-"

At that statement he jumped back and cast his protection circle again, and she winced as the bright dome once more sprang up around him.

"I live here? With my Uncle. Dr Harmon?"

For a long time he just stared at her; for such a long time, in fact, that she started getting bored. He sure was jumpy. She wondered what was scary about saying she hadn't got past any walls?

"Um, what's your name?"

Again he swept the glowing protective circle away and stepped forward, this time looking a little cross.

"You don't know?"

"I think it starts with G."

He blinked. Said something, under his breath.

"Sorry, I didn't hear you," she told him, pointing to her ear.

He looked annoyed, but spoke up louder. "I said I am God's Son," and then paused, like he was expecting her to react in some way.

"Um, that's a nice name. Why did you try to blast me with magic fire yesterday?"

"I – why did you say you live here? Alexander is your uncle? You don't look at all like him."

She giggled. "You call him Alexander? Doesn't he get cross?"

Mr G smiled. He had a really nice smile. "Sometimes,

yes. That's why I do it."

She giggled again. "He adopted me."

"But surely that would make you his daughter?"

She looked away, suddenly not feeling so giggly. "No. I'm his ward." She looked back through the window at Godsson. "He said I can call him Uncle, though."

"Ah. Of course. Yes. I see."

"So why did you get all scared when you first saw me? And why did you try to fireblast me, yesterday?"

"I – well, a young girl like you... you were the last thing I expected to see, here. So I, ah, assumed you weren't what you seemed."

"What did you think I was?"

"I... thought you were something that had followed me here."

"Um, I don't mean to be rude, truly, but I think you're an in-mate? I think you were *put* in there."

"Not *here*. To this world."

She could feel her eyes go big. "Oh, wow! So you're an *alien!* That is so cool!"

"No! I merely visited another... place. And there I dealt with... a bad person. But part of her death... attached to me. Followed me back."

"Wow." She thought about that. "Part of her death – you mean, like a ghost?"

He blinked, looking a little surprised. "In a sense; in a sense. In that Place, actions have consequences. And killing Melisande d'Artelle had consequences."

"Oh! I know her!"

Godsson jumped back from the window and once again the golden-bright circle sprang up around him.

She blinked, crossly. Why did he keep *doing* that? "We learned about her in.... Anyway, she was a real bad magician...."

She stopped, realizing he couldn't hear her, again. When he finally stopped his spell, he strode right up to the door. "What do you know of d'Artelle? Speak quickly, child!"

"I'm not a child! I'll be nine in December!"

"What do you know of d'Artelle?" he growled at her.

"I already told you, but you couldn't hear me through your stupid spell." That only made him look growlier.

Probably because it was true. Grown ups didn't like looking stupid. "Fine. Melisande d'Artelle made the Second World Storm, the one that came in winter time, and the Melt plague, and who was all pretending-to-be-good even though really she wasn't, she was really bad." She stopped, pleased that she could show off how much she knew. "Oh! You thought I was *her?* The Enemy of Mankind? Really?"

She wasn't sure if she was cross about that, or pleased. "Do I look like her?"

"No. It was merely – I didn't expect to see a child here, of all places. You shouldn't be here. How did you even get in?"

"Stop calling me a child! And I'm pretending to be a repair girl so the computer thinks I'm usual. I've got a broken bot and a red toolbox and I taught the computer you hold broken bots up to windows after you stand on a chair."

For a long while Godsson said nothing at all, but eventually he smiled. "You know, Sara, I think I like you."

They chatted for a long time. Godsson was fun. He even made up a secret new word: 'Grups.' It meant normal, boring grown-up people. Not like her, or Mr G.

CHAPTER 10

Sara prowled silently behind Dwayne as he spoke on his wristcomm.

"Yeah, I'm heading to the warehouse lift now. The truck's just entered the main gates."

She couldn't hear the response, but saw him check his netpad.

"Yeah, four Tik Tek Nursoid sixes, and two more Honda dombots." Again, he fell silent. "True. When the next gen Nursoids are released, there'll be no excuse for us to hang around."

Probably he was talking to Nerida.

"Looks almost time to head back to the city, babe: pick up a job in a normal place. It'll be a relief to be away from the creepy nuts around here."

Creepy nuts? That's just mean! Her eyes narrowed and she streaked bare-footed down the corridor at her very fastest speed. She was a swift and silent cheetah, eyes fixed on the unsuspecting sheep ahead in its white coat. But at the last instant, she decided the prey was too easy. That wouldn't lessen its fear, though, as the deadly predator flashed past it. The people here had learned that much, over the last few months. Not like the stupid robots, who just got confused and stopped if she hunted them.

She *Growled* him as she raced past, grazing his jacket and delighting in his startled cry. With a fierce grin back at him as she slowed for the corner, she darted out of sight.

His angry voice pursued her, though. "It's no wonder you don't have any friends!"

It almost made her stop and go back. She did too have friends! She had Faith, and her uncle, and Mr Shanahan. And Godsson. That was lots of friends!

But somehow, she didn't feel quite so Growly any more.

She scuffed through the gravel outside, wondering whether she ought to put some shoes on. That was how bored she was: she was thinking about shoes.

What to do? Faith'd still be doing her rounds with Mr Shanahan for another hour. And inside the building was just a handful of Grups in white coats roaming from one place to another doing boring Grup things. And they were all either too busy to talk to her, or too boring to talk *to*. She considered *Growling* Nerida – but she'd done that yesterday, and Dwayne today: it was too soon to stalk either one again.

And then it started to rain. She said Dwayne's curse word: in the cold rain the Forest would quickly turn into a big wet empty zero.

She could try sneaking into the Dungeons, where the in-mates lived. She could visit Godsson once she got past the security cameras....

Godsson was nice. Maybe they could make up more secret Hunter's language. Remembering him naming the grown-ups 'grups' made up her mind.

Yeah. She'd visit Godsson. He was always so serious she felt sorry for him. Even if he didn't approve of her hunting, he was interesting to talk to. Strange, but – he thought his father made *everything*, just like she made rivers and mountains and dams in the Forest. He said his father, as a test, made people put him in the Dungeon. She didn't understand why, though. But then, lots of stuff he told her about his father didn't make sense. Like listening to sparrows falling out of trees. Or hiding from people and seeing if they believed in him. It was weird, too, how some of the things he said made her think of old women dressed in black and white, serious like him, using some of his words. Actually, it was sort of confusing. Maybe it was a dream she'd had.

Sometimes, she felt sure, Godsson just made things up. He was the one who made her realize that Grups made things up too. They wouldn't ever admit it, but. Like the way none of them – except for Uncle – would admit that *It* existed in the woods outside. They'd just look blank, and pretend they didn't know what she was talking about. Scaredy cats.

-

"... forty days and forty nights, until the whole world flooded."

Sara giggled, leaning against the closed door to his room as she stood on the broken chair.

Through the thickened glass of the small observation window, Godsson looked offended. "Nearly everyone died, Sara. It's not a *funny* story."

"No, I wasn't laughing at *that*. I was just remembering when I built my dam in the Forest, and it broke and flooded all the roses and washed into some of the Castle's rooms. Boy, did I get into trouble for that! There were cleaning bots *everywhere*, for days.

"Anyway, they were all bad, the ones who died, so it doesn't matter. And I don't see why your father made all the other animals drown too. And what about other people on boats. And why did he kill all the animals, but not the fish?"

Godsson opened his mouth, then shut it. Then did it again.

"It's raining now, you know? Maybe it'll last for forty days and nights, and the whole *Castle* will flood! Hey, I could probably build a *great* dam today. Why didn't I think of that before? Thanks! Bye!"

She waved; hopped down from the chair; dragged it back down to its usual place at the end of the corridor; then raced off.

CHAPTER 11

That winter passed slowly, with only Faith to play with, and Godsson to chat to just for fun. Chats with her uncle always seemed to turn into lessons.

Apart from Mr Shanahan, everyone except Sara preferred to stay warm inside. Even the security officer stayed mainly in his small house, set off to one side and behind the bigger, sprawling building. She was the only person who spent the better part of each day outside, most of it with Faith.

Best of all was when it snowed, since then there were snow tunnels and snowmen to build. She always built two or three, since that way they could all talk and she could pretend they were real. It was nice being able to make new friends. The first one always got to help her decide who to make next, and got to suggest names for them, and help decide whether each would be a boy or a girl.

Except it was awful sad when they melted. It was almost enough to stop her making them.

Almost.

She didn't tell Uncle, though. Somehow, she just knew he wouldn't approve. And he'd probably do his stupid wiggly-finger thing and then give her a lecture.

The snow was also great for following tracks. They were like story books written in a secret language that showed where the animals lived, and drank, and ate.

She'd also learned that her arrows, even now she'd removed the dumb cups, didn't really hurt the animals. She'd looked on the net and found out you needed wicked-looking metal tips to do that. She wasn't sure she wanted them, though. She was kind of glad when her uncle said he wouldn't buy any for her. It meant she only scared the animals – or made them cross! – when she shot them.

Also when it snowed she could drag a sled – another gift from her uncle! – up the gentle hills in the Institute grounds to whoosh back down. She could do that for hours. Warmly clad, she'd play outside for most of the day. That was another good thing about being here. Her uncle wasn't as strict as the nuns had been in making her do her net lessons as... they used to be.

It was on a crisp winter day, after Faith had been called away and she was by herself, that she first felt them: felt there were things invisible, around her. Not really watching her, just... doing their own stuff. Not even really aware of her.

She discovered that if she looked, though, she lost them.

But as the days passed and she practiced her not-looking, the more she started to see them. Well, not *see* them, exactly. More like, see or hear their shadows: how they affected the plants and stuff around them. Sometimes she saw their traces in the clouds; sometimes in the wind as it raced through the trees, bending their trunks or twisting and dancing in their branches. Sometimes they flowed softly and gently over the trees and through them, stroking their leaves and petting their trunks, sliding up and around the rough silvery bark, rubbing and scratching themselves against those slow and patient warriors and wardens.

She realized these must be the invisible spirits that her uncle had told her lived in the Forest.

Sometimes, when they were playful, she danced and played with them. She'd pretend they could see her, and were dancing with her. And she'd spin and twist alongside them till she was dizzy; leaping and tumbling and even touching them, imagining their surprise as her fingers shivered over them, while they flowed and coiled around her in turn. And then they'd leap and race and dance together, swooping down the green pathways that tunneled between tall trunks, kissing and brushing over the feathery outstretched fronds of fern or the green-budding leaves, until finally they'd gyre up into the trees to leave her laughing below, breathless and excited, blowing a farewell wish.

Once or twice, Faith raced with her, a faint air of confusion on her doggy features even as she enjoyed the thrill of the chase, or the dance, whichever it was.

But the monster was quite, quite different.

For it, clouds would usually be the first sign, as they darkened the sun: as if that somehow made a space, a hole where the monster could slip out from its hiding place and into the world. The next sign was always a stillness, a silence. And a coldness, too. Always, then, the others fled, leaving the wind curiously hollow: just air blowing, joyless and busy, hurrying on its way from somewhere to somewhere-else.

The sounds would drop, too. First the birds and other animals. Then the insects would falter and fall silent.

Usually, it would just move in a straight line, before fading out. Or, sometimes, it would instead double back, and she'd sense it marching back the way it came, then reversing its path, over and over again. Times like that, she thought it was confused. Or, maybe, not properly awake.

She called it Robo.

A few times, when it was doing its silly back-and-forward sleep-marching, she'd fired her arrows at it. Though she still wasn't sure when it was that her uncle's magic *worked*, and when it didn't. It wasn't always easy to know when she'd shot it, of course, since it was *in*visible. But often she was *sure* she'd hit it, yet it would just march straight on anyway, completely ignoring both her arrow and her. 'Course, that might just be because it was hard to know whether she'd shot it in a deadly place or just 'winged' it. After all, it *was* invisible.

Sometimes, though, it was very much awake. Then, there'd be an extra coldness to it and a purpose. And she knew it Hunted, then. Then, it didn't seem either silly *or* harmless. Then, she sensed a strange kind of danger to it like her uncle had said. A wrongness. She'd follow, as silent as she could be, stepping carefully and breathing lightly. Not looking at it directly, 'cause then you'd lose it. You had to see it by its edges, by how the things around it moved; or stopped moving; or slowed and kind of saddened. It always moved in straight lines, though it could angle off in a new direction at any moment.

Mostly, she felt a bit sad for it and just followed.

This one day, though, it seemed different: really intense. Determined. Brutal in the way it stomped through the Jungle, bringing Winter early, to turn it into the Forest. It was a little scary, to tell the truth. She wanted to fire an arrow, but she wanted even more to know what it hunted with such concentration. Besides, she still felt kinda sorry for it, for all the times it had prowled, confused, back and forth like a broken cleaning bot.

And, yeah, maybe she was just a little bit scared to shoot.

And as she followed, gradually she sensed something else.

Something else, with sharp edges; which twisted and coiled through the trees more like oil flowing in air, showing off as it tweaked the world that had stilled and hidden, hoping to escape its notice, but jerking and quivering when it jabbed, or it looped and tangled and squeezed. Twisting and tying fronds. Tumbling and trapping drier shoots. Blowing leaves into the middle of spiders' webs, or just pinching the wind to make it gust and tear them. It felt not just Wrong, but Bad. Wrong, and mean, and cruel.

And then it found her.

She looked around, but too hard, and suddenly she couldn't see it anymore.

«Oh. You're like me. Did you know?» Sara wasn't sure if she had thought that, or *it* had. She giggled, inside, but again wasn't sure if that was really her.

«Yes, it's just me. I've thought of a new game. I'm just talking to myself. Pretending.»

Sara wasn't sure. She didn't really-

«Oh, poo,» she interrupted herself. Or did she? She didn't say *poo.*

«Oh, don't be silly. I'm just playing a new game I thought up. A fun game. I'm pretending she's my sister. A lovely little sister. I want a sister. Sisters are fun. Much more fun than boys.»

A little sister *would* be wonderful...

«That's right. And I'll grow up fast. I'm already growing. Soon I can be your big sister. Then I'll teach you grown up things.»

She frowned. She wasn't sure Grup stuff would be fun. Godsson didn't seem too impressed by-

«Godsson? I think I know Godsson. Bent Son... Naughty Godsson. Bad Godsson.»

Godsson's not bad!

«In my pretend he is. He has secrets. I remember. Godsson's mean. Not like you, big sister. I like talking to you. It makes me remember things. All sorts of things. Like how to get people – men, especially – to do what I want. Anything I want. And all I'd have to do would be to imagine my sister a little harder, let her speak to me just like this, tell me secret things. Teach me-»

And then, the other one, scary Robo, came marching straight into her and over her and the daydream ended, leaving her slightly stunned, with a fading memory of an angrily-silenced shriek. She blinked, dizzy, feeling like she'd just jumped from a too-hot bath she hadn't known she was in, into ice water.

What had just happened? Just ahead, on the path, a tiny tornado of confusion, of thrashing and flailing edges, felt rather than seen, spun, and dwindled, and collapsed.

She felt kind of... icky.

She realized *her* monster, the one she Hunted – Robo, or scary-Robo – had driven it off.

That night, she tried telling Uncle, but though he'd listened at first, the more she explained, the more annoyed he got. His fingers twisted and turned in odd patterns, like he was spelling out some signal with them, and then he looked away and went still. Just for a moment, she thought he was excited, and she remembered 'seeing' the invisible creatures, but he frowned straight after, looking angry.

She found herself thinking about what had happened, the memories shuffling past her mind's eye like a deck of cards, and then he turned back to her and opened his eyes, looking straight at her.

"You can't be a Hunter, Sara, if you spend all your energies on make-believe. Don't fool yourself into seeing patterns where there are none. Human beings are far too good at self-delusion. Frighteningly so. Don't start imagining that *spirits* are talking to you, girl. They simply don't do that. That's just the sort of thing too many of the inmates here believe. The *crazy* people. Do you understand? I won't have you of all people walk down that path."

She pursed her lips, biting down on the desire to tell him he was wrong, that they were real. She knew that would only make him angrier. He hadn't believed a single word she'd said. He'd made up his mind already.

He suddenly looked even angrier, like she'd said that aloud.

"Bah." He threw his napkin down and stood up. "Why should I expect reason from a nine-year-old girl?" he said as he stalked off.

At the table, fists clenched tight, she watched him go. *Just for that, I won't tell you about any more Hunts in the future. Not ever!* That'd show him.

Spring brought its own joys – fresh green shoots on the trees, strange creatures emerging from tiny cocoons, life bursting forth all around her.

Though all the time, mixed in with the net-based schooling and outdoor activities, were the tests and strange exercises her uncle set her. Chores that made no sense to her. Like concentrating on candle flames, or counting backwards from a hundred while she imagined the numbers getting smaller and smaller, or picturing herself walking around and around and down and down long flights of stairs, going deeper and deeper, darker and darker. At least he didn't get cross at her when she fell asleep doing them.

She'd been there almost a year before she finally asked him what he actually *did* at the Institute. He looked surprised – maybe at her question: maybe that she knew the word 'institute.'

"I study things you wouldn't understand."

"Yes I would."

"Really," he sniffed. "Well in that case, I'm happy to tell you that through subtle applications of paranormal patterns, I am endeavoring to unlock the secrets of the collective unconscious, examine the validity of the concept of racial memory, and clarify and possibly *expand* the set of Jungian archetypes."

She blinked.

"Well. Now you know, don't you?"

"Yes. And *I* know *lots* about... about young Arga Tipes. And *grown-up* ones, too. But I'm not telling *you!*" and she'd stalked out of the room and then headed into the Jungle to hunt Arga Tipes, a kind of small but fierce brown tiger.

Later, she'd forgiven him and offered to take him into the Jungle to help her hunt the fiercest Arga Tipe of them all.

She was surprised when he'd agreed. They had an exciting hunt, because the Arga Tipe was cunning and led them on a long and tricky chase: through quicksand, up trees, and into its secret tunnels. But in the end they'd won, since they'd driven it away and made the Jungle safe again.

Then, all through dinner, she told her uncle the story of all the things they'd seen and all the things they might have seen if they'd been luckier. She'd stomped around the dinner table, advancing on him with big lurching steps, arms stretched up high and fingers curled into claws, to show him how a Giffen looked when *it* hunted.

He put her to bed, but she was too excited to sleep: maybe Uncle had had so much fun with her, he'd want to do it *every* day! And suddenly the idea to *pounce* Uncle himself leapt into her mind in vivid color.

She got out of bed, and tiptoed from her room and to his door.

Sneaking through his darkened office, she quietly opened the inner door, behind his neat and almost-bare desk. That door led down a short hallway with three other doors opening off it, all dark. The only lighting came from an Exit sign in the corridor.

Now what?

Through the door beside her, a toilet flushed from somewhere further inside. Quickly opening that door, she slid inside, hearing it *snick* shut behind her. Dim light escaped under the crack of another door across the room to her left, just enough to make out the rumpled bed in front of her on the far side of his bedroom. Then the door to her left opened and she froze as light flooded in. But only for a moment. Her uncle must have turned it off before he'd even left the bathroom, trusting himself to find his way to his bed in the dark.

In the now pitch darkness she heard his heavy footsteps cross from her left, deeper into the room, then heard the bed creak under his weight and the blankets drawn up.

He didn't see me!

She let dark seconds flow through her as she slowly but surely became The Monster-Under-The-Bed. On bare feet, then, she crept slo-o-owly across the room, step by cautious step. *This was going to be so good!* She wanted to laugh, but forced herself to stay silent. Briefly, she had to halt, hugging herself in delight as she fought to stop the giggles from escaping and ruining the Hunt. She even kept her breathing soft and gentle, so he wouldn't hear her. The fuzzy cloth of her pajamas made no sound as she stole across the room, testing the ground ahead with her toes so she didn't accidentally kick something. But the floor was clear, no mess on it at all – just like his office – and after only a minute she stood while the sound of his breathing came from right in front of her.

He shifted position, the bedclothes rustling, and she froze. She was close enough. Now to get under his bed. What she *wanted* to do right now was bounce up and down, but by biting her lips and clenching her hands into fists she locked the excitement inside.

She carefully bent down, one hand reaching out to the floor. V-e-r-y carefully stretching out on the carpet tiles she slo-o-owly eased herself under the bed. There! She was in position. Her cheeks were aching from how wide her grin was!

The Monster Under The Bed breathed in, then: a long, soft, breath that her prey probably couldn't even hear. But it was a really *deep* breath, because the Monster was big, so it had big lungs. Above her, the movement of her prey hesitated, as if it had sensed something was wrong, that something had changed. That it wasn't alone. Now?

Now!

Softly but quickly she slid out from under the bed. But not silently: she needed her prey to know that *something* was nearby, moving in the night. There was a satisfying sudden stillness above, as her prey froze.

Now the darkness seemed alive, filled with her menace as she invisibly loomed over the bed, arms stretched out with claws at the ends like a Giffen. She paused, shaking with excitement and anticipation as she held her breath at the side of his bed. So quietly it was barely a whisper, she growled her softest Warning Growl.

Then *Pounced!*

And oh, his shouts, and her screams!

Laughing shakily, he turned on the light. Shook his head. Her eyes gleamed with delight at her success. He lifted her up and bounced her on his lap. "Sometimes, I swear, you behave like such a wild little thing, I think I must be your keeper."

"Yes! Yes!" She clapped her hands. "I'm Wild Thing! You're my Keepie Keeper!" She bounced up and down on him, relishing the physical contact.

He even stroked her hair, when she paused in her bouncing, to stare at her almost like she was something wonderful, and she snuggled in to him.

"But this Keepie is much too tired to play now. So his Wild Thing will have to go back to her lair."

Despite her protests, he took her back into her room and put her into her bed.

They spoke for a little while longer as she settled down, and he warned her again to be careful in her exploration of the Institute. "Brian Shanahan mentioned an odd thing today. It seems he's been noticing more and more strange glitches in the security systems for the permanent patient section. Odd shadows at the edge of the camera-sweep zones. You wouldn't know anything about that, would you, Sara?"

She shook her head, making her eyes as wide and innocent as she could.

"Good, good. He tells me that they're updating the system soon, because of it. They'll be using infrared sensors to direct the cameras."

"What's that?"

"Heat. The cameras will be able to detect body heat."

"Oh," she said in a small voice.

"You visit Mr Shanahan, don't you? Down in that small building near the pond. I'm sure he'd be happy to explain it to you, if you told him you were interested. I imagine he gets quite lonely down there. On second thoughts, though, you may need to avoid talking about the new security system. When people get new equipment, they'll often bore visitors by telling them all about the things the new system can and can't do."

Oh! she thought, as a brilliant idea struck her, then quickly tried to hide her excitement.

Tucking her in, then, he headed for her door.

"But, *Wild Thing*, best not to sneak in on me like that again: you don't want to give me a heart attack. For a moment I thought an inmate had escaped: and the next moment I was being attacked by a wild animal!"

But he smiled when he said it.

He put the light out and closed her door, and she rolled over onto her side, hugging the memory of his departing smile to herself.

CHAPTER 12

Having run the gauntlet of his weird neighbor – yet another new one – Sara was visiting Godsson again. Taking off the cold wet towel and dropping it on the floor, she had a quick look at the cells on either side of his. Nowadays she always checked – it was better, she'd decided, to *know* what was nearby than to ignore them and hope nothing bad would happen.

First though, of course, she dragged the chair up and held Bork up to each window, her red toolbox in her other hand.

The farther cell was empty, again. *I guess they couldn't find someone horrible enough to put there to try and scare poor Godsson.* Funny how at first his neighbors usually seemed just silly, or even nice.

She banged on the heavy glass of Godsson's window, and he got up from the desk he'd been sitting at, smiling when he saw it was her. He made his usual greeting gesture. *Could that be a spell?*

"Hi, Godsson."

"Hello, Sara. What can I do for you today?"

"Oh, nothing. I just came to talk. How are you?"

"The same, Sara, the same."

"Oh." She paused. "Don't you get awfully bored in there all day?"

A funny expression crossed his face, like she'd said something wrong, but he just shook his head. "I'm sure I *would* get bored, if I didn't have my work to do."

"What work?"

"It's a secret."

"Can't you tell *me*?"

"I'm afraid not."

"Does it have anything to do with your father putting you in here?"

He paused, considering whether to answer. "Yes, I suppose it does."

"Something to do with the way he's testing you?"

Godsson smiled. "He's not testing *me*, Sara. He's testing *you*."

"Me? How is he testing *me*?"

"Well, perhaps not you specifically, but all the people who put me here, and, by extension, everyone who does not act to get me out. Which of course means everyone, in the final analysis."

Sara thought about this. She frowned, tilting her head to one side. "Do you mean, you'd like me to try and get you out?"

"No, Sara. I want *everyone* to want me released."

Godsson was often confusing. But something he'd just said.... "You just said *people* put you in here. But you always *used* to say your father put you here as a test."

"Yes, Sara. Both are true."

Huh?

He smiled at her. "My Father acted to magnify the cowardice of one man. That man influenced others, persuaded them to share in his fears. They, in turn, drew in others. It is these fearful men who keep me here, but they are all, in effect, working according to my Father's plan."

"Um, I see, I guess.... What are they afraid of?"

"*Me.*"

"Of *you*, Godsson?" she asked doubtfully. "Why would anyone be afraid of *you*?"

"Because I am God's Son," he answered, sounding just slightly annoyed by her question.

"Yeah. Right. They're scared of you *because* you're Godsson?"

"Yes." He chuckled. "And because I learned how to bring people to rebirth. Or as some crudely put it, I learned how to reboot people, load a new operating system for their memories. A gift from Melisande."

She was pretty sure Godsson was being silly again. The Enemy of Mankind wouldn't have given him any gifts. *And how could people be re-born?* You only got born once. *Plus* she was pretty sure people didn't have that system stuff in their memories. She looked at him. Maybe he was just joking with her. It was hard to tell, with Godsson. "Will you do some more magic?"

He laughed. "I'm doing some right now. That's how *we* can hear each other, but the microphones in my room can't." He tapped the solid glass in the window, which was as thick as the door itself.

"Oh." She hadn't thought of that. "But I mean *real* magic."

Now he really *did* look annoyed. His expression hardened. "Put your hand up against my window, Sara."

A little unsure, she pressed her right palm flat against it, while he brought the back of his right hand up to match hers from the inside, but holding it a short distance from the glass. She wasn't so sure this was a good idea....

With his other hand he began a series of complex gestures, his expression becoming steadily scarier. Beads of sweat began to appear on his forehead. She'd never seen that happen, before. He slowly pushed the back of his hand against the window. She knew there was an invisible magic barrier spell, 'coz he'd told her about it – a real, live Dragon had made it, he said! It kept his magic locked inside. She'd kind of expected his hand not to be able to touch the window. But maybe his hand wasn't magic.

Keeping the back of it pressed flat against the glass, he flexed his hand in a kind of beckoning gesture; then twisted his hand as if tossing something straight up, or sideways, or... she wasn't quite sure, the twist hurt her eyes. His eyes met hers, but he wasn't looking at her, more like he was *pointing* at her with his eyes.

Something about all this was feeling creepy, all of a sudden.

But she wasn't a scaredy cat. Uh-uh. She shook her head. *I'm not scared.* She wasn't frightened. Not really. She pursed her lower lip and kept her hand pressed up against the glass. Like a shadow of his hand, only smaller.

Then something happened: wisps of a sort of translucent shimmer began streaming in toward her hand from her side of the window, coiling up and around her arm. Godsson dropped his hand from the glass. A small part of her noticed him making his greeting gesture again, except real slowly, like he was tired. But mostly, she was feeling the shimmer. She stepped back, pulling her hand away, but the ripple in the air kept coming, following her hand, more and more of it. She couldn't see where it was coming from, it was just *there.* Gradually it grew more real, colder, kind of clinging to her arm even as it sort of swelled, beginning to droop from her arm. And as it did, she started getting a bad feeling. She was really scared now. Like something awful was getting closer and closer to her.

She looked quickly behind her – but the beige-painted corridor was still empty. Nothing was creeping up on her. Fighting the fear, she turned back around, and suddenly the rippling air *blinked*, and she sensed three cold eyes staring at her.

It was too much. She screamed, tearing at it, suddenly frantic, raking it equally with her nails, her anger, and the need to kill the horrible thing. Something inside her seemed to shudder into life. Her anger grew, the feeling inside burning hotter as she worked even harder to tear it apart, kill it. It began writhing as though in pain.

Finally she stood panting, as the last wisps evaporated. Nothing at all remained of it – only a few long weals on her arms left by her own fingernails showed it had ever been there. She remembered Godsson and glared at him.

He looked dumbstruck.

"What was *that*!" she demanded.

"You... my...." He looked surprised, maybe even shocked. "You're not mundane at all, Sara, are you?" he said. "How did you-"

He gave her a look like he thought maybe *she* should be in a cell, too. She ignored it. "What *was* it?"

"Oh. That!" He shook himself, and managed a laugh. "I'm sorry if I scared you. It was only an illusion." He looked down at his feet. "I became angry when you seemed to be saying I couldn't do real magic, and decided to frighten you. I'm sorry, Sara." He looked up at her, his unlined face open and innocent.

"It sure *felt* real."

"Well, yes. The best illusions do."

She still wasn't convinced it *had* just been an illusion. It had sure felt real. "You said the Dragon's barrier stopped your magic going through!"

"That's true. And my magic didn't go Through." He smiled. "It was just an illusion, Sara, not real magic. Are we still friends?"

She thought about that for a while, then an idea struck her. "We are if you tell me about your secret work."

It was his turn to pause. "Well... I will tell you what it is, but not any details. Provided you promise to never tell anyone else: not of this conversation, nor of the Illusion I just cast. Especially your uncle. You must promise not to even tell them that you visit me down here. Is it a deal?"

"Um, okay! Now, what's the secret?"

"I can only tell you this: that it is the Final Redemption." He looked very solemn.

"I don't understand."

"You will, Sara. You will. I promise you."

She didn't let the matter rest there, but no matter how she argued, she couldn't get any more details from him. Eventually she wrapped herself back up in the heavy, sopping towel and stalked off, deliberately not looking back.

-

Godsson hardly noticed, thinking both about what she'd done, and about how utterly oblivious she was to anything beyond herself. She was a good example of humanity's terrible flaw. Self-centered, erratic, emotional.

An impeccable animal, really.

But perhaps that gave her a special place in the great plan. As first fuel for the Redemption.

But how had she dealt with... *It?* How could she have harmed it? Such creatures were unknown to this world.

His eyes swept the physical bounds of his room, then deeper senses washed against the cell's Imaginal barriers – those drains and cutoffs that broke the circuit, that earthed the truths that mages called spells. He smiled, imagining their reaction if they knew he'd managed to... avoid those Barriers. At least in one 'direction.'

Crossing to his sleeping pallet, he slipped into a state of deep meditation, then let go of his *self* and sank into the dissolving chaos below the Imaginal to work a more subtle kind of magic.

Hours later, with his Self re-formed, he sat up on his simple camp bed, surprise echoing through his mind as he mulled over what he'd learned. He recognized the hand of Harmon's craft, and recognized the patterns of Sara's essence. What he had *not* expected was to find traces of Dr Alex Harmon's influence in the depths that he had thought only *he* and the dragon lord could visit; to find connections from Sara into that primal chaos. And especially, one strong connection to something that did not exist. Not yet.

But what a wonderful opportunity. Perfect, in fact. Though even for him, it would be a challenging piece of work. Still, now he saw a very clear path forward, despite his incarceration.

-

That night, at dinner, Sara carefully questioned her uncle,

mindful of her promise to Godsson. "Keepie, are ghosts real?"

Harmon raised his bushy eyebrows. "Why, do you think you've seen one? Here, in the Institute?"

She rolled her eyes. "*No.* I was just thinking about the unvisible thing, is it-"

"*In*visible."

"Huh?"

"Not *un*visible. *In*visible. You were thinking about the *invisible* thing...?"

"Yeah. The *in*visible thing. Is it a ghost? The spirit of a dead person?"

"No, Sara. Spirits – we call them *organic* incorporeal beings – are not ghosts. They are not spirits of dead people, but something incorporeal – that is, something non-physical, something Imaginal – either embodied in a location, or drawn into being through a magician's will acting *upon* a location. There is still argument about which interpretation is correct."

He noted her eyes had gone slightly glassy at his explanation. Indeed, she actually shook herself when he stopped talking, and he frowned, mildly irritated. *She's only a child,* he chided himself.

"Can you make spirits?"

"'Summon' them, we say. No, shamans summon spirits. Mages such as myself, with the appropriate procedures, summon *inorganic* incorp-." He stopped himself as she started fidgeting. "Ah, if I learned the appropriate spell, I could summon 'elementals.' They are like spirits except they are tied not to locations but to what alchemists called elements: fire, water, earth, or air."

"Are they dangerous?"

"They can be. Yes, any kind of spirit can be dangerous. It depends purely on its potency. How big it is. Small ones are easily dealt with, by anyone, mage or no. It just requires courage and force of will. Larger ones, though, are certainly dangerous. Each in its own way. So much so, that magicians have developed special means to get rid of them. To Banish them."

"Can *you* Vanish them, Keepie?"

"*Banish,* not *vanish.* And yes, Sara, I can. Some of our inmates are very good at Summoning."

"Is the un-, um, is the invisible monster something one of the patients summoned? Why don't you just Banish it?"

Harmon blinked. "It's too fast for me."

She looked doubtful.

He let his voice sink lower.

"Nor is it something a patient summoned. Whatever it is, it is more subtle and dangerous than that. I am not even entirely sure it is either spirit *or* elemental. I suspect it may be some other kind of incorporeal being: some new kind."

"Ohh! Does it have three eyes?"

He blinked, again, several times, impressed afresh by the imaginative capabilities of children. Then nodded, solemnly. "It may well have three eyes, Sara, yes."

"Wow!"

For a while, she busied herself with her food, thinking hard as she sliced the processed meat, swirled it in the gravy, and followed it with an equal amount of green beans. At last she looked up.

"Do you think it could be Godsson's?"

Harmon carefully failed to react to her bombshell: that she had met and spoken with their most dangerous inmate. How on *Earth* had she bypassed their security? He blinked. She really was quite remarkable.

"Could Godsson summon up something that wasn't a spirit or an ella-mental?"

By god, if anyone could, thought Harmon, horrified by the idea, *it would be Godsson. Or the Dragon Lord.* Although, thanks to the Wards around his cell, Godsson could only summon them inward, upon himself. And except during his mostly-annual *episodes,* he was not so insane as to do that. Only when he felt he deserved such punishment. At each anniversary of the killing of d'Artelle.

But Sara still waited for an answer. He considered. It certainly made a good story, fitted his plans, and would also amplify the self-generated stress from her own imagination.

"Well, the Barriers around his cell are enormously powerful. So he should not be able to." He shrugged. "Although with Godsson, it is very hard to say what is possible or impossible."

Sara nodded, looking fully satisfied with the new information, and went back to her food, thoughtfully.

For his part, he took the opportunity provided by her inattention to slip his senses to the Imaginal, re-cast the mindmeld, and check that his recent alteration was still secure, still feeding any fear back into the part of the brain which – he hoped – would form a complex to focus her will inward, increasing the pressure necessary for her eventual Unfolding.

Indeed, it looked surprisingly well-developed and healthy. As if exercised regularly.

He slid his psychic probes back out, well-satisfied. She was sitting a little stiffly, he noticed. Her thoughts had slowed, too, growing strangely heavy. Time to withdraw. He checked the new mental complex one last time. Really, it looked remarkably complete, perhaps even more intricate than he had anticipated. As if she herself had been extending it.

Amazing, how potent a child's imagination could be.

Briefly, he allowed himself to consider the possibility that the 'invisible monster' was something more than merely his spur-of-the-moment invention. The possibility, even, that it really was some creature summoned by Godsson.

He shuddered. Fortunately though, even *could* Godsson summon something unnatural from the realm below the Imaginal – from the collective unconscious – he could only bring it forth within his own cell. Within the layers of those impossibly-potent Barriers which Lao Pi Shen, with his own small assistance, had created over five years ago; which still stood, as firm and strong as the day they'd set them in place.

That was something he checked at every visit.

Without fail.

Perhaps it was time for an unscheduled visit. Just to be sure. Though first, he would review the security files, since clearly she *had* somehow spoken to him. Perhaps she had distracted Shanahan, then used the comm channel in his office?

The video from Godsson's cell should tell him.

Ten minutes later, Harmon sat back in his chair, astonished. She had visited him *physically*.

He didn't understand the charade with the broken

cleaning bot, nor why there was no sound for the video, but those things were of lesser importance.

It also explained the weals on her arm that he had casually healed before dinner. '*Scratched it in the forest*,' indeed. But what had Godsson said to her, for her to react with such horror? He suspected her reaction was in some way related to his own recent alteration of her mental landscape.

It seemed that *Godsson* was now providing an excellent stress source. As well as stimulating her considerable imagination.

And Godsson himself had been more engaged, this year. Less aloof. Presumably, a result of her visits.

No, the most intriguing thing had been Godsson's reaction. What had Sara done to so astonish him? It was as if, by tearing at her arm, she had subverted Godsson's own delusion.

He considered. Their interaction clearly benefited both. It would be important for them to feel it was their secret.

He would simply monitor. And watch carefully what grew from their relationship.

CHAPTER 13

Sara liked to roam the Forest – which had turned into the Jungle, now it was summer – with her bow and arrows. She got to know the busy beetles, the always-foraging and hunting ants, and the birds in their huge variety.

The birds especially loved the blackberry vines with their sweet fruit – *if* you could avoid the horridly prickly branches – and the much easier grape vines with their juicy berries. She also noticed how the squirrels and the birds seemed to get annoyed with each other when the berries plumped up. Mostly they'd squabble over the grapes though, since the birds took the outermost black-berries, while the squirrels took the ones deeper in the nee-dled thickets of twisty whip-like branches. Both groups seemed happy enough with that arrangement. Sara only got the left-overs.

Sometimes *She* would toy with them, making the birds drop the berries so the squirrels could snatch them up; or tugging a branch aside so a leaping squirrel would miss, and fall down into the tangled, spiky vines. It made Sara giggle, seeing the animals tripping or fumbling. Though once, a crow got caught and started panicking, and that hadn't been funny. She'd had to burrow in through the thorny stems and try to get it free without hurting it, while it flapped about like crazy and hurt itself more.

As she'd awkwardly crawled free, getting tugged and scratched by the brambles while the frantic bird squirmed and panicked in her hands, She got cross.

«Don't be silly. They're just animals. And they're tak-ing berries you could be eating. It serves them right!»

Don't be so mean! She tried to ignore Her while keeping her head down, wriggling under the prickly whip-like branches with the large bird clutched in her hands, its heart beating so fast she was afraid it'd burst.

«I'm not mean. Nature's mean. Besides, it makes them stronger. The survival of the fittest. The fittest get fattest. So I'm really helping them.»

Sometimes, She seemed really mean. It was much nicer being with Faith.

It was always best with Faith by her side. As a proper guard dog, she was both real good at staying quiet, and also great at spotting animals – and could even shine a red dot on them if you gave her an exaggerated-enough

"*Where?*" look. They hunted real well together.

Though she had to admit it hadn't been such a good idea to hunt *Faith* herself.

To start with, it had been pretty easy: after all, she knew Faith's routine and the areas she was 'sposed to patrol. The hardest bit in *that* part had been not giggling when Faith padded past the bushes where she'd been hiding. Downwind of her, of course.

Sneaking out from the bush silently had been a bit tricky, but she'd thought ahead and made a kind of little burrow on the side away from the track, and had also brushed the leaves away when she'd wriggled in to wait in the first place.

It had been harder to follow her quickly enough while staying silent, since Faith moved pretty fast. But from watching how her companion maneuvered through the undergrowth, she'd learned to keep pretty quiet herself. And to freeze, the instant she saw Faith's ears twitch in her direction.

The hardest part had been *catching up* to Faith without her friend sensing her. Especially since she had to concentrate on where the wind was blowing from: Faith's nose was practically magical.

In the end, she knew she'd have to cheat if she was going to successfully Pounce her. So when they reached the area of rocky hills behind the Institute, instead of following along behind, she clambered up and across, waiting on the small bluff on the other side for Faith to come trotting into view along the trail.

She had to keep her head down, since she knew Faith's laser eyes were real sharp, and super good at detecting movement.

She shut her own eyes while she waited, concentrating extra hard on her other senses. Her fingers and limbs were trembling, a tingle thrumming through them, so sharp it was almost distracting.

Finally, she heard the softest padding sound; then nothing; then the padding sound again, much closer. She'd have to time it, she realized, picturing Faith trotting along. She tensed, readying herself to spring.

Three, two, one-

She leaped, clearing the rocks, Faith immediately below her. She just had time to think, *Perfect!*

In slow motion she saw Faith stiffen, the red glow from her eyes brightening, the head turning toward her even as the animal twisted and leaped sideways, dodging as her laser mounts snapped out, already aiming....

Sara felt her eyes widen as she suddenly realized this had been a *very bad idea*. Curling and contorting, she tried to wrench herself around, away....

The blast seared through her shirt, rock exploding from behind her. Faith *yelped*, and then Sara was crashing down onto her friend, knocking her off her feet. Both of them went rolling and tumbling down the rocky hillside, the hot barrel of the laser burning her as they jumbled together.

She came to, to Faith's distressed licking of her face, and for a moment she wasn't sure where she was or what had happened. Faith whined, so she cuddled her to reassure her everything was all right.

Her back and sides *really* stung, though, and she had scrapes and bruises on her hips, elbows, and forearms, she saw. What...?

Oh. That's right.

Once Faith had calmed down enough, Sara stood up to check out her shirt. Astonishingly, most of the right side was simply *gone*. The edge was just a little bit dark, hardly even looking burned. More like it had been cut. "Wow, Faith, you sure have a powerful laser, don't you?"

Faith whined again, saying she was awful sorry. But then looked annoyed.

"Yeah, okay, I guess that *was* pretty dumb," Sara admitted. "I just thought...."

From the look Faith was still giving her, she knew she'd better just hug her again. So she did, kneeling down. Her side, and back, and arms stung, but she concentrated on reassuring her best friend.

Faith yipped – and when she pulled back to see what was wrong, stared at her real seriously. Then, when she still looked confused, Faith's expression grew impatient. She pointed her nose back up the hill, and finally, put her red laser dot on a particular point far above them.

She looked up, tracing the disturbed earth and fallen rocks that led up from where they both now rested, to the trail above, and the point where she'd tried Pouncing Faith.

There was a big hole in the rock up there, like something had exploded out from it.

"Oh, wow!" She looked back at Faith. "That was you?"

Faith dipped her head fractionally, agreeing.

"That is *so cool!*"

But Faith *yipped* again, and even tilted her head to one side, like she was saying "*And, dumb-head, that means...?*"

But what *did* it mean?

She'd never seen Faith shoot her laser before. A shiver ran through her as she remembered the missing part of her shirt. Would Keepie've been able to heal her up if she hadn't dodged? *Or if Faith hadn't un-targeted her at the last moment?* Whichever.

"Come on, let's climb back up and have a closer look."

Faith still seemed worried about something, but scrabbled up the hill behind her. At a few places, Sara had to tug on her to help her up. But she just *had* to go and see the blast.

The hill wasn't that steep, though having her shirt flap against her side felt a little strange. Lucky it'd been a hot day and she'd worn something loose for Faith to target, rather than something tight-fitting.

While she climbed, she checked herself out. She had an oval-shaped burn on her side, which had really started to hurt. *From pressing against the barrel of the laser pod.* It sure must've heated up quickly! She also had lots of little cuts, and she winced as she found and scraped out some splinters. Of stone. Tugging the back of her shirt around, she saw it was punctured in a whole lot of places by a lot of tiny tears.

When they got back up to the trail, she figured out why.

She'd expected the rock to be melted from the laser, but instead it looked like the stone had simply *shattered*, exploding outwards. There were a whole bunch of shards scattered around.

"Wow, that is one great laser blaster!"

But Faith *yipped* again, shone her red dot into the crater in the rocky hillside, and even popped her laser pod out and then back in, and finally resorted to looking at her like she was stupid.

It was only then that she noticed the flashing blue light on Faith's collar. It looked kind of insistent somehow.

"Is that... a signal from Mr Shanahan?"

Faith yipped. *Yes.*

"Because you fired your laser. Because it means you found an enemy in the grounds. So Mr Shanahan will want to know what you shot at."

She thought some more. "And he knows where you are. So he's probably on his way right now. And if he thinks you fired at me, I'll get in big trouble for trying to Pounce you. And they might stop us from playing together. Oh, no!"

She plunged down to hug Faith again, just to reassure her. "Gosh, you are *so* clever! But don't worry, I won't let them find out!"

At the pain from her burns, and the stinging pains in her side and back, she also realized she couldn't ask Keepie to heal her, either. He was pretty smart. And he didn't like them playing together. He said Faith was too dangerous.

Which was just stupid. Even when she'd almost Pounced her, Faith had aimed aside! But she didn't like the idea of trying to explain that to her uncle.

Faith suddenly pricked up her ears, and Sara heard a faint sound, so with one last hug, she got ready to climb back up over the rocks and away.

Quickly.

Faith looked up at her.

"I know," she whispered, "you've gotta stay here for Mr Shanahan, haven't you?"

After one last shared look, she darted up the rocks and out of sight.

It took weeks for the burn to heal up fully. The other scrapes and punctures got better much faster. It would've been much nicer to be healed by Keepie, but it served her right for hunting her friend. Faith was, after all, a proper guard dog, who kept everyone safe.

It had been super hard keeping her face all innocent when Mr Shanahan sat her down to warn her not to roam the grounds for a few days while he checked out 'an intrusion.' He said it looked like Faith had been tracking a wild animal. It was possible a coyote or even a mountain lion had somehow got inside the grounds.

He spent a week searching the grounds with his drones, and Faith too, of course, before things had gone back to normal. She felt a bit guilty about causing them so much more work. But it was probably good for him to have some extra practice exercises to make sure everything was working properly.

She explained that to Faith. Faith just grinned. *She* was getting heaps more time hunting and patrolling with Mr Shanahan, and that was good for them both.

Though not quite as good for *her*, since she wasn't allowed out to continue her own hunting while the 'wild thing' was loose.

Hardest of all was letting not the faintest hint, not the tiniest thought even cross her mind, whenever Mr Shanahan discussed the hunt with her uncle at dinner times. The first time they'd started talking about it in front of her, she'd wanted to just sneak quietly away. But then she'd decided it'd be better to beg to be allowed to join the hunt.

"I've already got my own bow and arrows, too, so I could help!" Plus, it would've been nice to go with them.

It had been kind of strange, arguing to be allowed to hunt herself while pretending at the same time she didn't know what was going on. It almost made *her* confused!

After several ages, though, things eventually quietened back down and everyone decided that the animal must've got out the same way it had got in. Or died. Maybe it'd just been a rabbit, or something, they decided, and Faith had let her 'in-stinks' run away with her. Mr Shanahan increased the sensitivity on the sensors on the walls, and that was that.

She hadn't even known there *were* sensors on the walls. So really, she'd learned quite a lot from trying to Pounce Faith. Like the fact that Faith had a radio 'inplant'. Plus, sharing the secret had made her and Faith even closer.

But when Faith had her other work to do and Sara had to Hunt on her own, at least it meant she didn't have to stay quite so alert for danger and thinking up special missions all the time, and could just play.

Out in the woods a few weeks later, she was imagining talking to Her again. If it *was* just imagining.

I should give you a name if you're going to be my little sister. I think-

«*Lily. I should name her Lily.*»

Lily? No, I think 'Mirella,' 'coz-

«*No! Lily! And soon I'll be your big sister. That's how fast I'm growing!*» She giggled, inside, though she wasn't sure why she did. Or if it was really even *her* that giggled.

«*Godsson will go ballistic if you tell him you talk to an invisible sister whose name is Lily, trust me.*»

But why would I want *Godsson to go bull-istick?*

«*Because he'll get very scared and do lots of exciting magic.*»

But I don't want *to scare Godsson.*

«*It'll be good for him: teach him a lesson. Why are you always such a little baby? Look, let me show you. All you have to do is give me a ride. Just imagine I'm on your shoulders, steering you. It'll be easy-*»

She felt *Her*, Lily, kind of slide behind her, then a sudden surge of hate – except it wasn't pointed at her, but at something behind her.

She spun around even as a wave of kind of cold, 'want-you-dead' sort of seriousness washed over her. She had a bare moment to see a bunch of straight line movements of ferns and leaves right in front of her, then Robo was on top of her.

Things got very confusing very quickly. *She* shoved forward against her, an awful heat pressing down like Lily thought *Sara* was hurting her. Lily pushed down so hard Sara went all swimmy in her head, swaying on her feet. But it was Robo pressing into Lily, squashing them together. She gritted her teeth, scrinching her eyes up real hard and *grabbing* Lily. Instantly, Lily went crazy: twisting and whipping at her, and Robo went all, well, a sort of *Ending-with-a-capital-E* kind of determined. But then Lily slipped free, and Robo was all super-fast stompy-dodging around her, chasing after Her. The two disappeared *much* faster than she could follow, on foot.

Of course, she was partic'ly careful not to tell her uncle

anything about the Big Fight. Was careful not even to think about it in front of him.

To be honest, it was all just a bit scarier than she liked.

CHAPTER 14

It was mid-summer when unusual things started happening at the Institute. First, Uncle started getting cross easily. That wasn't actually the unusual part; the unusual part had been that when she'd asked if she'd been bad he'd actually looked surprised, and sorry, and patted her on the head! That had been nice.

He'd explained that there was a special thing happening soon, that happened every year at this time, and he was a little bit worried about it.

He actually asked her to forgive him!

He'd also explained that on the Special Day she'd have to stay in her room and not come out: "No matter what!"

She was super-extra interested, but she'd been careful to just nod, and shrug like she didn't really care. "Well, it's too hot, anyway. I'll just stay inside and read books. Maybe Faith could come inside, for once? I could keep her inside my room for the day."

Her uncle had shuddered – just as she'd expected: he was always *so* worried by Faith's weapons. And that was even though he didn't know about her mini-rockets! But the real reason she'd asked was to find out if the Special Day was also a Danger Day, that needed Faith's help.

So that was how she worked out it was. So when he'd said 'No' she made sure she just humphed and looked annoyed but bored, and didn't ask her uncle anything more. She made especially sure to *not* look like she'd already started planning her escape.

The next person she talked to in her investigation was Mr Shanahan, and straight away she could tell he was involved, too. He looked almost as worried as Uncle, and seemed unsure about even letting her into his house, let alone his security *office*. She'd had to sigh, and wave her hand at her forehead to make out like she was *so* hot and couldn't she just come into the cool for a little bit? She'd asked if there was a secret security emergency he was involved in. He'd instantly said "No, no, everything's normal," and finally let her in.

But she couldn't find out anything more from him, and he'd even hesitated when she'd asked if she could take Faith on Patrol. He'd thought and thought before finally relaxing and agreeing. So that made her extra-double-sure that Faith would be involved in the Super Special Danger

Day.

The *next* person she investigated was Godsson, and he was worse than Uncle or Mr Shanahan! He'd looked *real* worried. Maybe even a bit scared. Which was a bit frightening in itself, since Godsson *never* looked scared. When she'd stopped by, at first she'd thought he was going to put up his super magic shield. He'd shook his head, and muttered something to himself, before he'd done his greeting-gesture so they could talk.

He had dark circles under his eyes, and his long brown hair was unusually scraggly and greasy-looking. She thought maybe he hadn't washed in a while, either.

He looked sad, and strong, and brave, though, and promised he'd do his best for her. For everyone. That sure sounded serious.

But after talking to her for a while, he said he felt tired, and needed to sleep. "To prepare himself." It all sounded real onimous.

So that was how she found out it involved Godsson, too, which meant that the Danger must be a Magic Danger. Which made it a Super Special Magic Danger Day! She wondered if the invisible monster was involved, and almost asked Godsson. But at the last moment, she decided not to.

Instead, she decided to help.

She did more investigations, though. Just like Miss X, as if she was in her very own eXtro episode!

She found out it was going to happen on the 21st, at the summer soul's-tess. It'd been tricky finding out what that meant, but her net unit eventually told her it was spelled 'solstice,' and it just meant the middle of summer. But more important than that, she learned from Miss Nerida that the *Eff-Bee-Eye* would be involved, and that they'd bring *lots* of their people, with guns and everything, plus extra magicians – special ones called 'battle mages' – as well as some kind of shaman team. And that she had to be extra good, and extra quiet, and stay in her room. For her own safety.

Well, she was certainly going to be extra *good*.

She'd certainly been good by not bursting with excitement when Nerida said they'd have *battle mages* coming. She'd just blinked, real fast, while she concentrated on keeping her expression still, and not exploding. She'd tried to think of something clever to say to make it sound like she didn't care, but her thoughts had just started running round like a bunch of crazy squirrels, and all she'd managed to say in the end was "Oh."

Nerida had looked at her strangely.

Battle mages. She bet they'd be able to fly, and go invisible; and they'd be super strong and super fast, and shoot lightning from their eyes.... Then she wondered why they *needed* battle mages?

She talked it over with Faith.

"At first I thought, *monsters*, then I thought maybe *aliens?*"

She looked at Faith, but Faith just grinned back, not giving anything away.

"Well, I know it's not invisible things 'coz you're not so good with them."

But from the corner of her eye, she saw that Faith just ignored her gentle dig. Which wasn't too big of a surprise – Faith was a trained security dog, and knew how to keep a secret.

That night, she heard a helicopter land. She crept from her room in her pajamas. From the top of the stairs she could hear her uncle and Professor Sanders talking together in low voices, below, and in bare feet she tiptoed down each flight until she could see them. They were standing in the big area just inside, that the front doors opened onto. They were just talking and waiting.

There was the sound of crunching gravel, then a bunch of soldiers in black stalked in. They didn't say anything, just spread out, looking around. She ducked back to make sure they couldn't see her, but in the glimpse she'd caught, she saw they had guns and scopes and all sorts of gadgets.

She heard the doors swing open again, and when she next peeked around, a cross-looking man with a dark suit and medals and short, oily-looking hair was spitting out something about "Benson," and money, and trouble, and facilities.

She'd peeped out a little bit further to see if she could see what Uncle or the Director thought, when one of the men with the gadgets spun round and shouted "freeze!"

She jumped back, and then they were all pounding up the stairs, and Keepie was shouting, and the Director was trying to calm everyone down, and the angry man started shouting about spies and stuff.

But she'd already made her eyes big and round, and looked scared – which was actually pretty easy, 'coz she kinda *was*. She pushed her lower lip out and made like she might cry. Just like Lily had told her to do, if she wanted to make men feel sorry for her.

But she also raised her hands up, 'coz she knew that was what you did when people pointed guns at you.

It all seemed to work, though, since even while all the shouting and running was still going on, the first soldier up the stairs didn't look like he'd planned to shoot her.

He'd actually looked kind of embarrassed.

He had an armband that said 'FBI,' she noticed. *Ohh: Eff-Bee-Eye!*

The angry man got extra angry, though, going red in the face and talking about "slip shot operations" and lots of other stuff she didn't understand. But Director Sanders just calmed him down while Keepie led her off to her room.

She thought he must be super angry with her, and got ready for something awful to happen. She held his hand real tight, hoping that that might somehow keep him. She couldn't bring herself to try all the stupid big-eyes and trembly-lip stuff, though, she was too upset....

But amazingly, when they reached her door, he lifted her chin to make her look at him, and smiled, and then *winked!* Then he'd patted her on the head, opened her door, and tapped her on the bottom to scoot her inside.

"Consider yourself reprimanded, Sara," he said, still smiling, as she turned around. "But I should return and help calm down Mr Smith." And gently shut the door.

She wasn't going to be sent away!

She turned and slumped against the door, and her bones went all loose and she just slid down to the floor. For some reason, then, she started crying for real.

She discussed it with Faith the next day. The soldier part – not the getting into trouble part, or the crying.

"Which army do you think 'FBI' is? They must be goodies, since we're goodies here, an' they talked to Uncle and the Professor."

Faith didn't answer, just looked doubtful, so Sara explained more. "FBI wasn't their names, 'cause they had littler name badges on their shirts. Plus, they wouldn't all have the same name. And Miss Nerida had said 'The' FBI."

Anyway, from everything she'd learned from her *secret investigations*, she told Faith, she was pretty sure they'd lock her in her room, 'cause probably they thought she'd want to know what was going on, and help.

But she didn't tell even Faith about her secret plan.

The day before Super Special Magic Danger Day she made sure to act all bored, and even pretended to be tired, complaining about the heat – until Keepie got worried and asked if she was "coming down with something" and checked her out magically. She realized then that she shouldn't pretend quite so hard. But none of them knew she'd already noticed how Mr Shanahan made all his security camera 'sweeps' of the outside of the building take exactly one minute.

Which was a very important part of her plan.

Uncle had been surprised at her request for a watch – "so she could time herself running" – but thought it was a good idea. A shopping drone had delivered it the next day.

As soon as she'd got it, she made sure to visit Mr Shanahan. At first she'd thought he wasn't going to let her in at all this time. Which would have been a disaster! But in the end he did, for a little while, and she carefully noted when the security camera on the western wall started its sweep.

So now her plan was all ready.

She'd even come up with the idea of asking for all her favorite sweets and treats, and some grown-up movies to watch on the day when everything was supposed to be happening, and had to giggle at the way Keepie agreed so easily to it all. She'd even talked him into letting her get *Death on Blood Mountain,* which the net said was only for kids who were at least fifteen!

She was glad she had, though, since it wasn't 'til almost the evening that she heard some kind of truck or something arriving; and then, maybe half an hour later, *two* helicopters, one after the other!

The trid had actually been a little bit creepy, and also a bit horrible, with the way all the blood would explode from their chests when the monster squeezed them; but it sure was exciting! She'd watched it twice.

But when the helicopters arrived, she was pretty sure it was finally time to use her secret route. So she put on her new watch, got her little flashlight and dragged three chairs into her bathroom, stacking one on the other so she could reach the secret trap door in the ceiling.

She climbed up on the chairs and pulled down the spare sheet which she'd put knots in and then tied up there, earlier. Then climbed down from the chairs and put them away. Then she lumped up some pillows and stuffed them under her blanket to make it look like she'd gotten bored and gone to bed early, just in case anyone checked on her.

Back in her bathroom, she climbed up her 'rope,' and shimmied up into the tight and dusty space, pulling the knotted sheet up behind her and sliding the secret trap door shut, making it super dark. The first thing she did then was tie a cloth around her face. Not for a disguise: just to keep the dust out of her nose and mouth. That's how bad it was.

She turned on her flashlight then and very carefully and extra, extra quietly, started making her way across the wooden beams toward the western wall, and the unused room with the window near the drainpipe. Which was another trick she'd learned from Miss X.

After she'd climbed outside – first checking the second-hand of her watch – the hardest bit had been reaching the next window, from the drainpipe. It sure had looked a lot closer, from the ground. Her toes reached, but then she'd had to push free of the pipe and grab real quickly at the window frame to avoid falling, and it'd actually been pretty scary when her fingers had been scrabbling on the painted wood trying to get a grip. But exciting!

As soon as she'd gotten both feet on the sill and both hands on the join part in the middle, she'd just hung there, panting, before remembering she only had a few seconds left before the camera would swing back and see her.

But the window slid down easily and she tumbled inside. No one ever went into the dusty old office, and she'd unlocked the window and slid it up and down lots, two days earlier.

Out in the hallway, then, she listened. She considered sneaking back to the corner and looking around it to see if anyone was on guard in the corridor outside her room, in case they were treating her like she was a *real* prisoner – but decided not to risk it, in case no one was guarding it after all. That'd be pretty disappointing.

Instead she'd gone the other way, to the room with the chute where the bots tipped the dirty sheets and clothes in to slide down to the laundry room on the ground floor. Luckily, the laundry room also had a small chimney thing that went further down, to both of the basement levels where some of the patients were kept. Probably to bring the inmates' dirty stuff *up* to the laundry. Uncle had said it was important for some of the inmates to be surrounded by living earth, and that was why they were kept underground.

She wasn't sure what living earth was, but it sounded pretty cool.

And so, perhaps twenty minutes after she'd set out, she was creeping once again through a tight and squeezy ceiling space, this time above the lower basement as she made her way toward Godsson's cell. She was pretty sure it was his, because her flashlight showed a really strangely-glistening kind of wall at one point, near the middle, plus there were some kind of worrying groans.

They sounded like Godsson!

They were coming from his area, too. It sounded kind of scratchy, though, like his voice was coming from a speaker.

Super extra carefully, she slowly made her way to it. She even turned her light out when she got closer. Which was how she saw a small glow in the darkness of the roof cavity. Making her way to that, she looked down.

There were men in the corridor below her. Their jackets said 'FBI.' Three other men were there too, but they were dressed just *weird*, with cloaks with feathers, and wearing beads 'n stuff. It woke a dim memory that scratched and annoyed, but she couldn't work out what seemed so familiar. One of the FBI men stood close by those three. Probably three magicians, she decided. She wondered if they were the battle mages? They didn't look anything like as cool as she'd expected. She wondered where her uncle was.

Sounds of Godsson, in torment, rose up again from below.

And with horror, she felt the Wrongness. From the corner of her eye she saw Lily's smoothly-curving edges slip around the FBI man standing opposite Godsson's door, directly beneath her. She could feel Her coiling over him, and could almost hear the familiar voice, whispering. Encouraging.

Tricking.

She saw the man raise his gun, slowly, as if he'd fallen asleep. She saw he wasn't pointing it at any*one*. He was pointing it at the small glass window in Godsson's cell.

It was a very big gun.

Godsson screamed louder, horribly, and from the way the people who could see into his room reacted, even *they* looked worried.

For just a moment, she felt she saw a movement in the dark up in the ceiling cavity with her, in the dust: a familiar cruel, curving set of slicey edges in the tiny motes of dust that twisted and raced around the glistening wall. Once she'd seen that, she saw several more, all braiding together like jellyfish tentacles draping invisibly down from... somewhere, to wrap and coil around the man below.

She saw his arm tense.

The ceiling here in the basement was just as thin as it was up on the higher floors. Without thinking, she shoved both legs down, hard, feeling the stuff rip as she threw her weight onto it, thrilling as she plunged through, like a baby alligator smashing through its egg. With a cry like Hyper-Girl flying into battle with Argon she dived down onto the man under attack.

Fingers out like talons already tensed to claw and shred and rend, to tear it from him, she imagined lasers like HyperGirl's shooting from her fingertips. Then she was on him, feeling the Wrongness wrapped around him. Growling, she tore into it, even biting at it as the man suddenly reacted, shooting.

All at once everything was shouting and confusion. She held on desperately as the big FBI soldier spun round and around, trying to reach back to throw her off, but she dodged his arm and wriggled lower and screamed while she clung to his back and fought She who'd wrapped around him.

She wasn't her sister, Sara realized in that moment. That had all been a trick, and she cried at the pain of the betrayal and lashed out even harder, from the depths of her heart. Someone was shouting about holding fire, Godsson screamed again, in pain or joy, she wasn't sure which this time, and other men were diving toward her. The three strange-dressed men were doing spell-y things, she saw her uncle's face white in shock, and then she felt a sleepy blanket flow over her.

She struggled, as hard as she could, still tearing into the last wisps of the shocked thing now shriveling and van-ishing beneath her fingers, then everything slowed right down, and she saw the ground swimming up to her in a dream.

CHAPTER 15

Something stung in her nostrils. Aching, she blinked and stretched-

Uh oh.

She was curled up in a leather chair in Director Sanders's office. Her uncle was closing the lid on a small bottle as he moved back from her. She sat up and saw Mr Shanahan and the three weird guys with the feathers and beads hanging off their animal skin coats. And there was a really stiff-looking man in a dark suit with medals on it. The same man who'd spoken to her uncle and the Professor the other night.

He still looked angry.

She was absolutely filthy, she saw, but her legs where she'd scratched them going through the ceiling were undamaged. It made them look odd, with clean patches where her uncle must have healed her, then wiped the blood off. Her eyes and face felt surprisingly clean, too, she decided, as she licked her lips.

Then froze. *What if they decide to send me away?* She fought down tears that suddenly welled up.

The men looked at one another, and she wondered what they were waiting for. She looked at her uncle, letting him see how worried she was.

They must have been waiting for her uncle, 'cause at last he squeezed his eyes shut, pinched his nose, and spoke to her. His voice was very calm.

She sat up extra straight; even put her hands together in her lap.

"Sara, what did you think you were doing?"

What did she *think* she was doing? She *knew* what she'd been doing: saving Godsson, of course. But in the moment before she blurted that out, she stopped herself; and grasped for an excuse instead. "Um. I just wanted to see what was happening."

"But how did you get there? We even had a guard outside your room."

"You did?"

How good was that! But when she saw how the men reacted to her smile, she quickly made her expression all serious.

"And I had explicitly told you that you had to stay in your room. You even said you-"

He blinked, slowly, interrupting himself. "You had planned it all out. You even left the trid playing, and made it look like you were asleep in your bed in case.... But how did you- oh. Oh!"

Everyone looked at him, wondering what he'd just realized.

Remembering the trickiest part, climbing through the window, she hoped he wouldn't find out about that. He'd be cross. But strangely, he seemed to be almost smiling, now.

"How did you get out of your room?"

Somehow, the calm look in his eye made her think he already knew the answer somehow. But if he did, why would he ask her?

"Um." She looked around. "I-, um, there's a secret door in the ceiling in my bathroom. I climbed up on some chairs and tied some rope up inside, then put the chairs back."

They made her tell them every detail. Climbing down the drainpipe. Getting down to the basement....

As the questioning went on, she tried to work out how much trouble she was in. Of course angry-man, the one with all the medals, looked the angriest; though he kept shooting looks at the Director as if he wanted to complain, but was scared of him. Which was silly: Director Sanders was a softy.

Mr Shanahan looked real worried though, like he thought *he* might get in trouble, and she suddenly remembered how she'd found out about the one-minute sweeps of the outside cameras, and how she wasn't supposed to even be allowed *into* his security office; and how she'd had to get a watch so she could time it perfectly....

She'd just have to pretend not to know any of that, she decided, and hope they'd think she'd just been lucky; and hope that Uncle's excellent guessing didn't stay excellent.

And luckily, that's what happened; though the whole time, it seemed to her that her uncle was trying not to smile.

Maybe she *wouldn't* get into too much trouble, after all?

But when she got to the part where she was watching from up in the ceiling, the three feather-men got all interested. They all stared at her, real hard.

"-and there was this little hole, but big enough to see the man with the really big gun outside Godsson's room-"

"How did you know it was Godsson's room? How do you know Godsson's name?" That was one of the feather-men.

"Um." What could she say? They were all looking at her. That she'd learned about him in school? That she'd seen pictures of him on Mr Shanahan's- but then *he'd* get in trouble. "Uh...."

"She's clearly been sent here." That was Mr Angry with the dark suit and medals. "Our foreign friends have been clamoring to 'observe' one of Benson's episodes for years, no doubt to see what they can learn."

"Oh?" Director Sanders asked. "Does that mean you've decided these costly exercises *are* a worthwhile expense for the tax-payer after all, Mr Smith?"

This was like watching a ping-pong match!

"Sara is not some foreign child-prodigy super-spy," Uncle said.

Sara blinked. She wasn't sure what a protajee was, but Angry-man thought she was a *super-spy?* Yeah! How cool was *that!* She tried, but couldn't stop the smile from spreading across her face. Desperately, she fought it down before Mr Angry *Smith* looked back in her direction.

"My questions stand."

That was the feather guy who'd asked her about Godsson, who was still watching her. Carefully. Um...

"Just tell the truth, Sara," Uncle said. "I promise, making up lies is not something you should be doing for these gentlemen, at this time."

His voice was strangely encouraging, and she wondered if perhaps Keepie somehow already knew she talked to Godsson. But how could he know that?

He nodded, and looked across at the three feather-men.

"Um, 'cause I talk to him sometimes?"

Everyone – except Director Sanders and her uncle, she noticed – went instantly still, like she'd just said something really amazing.

"He speaks to you *telepathically?*" hissed the feather guy who'd asked her the questions.

"I don't- I don't know that word. Sorry."

"In your head. He speaks to you in your head. While you are in your room?" He lurched toward her, looking like he wanted to grab her. She shrank back into her chair. "*When* does he speak to you! Is he speaking to you even now?"

"Uh, no, only when I go and visit him."

No one said anything.

"I stand on a chair," she added, to help.

Suddenly everyone was looking at Mr Shanahan, who was shaking his head. "No, that's not possible. I couldn't miss something like that. The EyeNet would have flagged her presence as unusual, I couldn't have missed seeing-"

"Um, mister Shanahan, I, uh, I kind of tricked the computer."

Everyone turned back to her.

Then she had to explain about Bork, and the stick, and her red toolkit, and being repair-girl. Everyone just kept staring at her. They didn't even believe her, not until Professor Sanders called up the security footage and they manually searched through to find the last time she'd visited. Then they were all saying stuff like, "My god, it's gray-flagged," and she'd had to hide her smile.

Mr Shanahan had looked amazed, and relieved, and Keepie – Keepie's eyes were practically *sparkling*. The corners of his eyes had even crinkled up!

A bit like Professor Sanders's.

She had the strong feeling, then, that everything really would be alright.

And yeah, after that, things improved a lot. They were all looking at her *properly* now, too, like they weren't just seeing some silly girl any more. All the grown-up attention made her sit up extra straight.

There was a bit after that where Keepie and Mr Shanahan – and especially Mr Angry – were all like, "But you could have been shot," to her, as well as "If my agents weren't so highly trained at telling good guys from bad guys" and stuff. Though they'd all used much bigger words than that. But she just said 'sorry' over and over, and tried to look it. She even made her eyes go big and round, and pushed out her bottom lip a lot. Before remembering who'd taught her to do that, and stopped doing it.

Finally, they wanted to know why on Earth she'd jumped down, since she'd been hidden?

And so she had to explain about seeing that the man with the big gun was being tricked and was all wrapped up by Her, and how she could tell She was attacking Godsson too, from the way he was screaming. So then they *all* had a big argument and she was shouting at them for being so mean to Godsson and anyway she'd helped, because the FBI man was about to shoot Godsson through the window!

They all stopped the argument when she said that – it was weird, like they just paused a trid. Then they all had to look at the security recording. Watching it, it was obvious – and she *totally* looked like a super spy-girl for real when she jumped through the roof! She looked so fierce it even impressed *her*! – but *they* all said the man had just heard her in the ceiling and was lifting his gun up toward *that*, and she was all "Don't be so stupid!" but then *they* were all "Clearly Godsson has man-ipillated her into joining Godsson in his dis-show-tiv fantasy." They didn't change their minds even after she'd pointed out that as soon as she'd killed the monster, Godsson had cried out real happy and then suddenly was winning *his* battle inside his cell. But no, they were all still like, "that's just a coincidence."

Even while she'd been so cross with them, though, it'd been pretty cool to learn she'd been hit by a Sleep spell by the feather guys. They'd had to use magic to stop her!

She couldn't wait to tell Faith all about it.

In the end, after arguing forever using all sorts of big words, they'd decided Godsson was just imagining things, and that he'd taught her to imagine the same things. How stupid was that? But Uncle told them how her talks with Godsson seemed to be good for him. Then he'd pointed out that it was all imaginary and no harm had been done, and everyone had to agree, though Mr Angry had grumbled about that.

Even Professor Sanders said he wasn't sure it was entirely safe, though in the end he'd said "Very well, doctor, but I'll be holding you responsible if anything unfortunate happens."

It wasn't clear just what they were allowing – was she allowed to keep visiting Godsson, or not? She decided it'd be better not to ask. And to keep sneaking in, even if she wasn't allowed.

Then Mr Angry said something about a dragon. The Director answered him.

"Mr Smith, we know the Dragon *does* still take an interest, from his reaction each time someone suggests relocating our problem. Or terminating it." He looked at Mr Angry when he said that.

But she was more interested in the talk of a dragon. A *dragon!* How cool was that? The Institute was the best place *ever,* to grow up!

Anyway, in the end they'd all agreed that since there'd been no harm done – she'd wanted to shout at them, then, but her uncle gave her a look that warned her not to – that since there'd been no harm done, this time there wouldn't be a punishment except for being 'grounded.' Which meant really having to stay in her room. For a whole week.

-

After all his visitors had left, Director Sanders turned to his screen, and sighed. The man looking back at him quirked an eyebrow up. "Not bad for a nine-year-old girl, eh Sanders?"

Director Sanders shook his head. "I was sure you'd have to use your veto, sir. But in the end, I think even Smith was impressed by her ingenuity."

"What did you think, Sanders, of her story about *She*?"

"Worried, frankly. Neither Dr Harmon nor the three very impressive shamans you found for us this year saw anything incorporeal at any stage. But still, and I can't pin down why I feel this way, I'm worried."

"And her story of hunting invisible things like that in your grounds?"

"It's a horrifying thought, isn't it? If it were true. Frankly, sir, if it were anyone other than Godsson and d'Artelle involved – and Lord Lao Pi Shen, for that matter – I'd dismiss it out of hand. It's far more comfortable to assume it's just shared fantasizing."

The man nodded. "But whether this is some game by the Dragon or not, it is still in his best interests to see Godsson contained. Just as it is for everyone else on the planet. So, whether these annual attacks are real or just Godsson's fantasy, I feel we can still be sure that our containment of him is still effective."

"So, nothing has changed, sir?"

"I don't believe so. Don't lower your guard, though. Neither of us wants to use plan B, do we?"

"*No, sir.*"

A bead of sweat at his brow at the thought, Sanders signed off and eased back in his chair. Hopefully, next year's anniversary of d'Artelle's death would be less dramatic, if the usual three-yearly rising-then-falling pattern held.

CHAPTER 16

They'd glued shut her secret door and made her promise not to go up into the ceiling again. But it wasn't till the next day that she discovered what 'Grounding' really meant: when she stepped outside her room to go to breakfast, and suddenly sirens were going off.

Her uncle hurried out of his office. And then explained that, yes, for a whole week, she was not allowed out of her room unless it was an emergency. And he'd narrowed his eyes as if he knew exactly what she'd been thinking when she made the mistake of looking happy about the 'unless.'

And Faith wasn't allowed to come *inside*, either.

Grounding was *awful*.

Her uncle brought her breakfast, and a dombot came and collected the dishes and stuff. Nerida brought her lunch, and for some reason said she hoped she wasn't going to waste "all that food." Which was weird: why would she have asked for it if she wasn't going to eat it?

But Nerida had brought her own lunch and ate it at the desk, watching while she sat on her bed and had her soymeat, hash brown – yum! – and fish fingers on toast. Nerida just had a salad and a blueberry muffin. At first, she thought Nerida had stayed because she thought she was going to do something weird with her food, but after a little while Nerida started asking about what'd happened the night before.

So she told her, and it was kind of cool how Nerida kept going "No way!" and "You didn't!" but not like she thought she *really* didn't. It'd actually been fun talking to her. Nerida seemed to get less strange the more they talked. Though not completely not-strange, Sara discovered, when she'd tried to explain about the spirits in the woods and the invisible monsters.

That evening, at the knock on the door at dinner time, she toppled down from the wall, her hands and arms aching from holding herself upside down. "Coming, Nerida!" she called out as she bounced over and threw open the door.

And found Keepie standing there with her dinner tray. He didn't look too happy, either, she thought. She blushed, annoyed at getting it so wrong, then remembered to step aside so he could come in. He looked sideways at her, with a little frown.

"I thought you and Nerida didn't get on?"

"Oh, she's not so bad once you get to know her."

He just looked at her, thoughtfully. He must've already eaten, since he only had food for her on the tray. He put it on her desk and made her eat it there, instead of cross-legged on her bed.

She was sure he'd come for some special reason, but for a long while he didn't say anything, just watched her while she ate.

She looked at him, trying to work out if they'd changed their minds and she was going to be in bigger trouble after all, but it was more like he wanted to ask her something. When he finally spoke, though, it was just to ask about Godsson.

"I suppose you and he talk about a great many different subjects, Sara?"

She answered around a mouthful of her seafood omelet – for some reason, she hadn't felt very hungry tonight. "Uh, yeah. I guess."

"Adam and Eve?"

She grimaced. "Yeah. That story didn't make any sense to me, but. A lot of-"

"Has he ever talked to you about Lilith?"

Huh? That sounded like... "Lily?"

"Never mind: no need to fill your head with fantasy and superstition. Did you ever talk to Godsson about "Her?""

She never had, 'cause she knew *She* didn't like Godsson and just wanted to upset him. "No."

Her uncle frowned. "What about 'Robo'?"

"No."

Actually, why *hadn't* she mentioned Robo to Godsson? More than once, she'd been *about* to. But each time, she'd just... decided it would be a bad idea. Like Godsson would approve of Robo. Too much.

At the odd look on his face, an awful thought struck her. "Have *you* been talking to Godsson, Keepie?"

Suddenly he looked *guilty!*

"Oh, no! And you told him about Robo, didn't you?" She wasn't sure *why* that was such a bad idea, she just knew it *was*. At her look, he got even guiltier. "Oh-! No, you told him about *Her*, too, didn't you!"

He actually *winced* – then shook himself. "It doesn't

matter, Sara, provided *you* don't get drawn into his non-sense. The man's fantasies get worse by the month.'

She felt her lips pressing together, and for some reason she wanted to hit him. "What fantasies?"

"You wouldn't understand."

"Stop treating me like a baby! I would *too* under-stand!"

He sighed. "I'm not treating you like a child. I scarcely understand it myself."

So he did *understand!* She glared at him.

"Oh, just some gobbledegook."

She kept glaring.

"Oh, some story about traveling to the Imaginal realm with his physical body, and about how Melisande d'Artelle's death in that place created a magical pattern which then followed him back. There: satisfied? Complete fantasy, of course."

"If it's just make-believe, why not let him go free?"

He made a strangled noise. "Do you have *any* idea how much harm a mentally unstable mage can do?"

"Godsson wouldn't hurt anyone!"

For a moment, she thought he was choking. Then he looked really angry. "I assure you, you're utterly wrong. Godsson *has*... 'harmed' people, Sara. I have seen it with my own eyes."

He seemed to think for a moment. Then shook his head. "No. No, you're not to see him anymore. I forbid it."

"Fine," she snapped, but inside she was thinking *You can't stop me from seeing my friend.* She pushed her plate away. It had gone cold, anyway.

Neither of them spoke as he picked up her tray and stood. She didn't look at him.

"You're still Grounded, Sara," he said, from the door-way.

"I know," she said, still not looking at him.

For several seconds he must've just stood there, watch-ing her. "Order your meals from the cafeteria using your netpad. A dombot will bring it."

"But Nerida-"

"Nerida has her own work to do, and doesn't have time to wait on you hand and foot."

"She doesn't-"

But by the time she'd turned back round, he'd already left and the door was shutting.

Why was he so mean?

She didn't see *anyone* for a whole day, after that, and thought she'd go mad. When her uncle opened the door, she jumped up before she remembered she was still cross with him. Except she wasn't; not really.

He didn't look all that happy to see *her,* though.

"Come along, Sara. We have... a *visitor.*"

He said 'visitor' like you'd say 'poo on your shoe.' "Come where?"

"Just to my office. Professor Sanders, and our visitor, Professor Roger Ahronian of MITM" – and again, he looked like the words tasted bad in his mouth – "are waiting to discuss my concerns over recent events. For some reason, the Director has decided he wants you present. But I suggest you keep your opinions to yourself."

He noted her lips thin. *Of course that wouldn't stop her.* "They are unlikely to be helpful to Godsson should you share them."

"Why not? What's so special about Professor, Ar...?"

"Professor Ahronian considers himself the world expert on the Incorporeal. And he is quite certain he has nothing to learn from Godsson."

So, she had to come and sit with her uncle while someone he hated was rude about Godsson? She considered staying where she was. "I'm not allowed out of my room."

"You are for this."

"Does that mean my Grounding is over?"

"No! Now stop being difficult and come along. We mustn't keep our *distinguished visitor* waiting."

"Can I bring my bow and arrows?"

For a moment she thought he was going to snap at her, but suddenly he smiled. Then chuckled, and his shoulders relaxed. "I'm tempted to say yes, but you had better not. Come along."

Maybe it wouldn't be too bad.

The expert certainly *looked* very expert: he was tall, with very black hair and a neat black beard and sharp black eyebrows, and wore a nice suit. He looked like he might be an actor, or somebody important.

"Ah, and this is the young lady in question, is it?"

She wasn't sure if that was a smile or a sneer, but the way her uncle and the Director winced when he said 'young lady' helped her remember she hadn't been bad.

She wasn't sure she was going to like him.

Her uncle went and sat behind his desk in his usual spot. The foreign-looking professor sat opposite him. He was leaning back in the heavy visitor chair, one very shiny black shoe bouncing up and down across his knee, and looking like *he* was the one in charge.

She decided she *didn't* like him.

Professor Sanders was sitting in another chair, at the side of the desk, like he was going to be an umpire or something. At a nod from her uncle, she saw they'd put another chair to the left of the Director's, at an angle to it. She went and sat down.

They talked about 'papers' for a bit and how her uncle hadn't written on any for a while, or something like that, and then the visitor – who had quite a long, and slightly bent-down nose – leaned forward. "Alexander – I may call you Alexander, may I?"

She expected her uncle to say 'No,' but he just tilted his head slightly.

"I've read your report, viewed the recent footage, and the Director has even kindly taken me down to 'Godsson's' cell for a personal inspection. Impressive Wards, I must say. Although my opinion has not shifted in the intervening years-"

She saw her uncle's lips press together.

"- and I still think the poor fellow could be treated a little less like a dangerous criminal and more like an actual patient."

She sat up straighter at that. Maybe he wasn't so bad after all? At the look her uncle was giving her, though, instead of saying what a good idea that was, she just nodded her head a lot.

"Your idea clearly meets with my nine-year-old ward's approval, which you must no doubt find reassuring – but he *is* clinically insane, Roger. I may call you Roger, may I?"

Huh? She tilted her head, watching the two men. They both had the same kind of smile on their faces, she saw. Like they wanted to punch each other. *What was going on?* Maybe this *would* get interesting, after all.

"Nor may we magically neuter him without his legal consent – even if that would work, for someone of his power.

"And perhaps I should also remind you that those Wards, and our precautions, are at the explicit recommendation of the Emperor of China. He warned us that *something* had made a link to Godsson, something that had been moving in their 'direction' as they left what they called The Deeps behind them."

Ahronian spread his well-manicured hands. "Dragons lie, Alexander..."

Dragons again? This was getting good! She wondered when she'd get to see him. Unfortunately, she'd been so distracted she missed some of what 'Roger' said, after that.

"I pointed this out to you, I believe, in the report I pre-pared following my *first* visit, all those years ago. My opin-ion is unchanged. In my view the evidence points more to Lao Pi Shen bringing you this fellow merely for his own amusement."

Things got a bit complicated after that, but she gath-ered that Roger thought the Dragon Lord was playing a joke on Keepie, one that'd take years and years before it got funny. Except it probably wouldn't be that sort of a joke.

But Keepie thought the Dragon wasn't joking at all, and was very serious about keeping Godsson locked up.

She wondered if Godsson scared the Dragon? Did Godsson know his weakness? Did dragons have a weak-ness? But if they did, and Godsson knew what it was, why not just tell Uncle? And she wasn't sure if the Dragon – or the Dragon Lord, it wasn't clear whether he was a real dragon or not – was a baddie or a goodie. They didn't talk like he was either, really. More like he was just kind of scary.

Which made sense if he was a real dragon. She decided maybe dragons *would* play tricks, though.

Then Roger was rude about Keepie's research, but Keepie just smiled, and kind of said Roger didn't do *proper* research, except not exactly in those words. Once again she had the strong feeling they both wanted to punch each other, even though they kept smiling at each other.

Professor Sanders didn't say anything, just seemed to watch everything, as far as she could tell whenever she looked at him. Which was mostly when she thought Keepie and the mean professor wanted to thump one another.

At one point, being careful not to let Roger see, she made a little gesture like she was shooting him with her bow and arrow, and for the first time, saw Keepie relax. For a moment, he almost smiled.

But then it got more interesting again, if a bit hard to follow.

Keepie asked, "So you discount the FBI agent's own reported impressions; as well as Godsson's reaction at the time my ward took her impetuous action?"

Roger smiled. "I thought for a moment you were about to ask me to take into account your *ward's* own story." He steepled his fingers. "Surely you're aware of Arizmendi's seminal 2008 paper...."

He started talking about communicating diss-show-tiv states, and psycho dramas, impetuous young girls – which she was pretty sure was a *good* thing, since he also praised her imagination – and 'Suggest ability.'

But maybe she'd got that wrong, since Keepie suddenly seemed to be asking if maybe there *might* be a third kind of Incorp Ory-eel being, and then he and Roger got all super-polite I'd-like-to-punch-you-*so*-hard again, talking about empathy and mirror new-rones and stuff, before getting interesting again.

Her uncle was saying, "your exhausting *Tax-onna-me of the Incorp Ory-eel* offers no scope for explaining the physical transport of living beings, such as Lao Pi Shen's mysterious arrival here in '47, or for that matter d'Artelle's still-unexplained physical escape."

But Roger didn't look impressed. "Mere trickery, Alex. Even before magic truly returned, 'magicians' performed convincing feats of physical translocation. Armed with real magic, how much easier must such deceptions be to pull off now, eh? If these imaginary new incorporeal beings of yours can cross the cell Wards, then presumably so too could Mr Benson. Yet there he remains."

Who was 'Mr Benson?' Godsson? Surely not!

"So you are *certain* there is no cause for concern?"

"Absolutely. Though perhaps you need to keep a closer eye on your ward, eh? Especially if you're bringing her up here, of all places. I wouldn't be letting *my* children climb around in roof cavities!"

Suddenly *she* wanted to punch him. "*You* wouldn't be able to stop me. You're mean. I'd run away if *you* were my uncle!"

She was on her feet, she realized.

They were all looking at her, but it was *true*: she would, and he couldn't!

But the mean professor just sneered at her like he was pleased that she knew it wasn't a real smile, and then the grown-ups were all politely rude to each other while they said their goodbyes – except Professor Sanders – and then the Director took the mean professor away.

Good riddance!

"Perhaps I should have let you bring your bow and arrows after all, Wild Thing, eh?"

And just like that, they were friends again. He even read to her before she went to sleep.

But Grounding was still absolutely *awful*. If it'd gone longer than a week, she reckoned they would've had to lock her up 'cause she would've *really* gone insane. Thank goodness for the trids and things. At least she got to watch *Death on Blood Mountain* a bunch more times.

But it was even better when she was finally allowed outside again. And Keepie kind of hinted that *he* thought she'd done the right thing, and that he was pleased with her.

So, really, it all worked out quite well in the end, apart from the fact that they'd glued shut her secret door.

And as for not being allowed to visit Godsson any more? She'd find a way....

PART II

(Two years later)

CHAPTER 17

Things were quite comfortable at the Institute – though sometimes Sara wished for other kids her own age to play with. Her uncle seemed happy with her 'progress,' even if she wasn't exactly sure what that meant. Though he did say he wished it was faster than the sea level's retreat. She'd made the mistake of asking "what sea level retreat?" – which led to a whole lesson on the 're-icing' of Antarctica.

Like how it was the old name for the south-most continent in the whole world. It was supposed to be covered real deep in ice, and was where all the penguins lived. But no polar bears.

Uncle said lowering the sea level was a dramatic demonstration of what the human race could achieve. But then he grumbled that if the governments had fixed the problem, Antarctica would still have its old name. He said 'Newtopia' was a stupid name.

But Sara thought it sounded nice: kind of shiny and new. It was also much easier to say, too. Maybe she'd visit it, one day.

For Godsson's 'episode' the first of those two years, Harmon had managed to broker a deal which everyone found acceptable: Sara would form a 'backup team' with Faith. She would observe with Brian Shanahan by video from the security office of his house-cum-bunker; and she and Faith would be called in should it become necessary.

When he had informed her, Sara had *glowed*.

She devoted weeks to practicing the run from Shanahan's separate out-building, down to level B2 –closely supervised, of course. She glued special 'bump mats' on the corners of walls, for her to bounce off, and attached short loops of rope at the turns in the staircase to fly around the bends... her inventions had seemed endless.

She'd even outpaced Faith, on two occasions. The other members of the Institute, too, took pleasure in her childish excitement, able to relax instead of being alert and tense, wondering what awful stunt she'd pull this year.

Her uncle even managed to get Professor Sanders to negotiate to leave her various modifications in place.

But fortunately, that year's episode – or 'attack,' as Sara phrased it – had been as undramatic as Harmon had expected. She of course remained unaware of the complexity of the true cycle, and also knew only of the midsummer attacks, at the anniversary of d'Artelle's death. She knew nothing of the tri-annual pattern: the steady growth in intensity over two years, followed by a slight fall the next. Nor did she know of the disturbing other pattern.

Nor would Harmon ever tell her of the 'king tide' expected in 2061, when all the cycles would coincide. Fortunately, that was still seven years away. By then, she would be seventeen, and presumably less trouble.

The second year went equally smoothly, although Sara's earlier intervention had clearly faded in Godsson's memory: his self-torture had continued to grow. The only issue had been Sara's reaction during the episode itself. Her distress had communicated itself to Faith, making it a fraught experience for all three of them.

Harmon was concerned: next year's event would be still worse, though it should still fall short of Godsson's suffering the year of Sara's dramatic 'assistance.'

That was a treasured memory for Harmon: the astonishing sight of the nine-year-old girl plunging through the ceiling like some tiny Valkyrie descending from Valhalla, teeth bared and fingers spread like talons, screaming like a banshee.

No, it had been a wonderful moment, despite thinking his heart would stop; and having to physically restrain the agent by his side from shooting her – notwithstanding FBI director 'Smith's' assurance of his agents' perfect and instantaneous threat-assessment skills. Neither Harmon nor the agent concerned had ever felt the need to correct the official record on that account, however.

Besides, if Sara and Godsson were right, and something could somehow leak past the Barriers, some incorporeal entity or magical pattern which was, impossibly, invisible to the Imaginal sight as well as to physical instrumentation – well, perhaps 'Team Sara' *could* somehow help.

Not that he would ever admit that. He could just imagine the response of that pompous ass, Ahronian, were the new arrangement run past him.

He was concerned how Sara would handle next year's event, however. Still, she would be twelve. Perhaps her increasing maturity-

Harmon caught himself. What was he thinking? Of course there would be trouble. There was no doubt at all about that.

CHAPTER 18

One day, three weeks before Christmas, Harmon was startled by Sara bursting into his office, eyes alight, bouncing with enthusiasm. Before he could speak, though, she had crossed the room and begun tugging him to 'come.'

"Keepie, Keepie! I've got a surprise for you. Come and see, come and see!"

Her excitement caught him up – he found himself genuinely curious to see what she planned, and decided to forgive her interruption. "Fortunately for you, little one, I should take a break anyway. Very well. Surprise me."

She squealed with joy, and with unexpected force, half tugged him from his chair. He schooled his expression to conceal his surprise. "You're getting quite strong, Sara, aren't you? It must be all your healthy activities."

His compliment seemed to please her, making her beam even wider. Her small frame straightened up and he needed no mindmeld to tell what she thought. She put her head back proudly and let go of his hand. "Yes. I'm very strong."

She turned and strutted off, making him smile despite himself.

He followed her down the long corridors of the Institute, admiring the healthy play of muscles in her back and legs. He wondered if her surprise related to her upcoming twelfth birthday.

They were in a part of the Institute he'd never visited. Nor had many others, by the look of things. A faint nervousness crept into his thoughts. At some clinical level he noticed this, and found it intriguing that she could provoke such a reaction, in him of all people. Her attitude, however, did not seem to involve one of her Hunting aspects; it seemed, in fact, unusually child-like.

"Where are we going, little one?"

She looked back over one shoulder. "A Special room," she said in mysterious tones.

Involuntarily, the nervousness strengthened. Annoyed at his own reaction, he resolved to no longer play her game, and asked no further questions.

At last they came to a tall set of double swing-doors. Pushing through them she spun around, spreading her arms wide.

"Ta-daaa!" Excitement shone in her eyes. He followed

her in some surprise into the very large room beyond. A gymnasium! He hadn't known the Institute had a gymnasium. He noted the faded beige walls, the paint peeling in places. It was chilly down here, too. Winter had reached in, making each of their breaths a small puff of cloud.

His eyes swung back to his young subject as she raced toward a springboard and vaulting-horse. She jumped and bounced up, to land running along the top of the horse. Racing over it, she leapt nimbly down to land on the long balance beam beyond. Speeding along that she jumped down, running then to the far wall where climbing bars rose up to the high ceiling. She flew up them – then, at the top, leaned out.

A rope from the ceiling hung a good three meters beyond her reach.

She leapt out into space.

For one long moment his heart stopped. Then she had the rope. It swung wildly as she climbed down, and his jaw clenched as he noticed the age of the fixtures. She jumped the last couple of meters to the ground.

Her eyes were glued to him, beaming with pleasure as she soaked up his every reaction. She sounded only slightly out of breath as she ran over to a large trampoline in the center of the room. As she clambered up onto it, she looked over her shoulder at him. "Just watch, Keepie: *this* is best of all!"

Bounding to the middle of the tight-woven blue netting, she began jumping up and down, rapidly building height with each bounce. The thing creaked alarmingly.

He winced each time she came down, but was drawn closer against his will. He fought down the protective urge that welled up, while his dispassionate side noted the reaction with amusement. At the side of the trampoline, it was clear that the frame was rusty, with parts of the elastic material pulled away from the edges. The padding had peeled off the rim and there were no protective mats on the floor around it. The thing itself squeaked and groaned in agonized protest with her every bounce. Yet, despite all this he found himself captivated by her simple grace as she leapt and tumbled in the air. And then the big finale, obviously: higher than ever, somersaulting over and over as she flew up, then straightening as she descended, her legs fully extended as her feet once more kissed the surface. Her slender legs folded dramatically, soaking up the entire impact, and the great arcing movements instantly stopped. One more tiny bounce, and then with unnatural suddenness she was still.

She stood above him, panting slightly, radiating pleasure; anticipating his approval.

"I practiced and *practiced* to surprise you!" she declared with pride.

He stood for a moment, expressionless, as he analyzed what would be the best reaction for his purposes. For once, though, he realized he didn't care, and simply grinned. He found himself applauding, which made her beam even wider.

"Well, Wild Thing, you were right: it *was* a surprise, from start to finish. And you know what, I think I've just worked out a Christmas present for you. Suppose I arrange some maintenance for this equipment so it's safe for you to use? Maybe even add an apparatus or two?"

For one disconcerting moment he had the illusion she had physically lit up, glowing with joy. He blinked, and in that instant she launched herself through the air to him. Automatically, he reached out and caught her as she impacted solidly against him, clinging tight. He staggered.

"Oh Keepie, you *do* care about me. I love you!" she exclaimed, burying her head against his neck. He stood, extremely conscious of the small, hot form pressing into him. Smelling her fresh personal scent. The sudden intimacy broke through his defenses and his arms tightened round her in the simple physical pleasure of contact. For once his clinical side lay silent.

He stood there, gazing unseeingly across the room. Simply feeling.

—

Within a few weeks, the gymnasium had been refurbished. Fortunately, Professor Sanders had been agreeable, once Harmon had pointed out that it was a good resource for all the staff – few as they were – and the patients. All but one, naturally.

Harmon had even had a holo-feed installed there: filtered to receive only appropriate programmes, of course. It meant that Sara had the examples of skilled athletes and gymnasts to follow. He remembered his purchase of the unit with some amusement. The salesman had been quite perplexed by the end of the sale, despite the smooth control with which he'd started...

"Yes, sir. All netcasts are introduced by a digital code according to their classification. We find that many parents find the built-in censorship of the Kyosei CX perfectly suited to their children's tender years."

Harmon had frowned, projecting an air of doubt. "I see. However, I think I want something a little more flexible. For instance, I may want to set it to receive only sporting programmes."

"Ahh. Sports! A very popular choice. Yes. The model ZX has a password-guarded category-selectable screening facility. For instance, you can program it to display only sports, but avoid blood-sports or sex-sports."

The device gleamed like a sleek black beetle.

Harmon waved dismissively. "Can I choose *specific* sports for it to receive, or select programmes by content?"

"Uh. Well, there *is* a digital abstract of the programme broadcast after its category identification, so..." greed began to gleam in the man's eyes "... so if you upgrade to the Hitachi AutoCrit software, you can even program it to select – er, historical dramas with a happy ending, for example. And for a small extra sum, you can have a verbal input module, which will respond only to your voice."

The salesman's encouraging smile was just a touch predatory. Harmon *did* rather like the sound of the voice-module, though. Oh well – a simple problem. "You will, of course, be able to give me a substantial discount to close the sale, won't you?" he Suggested. A highly illegal use of magic, but who would ever know?

The salesman blinked, looking a little confused. "Aah... yes... yes... of course... a substantial discount...."

CHAPTER 19

Early in the new year, Sara woke one morning with a cry of pain. For a moment she lay there in sleepy befuddlement, before the pain stabbed again, suddenly. Deep inside her.

"Oh!" she gasped.

She curled up, and for a little while that helped. The ache seemed rooted deep within her though, like something inside her was dragging downwards. She curled up tighter, hugging her sides. But the pain still built, tearing at her again.

"Aah!"

What was happening to her? The pain surged, deep within. It felt like something had torn. What was *wrong* with her?

A trickle of liquid suddenly ran between her legs. Her cheeks burned, shame piling on top of fear. She'd wet herself! "No!" she whispered, horrified. But somehow it didn't feel normal... she reached down, felt between her legs. Brought her hand back up, holding it before her. And stared at it in shock: blood. She was bleeding. Something inside her had broken, and she was bleeding to death.

A small moan escaped her before she could clamp down on it. She shook her head, disbelieving. *Why* did it hurt so much? What had she done to make this happen? *How* had she failed? *I must be bleeding all over my bed,* she realized. Her cheeks flamed brighter at the thought of her uncle finding that she'd ruined her own bed, too. She forced herself to move, to get out. Into the shower. Where she could at least wash off the blood.

So she went; hunched over, clutching at her stomach; stifling the sounds that tried to tear from her throat. Small cries escaped her lips, and she bit down on them, trying to face her death bravely. But tears streamed down her face at just how badly she was failing, what a mess she'd collapsed into. She made it to her shower stall, turned on the water, and finally gave in to her body's protest, lying down and curling up with the warm water raining down on her.

Harmon found her, a minute later, after hearing odd sounds from her room. As he entered the bathroom and saw her huddled form, the traces of blood, dismay smashed into him. Then she moaned, and moved, and suddenly the situation became clear.

Her eyes opened, staring into his in anguish for a moment before she looked down, curling away from his gaze. He hardly needed to slide his magical probe into her mind to know her torment. Kneeling over her, ignoring the spray that soaked him, he laid a comforting hand on her slim side.

"Oh Sara, Sara. It's all right, it's perfectly natural." He laughed, in genuine relief and sympathy. "Congratulations: you have just reached womanhood!"

She uncurled slightly, turned her head through the stream of water to stare at him uncomprehendingly.

"Don't be afraid, you're not injured. I'll get you some medication for the pain. Then I think it's time we had a talk about the facts of life."

Not to mention planning for a contraceptive implant eventually, he thought.

-

As winter ended and the warmer weather heated the old building beyond the capacity of its venerable air-conditioning plant, Harmon frequently found himself watching via the holovid as his young subject exercised in the gym, her movements matching the rhythms of the music she'd chosen. Today she was clearly hot, and it was visibly interfering with her performance. He had noticed previously that she seemed to feel the cold less than he, but the heat more. Yet still she practiced. Harmon knew she thought of it as 'play,' thanks to a Suggestion to make sure she followed a regular exercise regime. Briefly he wondered if his Suggestion had been a little *too* strong: ought she to exert herself like this?

He watched her bending, flexing, swirling around on the uneven bars.

She was beginning to mature sexually, he noted idly. He looked at her again, this time comparing her against his mental concept of the Huntress he was creating.

Something didn't fit. He concentrated, trying to pin it down.

She somersaulted off the bars, landing on her feet with a stagger, off-balance for a moment, which was unusual for her. His frown deepened. She looked tired as she trudged over to the trampoline, plucking at her damp top.

Slowly he realized what troubled him. The Huntress would not suffer senseless discomfort – if her clothes were too hot, too constrictive, she would remove them. False modesty was simply not harmonious with the Huntress archetype he was creating. His own societal prejudices had blinded him, had nearly made him fail in his duty to the experiment. Fortunately, however, he had the ability to free *her* of these illogical attitudes. He must alter her concept of clothing, foster the idea of dress as simply a means to achieve warmth. And, he supposed, to emphasize appearance – provided that did not conflict with its main function.

How would he put it to her? She had a fine body, even at this age. Perhaps he would appeal to her vanity. Suggest she should seek to make others more aware of her healthiness, offer herself as an example for others to follow.... Yes.

He brushed aside a slight uneasiness about the decision.

He could clearly see the new structure, the linkages that would form by adding this new element to the edifice he was building. Yes, he reassured himself. The change was necessary for the experiment.

Picking up the MetaStylus, he gestured the net-unit to call up the concept-model for the Sara experiment. Carefully, he created a new sub-tree, linked it into the main structure, then sat back and memorized it. With that held clearly in mind he would be able to make the necessary adjustments, perhaps as early as this afternoon, during the deliberately-soporific and confusing tests he had designed as part of her weekly 'mental strengthening exercises.'

And yet, later that day, as Sara blinked her way through her complex but tedious visualization exercises, guided by his own pre-recorded voice – to free his full attention for the magical manipulations required – the uneasiness returned. The whole process was both delicate and difficult. Akin to brain surgery, though working on the patterns encoded in the neuronal complexes rather than on the gross structures of the brain itself. He found himself dabbing aside a bead of sweat as the alteration drew to its conclusion, and reassured himself once more it was necessary for the experiment.

As usual when he needed to make a larger adjustment, Sara was exhausted by the end of the session. He read her intention to just go to her room and watch some of her trids. As outlandish as they were, at least they tended to have strong female characters. Even if some of them looked like feral pixies.

The shows she enjoyed were almost as fantastical as Godsson's belief in some ugly fractal reality-pattern which had formed when he had helped destroy Melisande d'Artelle, and which was now slowly replicating and growing, blindly seeking a path back to the key person in her death.

He chuckled, albeit a little uncomfortably. *That* would certainly be a challenge even for his Huntress Archetype!

CHAPTER 20

Dropped off by their cab driver just past Union Square on Market Street, Harmon began exploring the SoMa area, Sara holding his hand firmly.

Initially, after visiting one or two young-girls boutiques, Harmon had retreated in price shock to the street, where they meandered through the semi-permanent 'transient shopping district.' In happy contrast to the air-conditioned and glittering commercial palaces, the street vendors had perfectly reasonable clothing at remarkably low prices.

But when Sara tugged on his arm and asked for some 'scrip' to spend, and then complained about him being a mean 'wagie' – which Harmon knew was street-speak for a wage-earner – the researcher realized Sara's sharp ears were picking up more than he wanted her to. They retreated inside once more, each already laden with several bags.

"This one is nice, but why can't I wear my new hunting outfit?"

Her uncle ground his teeth, and took a deep breath. "I've already told you. You're *not* hunting now, for one thing, *and* you must try to blend in, so people don't realize you *are* a hunter."

But she really wanted to wear her hunting outfit. It didn't mean she was going to hunt today. "Can I just wear it till we catch the cab back home then?"

"NO!"

She blinked, swaying back on her heels at the force of his shout. Several of the sales ladies in the store turned around and looked at them. She noticed her uncle's hands were clenched, and he was breathing hard through his nose, his lips pressed tight together.

She saw his hands unclench, then he sighed and shook himself. Wriggled his fingers.

"No. Go outside. Go outside and wait for me quietly."

She shivered, feeling kind of strange and fuzzy for a moment.

"Do you hear me, Sara?"

It wasn't *fair!* All the same, she thought she'd better do what he said. She turned and went outside. But real slow, taking her time to feel some of the clothes on her way out. She didn't know why he'd gotten so grumpy all of a sudden. It was like the longer they shopped, the grumpier he got.

Outside, she turned and looked back through the front of the store. *He's not even watching me!* She stamped her foot. *Go outside and wait quietly*, she fumed. Still, at least she had some nice new clothes. She slid her hands over the slippery sheen of the clinging svelteene, enjoying the velvety feel of its nano-engineered microfibers, and had to smile despite her anger.

A little distance away was a bench, with people sitting on it. A bus stop, she realized. A boy about her age sat between two women, one really old and one just ordinary-old. A man in a suit sat further along, and at the end closest to the bus sign sat two young people dressed just like dangerous-looking go-gangers from the trids. But if they were go-gangers, why were they catching a bus instead of zooming around on their electro-bikes and out-racing the metro police? The girl was sleek, her skin a smooth, healthy green. Her partner looked cool and sharp, and his skin was slightly silvered. They were the first painted people she'd seen in real life.

They weren't *really* painted, of course.

The first time she'd seen one on the trideo, she'd asked Keepie about it, thinking she'd look good with deep blue skin. But by the way he'd snapped that it was a "stupid and dangerous DNA modification," she knew straightaway there was no point asking if she could do it.

There was one spot left on the bench, and suddenly she decided it'd be nice to have some company. Running up from behind, she leaped over the back of the seat, landing just right to fall gently back into the vacant space. Every head turned as she flashed into view, and the woman next to the boy literally jumped!

She looked around at them and smiled her sweetest smile.

Gradually they all looked away, except for the young boy, who continued to watch her, and who smiled back. Maybe they could be friends? She opened her mouth to talk to him, but at the very last moment decided against it. Instead, though, she smiled, except just for him this time. The woman, probably his mother, noticed. She looked Sara up and down, raised one eyebrow, sniffed, and moved protectively forward.

"Daniel, sit still."

What a grump. A grumpy grup. She stifled a giggle. She hooded her eyes a little, looking up at Daniel's sniffy mother, her lips pulled back in what she hoped was a sort of evil-pixie smile, like Sleena in *Sub-world*. A pity her teeth weren't longer and sharper, though, like the dark pixie. But the woman looked away, anyway.

Sara craned round to see if her uncle was coming yet, but he wasn't. At least it was a nice warm day. Sunny.

An insect buzzed round her head, and she brushed it away.

I wonder how long till the bus comes? For some reason, though, she didn't feel like asking the question out loud. Cars, alternately sleek and whispering, or noisy and smelly, flowed past the bus stop.

The fly buzzed round her head again. There seemed to be quite a few around. All the people on the seat were waving them away. One landed on her leg. It tickled. For a moment, she watched it, bored and glum, but then its sheer *ugliness* got too much for her. She smiled with momentary anticipation.

Her hand flashed out and swatted it.

Eww, she thought, grimacing at the red and black result. *Lucky I didn't squash it on my new clothes!* She flicked it off and wiped the remains away as best she could.

The woman beside her had a small smile on her face, but looked away when Sara noticed.

Even as she rubbed her hand to clean it, another fly, maybe attracted by the smell, landed right where she'd just squashed the other one. She froze, waited a moment, then lashed out again, but this time with less force. The fly, stunned, bounced off her thigh and onto the ground. She squashed it underfoot so it couldn't stagger up and try again, and then waited.

Less than a minute passed before another fly landed. Seconds later, it too was dead. She saw the young boy lean forward to see what she was doing. Sara began to enjoy herself. This was like a tiny, miniature hunt. Her speed, against the flies'. She concentrated.

Another landed – another died. She grinned. So far, she hadn't missed! This was *fun*. She leaned forward slightly, waiting for the next contest.

For a while, no more landed. Had she scared them all off? Along the seat, at the end, she saw the fake 'go-girl' seemed to be watching her with interest, too, even raised her eyebrows as if asking her to explain, maybe – but Sara really didn't feel like talking right now. The man in the suit was looking, too. Hey, she was getting an audience! Then a tickle on her thigh drew her back to her hunt.

Slap!

Five. The little corpses began to pile up around her.

-

Harmon looked at his watch as he left the store. Three o'clock already! Thankfully, that was now over with – and should suffice for some time. It had better. Even though he'd made them go over the bill item by item, he could still scarcely believe that such small amounts of material could cost so much. He winced. Though they weren't *all* minuscule outfits – he'd pointed out that sometimes she needed warm clothes, too, and heavier jeans: such as when she went picking blackberries. Or clothes that would allow her to blend in with the sheep, if necessary. *For example, at dinner time in the cafeteria,* he had thought, but very carefully not said aloud. She'd pouted, but let him choose several sensible outfits.

The whole experience, though, had been a tedious drain of his time. As much as he disliked the net, now he knew what measurements were necessary, at least he could shop electronically next time.

He looked around, wondering where the girl had gotten to? A flash of movement from the roadside attracted his eye. Ah. There.

Starting over toward the bench, though, he soon slowed and then stopped. Why were all the people at the bus stop acting so strangely? They were practically sitting in each other's laps to avoid being too close to Sara. All were staring at her, too, he saw. They seemed mesmerized.

He frowned in annoyance. Now what was she up to?

Slap!

The sudden movement startled him, and he noticed the people at the bus stop collectively flinch, too. What the devil was she doing? He couldn't see from here, but something in the set of her shoulders indicated that whatever it was, she was totally concentrating. Completely focused.

With an economical series of gestures, he patterned the shape of distant sight in the Imaginal, fed that certainty into the quantum sea, and cast the spell of clairvoyance. A moment later, he saw the bus stop as though standing directly in front of it, facing the waiting people. He watched carefully, keeping one eye on himself, farther behind them.

Sara sat with her right hand raised and bottom lip clenched between her teeth. A movement in the air, then a fly landed on her tanned thigh.

Slap!

He jumped, eyes widening involuntarily. He hadn't seen her hand move, it was so fast! She smiled as she brushed the smeared corpse to the ground at her feet, and his eyes followed it. He stared. Small black insect bodies littered the ground around her. There were dozens of them! Surely he hadn't been gone *that* long?

He looked back at himself, then shifted his attention to the would-be bus passengers. Their expressions ranged from fascinated delight – on the face of the girl at the far end – to something like horror on the face of the woman closest to Sara. There was something comical about the look. In fact, there was something comical about the whole situation! He stared at the woman a moment longer before her expression – a combination of shock mixed with a determination not to lose her seat – tipped him past the point of wry amusement.

The spell broke as his concentration shattered in gales of laughter.

People turned toward him in surprise. A moment later, Sara heard him and also turned around. As one, the people on the seat flinched away, which only made him laugh the harder.

Sara, clearly puzzled, cocked her head to one side, watching him. Slowly she began to smile, too. He doubted she understood his amusement, but simply seeing him laugh seemed to make her happy. She jumped over the seat and ran to rejoin him, hugging him silently. He casually ran an Imaginal eye over her, noting his own Suggestion to wait quietly was still laced through her thoughts, binding her.

Back at the bus stop, the people on the seat slumped in

relief.

Leading her away down the block, he looked back briefly as they rounded the corner, only to collide with a nightmarish figure as he turned back. One massive arm cushioned the impact before claws fastened on his clothes. The thing stood over two meters tall, its lupine muzzle only inches from his face.

The lower torso was goat-like, with hooves instead of feet. The head was like a wolf's, but the hands were black-furred and tipped with wicked-looking but clearly impractical recurved claws. Pointed ears, also furred, flipped up on his head, and yellow eyes squinted against the bright afternoon sun. Despite their extreme illegality, backyard 'furry mods' had proven impossible to eradicate, all across the world. Didn't these fools realize they could pose as much a potential threat to the human race as d'Artelle's mind-raped cadre of genetic engineers?

"Spare some scrip, fren. Any corp scrip."

The voice was low, a growling bass. Peripherally, he was conscious of Sara's gaze on them both, fascinated.

"No." He took a step back, but the man-thing's hand did not release its hold on his coat.

"Chit, fren, 'm no half-comp. Wagie like you, poz ya got scrip. You c'n spare some." The lips curled back from cruel yellow teeth, the canines fascinatingly long.

Instinctively, Harmon Percepted the thing's Imaginal state: vicious, and becoming more so as it started goading itself into anger. Some sort of drug in effect, too, one that blurred and blunted the normal beauty of the dance of the Imaginal form. He shifted his perception back to mundane reality, back to the foolishly mixed set of half-complete gene alterations the once-man had toyed with. New Humans indeed! "You're like a metaphor for our own modern society," he stated coldly. "A pathetic, will-less wreck of something once human. A sad waste of millions of years of evolution. Your kind *disgusts* me." He let his own anger sharpen the spell he flung. "*Go away.*"

The Imaginal pattern snapped over the man's confused and weakened spirit form like a religious revelation. The hulking figure jerked back as if electrified, then fled.

Sara gazed up at him in admiration, mouth working as if about to speak, when her expression shifted to a mixture of confusion and then frustration. Puzzled at first, he remembered his Suggestion that she should remain silent, just as her face screwed up and words burst forth again. "You spelled him, Keepie! You made him run away!"

He glowered at her, as annoyed by her incriminating words as the fact that she'd been able to snap the mild compulsion. "Shh, girl. Yes, I did, but I could get into trouble for using magic like that. Even charged with assault!" He turned and watched the figure disappearing from sight, then looked to see if anyone had overheard her. "Even for hopeless scum like that," he mused. He caught the eyes of his young charge. "Do you know what he was, Sara?"

"A troll?"

"Trolls and ogres are victims of the Melt virus. No, that was someone who thought his own shortcomings could be corrected by replacing highly-evolved human characteristics with more primitive animalistic patterns. Someone who thought the fears and weaknesses still remaining after those alterations, could be overcome through *drugs*."

She frowned, clearly not understanding, but also clearly refusing to admit it. "Where are we going, Keepie?"

"I've decided we'll take a cab back. You attracted too much attention back at the bus stop."

"I did? How?"

He rolled his eyes, but knew that until he explained she'd pester him. "Those people were sheep, Sara. Gray people, leading small, dull lives. Safety and security are all they desire. But you are not like them, are you?"

She shook her head.

"So they recognized you as something different: perhaps something threatening. But be aware: although such people don't matter individually, as a mass they can be dangerous. So it is best not to scare them too badly. Do you understand?"

"Uh huh, I do, Keepie," she nodded.

A few minutes later, freshly distracted, she tugged at his arm, pointing at a youth dancing around a light pole and hitting it with a silvery stick, shouting.

"What's the matter with *that* one, Keepie?"

For a moment he wondered whether they'd happened upon some fool's random psychotic episode, when he spied the glowing red armband that signaled the active use of a consensual AR system. Another educational opportunity! Perhaps the trip would prove to be worth the expense after all.

So he explained to her about Altered Reality, how the boy's optic nerves and other sensory inputs were being fed input from some remote multi-player game simulation. That the boy probably saw his stick as a magical sword, the light pole as some kind of threatening monster; while the red armband warned people he was immersed in an active simulation.

"What if he hits ordinary people?"

"The computer system portrays them as things to be avoided. If he did hit one, he'd be charged with assault."

In the cab back to the Institute, he took the opportunity to explain how life's challenges had to be met from within, not avoided through artificial means like drugs or AR or its worse forms, like the illegal and addictive 'NuLife,' that activated dangerously many parts of the brain, especially the emotional pleasure centers, amplifying them until normal life seemed pale and dull in comparison.

Sara listened, rapt, occasionally giggling. He was pleased to read her thought that such people were crazy.

CHAPTER 21

Sara admired her new clothes as she made her way to the basement. It'd been fun going into the City – the sights, the sounds, and especially, all the people! Buying the clothes and trying them on had been fun, too.

Sometimes her uncle had complained, since some of the clothes didn't have much cloth for the price. It was almost like the less cloth there was, the more it cost. But it was nice how the material fitted her snugly, instead of all sloppy and floppy.

Some of the saleswomen had acted kind of funny, though. Disapproving. And she was *sure* that Uncle had done magic on some of them, and they didn't even know! When he saw she'd noticed, it'd become like a secret game, just between the two of them. She'd been kind of sad when it was time to go back to the Institute. But Keepie had promised that as her figure continued to 'develop' they'd go out again and buy more.

She hardly had to think about bypassing the security systems, she'd done it so often. It was a routine now: stick, Bork, toolkit – plus the new bits, since they'd banned her. And today, she felt a new confidence in herself and her abilities. She felt *good* in the new clothes which Uncle had bought her, like she was at the center of things somehow.

She remembered his words with pride: "You have a very fine figure, you know, Sara. Very fit; very healthy. Your new clothes really show the good care you take of your body."

Now she was on her way to show Godsson her special new Hunting outfit. Made of soft brown imitation deerskin, the shorts clung snugly, plus they had fringes for decoration; and a halter top. It left her plenty of room for movement, and revealed much of her red-bronze tan. Some of the male workers had certainly seemed to admire her legs, she'd noticed. They *were* quite strong. She stood on one leg, and bent and flexed her other before her, watching the play of muscles.

On a whim, and just for fun, she put down all her visiting-equipment and kicked her left leg out and up, catching it in both hands as her knee kissed her nose. She savored the deep stretch in her 'glutes', then wiggled, just to feel the tickle of the fringe of her new shorts. Dropping her leg, she did a little jump spin, enjoying the tickle one more time.

But ahead of her was the start of the section of corridors with the IR sensors, so she picked up and then unfolded the damp blanket, wrapping it around herself before picking up Bork, stick, and toolbox and moving on. Once she'd realized they'd just told the computer she was interesting, it hadn't been too hard to work out how to fool it again.

She couldn't wait to show Godsson her new outfit! After she'd unwrapped the damp and tatty blanket that hid her body from the heat cameras, of course. They'd changed all the access codes, of course, but because they hadn't actually asked how she'd worked them out in the first place, it hadn't been hard to follow her uncle and watch as he'd entered the new ones. Though he had got more careful, and kind of moved his body to hide the panel with the buttons. But he didn't notice the small mirror she'd temporarily stuck to the ceiling directly above and angled just so. It took a few days, 'cause it took time to move and position the mirror as she learned each new code. She was glad there were only three doors. She'd also guessed that they might have undone her training of the computer, so she'd carefully done her repair-girl exercises, but this time in disguise. She wore a workman's cap and a pair of high heels, all of which she'd got Keepie to buy for her, as well as sunglasses. All just in case they'd told the computer to pay special attention to *her*. He'd looked especially unsure about the high heels for some reason, but hadn't been too hard to convince. Of course, she didn't tell him they were just to make her taller. She'd studied on the net about how computers recognized people. There was heaps and heaps of stuff about it, though it was harder to find things that weren't all scientific impossible-to-understand words and tables and graphs.

She wondered if Keepie knew science-y stuff like that?

After gathering all the pieces of her disguise, it'd taken a whole week to re-train the computer to recognize the new, not-Sara repair-girl, but it'd actually been kind of fun breaking the improved security.

She could see Godsson's cell now, and checked her new clothes one last time as she moved to one side of the corridor, staying well away from the room opposite his. The new inmate in there was… upsetting. He always seemed to be hurting himself. She felt sorry for Godsson, jammed up against someone like that. It gave her the creeps just to think of being so close to him during her short visits. What must it be like for Godsson, who spent all day next door? And the woman on the other side, labeled 'AS' on Mr Shanahan's security cameras, was worse. Sometimes she was brought upstairs so Uncle could heal her. She had creepy eyes; always darting around like she was seeing things sneaking up on you, but even if you looked, real fast, there was never anything there.

When she got to Godsson's door she knocked hard on the thick window. In a little while he came out of his bathroom and smiled.

'Sara,' she thought he said, watching his lips move. He made his special greeting gesture, which always reminded her of someone who was a bit deaf, holding a hand up to his ear.

"Godsson! Look at my new clothes!" She stepped back from the window so he could see more of her, then threw open the damp blanket so he could see, but the security cameras couldn't. "This is my special hunting outfit!" She held still so he could get a proper look. But his face kind of froze into a weird, stiff expression.

"Sara! That is hardly seemly. Especially on one so young." And then, he deliberately looked away!

She was dumbfounded. Frowning, then, she looked down at herself; held one leg out to one side to admire the slim muscles and smooth skin; with her fingertips, she dusted the silky surface of her stomach, prodded to check its firmness; and looked back at Godsson in puzzlement. *Maybe he'd actually said he could hardly* see *me*, she thought? Maybe he thought she'd been teasing him.

"Where do you want me to stand? I thought you *could* see me from there." She stepped a little closer, stroking the tight material of her top. "It's real imitation *deer-skin*," she pointed out.

"The problem is, Sara, that I *can* see a great deal of you. I should not see so much."

"Huh? Why not? Don't I look good? I know I *do*; I do *lots* of exercise."

Godsson began to sound cross. He hardly *ever*

sounded *cross*. "Sara. You are clearly at the age where you have to pay special attention to dress with proper modesty, so as not to encourage lascivious thoughts in men. Dressed like *that*, you are an invitation to... to...." He sputtered to a stop.

"To *what*, Godsson?"

"To rip those clothes off you! To engage in unsanctified and wanton sexual acts!"

He was actually panting, she noted in surprise. But more interesting were the strange words he was using. She knew 'sex' was some secret grup thing. She *hadn't* known, though, that it involved taking off clothes.... which led to another thought....

"You're saying that some man, seeing me in *these* clothes, would just decide to try to rip them off me?"

"Yes! That is *exactly* what I mean," he said, relieved at having at last gotten his message across.

"But no one would do *that*. Why would he?"

"He wouldn't be able to *help* himself!"

"Well, in that case it sounds to *me* like he's the sort of person no one would even want to *talk* to. Not if he goes round ripping people's clothes off them for no reason!"

"But many men are *like* that. You don't know."

"Well. In that case I guess I don't *want* to know. And anyway, I can look after *myself*."

"Can you?" he asked, clearly thinking she couldn't. "And what of the men you would lead into temptation, dressed like some under-age street whore!"

She wasn't exactly sure what he meant, but she wasn't going to let *him* know that. "I don't look under-age, I look good! And I just think you're being mean. Maybe it's *you* who wants to rip my new clothes off!" And she strode away, so angry she almost forgot to wrap herself back in her stupid wet blanket and pick up her stupid stick, and Bork, and her red toolbox. *She* liked her hunting outfit. She'd go out into the forest and hunt something right now!

-

Even with the 'summer solstice' approaching, it took several days before Sara's temper cooled enough to consider helping him again. But she couldn't forget Godsson's lonely battles; so she began watching her uncle carefully, waiting for the right time to bring the subject up.

The two ate together in their usual corner in the cafeteria. The handful of other members of the Institute sat at the scattered tables, eating and talking. Perhaps a little nervously.

Tonight, Sara judged Harmon's mood as tired but satisfied. Already, though, the young girl thought she could sense the beginning of the tension about the upcoming attack on Godsson.

"Keepie?"

"Mm, little one?"

Sara knew that was a good sign. "You remember that year when I helped Godsson fight off the invisible monster?"

Suddenly, Harmon didn't look so relaxed. "Indeed, I think the risk that any of us will ever forget that is quite minimal."

Which meant, yes. "And you remember how I promised not to sneak in again?"

"Yes. Very clearly. Fortunately, I know that you understand how important it is to keep one's promises."

But Sara had become quite a good actress, and merely shrugged. "Yeah. But you remember how I helped, right, and how Godsson was losing until I jumped down and attacked-"

"Sara-"

"Even if no one believes I saved the FBI man, Godsson *did* start winning his fight straight after-"

"Which can easily be explained by Godsson hearing you through the open intercom. That simply served to reinforce his dissociative episode whilst acting as justification for a rallying of his own efforts, providing a plausible rationale for the battle to turn in his favor."

At her annoyed expression and opened mouth, he held up one hand. "Let me continue. An *alternative* interpretation, favored by a certain twelve-year-old girl I know...."

Sara pouted. "Twelve and a *half.*"

Harmon ignored her. "...is that Godsson was battling an invisible monster from some realm far below the Imaginal, a creature somehow magically connected to him at the moment of Melisande d'Artelle's death; that this incorporeal entity had somehow escaped the extraordinarily powerful magical Wards created by the Emperor of China himself – with some small assistance from me – and was now subverting people outside Godsson's cell. Despite the fact that three powerful shamans, and myself, all watching very keenly on the Imaginal, failed to see or sense any trace of such a creature. Yes? Have I summarized the alternative theory accurately?"

Sara's tightly-pursed lips said she could not argue with that.

"Now, if the latter theory is correct – and I am not saying it's wrong – it means that everyone in the Institute is in grave danger. Further, if it can escape the different Barriers built into every centimeter of the walls encircling the grounds, everyone in the *world* is in that same danger."

"Yes! That's my point! So you should let me help in case it gets through again. I already killed it once!"

"Sara, if your theory is correct, then don't you think there might be *even better* help we could find, than a certain twelve-year-old girl? Even one who occasionally demonstrates some quite... impressive ingenuity?

"For example, if the entire world is in danger, perhaps the Dragon Lord of China might send some assistance; or if things were truly desperate, might even offer his own help? Don't you think that the defense of the world would become quite a big 'deal,' and would most certainly be taken out of our hands?"

Sara pouted. "I could still help. I did once."

Harmon shut his eyes, massaging the bridge of his nose. *Why was he trying to reason with her? Or protect her?*

"And if no one else thinks it's a big deal an' it's all just our imagination, then you should let me help since *Godsson* thought it helped, so I could help again."

"No. I refuse to put myself in the position of having to explain to Professor Sanders, let alone to the Director of the FBI and a coalition of three of the top shamanic Traditions on this continent, why we will need a twelve-year-old girl there to assist them."

She thrust her chin forward. "But I wouldn't be there to help *them*. I'd be there to help *Godsson*. With his 'imagining'!"

Harmon blinked, amused by her use of the 'bunny quotes' despite his irritation. "No, Sara. You will be on standby, as usual. We are not discussing this any further. Be grateful I have negotiated that *should* the on-site commander decide your assistance is required, the doors will be unlocked and you will be called in."

Sara, of course, looked unconvinced.

Just as Harmon had feared, the pattern of the tri-annual increase in the intensity of Godsson's attacks had caused trouble that year. Fortunately, being alert and forewarned, Shanahan had been able to grab her as she'd tried to run from his security office heading for his front door; although it had clearly distressed all three of them – Sara, Shanahan, and the cyborg dog.

Whatever Sara's other character flaws, lack of empathy was not one of them.

Given that her intervention three years earlier had seemed to help the fellow, though, and considering her growing distress, it occurred to Harmon that a legitimate approach to treatment would be to include Sara. Especially given the continued insistence by so-called experts such as Roger Ahronian that so long as Godsson were contained, the episodes were harmless.

Having Sara there to provide emotional support *should* help. It was also far preferable to having her attempt to physically fight her way in, all efforts at subtlety thrown aside. Heaven knew what mad scheme she'd come up with, otherwise.

Which according to his understanding of her psyche was basically a given for the year ahead.

CHAPTER 22

Now that she was practically thirteen, Sara had a busy schedule. Morning started with breakfast, followed by her stretches and exercises in the gym. After lunch Mr Shanahan would bring his netpad from his office and give her a swimming lesson, or maybe unlock some tools from the always-deserted 'wood-working therapy room' to show her some stuff.

Mr Shanahan had become much friendlier. She almost considered inviting him along on some of her patrols with Faith, but then decided it'd be better not to mess around with a perfect team. Not that she was *HyperGirl* or anything, but still....

Before, Mr Shanahan wouldn't leave his office: spending his days watching all his security monitors. But in winter, the Institute had got six new Tik Tek gynoids and androids, and after training the dumpy-looking 'bot women and men, most of the staff had gone off to work in big hospitals and other places. And for some reason, Mr Shanahan now went outside more often, not just to go into the main building for meals. She thought maybe because he missed talking to people. He'd started talking to Nerida and Dwayne heaps more since all the other orderlies had left. Now, he joined either them, or her and Uncle, for most meals.

For herself, she'd hoped the new robot helpers would be fun to hunt, but they were actually a hundred times more boring than even the boring old white-uniformed people they'd replaced. There was hardly anything interesting to hunt inside anymore. Though strangely, more and more often she sensed *It*, lurking. Looking. It never came close though, anymore. At least, not while she was inside.

She'd bumped into Mr Shanahan one day, with Faith trotting at his side, down by the lake. She and Faith had shared a grin, pretending they weren't a closer team than Faith and Mr S. The weird thing was, Mr Shanahan actually invited her back to his security office. There in the front room of his house, with its rows of monitors and equipment and its thick windows that gave him views on three sides – including the rear of the Institute – he'd seemed kind of sad, only looking up at his screens when one of the new 'droids trudged into view, then looking quickly away again. Even Mr S thought they were boring, she guessed. Most of them were used as nurses, but he had one that he had 'configured' to do patrols in the grounds, like she and Faith did. Only not as good, of course.

Most afternoons after that, when she went to get Faith for their patrols – which they'd do until she had to come in for her evening meal – she made a point of stopping by his sturdy little house like she'd used to. Some nights they'd finish early – or Uncle would forget about dinner until late – and she and Faith could play catch-race, or Pounce, or chase. She liked Pounce best, because usually it ended with her snuggling Faith, nose buried in the welcoming fur, appreciating the pungent doggy smell. But always careful not to squeeze Faith's tender bits, where the machinery joined her flesh.

And always very careful to make it clear when they *were* about to play Pounce.

Sometimes, mostly in the afternoons, she'd work on the wooden Wing Chun sparring dummy she was building with Mr S's help. When she told her uncle about it, at first he'd been pleased. She'd explained how you used it, and even showed him some vids, explaining how Mr Shanahan said he'd show her a few things. Uncle had frowned then, pointing out that the security guard had his own work to do, and hadn't she gotten him into enough trouble already? And that it would be safer for some reason to have the dummy in the gym, as well as having a lot more room to use it than she'd have inside Mr Shanahan's place.

They'd actually argued about it.

"But Mr Shanahan used to be a marine! He and Faith even fought in the Amazon Jungle together! He could teach me all *sorts* of cool stuff, not just-"

"Enough, Sara! Brian Shanahan does not work here at the Institute simply to be at your beck and call. He has his own duties. Or are you trying to undermine him, make him fail at his duties so that he loses his job?"

For a while she wondered if her uncle was jealous of Mr S. Though by the time they'd talked about it a few times, after her weekly mental exercises, she did see it wouldn't be fair on Mr Shanahan, and how it would be better to study from trids so she could get a wide set of teachers showing how to do it, and not maybe pick up bad habits from a single instructor.

Mr Shanahan had seemed a bit sad, though, when she'd explained all that after they'd finished the sparring dummy. For a while, she felt uncomfortable, like she'd done something bad.

She didn't visit Mr Shanahan quite so often, after that.

One day, Faith by her side, she knocked on his door. She'd had a rather awful thought: what if, during the upgrades to the gym, they'd added a security 'feed?' Mr Shanahan had seemed a little surprised to see her, but let her in.

She casually checked out his security screen, looking especially to see if there were any new codes that might stand for the gym. When she'd thought of the possibility, at first she'd felt pleased that people might be watching her when she was working out; then embarrassed to think of them laughing when she made mistakes or her ideas didn't work out. Then she grew hot, at the idea of Mr Shanahan watching her practice on the Wing Chun dummy they'd made together; seeing her using training vids instead of him to instruct her like they'd talked about during the long hours they'd spent building it together. That would've made it even worse.

It was a huge relief, then, to see that no new code had appeared in his list, like it did when they got a new inmate. She'd turned back to Mr Shanahan, then, afraid she'd been too obvious, but he'd just seemed kind of sad, and looked away.

She hadn't quite known what to talk to him about after that, and the visit turned kind of embarrassing. She hadn't stayed long. Mr Shanahan didn't try to stop her leaving.

She found herself focusing more time and energy on her morning routine instead, to make up for it. Straight after breakfast with Uncle she'd spend an hour or two in the gym 'working out' – that was what the grups called it, she learned from her vids. She had a private little dream centered around this morning ritual: if she could just do each of her routines perfectly, without the slightest stumble or ever being off-balance, something wonderful and magical would happen to her.

And if she could get outside without anyone seeing her, and *then* stalk something perfectly, leaving no trails... then,

something even better would happen! Something involv-
ing a woman with long black hair and deep, deep eyes....
And a fierce smile.

So every day, she tried to be perfect. She knew it
pleased Uncle – she knew she had to be perfect, to be good
enough. She *so* hoped she was going to be beautiful when
she grew up. She was strong, and healthy, and that was
real important. But somehow, she knew she had to be
beautiful, too.

CHAPTER 23

Sara turned thirteen and the year ended. Approval for Harmon's radical proposal had been granted only weeks before, but Professor Sanders had been happy to withhold the news until her birthday, at the winter solstice. Harmon was sure her thoughts would turn at that time to the summer solstice ahead, so it was with considerable relief he'd been able to gift her with the good news; long before she could start planning something unfortunate.

Her reaction had exceeded his expectations: he had never seen her so excited. Which said a lot, just in itself.

Her face had opened in astonished delight and she'd leapt across the dining table to wrap him in a hug, much to his embarrassment and the amusement of the other three diners.

She was an affectionate little thing, and despite the need to maintain his clinical distance, he'd felt his heart warm. He'd even hugged her in return, albeit a little awkwardly from his seated position.

The event had quickly turned into a surprisingly communal evening in the cafeteria, as he found himself having to explain to his co-worker, Simmons – and the last two of the human orderlies, the long-suffering Dwayne and Nerida – what had so excited Sara. At first they refused to believe that Sara would be allowed to be present literally outside Godsson's cell during the annual lock-down, provided simply that she behaved well and did not attempt to disrupt things. She would, after all, be only thirteen – "and a half!" But after laying out his rationale, they had all nodded, appearing to be genuinely impressed and agreeing it sounded potentially good for both Sara and Godsson. Though Sara herself, he noted, looked annoyed by his explanation. No doubt, she itched to point out that it was all real, not make-believe.

He would have a quiet word with her later to explain that *secretly* he was relying on her to support Godsson should the attack prove real. It would fit very nicely with the stress induction system he'd put in place for her own hunting of the Institute's 'invisible monster' with her bow and 'magical' arrows.

Though heaven help them all if the creature were real.

Winter turned to spring, and spring to summer. In just the

last four months, Sara's body had begun to fulfill the promise of richer curves concealed within the slender lines of her adolescent frame. So much so that another trip into the city was required, and one that again needed her actual presence: Harmon didn't wish to waste money on ill-fitting garments. It would be only the second time he had taken Sara into New Francisco.

Today, Sara wore her favorite clothes – her huntress outfit – even though it was more than a little tight on her now and showed obvious signs of hard wear. Harmon watched her playing with the security guard's 'dog' while they waited for their cab to arrive. The idea of her playing with the cyborg animal still made his hands sweat. Suppose it activated a weapon from its arsenal? It supposedly had armaments sufficient to deal with any individual here, even 'Godsson' if it took him unawares.

Still, he could almost certainly just heal her, since Sara was most unlikely to trigger a response at that level. And playing with the weaponized dog lessened the chance she would focus her attention on the Institute's walls and the act of leaving. He had been most carefully conditioning her in this regard. To her, the Institute was enough: more than a home, practically the world as far as she was concerned. He had conditioned her to this disinterest for his own convenience. Soon, though, he would need to undo it lest he end up with the magical archetype of someone scared to leave her room.

At last, he saw the yellow cab in the distance on the curve of road leading to the main gates. He went to the security panel just inside the front doors, identified himself, and authorized the cab's entrance. As the gate swung open he re-emerged, calling Sara as he descended the steps.

She looked up, surprised, then stilled in confusion. She took a hesitant step toward him, then stopped.

He scowled. While conditioning her toward disinterest to the outside world was working well, his Suggestions toward obedience had not shown the same improvement. So, while one result seemed to support the effect predicted in that very recent paper from Spencer, her disobedience was evidence against it. Either way, her recalcitrance was irritating.

"Sara!" he barked out, letting a little anger creep into

his voice. "Come here! Now!"

She seemed to come awake, but instead of running over to him, she first bent down to hug the 'dog' farewell. Harmon scowled. She should not have been able to do that.

The creature followed at Sara's side as she trotted over to him, escorting her as far as the gravel area, then stopping. Its red eyes seemed to stare knowingly, as its gaze locked on his. Not for the first time, he wondered just how intelligent the cybernetically modified animal was. Its stare was almost unsettling. He was glad to turn away from it and face the approaching vehicle.

Sara bent down to it again. "Bye, Faith! We're going to New Francisco! To buy presents for me!"

As she turned, straightening up in her overly-tight 'hunting' outfit, Harmon noticed the disapproving look the cabbie gave her before swinging the car round in a swift circle on the little-used area.

But as the vehicle slowed, Sara flashed past him, angling toward it. The day was hot, but Harmon went cold as she ran straight at the moving car, then launched herself at it.

She sailed in through the open rear window, bouncing heavily on the back seat even as the driver slammed on the brakes. The car juddered to a halt, throwing her small body forward, onto the floor.

Harmon's mouth was still open in stunned disbelief as Sara got up from the floor looking annoyed.

He started to breathe again. Gods! *She can still surprise me.*

He moved over to the vehicle, noting that the driver's initial shock had quickly turned to cool suspicion. "The girl seems mighty keen to get going. You in a hurry too, maybe?" he drawled.

"I am Dr Harmon, and the over-excited young lady is my ward. If you're worried that our departure from the Institute might be... unexpected... why don't you check with them?"

With ill grace, Harmon endured the delay as the driver used his cab-link system to do exactly that. Harmon fumed, but could hardly reprimand Sara for following the dictates of other parts of her conditioning. Even if her sheer *exuberance* did sometimes exceed his expectations.

The cab swept south along the highway through the hills to New Francisco. As Sara chattered gaily at the driver, or exclaimed in delight at various farm animals dotting the fields, or leaned out and waved at the surprised occupants of the occasional car they passed, it became obvious that Harmon's concern she led too insular a life had been unfounded. This time he had the uncomfortable impression he wasn't so much taking her to the city as unleashing her upon it.

As they reached the Golden Gate, they both stared off across the steel-gray waters. A minute later Sara broke the silence as the cab sped past the huge sign welcoming visitors to New Francisco. "Where's Old Francisco, Keepie?"

"It's the same place as New Francisco, Sara. There was a very big earthquake in '44," – *the same year you were born*, he mused. "So much of 'Old Francisco' was damaged – some whole districts destroyed – that after all the rebuilding, people started calling it New Francisco. The older city used to be much more crowded, though. Everything was more tightly packed back then because of all the extra people."

Although she had asked, Sara did not seem all that interested in his answer. Harmon stared out the window, remembering the Turmoil.

For those who believed in signs and portents, that year had seen a surfeit of them. It had been a terrible time, the start of three unbelievably bad years. The long-feared but never expected Big One; then the first deaths from the Red Plague, followed by the Second World Storm. The fear that *this was it, the world really was ending*, had loomed like a vast cloud-bank on the horizon, overshadowing everything. Hardly surprising, as the death toll grew to *two billion* people worldwide.

And then the Melt virus. He shuddered at the memory of those appalling days and nights: the dreadful, oppressive fear felt by everyone, week after endless week, himself included. Wondering day by day if you would be the next victim as you mutated into some repellent parody of a human being.

Then the final discovery that most of those billions of deaths had been caused, directly or indirectly, through the manipulations of one magically-active woman, Melisande d'Artelle.... It had been a bad time for humanity, but a terrible time to be a mage. No wonder people's first reactions still tended toward fear and distrust. Though things could become grim again soon, if Spencer's latest research in *Nature* was correct: that repeated exposure to a single magician really did make the recipient more *susceptible* to that mage's spells. He winced, knowing the outrage that the discovery would provoke. Even pedestrian healing magic would acquire a taint. And the masses were foolish beyond belief. Look at that whole business of global warming. "Why didn't the scientists warn everybody *properly* about the dangers of climate change?" People were fools.

He shook himself out of the reverie. "Look, across there," he said, pointing off to the south east as the row of shattered concrete pylons spotted across the bay came back into view. "That's the Oakland Bay Bridge. It was destroyed by the earthquake."

Sara scampered over him to the left side of the cab, and stared out the window.

"Be finished in a coupla years," the driver suddenly interjected. "They're rebuilding it. Taken 'em long enough, but." He lapsed back into silence.

Later, as Sara was lamenting the fact she had not been allowed to bring her hunting bow, Harmon's eyes met those of the cabbie in the rear view mirror.

"You often take her hunting in the city?" he inquired, ironically.

Sara pulled her head back inside, from where she'd been watching an eagle high above. "No. Uncle says I'm too young, yet."

With difficulty, Harmon masked the dismay he felt as the driver went suddenly still. The cabbie's eyes met his again in the rear-view mirror, taking a careful look at both of them. Sara, pressing in against her uncle's side, smiled sweetly back at the driver while Harmon stared fixedly ahead.

The driver opened his mouth to ask a question, but suddenly seemed to think better of it and simply turned his eyes back to the road ahead.

A talk seemed to be in order, Harmon thought. And the sooner the better, judging from the driver's reaction.

CHAPTER 24

Finally, the summer solstice arrived. Sara's demeanor was very composed, bordering on mature, as she accompanied Harmon past all the military and FBI personnel. He was highly conscious of her small hand in his as they made their way in the late afternoon, down the stairs to basement level two and then along the passages leading to Godsson's cell. Harmon observed her closely. It was two years since they had upgraded the security and she had been forbidden to come down here. He had expected her to be either excited, or avidly studying everything as she sought to identify weaknesses. For once, however, she surprised him by behaving with a gratifying maturity.

For a moment, he wondered whether she could possibly have continued to visit? *No. Inconceivable.*

Briefly, he considered asking Shanahan to review all the security records anyway – until he pictured the laughter *that* would provoke: "She's even got *you* believing she can work miracles now, eh, Doc?"

It felt extremely peculiar to be introducing her to the agents who waited, alert and armed in the corridor outside Godsson's cell. There was something more than surreal in seeing the child's hand enveloped in the armored glove of each of the heavily armed men and women, soberly shaking hands. As usual for these more intense tri-annual episodes, the Director of the FBI, 'Mr Smith,' was attending in person.

Although the man's lips had turned up in something of a sneer as he too shook hands with the young girl, thankfully he said nothing.

The three shamans, strangely, seemed to treat the introduction with genuine gravity, and he noticed that each examined her quite carefully with their Imaginal senses, before eyeing Harmon himself speculatively.

To Godsson, he had explained earlier that Sara had become so distraught that he had been presented with a choice of either sedating her, and permanently damaging his own relationship with her, or allowing her to be present to 'help' if necessary, as she had three years earlier. Harmon had simply laid out the rationale he had used to convince the higher-ups to authorize her attendance, knowing that his patient was well aware of the standard interpretation of his mostly-yearly battles.

As he had expected, Godsson, in contrast to everyone else, grew quite vituperative, calling him ignorant, arrogant, high-handed, and uncaring for his 'daughter.' Did Harmon not see the risk he took? Did he not know that these were real, if abnormal, entities intangibly manifesting within the Institute grounds, judging from what Sara had told him?

Abruptly, though, at that point he had simply stopped talking, and Harmon was certain it was not because he knew he would be unable to convince him to change his plan, but because there was something Godsson did not wish to tell him. Some dark secret he concealed.

Rationally, Harmon knew this was all simply part of Godsson's elaborate delusion. Knew that they argued over fantasies.

One small part of him, though, continued to whisper, "but what if...?"

Now they all waited, tense, not quite certain when the episode would begin. The *attack*, as Godsson and Sara would say. The mad mage, however, was very clearly far more worked up and nervous than was normal even for a tri-annual attack, and Harmon was sure this was because he was genuinely fearful that something would happen to Sara.

It was gratifying, if a little surprising, to see that Sara had apparently succeeded so well in gaining the madman's affection.

For her part, she stood on the sturdy wooden bench that had been set up against the side of the corridor opposite the cell, as solemn and alert as any of the adults as she stared at the small window.

The intercom system was turned on, the sound of Godsson's measured pacing a wearing beat against the collective nerves of the watchers.

And at the instant of sunset, the attack began.

The only sign was Godsson's invocation of his dauntingly-powerful protective circle, its golden light blazing forth from the small window. But as usual, the barrier appeared to offer little protection to him, and soon Godsson was writhing, twisting and dodging, muttering incantations, prayers to his heavenly father, and physically fighting something only he could see.

Harmon saw Sara flinch, her little hands closing into white-knuckled fists, and she stared at him accusingly, the thought "*why don't you go in and help him?*" clear in her expression.

She was too young to learn what had happened on the one occasion they *had* tried that. That would be something to share with her when she was older. Perhaps. There *were* limits to the stress levels he wished to subject her to.

Seeing that no one was offering to help her 'friend,' she turned her small face determinedly back to the window, squinting against the glare. He and each of the shamans stepped forward to look through the window, taking their turn at trying to See what bedeviled the solitary figure. But there was just the man, magic flaring from him as spells of daunting power shocked through the air of his cell, to no obvious *effect* – and with even less *meaning* to their strange shapings. Some, Godsson directed inwards at himself, and it was generally at those moments that his cries grew desperate.

Though as the grunts, moans and shouts continued, they did not build and build as they had three years ago, just before Sara had interrupted. Despite himself, despite the obvious self-torture, Harmon found himself relaxing slightly. He ached for Godsson, yes: only the stoniest heart would remain unmoved. And he himself, Godsson's therapist, who knew the man's mind better than most, felt the pain more keenly. But still, this episode looked to be less intense even than the episode six years earlier, bucking the generally upward and worsening trend.

Probably due to Sara's 'help' three years earlier. Though whether that help had been real or simply a kind of placebo effect was impossible to say.

He hoped it was only the latter.

For a short while, then, Godsson's cries eased, as they sometimes did, and the man seemed to use the time to gather his breath and resolve, his hands held out before him as if he gripped something.

Harmon jumped – everyone in the corridor did – as suddenly Sara cried out. "That's it, Godsson! You're winning! Push her back, push her *back!*"

She stood, vibrating with tension, every muscle clenched, sweat on her brow and her face red and screwed up, but she stayed where she'd been told, there on the simple wooden bench, and shouted encouragement to her friend. "I know you can do it! Force Her back! *Hurt* her! Tear Her up into little pieces!"

Sara's hands, he saw, were once more clawing unconsciously at the air, as though she imagined herself in the cell with Godsson, fighting alongside him. The image of Sara suffering the same fate as either of the previous two poor souls who had once tried that was suddenly so vivid he sagged against the wall.

Tears streamed down her face as she continued to shout, bouncing slightly on her viewing stand as she stared inside. Harmon watched her Imaginally, noted the intense patterns of emotion, her aura vivid and reaching out slightly. Nothing magical, however. Just a small soul utterly focused on her friend in his hour of need.

Harmon looked along the corridor, noting the emotions and auras of the shamans, the agents: all, in varying degrees, in empathic pain; suffering and emoting along with the madman raging in his cell. All except Mr Smith, who registered faint amusement.

Harmon had always suspected the man to be emotionally impaired.

The attack continued.

Strangely, though, Godsson seemed to be gaining ground, gaining the upper hand rather than 'winning', through sheer endurance. That served only to stir Sara to more extravagant cries of support, of caring; dare he say it, of love. Was she so desperate for affection she dreamed she could get it from the madman?

More surprising still, the attack finished after a mere two hours, when the golden light finally winked out. Usually, Godsson's episodes lasted until 2 or 3 a.m. And until Sara's dramatic intervention three years before, they always ended with the inmate a worn wreck, collapsing unconscious onto his bunk, or even the floor, as if only sheer willpower had kept him going. But Sara's earlier help had eased Godsson's need to exhaust himself so severely – though that positive change had eroded with each passing year.

But now, he staggered to the window of his small room, and Harmon saw his eyes meet Sara's. For once, though,

Harmon found himself unable to read the expression there. Godsson's eyes then turned to Harmon, and he frowned, clearly thinking dark thoughts.

For her part, Sara slumped back against the wall, panting hoarsely, as if she had driven herself to her own limits.

When Harmon looked back at Godsson, he saw the man nod to his ward, as if acknowledging her *support*; surely not her *help*? Then he simply turned his back on all his watchers and laid himself on his bunk.

Harmon went to Sara, who collapsed gratefully forward into his arms, falling asleep almost at once. "Gentlemen. Ladies. I believe the episode is over for this year. I will put my daughter to bed. If you need me, call."

In complete silence, then, he walked between the agents and the three shamans, who parted silently, as he carried Sara up to her room.

The next morning, Sara had not been in her room, and he began searching for her, concerned regarding possible traumatization, especially considering how extremely she had reacted, how deeply she had engaged with Godsson's grueling theatrics of the night before.

Instead, the moment he stepped through the doorway of the cafeteria at breakfast time, she'd flung her arms around his waist, bow and arrows clutched in one hand, and proceeded to gush thanks for letting her 'help Godsson'; demanded to know if she'd been good enough; and asked whether she would be allowed to help each year. Before he could answer, she then explained that she and Faith were going to be hunting the invisible monsters; and pleading for him to buy and 'magic' some more arrows for her.

He had barely responded to all that, in a generally positive sense, before she had flashed a grin and darted from the room on her way to the front entrance.

He felt rather as if he had just been spun around by a small whirlwind.

Looking around, he saw her bowl, plate, glass and cutlery already being stacked back in the glass-fronted cupboard by the washbot, and the male orderly – Dwight? – raising one eyebrow in question.

"How'd it go last night, Dr H? Well, I reckon? Sara looks extra full of beans this morning, if that's possible."

"She does, ah, Dwight, doesn't she?"

"It's Dwayne, Dr Harmon."

"Ah. Of course. Yes, I had planned to give her a thorough examination, but I think that can wait until later in the day. Yes, her attendance at the episode seemed to be a definite positive."

"Chill. What'd she mean about magic arrows? What monster?"

Harmon waved a dismissive hand. "Merely a game, Dwayne. Something to keep her amused, active, and shooting at things other than orderlies."

Two steps forward, one step back, Harmon later mused as he ascended the basement stairs on his way back to his office. Worryingly, Godsson had begun equating the biblical figure of Lilith with d'Artelle, and seeing signs of Sara's 'infection' by the thing spawned from that death. He had even urged Harmon to bring Sara into his cell so he could check her for himself.

Over my dead body, Harmon had thought.

CHAPTER 25

Sara had taken to hunting the invisible monsters on her own. It was getting too dangerous to take Faith along with her: too dangerous for *Faith*. Faith seemed not to really understand what they were doing, and mostly just followed along looking puzzled while Sara dodged and twisted to avoid their touch. And Faith was just hopeless at avoiding them. Robo had even wrapped around Faith once, and made her go all strange. She'd actually *whined*; then gone sort of dopey and just trotted off.

She'd acted weird for days, afterward. Even Mr Shanahan had noticed. He'd wondered if Faith was getting older, less wanting to play. But with enough teasing, and pleading, and begging, and offering to play Faith's favorite games – which mostly involved chasing – after a few days she'd come back to her old self.

Since then, Sara went on her special hunts *solo*. Which meant alone, but sounded a lot more grown up.

It was still rare for her to find either one of the invisible monsters – either *Her* or Robo – but *She* wasn't around much any more. Thank goodness. The trouble was, she wasn't sure Robo was, either.

At least, not really around. 'Cause either Robo was getting creepier, or he was changing. She wasn't even sure Robo was really Robo anymore. He seemed colder. Not at all funny. *Sticky,* somehow, like he'd learned from Her how to wrap around people. He was actually getting kind of scary. As scary as Her, only in a different way.

And she was pretty sure her magic arrows weren't working anymore. Not at all.

Even the thought of being *touched* by the new Robo made her skin kind of shrink. She found herself shaking her head just at the thought. Somehow she knew it'd be real bad if she let the new Robo get her.

She wasn't quite sure why she was even hunting it, anymore. The game was no longer any fun at all. The new Robo had even started to act like it was maybe hunting *her*.

She'd also discovered that if she showed any fear, it seemed to see her better. Actually, it was the same if she got angry with it, too. She'd learned she had to stay very Huntress-y: very calm. In its own way, the new Robo, or the grown-up Robo, was almost as creepy as *Her*. But at least he never tried to talk to her, asking to go for 'rides.'

Okay, so maybe the new Robo wasn't quite as creepy as Her. But she wasn't so sure it was really a good idea to be hunting either of them, anymore.

She was worried about Godsson, too. Sure, it was cool that she was allowed to be there during his battles – but also, awful. It just didn't make sense, the way they all simply stood around and watched. Why didn't they help? And couldn't they see *She* was getting stronger?

Sure, last year hadn't been so bad, but she just knew, somehow, that this time was gonna be a lot worse.

And she still hadn't thought of anything she could do, even now she was practically fourteen! There oughta be *something* she could do to help her friend.

CHAPTER 26

Six months later, on a cold, still winter's afternoon, Sara sat in Harmon's office, completing the history quiz he had set her. With little more interest than she herself displayed in performing her studies, he reviewed her results. The logs of her online sessions showed, as he had expected, an improvement over her previously minimum 'attendance' efforts. He had let her choose her own avatars for her synthetic instructors, and was hardly surprised to find she'd chosen popular figures from the trid shows she favored. The monthly license fees were well worth the hours they saved him from otherwise having to spend instructing her himself.

He did wonder, though, why she had chosen 'Sleena the pixie warrior' for her math instructor. The small creature looked quite feral, with those long teeth. He couldn't see the connection.

The female adventurer/investigator 'Miss X,' whom she had chosen as her Science lecturer, at least made a modicum of sense. Perhaps, though, the choice of the cyborg dog 'Argon' as her English teacher was most surprising. Yet he did not think she had made that choice from any sense of irony.

He put the smartsheet down, satisfied with her results this month.

History, of course, was an entirely different matter: far too dangerous and open a subject area to leave to any kind of automated or self-directed study. No, *that* he made sure to cover himself. There were far too many potential information sources that would interfere with his own aims for her.

He had carefully designed today's history test to ensure she would meet the minimum standards required for a pass mark. It was somewhat difficult, considering the areas in which he saw negative value should she learn too much.

As she completed the quiz, her final score, 62%, transferred across into her online records, and she smiled at the pass mark.

"Can I go now, Uncle?"

"Your history results are a little low, Sara. I wondered perhaps whether you'd like to know more about what happened after the magic returned?"

At that suggestion, she sat up straighter. "Yeah!"

"In some ways, we could perhaps have predicted it, after the Week of Miracles. Can you tell me when that was?"

"Um. March 31, 2036."

"Good! You remember, there was an even mix of good and bad 'miracles' in that first week: as many people doing terrible things as wonderful things. Yes?"

She nodded. Briefly, he considered using it to illustrate the lesson 'power corrupts,' since the even mix of good and ill did run counter to normal patterns of aggregate behavior; but decided that was probably a lesson best left for later years.

"And what catastrophe followed the Week of Miracles?" At her blank look, he added, "What big disaster?"

"Oh! The First World Storm!"

"That's right. And why did so few people die in the First World Storm compared to the Second?"

She thought for a moment. "Because the Enemy of Mankind made the Second one!"

He winced at the simplistic answer. "Well, in a sense I suppose that is true. Although *how* she did so, no one is quite sure even today. There is some evidence she influenced elemental beings at the global scale."

Sara looked lost.

"Some people think there are elementals so big they can affect the whole Earth, and they think D'Artelle deliberately *arranged* the Second World Storm to start during the depth of winter in the northern hemisphere. The First World Storm lasted only a week; the Second, four terrible months."

At her wide-eyed nod he continued. "So the death toll from the First was so much smaller because India, South America and Africa are more tropical continents, and few people live in Antarctica." For a moment he had a strange feeling, something related to the Australis Ocean, but dismissed the tangent thought. "So, because the First Storm covered the whole world during summer in the northern hemisphere, the death toll was 'only' about one hundred thousand. In stark contrast, in the Second World Storm *ten thousand* times as many people died: over a billion people."

"Ohhh. That's a real lot, isn't it?" She looked sad, before brightening. "But Godsson killed her in the end, and saved everyone, didn't he? With help from the Dragon Lord! Is Lord Shen really a dragon?"

"Well, he *looks* like a normal human man. Chinese. Very intense eyes. With flecks of gold." Harmon thought back to their one and only meeting. "I simply don't know, Sara. Certainly, a living, breathing dragon did help him reclaim the position of Emperor of China – with some extremely deft political maneuvering of his own. It is also true that that dragon and Lord Li Pao Shen have never been seen at the same time. And Lord Shen claims he has a draconic form. I suppose it may be possible."

"Wow. How do you become a dragon, Keepie? Could I?"

I certainly hope not! "I don't think you could, no. Even if there is a way, I think it would be a closely-guarded secret. But I was telling you what happened when the magic returned."

"Why did it return, Keepie?"

"A good question!"

Sara beamed.

"I have heard many theories, all unconvincing. Personally, given the fact that all the supernatural creatures and beings which have reappeared in modern times have also featured in myths and legends for hundreds, and even thousands of years, I would not be surprised if that continuity of existence across the non-magical period were somehow a significant point."

He'd lost her, he could tell. So instead, he recounted the story of the return of the being *Kali* in July '36, and the terrible consequences as other members of the Hindu pantheon 'returned,' leading inexorably to the Great Conflict: Science opposing Magic.

She listened, absorbed, as he spoke of that awful struggle and the terrible sacrifices, as the Indian people rejected the demand to *worship or die.* He spoke of the first use of the atomic bomb as a weapon of war for almost a hundred years.

But the worse history lesson – Melisande d'Artelle's treachery – could wait for some other day. He shook himself. "Come, Sara. I see it is now 6 pm – I've kept you a little longer than I intended, I'm afraid. I think it's too cold for you to be patrolling tonight with Faith. Time for dinner, anyway. I'll read you a book afterward, if you like."

Disappointment at not patrolling with Faith was replaced by pleasure at his offer, he noted.

It felt strangely good.

CHAPTER 27

Godsson turned even before she reached his door. Frowning, he made his greeting gesture. "It's rather late, Sara."

She shrugged. "I wanted to find out more about Melisande d'Artelle."

"Really. Perhaps if you take off those sunglasses I will. I dislike being unable to see your eyes. You have nothing to fear from me."

"I know. But I can't take them off. They're not for you, they're so the stupid computer won't recognize me. That's why I wear this dumb repairman cap, too. And the high heels."

For a long while he said nothing.

"Why this fascination with the Enemy of Mankind, Sara? Do you find yourself drawn to these stories? Do they call to you?"

"I'm just tryin' to understand why she did so much bad stuff. Uncle said she killed a zillion people in the Second World Storm."

"A fair statement. Did he also tell you that it was at her behest that the Melt retro-virus was created? And the Red Plague?"

She shook her head, and even through the sunglasses he could see the whites around her widened eyes.

"Why was it called the red plague?"

"Can you not guess? What color is blood?"

"*No way.*"

"And all while she ran the Helping Hand organization, working closely with the WHO."

"Who?"

"Some call them that, yes."

Godsson should have expected the misunderstanding which followed, and just given the organization its full name....

"But *why* was she so evil? Was she always that way?"

"It's possible she became evil while still quite young." He watched her as she digested that.

"But to be *that* evil, something must've happened to her!"

"Evil people don't think they're evil, Sara. That is the tragedy." Again he just looked at her. Then sighed. "Even Melisande, at the end, claimed she did what she did to save the human race from an even greater threat."

"No way! What threat?"

"It doesn't matter."

"*What!* Are you- I mean, of course it matters. An even bigger threat to the *whole human race?* What was it?"

"It doesn't matter. She was merely trying to deceive us."

"What. Greater. Threat?"

"*It doesn't matter.*"

"If you don't tell me, I'm not gonna visit you any more. Not ever."

Godsson considered that, for long enough for Sara to begin to scowl. "Very well. But if I tell you, you must promise to do me a favor in return."

"Okay."

"Do you promise?"

"Yeah, I promise. Now: *what greater threat?*"

"Aliens."

"Huh?"

"Melisande said she did what she did because aliens were invading."

For a long while Sara said nothing.

"You're just making that up."

"No. By my Father's Name, that was what she claimed. What she even appeared to believe."

Sara digested this. "Wow. So, what kind of aliens? What do they want? How long-"

"I'm sorry, Sara, that is absolutely all she shared on the subject. But now, you made a promise to me."

She sighed. "Yeah, okay."

"Good. I need you to help me get out of here. So I can fight Her properly. With you by my side."

Sara was shaking her head. "I can't do *that!* I'd get into awful trouble. I'd be Grounded for weeks!"

"So you would break the promise you swore mere minutes ago. How typical."

"But you said your father said you couldn't come out till everyone wanted you out."

"Everyone will. After I'm out."

"No, Godsson, I can't do that. I'm sorry, I just can't!"

"Go, then. I will Call some...one else."

"Don't be horrid. I said I'd do you a favor." She thought. *What might Godsson like?* "Maybe I could get them to get you a pet or something?"

But he ignored her, and began pacing – almost *marching* – back and forth across the room.

"Godsson! Wouldn't you like a kitten?"

Still he marched. Strangely, the glass misted over, making it harder and harder to see him, gradually hiding him from her sight.

"Well, fine, see if I care!"

She stormed off.

Behind her, the frost continued to build.

There was no way she could sleep after that! She rugged up extra warmly before sneaking out of her room, her flashlight defocused to throw a diffuse light. Faith had been surprised but pleased to see her after she'd crept up to Mr Shanahan's place, quietly calling her out of her cyber house.

They'd patrolled for almost two hours, and now Faith's breath panted out in steamy puffs beside her as Sara skipped through the pines leading down to the Institute, occasionally sharing what she'd learned in today's history lesson. She and Faith had finished their patrol in the area where helicopters sometimes landed with new patients, or grumpy FBI men.

She stopped when Faith halted with a queer half-whine, staring ahead through the trees at the Institute, its light just visible between the trunks. A strange sound of cracks and pops in the trees began, moving closer then suddenly rising all around them. Arctic air rolled over them in a wave, Faith's fur crackling, frost feathering her coat and prickling against Sara's skin, shivering in her hair and eyelashes.

Then all was still.

"Faith, what-" Sara stopped at the sight of her own breath puffing out in a white cloud of tiny crystals. She gasped, and the air rushed back into her lungs, searing with intense cold, so cold she had to just *sip* at the air. Her eyes hurt, watering, and she blinked swiftly, feeling the tears instantly freeze. Her eyes narrowed to slits.

"Maybe we should get inside? I d-don't think this is n-normal." Lips already numbing, the cold sliced through her winter jacket and pants. Her fingertips tingled, aching.

"Come'n."

Faith whined once and moved forwards, and Sara followed, each step crunching through sudden frost, each breath puffing out in frozen plumes. The air had misted white, and Sara realized it was snowing tiny little flakes, so small she could hardly see them. Sharp snaps and cracks sounded from the branches above.

Her teeth started to ache, and then to chatter. She could feel ice in her mouth, and her toes hurt. "F-F-Faith, I th-think we'd b-b-better hurry." She started to trot, to run, but stumbled and almost fell. What was wrong with her legs, with her feet?

She couldn't see properly. One eye had shut and now she couldn't open it. Rubbing at it with fingers that wouldn't bend properly, she felt eyelashes snap, and stopped in confusion. The white mist was thinning, but it was so pretty, drifting down like dust from angel wings.

So cold. She wavered on her feet. Her teeth were chattering so much she couldn't hear her breath freezing anymore. Through the still, clear air she could see the lights of the Institute, closer now. Faith whined, ahead, and she forced her legs to move forwards. Like lumps of lead, she swung them now in a tottering wooden gait, keeping her balance more by luck than skill.

She couldn't bend her tongue anymore, and it was getting harder to move her legs. Each step was a swaying shuffle, each root and tussock a barrier to haul a leaden foot over, each breath an icy knife in her chest. How had it gotten so cold, so fast?

The warm lights of the Institute seemed a mile away.

When Sara and Faith finally staggered from the trees, the cold – already arctic – worsened. Two steps later her legs stopped working entirely and Sara fell, toppling stiffly to the icy ground, snapping grass. Eyes frozen shut on angry tears, she wrestled distant limbs that ignored her. Her hands were fists, clubs she couldn't feel. Elbows digging stubbornly into rock-hard soil, she worked her hips, inching along the ground, carving a path through splintering grass.

A sound beside her: then stiff fur brushed against her, low, and she managed to unbend an elbow enough to throw one arm over Faith. Together, the two struggled forward toward the light. Faith staggered each time Sara shifted her weight, knees slipping against the ground. The two fought on, step by draining step. No thought, just the endless dragging effort. Faith's turbines made strange, tortured sounds as they tried to spin up, while she moved as if in pain.

Then warm air, bringing life into her lungs instead of cold death: her skin, her lungs, burning as sensation returned. They collapsed together, sharing the life-saving warmth.

Rubbing at her eyelids, the stinging heat brought a welcome rush of tears, and she stared blurrily around her. By the Institute's lights she saw they lay just inside a circular perimeter enclosing the buildings. Beyond, frost crusted the ground and made the trees stand out against the dark. Her muscles started working again, in violent shudders that shook her small frame. She sat up.

They were a hundred meters from the main entrance. Strangely, the white-dusted trees were fading quickly into darkness, the snow already melting. Looking back at the end of their trail, she saw remnants of frost disappearing, and got shakily to her feet. Tottering back to the curving boundary, she gingerly stretched out one shivering hand, ready to snatch it back. But no cold came. The air was normal.

"W-weird." She could see Faith agreed. "Uncle said the Institute's inside a big magical circle, a 'Ward'. So that must have been magic c-cold!"

She unfocused her eyes, *not-looking* out into the dark, like she always did when she was hunting *It*. Took a step outside the magical Ward, and *stretched*... instantly her stomach lurched, and a fierce tingling burned over her skin. It *had* been here. She opened her eyes and turned back to Faith.

"C'mon, let's check the b-boundary!"

Faith looked up at her doubtfully.

"It's all right, we'll stay close. Oh." Sara dropped to her knees, hugging her friend fiercely. "Thanks for saving me, Faith."

CHAPTER 28

Four thousand kilometers east, Marc Disten stretched, trying to work the knots from his shoulders. He allowed himself a small congratulatory pat on the back as the elevator started its long descent. Today's trading had gone well. Spotting the implications of an abstruse piece of theoretical physics – even if it was something as curious as an article in an obscure journal with evidence that some arcane 'universal constant' had changed, and which explained why the packed-light network had so catastrophically collapsed back in '42 – was the reason traders like himself still had jobs. He'd seen that a few savvy investors would reason that a breakthrough like that might lead to a *return* to those glorious days of truly high-bandwidth global communications, which meant in turn that he and his software agents had got a jump on the market, earning his investors a return three points above the average gains across the day.

His fists clenched. It would have been nearer five points if the fools in IT could actually do their jobs. What part of the word 'uninterruptible' did they not understand? He'd seriously considered helping them 'test' their fail-safe systems by going down into their troll cave and putting a bullet through some equipment – or some people. For a supposedly top team in a top New York brokerage, they were a joke.

A spasm in his neck warned him to let it go, and he forced his mind away from those pasty geeks with their smirking superior airs.

His neck spasmed again. *Right, right. Think of Julie-*Fuck.

Jules was gone. Taken up with that prick DJ. He should've seen the signs when she kept wanting to return to the Seal Club – and what sort of prat thought *that* name was funny for a nightclub, anyway? – because she liked the 'vibe.' Vibe. Meh. If you called an underground pit full of poseur anthros and rainbow-colored people jacked up on god knows what kind of brainstim-

The elevator dinged, finally, and he rolled his shoulders again, reaching up and back to knead the tense knot of muscle as he strode across the half-empty underground car park. 22:13, he noted, checking his peripheral link. Nice to be leaving at a reasonable hour for...

No way.

He stopped as suddenly as if his boots had frozen to the slick cement floor, staring at the long scratch down the side of his sleek black Ferrari T4SX Quattropotenza.

No. Fucking. Way.

This carpark was supposed to be covered by top security, and someone keys his T4? No. Just, no. It was a joke. Someone had merely drawn on it in white marker to make him panic.

He ran the last meters to his car, fingertips feeling-

Shit!

He looked up and around at all the security cameras. He'd make sure someone lost their job for this! He stared back down at the long, undulating score mark. That'd be close to a thousand-cred paint repair, and he'd lose half his goddamn NCB unless he could identify the shrivel-souled, dirt-eating, envy-drowned, piss-drinking, bottom-feeding, scum-loving son of a meltie who'd done it.

Why me? Why does this kind of shit always happen to me?

He was so angry, the car at first didn't recognize his brain pattern, and he had to fucking stand there counting to fucking ten before his god-damned car would allow its own fucken owner inside. Even the power-laden hum as the four wheel-turbines cycled up to speed failed to ease his mood, since he knew that only a meter or so to his right a huge, ugly score marred the pristine mirror-black finish, like a sign saying 'He owns it but he can't protect it.'

He amped up the volume on the synthetic exhaust and felt the harsh bass rumble through the seat of his spine, echoing through the underground carpark like some suddenly-revived saber-tooth tiger growling in its underground cave. A smile flickered across his lips. Disengaging auto-drive, he accelerated and then braked, hard, spinning the steering wheel and almost fish-tailing despite the smart-hubs, then tore up the first up-ramp. Adrenaline surged as he spun into the tight corners, powering up and out of the bowels of the building like a barely-controlled missile.

By the time he reached the exit ramp onto the street, he knew he should slow.

Fuck it.

He roared onwards, glimpsing startled faces as he sliced through a momentary gap in the pedestrian traffic. Spinning the wheel hard right he stormed onto the road like the angel of death. iCars abruptly braked or slowed as his car surged into the flow, a shark scaring minnows from its path.

His teeth peeled back in a grin. He'd get another ticket or two tonight, but on his income it was worth the thrill. He twitched the wheel left and floored it, surging past the other vehicles as if they'd all suddenly stopped, before plunging back into the stream fifty meters later and ten cars ahead. Behind him, seconds later, came the sweet accompaniment of horns. But his eyes had already narrowed to identify the next opportunity.

Gradually, though, he calmed, regaining control of himself. *Shit, at this rate, I'll wind up writing this beauty off altogether.* Which was possibly just what the fucker who'd scored it had hoped for.

With a major effort he relaxed his grip on the leather-infused steering wheel. Almost, he opted to release the car to auto, but he'd be damned if he'd give up the simple pleasure of driving. Even just sensible driving. He flushed, remembering the startled faces as he'd rocketed out of the building and onto the street like some maniac. What if he'd hit someone?

Shit, he really had to get control of his temper.

That'd been half the reason Jules had left, hadn't it, if he was being honest with himself?

How long had it been since he'd seen his counselor, Jackie? Too long. As he drove, he Linked, requested an appointment. As an afterthought, he also added an apology for the last session.

With that decision, he felt the tension in his neck ease. As if deep down he knew it was the right thing to do. Maybe he could even turn the wanton damage to his T4 around, use it to learn something, for a change? Grow.

But for tonight, he decided, he needed company. Shaunessy's, downtown, didn't have pretensions and wouldn't take shit from him, either. Which he respected. He could almost taste the micro-brew already. None of that trendy synth crap they served up at places like the Seal Club. He almost set course for it then and there.

But Mr Muggles was at home, and needed company as much as its owner did, auto cat-feeder or not. Yeah, he'd defrost some of that Australis Ocean salmon and they'd have a little quality time. Then maybe he'd hook up online and take some negotiable honey down to Shaunessy's for a long, slow cool down. Then a nice long heat-up.

But Mr Muggles came first. He smiled, already thinking fondly ahead to the welcome he'd receive, looking forward to the kooky cat twining round his ankles and trying his best to trip him up.

He breathed out a long sigh, offering up a heartfelt 'Sorry' to the cosmos, along with a promise to try to be less of an asshole in future. Seriously. What was that saying? "Today is the first day of the rest of your life."

He even turned the volume down on the synthesized V16 engine sound.

They staggered out of Shaunessy's, leaning on one another to keep their balance as he led her back to the car.

"Whoa! Boy, I didn' wanna say before, but you really oughta get that fixed, you know?" she said, waving at the undulating white scar marring the mirror-black surface.

Red flooded his vision. Of course, they'd scored *that* side specifically, so any passenger he gave a ride to would see it. The calculated humiliation set his hands shaking, but this time he let the auto-drive handle the trip to her apartment. After his earlier touch of slightly aggressive driving, for sure he'd have been crowd-shared onto the cops' active-watch list for tonight. Spiteful little shits.

The bitch had better watch her mouth, though. "*You oughta get that fixed.*" What, did she think he didn't *know* that? Or maybe she thought he had to *save up* to pay for the repair?

But things improved once inside the car, as always. Malissa-with-an-A thrilled to the leashed power, the enveloping leather aroma, the lumbar vibe.

All the girls loved that lumbar vibe.

As the door folded smoothly away and he helped her up and out, he put one finger on those full, red lips to silence her when she glanced back down at the ugly score mark.

In the ride up in the elevator he slipped one hand down from her shoulder and up under her shift. Grabbing a sample of the merchandise he'd already paid for.

And suddenly she's telling him to *slow down*? As if they hadn't already negotiated the deal on her site. Did she think she could change the terms of the contract *now?*

But the final shitty straw came after they'd reached her bedroom, when she finally stripped off to unveil the repellent surgical *enhancement* she drunkenly flaunted as if expecting him to be *pleased* by it?

"What's wrong with your- *that's*- what *is* that, even? That's not natural!"

"What's the matter, baby? Selfish prick like you, should be glad I've made it easy for ya! You've probably never satisfied a woman before – this way, even you can't-"

His hands wrapped around her throat, and it felt so good, choking off the lies. Bitch. But even then she smiled, thrusting herself into him as if this was just a game. As if she could change his mind.

It made his blood boil all the hotter.

It wasn't till she fell limp, her weight pulling him forward onto her bed, that he unlocked his hands from around the whore's throat. He felt drained, the anger gone as completely as the woman's life. Crouched over her, frozen in shock, he stared at her. At her body.

What have I done?

He gazed in disbelief at the woman; at his hands. One outburst of passion. That's all it had taken. Now his whole life was ruined.

Stupid fucken bitch! What'd she think was going to happen, when he saw the weird *work* she'd had done? If only he hadn't come here, to her apartment, in the first place. Or hadn't picked *her*. But when he'd seen the vid-snippets on her profile: those gorgeous legs; that cleavage....

He closed his eyes, wishing with all his heart that things were different. That he'd kept control. If only he could keep control...

And it was at that moment, holding exactly that thought, that the new Pattern eddying in Imaginal space found him. Like lightning finding the tallest spire, the essence meshed with him in a flare of dark energy. Heat drained from the room, and in that moment Marc Disten the stockbroker died.

A different consciousness rebooted.

Clear blue eyes reopened and looked around the bedroom, everything made suddenly strange by a faint layer of
frost on every surface, even those of the woman's naked
body and the teddy-bear motif sheets it rumpled. The
small room was colder than an icebox. Bedsheets crum-
bled as Disten reached out to the lacquered bed-side cabinet and wiped a finger down the chill surface, leaving a line
through the dusting of frozen water vapor. Puzzling. But
unimportant.

Disten stared down at the body, considering the problem it presented. Several options presented themselves for
inspection, and he wandered into the small kitchen with its
black marble bench-tops and began opening the pale
wooden-faced cupboards.

A little later, with the deep fat fryer heating on the
stove, he stood in thought, visualizing the imaginary sce-
nario.

She would be reading, dressed in her flannelette gown.
First, smoke would rise from the oil. Smoke detector? Yes,
there. He took it down, flipped out the battery, and while
the fat continued heating, he patiently shorted the termi-
nals together, draining it before replacing it in its snug
compartment. What would she be cooking? Checking her
freezer and utensils, he soon had chips frying.

That done, he fetched the body into the kitchen,
checked the oil, and thought.

Smoke would rise, undetected, from the fryer. The
woman would be seated at the table, her back to it, still
reading.   The flames would burst upwards from the
saucepan. She would sense it and jump up, panicking,
knocking over the chair, tripping as she reached out....

He realized he was still holding the dead woman. Had
been, for some time, unaware. He considered this. With
effort, he could sense some muscle fatigue, though it was
distant.

Interesting.

She would be reading, her back to the stove. Reading
what? Kicking over a chair, he draped the body over it,
then fetched a book to place by its side.

Waited.

Twenty minutes later the oil caught fire. Using two

oven cloths decorated with baby animals he lifted the fryer off the stove, bending his head to one side to avoid burning himself.

Flame sheeted upwards as he carefully sluiced the burning oil over the body. It made an interesting pattern in the air as it fell, not one he'd seen before.

Stepping back he dropped the pot in the location chosen earlier, putting the oven cloths back on their place on the work bench. The heat was intense now, flame spreading rapidly through the kitchen, devouring the last of the frost. He watched for several seconds, considering.

At last, judging it satisfactory, he turned and left the apartment.

CHAPTER 29

Harmon stared as Sara entered the cafeteria, clearly excited: her somersaulting roll toward the meal dispenser gave it away. It wasn't until she had bounced to her feet that she noticed him, and froze. He could see the thought: 'uh oh' as he checked the time. After 10 pm: over two hours since he had put her to bed.

Strangely, though, her excitement returned. Indeed, she ran over and jumped onto the bench seat opposite him, leaning forward conspiratorially before he could reprimand her. "*It* attacked Faith and me tonight! With cold!"

He looked around the room. Five empty tables, two garish junk food dispensers, one large white food processor and a tall thin dishbot waiting patiently for him to finish his coffee, reassured him they were alone. Most others left at 5 pm. Now that they'd automated the patient care, only Simmons, Shanahan, and the Director still lived on site; and *they* ate much earlier.

"Really? That's interesting." He kept a smile off his lips with difficulty. "That was lucky, considering how little you feel the cold."

She peeled off her jacket, revealing a tight-fitting black top edged in white fur trim, and ran over to stand in front of the dinner machine. Head tilted to one side before punching in several codes, she turned to talk to him over her shoulder.

"I guess so. But it would have got me if it hadn't been for Faith."

He frowned. It was good that she imagined enemies for herself, bad that she was telling herself she needed external help to overcome them. "Really, Sara, you must learn to defend yourself. You're telling me that it got a little cold, and Faith kept you warm?" He let his disdain show.

She scowled round at him. "It didn't get a *little* cold, it got *super* cold. My breath froze and fell to the ground, and my eyes froze shut. It got so cold I could hardly move, and Faith half dragged me till we got back inside the barrier."

Her breath froze – what an imagination she had! Her face did look a little reddened, though, he noticed, as she returned with a tray loaded with a plate of soy fries and a large mug of hot vegetable soup. She angrily thumped them onto the table, making the soup splash and the dishbot jerk forward in readiness. Her eyes also looked a little red, and there was something odd about her eyelashes. Were they shorter?

"Well, a cold snap is possible, but what made you decide it was *It* attacking?"

"'Cause the frost ended in a big circle about a hundred meters from the main doors. I remembered you said there was a magic barrier that kept us safe, inside. That means it must of been a magic attack. Plus, I sensed something out there, afterward."

"Must *have*," he automatically corrected as she shoveled a handful of fries into her mouth, looking pleased with herself. He considered. The Warding did extend that distance from the buildings. Which suggested that she had somehow sensed the barrier – quite encouraging, really – and woven the fact into her fantasy. Unless there *had* been an incident outside? He took out his MetaStylus, traced 'Shanahan' on the table, then pressed the connect button.

"Problem, doctor Harmon?" Shanahan's voice sounded tinnily in his ear.

"Probably not. Has it been quiet this evening? Any incidents?"

"Nope. All inmates snug in their rooms. And nobody trying to break in, either," he laughed.

Sara scowled, leaning forward as she obviously tried to hear the other end of his conversation.

"Ah, good. Has it been unusually cold outside, perhaps?" Harmon asked.

"Well, the sensor in the entry hall did register a twenty degree drop a quarter hour ago. Only lasted a few minutes, though. Probably a faulty thermocouple. And a sensor out front, too. Hmm. That's odd. Looks like Faith headed out on an extra patrol on her own after I'd settled her; and I see here that her telemetry went offline for maybe half an hour, an hour and a half later. Hang on: there was an accompanying heat signature at her kennel when she headed out... Wait: are you there with *Sara*? Did she sneak Faith out again? Did she-"

He paused, and when he continued, his tone of surprise had shifted to anger. "Ah, shit: she did something to them, didn't she? To Faith's sensors. Which means I've ordered replacements for no good reason. Dammit! Tell her to stop fucking with my security systems: they're there for a reason. Maybe I should charge the replacements to you."

Harmon sighed. "I will speak to her." He disconnected. So. She must have decided that *It* could attack via cold, and done something to the sensors to fit the fantasy, constructing her small adventure. Quite well thought-out and executed, really.

"Well?" Sara demanded, taking a mouthful of her soup, fries already finished.

He smiled, rather pleased that she had been able to manipulate the security system without Shanahan's knowledge. She was becoming quite resourceful. "Yes, a sensor did register a temperature drop," he told her, not wishing to weaken her fantasy, then changed the subject, indicating her plate. "Still hungry? You ate quite a large dinner."

"I got cold. From *Its* attack. This is just to warm me up."

He eyed her figure. It was a good thing she stayed active, or with the quantity of food she ate she'd soon be overweight.

Sara just smiled at him over her mug of soup, looking self-assured, even more so than usual.

A scan of her in the Imaginal supported her account. She looked as he would expect had she faced an ordeal. But fantasized or real? If there had been a twenty degree drop in temperature registered in the entry hall, then there *could* have been a larger drop, outside. But what could do that? A weather elemental? But elementals and 'foreign' spirits would be unable to penetrate the external Wards. He examined her again, hoping for a hint of magical Unfolding, but there was nothing, as usual: she remained stolidly normal.

Did she look *too* pleased with herself, though? Planning some mischief, perhaps? He cast mindmeld and skimmed her thoughts, but she was focused on the warmth and taste of her soup; just an occasional darting memory of cold, of struggling on leaden limbs. Nothing else. Surely...?

"Sara, you haven't been visiting Godsson, have you?"

Bizarrely, she immediately pictured the vintage 'Mario Brothers' cap she had begged him to purchase, a long time ago – and which he had never seen her wear. Then she grew angry, remembering herself standing on the chair which had been removed, holding up the broken cleaning bot which had also been taken from her.

She slammed her mug down on the table, soup splashing out. "I'm *not allowed* to!"

Then stormed off.

For some reason, he was not as reassured as he should have been. The mind link, of course, snapped as soon as she disappeared from sight. He sighed. She couldn't be visiting Godsson. Shanahan had tightened the security. They'd changed all the passcodes. And he had just probed her, too.

He shook his head. She was beginning to make *him* think of her as something more than a mere child. If only she would Unfold! He brought his mind back to the matter at hand: her 'ordeal' tonight.

Just her fantasy. He would have to watch that: if she began taking too much satisfaction from make-believe activities, such a relief mechanism could interfere with his own experimental programme.

A part of him, though, worried. *Could* there have been some kind of magical assault? But from who, or what? Nothing supernatural could penetrate the Institute's Wards − at least, not without such a massive display of power that it would be noticed. And the imaginary creature was just imaginary.

Surely?

She, however, still remained utterly convinced it was real; he knew that from his mindmelds. Her 'Robo.' A most peculiar choice of name, given his suggestions of an unsettling invisible creature. Odd that she was imagining robotic behavior for the thing.

It was also odd that she was still so certain it was real, since in many ways she was quite the little pragmatist. It had been years since he had used his telekinesis to encourage her belief.

Then, too, there had been that singular occasion very early on, when he had secretly followed behind her, reading her mind, and felt what seemed like some kind of backlash effect. Even, for a moment, had felt he sensed the same thing she did.

Something about the situation definitely made him uneasy. But in the end there was little he could do except stay alert, and keep an open mind.

At least she had appeared uninjured – even unconcerned. Indeed, she had seemed in very fine fettle. And by her own account, Faith too had come through unscathed. So even if something odd had happened, it had not been dangerous.

At least, not at this stage.

He felt a shiver run up his spine.

CHAPTER 30

I am so *ready!* The last six months had taken *forever,* but finally, it was the summer solstice.

The FBI man watched her carefully as her uncle concealed the keypad from her sight. She looked away while he entered the code, hoping it'd make him go faster. *Why was he so* slow? She always did it much faster. She bounced up and down on her heels: the sun had already set and she was sure *She* would already be attacking.

Sure enough, as soon as the final door was opened she could hear Godsson's cries from below. Wrenching her hand free from her uncle's grip she raced down the stairs. Thanks to his shouting, the FBI agents along the corridor swiveled to face her as she sped toward them.

Maybe some of them recognized her from the year before, because no one shot at her as she dodged between them to press her nose up against the bottom of the window into Godsson's cell, squinting against the terrible golden glare.

It was bad. He was turning, not quite spinning, as if She were coiling around him, trying to make him dizzy.

"Don't let her trick you, Godsson! She's just tryin' a confuse you!" *She* had learned spinny things recently: how to make things whirl and flash in bewildering ways that were hard to look away from. "Just shut your eyes!"

She felt a wave of hatred, from *Her* of course, and pulled back, even as masculine arms pulled her away from the window and lifted her onto the bench opposite, which she didn't really need.

The man who'd lifted her so easily was a tall stranger she hadn't seen before. He was dressed in actual skins, with pale gray fur still on them, the edges curling loosely open over a broad, tanned, and well-muscled chest. Complicated feathery knots and little tiny dangling jewelry things hung from the skins, and around his neck a leather cord held up a small lumpy bag drawn tight shut.

His eyes were a dark brown, very clear, and she realized he was studying her just as closely as she was studying him. For some reason it made her blush.

He looked well-fed, and for some reason he was sweating slightly, as if the air-conditioned corridor was too hot for him.

Past him, looking on, were two others almost as

strangely dressed, a man and a woman. The man was bald, his face painted in bright and dark stripes. The woman had long blonde hair and a slightly cross face. Both looked older than the man who'd moved her away from Godsson.

Whose cries had eased after she'd warned him. But only for a while. Soon enough, *She* attacked again.

And it kept getting slowly worse, hour after hour. She called encouragement till her voice grew hoarse; and then kept calling. But by midnight, it had gotten worse than she ever remembered it being, worse even than that awful first time she'd seen him being attacked.

She went quiet, *willing* him to win, to keep fighting, to not let Her beat him. She eyed the keypad, wishing she'd managed to spy out the combination.

If only she could get in there somehow! Then she'd *really* help. But entering from above wouldn't work: even if she *could* still get in undetected past all the new security gadgets they'd sneaked in up there, she remembered how the area over his cell had been super strong. Real different to the rest of the old, thin ceiling tiles.

If only she could get *in* there! She kept willing him on. It felt especially awful now that she'd gone quiet. But she had to: she felt suddenly sure that something was creeping up on her, and she had to stay still and quiet to hear. Waiting in the silent moments was horrid, like she could feel hooks or barbs trying to sneak into her own flesh.

She looked carefully around. Godsson's agonized grunts and howls gripped them all. Everyone had their eyes focused on the speaker where the terrible sounds escaped the cell.

But it felt different. It felt wrong. Like *She* was tricking them. She looked around, trying to see... and like a puzzle coming into focus, saw how the edges of the skins the handsome shaman wore curled too sleekly against his skin.

"It's here! She's here! She's come through!" She screamed and threw herself onto the strange shaman, tearing Her off his clothes. Clinging to him with her legs, she felt seams and ties rip and tear as she clawed at the invisible thing wrapped across his broad chest and round his waist.

At first he stood still like he was in shock, but she knew it was more because *She* was confusing him, probably whispering to him, or doing other weird stuff. She felt the man's arms wrap warmly around her, cuddling her, and felt something pressing oddly against her, before he jerked like he'd just come awake, and then started grappling her and trying to pull her off.

Inside his cell, Godsson shrieked and raged louder, the light suddenly pulsing and sucking inwards, disorientatingly, as if the burning light wasn't flickering but *fighting* an opposite darkness.

Still she struggled against *Her*, her hands scooping and twisting across the large man's now-bare back, wrenching and tearing at threads she could hardly sense.

When she felt the last wisp slip away, retreating, she slumped in relief against his chest.

But only for a moment. From behind her, the other two shamans finally reacted: started making weird words. *Tryin' ta cast a spell on me!* She pushed hard, squirming free of the well-muscled man's embrace, dropping between his legs then twisting and jumping up to cling to his back, putting him between her and the other two like he was a human shield.

She felt rather than saw the spell wash past her, and grinned. She hadn't been sure her maneuver would work.

No one moved.

It was suddenly real quiet in the corridor. Even Godsson had gone silent, now. But in a good way, she was sure.

The lights in his cell, like an aurora, winked out.

Still, no one spoke.

Finally, she dropped from the tall shaman's back and stepped back, dusting her hands with satisfaction. She looked up at him, a little bit surprised at just how completely she'd shredded his clothing. He stood there half-naked, tattered swathes of animal hide kind of dangling off him.

She turned, meeting several pairs of wide eyes watching her as she turned to her uncle. "See, I *said* you needed me!"

She saw his worried gaze move from her to Godsson's window. He frowned. When she looked, she saw Godsson's strained face staring out at her.

She felt her brow crinkle. She'd kind of expected him to look pleased, maybe even grateful. But instead he just studied her. Finally he looked from her to her uncle, and seemed to study him the same way, too.

Then all at once she was drowning in a torrent of questions.

She sneaked a look at her uncle, who was looking at her and shaking his head. But with the danger past, her eyelids felt like she'd somehow had lead weights glued to them without her noticing. The thought of her bed actually felt kind of nice.

The debriefing, in Harmon's opinion, was quite unsatisfactory. The consensus, reached only after an embarrassing admission from *Angakkuq* Yakone, the Aleutian shaman, was that his mind had drifted and he had begun thinking of his wife. Missing her.

This had provoked a physical reaction interpreted by Sara as evidence of an invisible seduction. She attacked; the physical assault snapped Yakone from his reverie; Sara declared herself victorious; and Godsson, overhearing, ended his self-flagellation.

It was all too glib. How could a grown man mistake a fourteen-year-old for his wife?

More and more, he suspected something new and unknown was at work.

But his had been a lone voice. That a fourteen-year-old girl and a madman agreed with him had counted *against* that interpretation, not *for*.

Still more worrying was what lay ahead three years from now. On top of the increasing ferocity would be another tri-annual high *and* a peak in the subsidiary cycle. A 'king tide.'

Worse still, Sara had looked like she had wanted to enter Godsson's cell tonight. He had seen the way she kept eyeing the electronic keypad on the cell door. *Heaven help her should she ever step inside.*

Perhaps, by age seventeen, she could stomach the footage of that first solstice? When his two co-workers had ventured inside to help.

He shuddered. He would have nightmares tonight, he knew.

But at least this time no one had tried to shoot her.

CHAPTER 31

As it happened, Harmon had underestimated Sara's determination to physically enter Godsson's cell during the next attack, even though it was still a year off.

"It's not fair, Keepie. Why does he have to fight it alone each time?"

"Because it's only a figment of his imagination, Sara." His own burgeoning doubts, though, made it hard to inject the necessary conviction into his voice. "Going inside his cell would not help."

"But I *can* help, Uncle! I can sense it, and I've felt it, ripped it in my own hands, twice before. I know I can help. If you let me go inside, Godsson and I together can end it, once and for all!"

"No, Sara. You don't know what happened, before. It was the most ghastly thing I've ever seen. Inhuman."

She said nothing, but sat forward eagerly, her whole posture urging him to continue.

"It was the first year. The summer solstice," and the start point – and maximum – of the strange secondary cycle: not that he would let Sara know of that. "We didn't know what was happening, what was wrong. Two of my co-workers, fellow therapists, both magically very capable, rushed into the cell despite my warnings. They thought me cruel, uncaring, for not joining them."

Sara leaned forward, hands gripping the air as if trying to drag the words from him faster.

"I stood in the doorway, uncertain whether I should enter, too. But Godsson did something to them, something terrible. They started... they *changed*, into monsters for him to fight, along with everything else he was doing to himself."

"It's not *him*, Keepie, I keep telling you! It's Her!"

He shook his head. "Suppose it *was* 'Her?' That changes nothing! Right before my eyes they started... *transforming*. And then Godsson had *three* opponents instead of one – and two of them were physically present in his cell.

"Poor fools. He destroyed *them* in seconds. Incinerated."

"But Godsson wouldn't hurt *me*!"

"You can't know that! He might. Sara, you need to understand that during his episodes, Godsson is not himself.

You cannot predict his actions based on his normal behavior."

"But it's not *him* that did it, it was Her. And I can hurt Her. So I can help Godsson."

"Even if you're right, that it's not Godsson but 'Her' who... altered my colleagues, what would protect *you* from suffering the same fate?"

"Godsson protects himself from Her. He'd protect me, too."

Her uncle kind of twitched forward, Sara saw, like he wanted to drop his head into his hands. For a moment, she almost felt sorry for him.

But it was his own fault for being so stubborn.

Ten full seconds passed before Harmon spoke again, extra slowly. "Sara, Godsson is mad. He is not your friend."

Sara's lips pressed into thin lines.

Harmon's hands twitched again. "He has begun calling Melisande '*Lilith reborn,*' and you her-"

Harmon stopped suddenly, shutting his eyes. Sara saw his lips purse, and his left hand clench. Finally, he took a deep breath, shook his head, and opened his eyes again; then started all over again trying to convince her that Godsson thought she was bad.

But Sara knew Godsson just got mad with her because he *was* mad. Not because he didn't *like* her!

In the end, Harmon stood up. "Fine. Come with me. If *I* can't persuade you, perhaps seeing the incident for yourself will convince you. I had not planned to show you this for some years, however."

Shanahan had been shocked by the request after bringing them in to his office, and looked from Harmon to Sara. But Harmon had to give the man credit: Shanahan took one look at the stubborn set of his ward's features, put two and two together with the request to view *that* footage, and shook his head.

"Sara, darlin', you don't want to go into Godsson's cell. No one goes into Godsson's cell. Least not while he's conscious. We even have-"

At Harmon's frantic cutting gesture the man caught himself, eyes widening.

"What? We even have what?"

Shanahan ignored her, spinning back to his monitors and angling them right around so his visitors could see them – and he couldn't. In seconds, both screens filled with views of Godsson's cell, and the room was filled with coruscating flashes of light and the mage's awful cries. Shanahan winced, his eyes glued to the girl's, desperately willing her to be convinced.

From the screen, a voice shouted: '*We have to help him, he's under attack!*'

The dialog played out exactly as Harmon remembered. Sara stood entranced, watching a younger Alex Harmon standing wide-eyed in the doorway of Godsson's cell.

The nightmare scene unfolded.

Crowded into the corners of the room by Godsson's protective circle, Abrams and Li faced the same direction as Godsson, blasting away as if they too could see what he saw: drawn into the shared delusion, wrestling the same demons he did.

Then Abrams began changing, and a moment later, so too did Li. Abrams *grew*, his clothes tearing at the seams, the limbs morphing, softening, lengthening, and between his legs, the obscene exaggeration there was echoed somehow in his other limbs. Skin, thickly pulsing veins, all recognizably still human even as he morphed into something utterly monstrous. Li, meanwhile, had changed into something... hungry. Multiple mouths, yet with monstrously *human* teeth; long shaggy hair... They had thrown themselves forward at the mage's barrier, and somehow begun distorting it – something Harmon had never seen before, nor since. Any Ward, no matter how weak, either remained perfect, or shattered. They didn't *bend*.

His hand twitched, remembering, and the younger Harmon on screen slammed the cell door shut, moments before a huge fireball whited out the monitors to perfect rectangles of intense white. Two, three seconds passed, then the light winked off, leaving just the golden glow of the now once-more perfectly circular Wards, but the room was now wreathed in a thick fog – the water vapor released from the two incinerated *things* his co-workers had transformed into, in the space of just twenty-seven seconds. Meanwhile, Godsson continued his raging fight against the unseen demons of his own mind.

Had it been enough? Harmon hoped desperately that it had. "Enough, Shanahan."

The videos stopped instantly.

Even Sara looked shocked. Her mouth worked, her fists clenching and unclenching. Finally, she turned and plunged from the room, her footsteps faint but accelerating.

"By the Holy Mother, Dr Harmon, I never want to hear or see that again." He crossed himself. "Did it work, d'you think? Should you go after her?"

"No, Shanahan. I *think* it worked. Best if Sara wrestles herself on this topic, not I. I *think* it worked."

"Let's hope so, Dr Harmon. She wouldn't want to be going into that room in the years ahead, by all the saints."

"I agree, Mr Shanahan. I *wholeheartedly* agree. And thank you."

Shakily, he left the office and then the small house, trying to wash the terrifying images from his mind. If that evidence didn't dissuade her, nothing on Earth would.

So, why was he still so fearful?

Sara didn't stop running until she reached the point where she knew the Ward encircling the whole Institute held out all bad magical stuff.

Like *Her?*

She hugged herself, suddenly scared of crossing the unseen barrier. Then got angry at her cowardice. She pictured her uncle sneering at her, and that was enough to force her across.

Besides, she wasn't sure the barrier really stopped Her. Not properly.

What if She grabbed me *right now; turned* me *into some disgusting monster like young-Keepie's friends?*

She shuddered, her flesh crawling so badly that for an awful moment she thought it'd already started happening.

She needed to get a hold of herself. Then almost sobbed, when she realized she *was* holding herself. She let her arms drop, and forced herself to go on into the Forest. Even if She did attack, she'd tear Her up, so there!

Besides, that happened ages *ago. Inside Godsson's cell.* If She could have done it again since then, She would have.

She sighed and shut her eyes. The image of the man who'd gone all swollen and *wriggly* inside his bloated flesh suddenly squirmed before her and she gasped and opened her eyes to focus instead on the trees. But each time she shut them for more than a moment, she saw the two human monsters inside Godsson's cell.

And Keepie still thought it was Godsson doing it? That She was just imaginary? How could he be so *dumb?*

"Agh!"

It meant she was the only one who could help Godsson.

And she still had no idea how to actually get into his cell, to fight alongside him. Plus, now Keepie *and* Mr Shanahan knew she needed to, so they'd both be working extra hard to make sure she couldn't.

Unless... unless they decided that seeing the video had changed her mind?

She tilted her head to one side, considering the idea. Could she just start *pretending* she didn't want to go into his cell any more?

The most horrible part, though, was that she didn't even really *want* to. She wasn't certain Godsson could protect her. Not really. She wasn't sure he'd even be able to keep protecting *himself.* Not if things kept getting worse each year.

Which meant that since she *had* to get into the cell, once she *did*, she might turn into some kind of disgusting monster like young-Keepie's friends had.

Or something even worse.

CHAPTER 32

She did a real good job of acting like she'd changed her mind and didn't want to join Godsson to fight alongside him anymore. Keepie had been super relieved, and so had Mr Shanahan.

And things went along just fine for months.

Though, early on, there *had* been one night. They'd just been eating dinner, and she'd been thinking about excuses for why she needed a spy cam. After all, she couldn't tell Keepie she needed it to stick to his shirt to record the secret code for Godsson's door! And straight after she'd thought that, he'd started choking on his food.

For a moment, she'd worried that *she'd* caused it, before jumping up to thump him on the back like you were supposed to.

He'd looked at her kind of shocked.

"Sorry, Keepie. I didn't mean to hit so hard. Are you okay now?"

But over the next few days, everyone started to act peculiar around her: they'd look at her, then look away quickly when she looked back. Like they all assumed she'd been *attacking* Keepie that night when he was choking, when actually she'd been *saving* him. *Why does everyone always think I want to* hurt *people?*

Plus, no matter what reason she came up with, Keepie kept refusing to get her the spy cam, too. And Mr Shanahan seemed nervous whenever she visited him.

It had taken months for everyone to go back to normal.

And then, months after *that*, at the start of summer the next year, just a month before Godsson's attack was due, Mr Shanahan said something shocking.

He was leaning back in his super-comfy black chair, and smiled at her. "It'll be grand having your company again this year. You and Faith: 'Team Sara' ready for action again, eh?"

"Whatever makes you think that, Mr Shanahan?" She laughed, and patted his arm. "Silly! I'll be right *there,* watching, to help guard against Her. Plus shouting out just to encourage him. That helps too, you know."

"Uh. Oh, yes, mmm, sure and I forgot."

But Mr Shanahan had such a guilty look on his face she'd gone straight to Keepie to check. And found out then that the FBI had said she wasn't allowed to go, this year!

"*No!* Why? No, they *can't*, that doesn't make any sense!"

"I believe it has something to do with your attack on the shaman last year."

"But everyone said it *helped* Godsson! Even though they all said it was just cause he thought it should!"

But her uncle just shrugged. "I'm sorry, Sara, but there is nothing I can do about it."

He didn't look sorry. In fact, he looked *guilty!*

"*When* did they decide?"

"Several months ago."

Several months ago. She just stared at him. "When were you going to tell me?"

"Don't take that tone of voice with me, young lady!"

He was really angry, she saw, though most people wouldn't have seen the signs. *But I can help Godsson! I just want to help!* Why were they all being so stupid, and so mean?

His eyes narrowed, just a fraction, and suddenly she felt a horrid shock, like she'd just been plunged into an ice box. *He's going to send me away! But he* promised *he wouldn't! Not ever!* Water started blurring her vision.

He frowned at her. "I think it best you go to your room, Sara. When you have calmed down we can discuss this further, rationally, when you have stopped behaving like a petulant child."

It's happening again. Finally. Her mind kind of slowed, then stopped. *He's sending me to my room, while he looks for somewhere to send me away for good.*

Numbly, she turned around, not even caring now about the water streaming down her face. She stumbled away.

"Sara."

She stopped. His voice sounded gentle. *He'll say 'this is really best for the both of us, Sara.'* She didn't trust herself to turn round.

"I am only sending you to your room, Sara. As soon as you can do so rationally, we can discuss this again, should you wish. But you *are* banned from seeing Godsson at this year's episode. *That* is not open to negotiation."

She froze. Was he saying...? Did he mean...? Wiping her face so he wouldn't see, she dared to turn around, hoping against hope that he might be telling the truth.

She sniffled, studying him. He wasn't angry any more, at least.

Her heart swelled. *He isn't angry! He isn't going to send me away!* For some reason, her vision was going all swimmy again.

Somehow, she found herself snuggled up against him, hugging him tight, her head pressed into his shoulder while he sat.

She didn't say anything; didn't trust herself to speak. After a while, she stepped back, and nodded. And left the room.

He'd looked... almost sad. She didn't understand. But at least she was sure he wasn't planning to send her away.

She was sure. She *was*.

But once in her room, she felt at a loss, all churned up inside. Fear about being sent away still pressed down on her, even if it was kind of squashed flat by a certainty that he really wasn't going to.

But somehow, she just couldn't stop thinking about it. As if something about it made her brain itch. And the longer she thought, especially at how quickly he'd gone from being real angry to almost-nice, something about it felt wrong. Like she was missing something.

For some reason, then, she remembered the night he'd almost choked on his food at dinner time. It had been straight after she'd thought about getting a spy camera to capture the secret code for Godsson's door. And just before everyone had started being real 'eww' to her.

Like they would have acted if they'd discovered I still planned to go into Godsson's cell with him?

And just now: how perfectly he'd seemed to understand her fears, and said exactly the right thing to reassure her. And he'd done that silly finger dance when she'd stormed into his office just now, hadn't he? The same weird twitching dance of his fingers. A bit like how Godsson did a different finger dance for his talking spell.

Keepie did that, too, when he did a spell. *Keepie had done a spell.* Tonight. On her. And then he'd gotten all nice.

He read my mind! Keepie's got a spell to read *my* mind*!*

The moment she thought it, she knew it was true.

She flopped back on her bed stunned, staring at the ceiling, remembering other times he'd guessed exactly right about what she'd been thinking; she even remembered a certain kind of *feeling* in her own head when he had. She'd felt that way tonight, too. Like there'd been a butterfly flitting about in her head, dancing around her thoughts.

He read my mind when I was thinking of putting a spy cam on him!

And he'd looked *guilty* tonight, too: when he'd said the *FBI* said she couldn't help this year. She thought about that. Why would he have felt guilty?

Oh.

He *was the one who'd told them I planned to break in; and* that's *why they said I couldn't go!*

She flung her arms wide, simultaneously amazed and excited and exhausted. And then she had perhaps the most important thought of all: that because she hadn't realized he could read her mind until right now, *he* didn't know she knew!

Yet.

So what she really needed to work out, was how to keep that a secret from him. She'd have to find a way to hide her thoughts when she knew he was doing it. At least now she knew he did that finger-dance first, to cast the spell.

Still, it sounded tricky.

But it'd sure show *him,* if she *could* do it....

CHAPTER 33

Two thousand five hundred kilometers to the east, the thing that had once been the stockbroker Marc Disten waited as his 'Link made the now-usual negotiation with the Robotel's admin facility and the boom gate opened. After the car parked itself in its assigned underground spot, Disten emerged, pausing just long enough to ensure the auto-locking completed correctly. It had begun to malfunction. As he waited, he noted the score marks on the vehicle's side panels. The car seemed to attract such damage. The frequency had dropped as the scratches accumulated. Presumably, then, the root cause was envy.

Foolish.

Heading to the elevator, the body's needs were assessed. There was little stiffness, thanks to the hourly isometric and stretching routines. But toilet facilities were required, as well as nourishment. The clothing could be laundered at the same time. Others reacted if this were not done every few weeks.

During the lift ride, the 'Link's nutrition app was used to order a suitable meal, then its directions were followed to the assigned room. Inside, the clothes were stripped and the Marc Disten financial accounts queried. Exhaustion of capital was now not anticipated until 2172, well exceeding the predicted life expectancy. The investments continued to do well.

A dombot arrived to collect the clothing, and by the time the self-cleansing had completed, another was waiting with the delivery of the food. While eating, the 'Link's mapping function was cast to the tiny room's meager smart frame, allowing study of the directions for the route. A twenty minute walk.

It was curious that Dr Callahan Scott's announced paper had been withdrawn from publication. The research had clear parallels to the superior new mode of thought. Had the paper been suppressed?

Later, striding through the extensive and well-maintained grounds of the University of Illinois, Disten noted the uneasy glances, despite the care taken to blend in. Meeting the gaze of two young women who had reacted particularly strongly, a decision was taken to alter course to intercept and question them.

They immediately changed direction and hurried away.

Disten briefly considered what non-verbal cues could have provoked the response, but failed to identify one. The issue was of minor importance, however.

After a five minute walk, the Beckman Institute for Advanced Mental Science loomed ahead. Three forty six, p.m. Like the University itself, the building appeared well maintained, with pleasing regularity and patterns in its design. He proceeded to the reception area.

But there, things became difficult.

"I'm real sorry, sir, but Dr Scott has taken a leave of absence," the middle-aged woman offered.

"Callahan Scott was scheduled to publish a paper, 'A New Cognitive Model for Human Thought.' Why was it withdrawn?"

It was exceedingly difficult to read human body language, but the receptionist's reaction was sufficiently pronounced that he felt confident she had just become agitated.

"Well, his wife died, three years ago, you know, and he didn't cope very well with that at all."

"Incorrect. The death of Scott's wife was a key enabler for his new research direction. Where is Scott? A discussion would be of mutual benefit."

"I'm sorry, sir, I can't give you that information."

Disten stared at her. A discussion with Scott should be very productive. There had been no success, so far, in communicating the new and perfect thinking mode to others.

The woman took a step backward, looking to her right, to the flimsy door which would be of little impediment to his entry into the office area from which she worked. She then looked... frightened, her eyes darting around, as if looking for yet another door.

"Dr Callahan Scott will be very pleased to see me. His work is correct. Together, a great advance will be possible. *Give me his address.*"

The woman's skin paled, and she put out a hand to the wall, apparently in need of its support.

"I can't. I *can't!* No one here knows! The *police* are looking for him, and *no one* can find him, and... *please don't hurt me, that's all I know, honestly!*"

Disten considered this, as the woman's emotions took

complete control of her and she collapsed backward into her seat.

"You have copies of his research. This Institute would keep copies."

The woman shook her head, tried to speak, but her words were almost impossible to decipher. What cues had scared her? How did she know that he had planned to take the information from her? It was curiously perceptive.

In the incoherent babble, however, she appeared to be saying that shortly before his disappearance, Scott had taken all his research and deleted all copies.

Disten turned the handle of the door – the steel bolt snapping as his grip exceeded the mechanism's integrity – and stepped into the room.

The woman stared at him: and fainted. Behind him, voices in animated discussion echoed through the large stone foyer, approaching.

With a last look at the woman, Disten stepped back through the doorway, closed it behind him, and walked out.

The two young students appeared not to even notice him. Disten turned, watching them disappear deeper into the building. They did not even glance into the reception area as they passed it.

Outside, returning to the Robotel, Disten tried once more to scent, or to sense, the elusive call that pulled westward.

Still nothing.

Yet it waited. The other half to the puzzle. The part that would be able to *communicate* the new knowledge.

Days later, Disten considered the problem afresh. Words alone still proved insufficient to share the perfected mode of thinking to others. Without training, it was difficult to design experiments in methods of communicating the new understanding. Scott's work on viral memes, belief systems, and indoctrination would have been most helpful.

Each attempt so far had only reconfirmed the challenge. Strong measures were required to displace patterns of thought learned over a lifetime. Disrupting those patterns sufficiently to allow replacement with the superior mode had so far proven unsuccessful.

Marc Disten let the latest subject collapse, shaking, to the floor, while considering what to try next.

The large man nodded once, briefly, then bent and picked the woman back up. Looking then into her desperate eyes, a new approach suggested itself: the new mode could be offered as a route for survival of the individual organism.

The only route to survival.

Afterward, considering the broken body, Disten remembered the first killing. Wakening into the wonderful new clarity had been startling, a magical experience never heard of, much less expected to have undergone personally. The memory of that awakening was still as powerful as ever.

That clarity demanded to be shared. Why was it proving so difficult to teach how to end the confusion? Was there, perhaps, something of real magic involved?

Disten considered that idea. The sense that the solution lay westward appeared to have no rational basis.

But one certainty still stood out, above all others – that there *was* a way to communicate the new clarity to all humanity.

Somewhere in the west.

PART III

(Two years later)

CHAPTER 34

Sara hiked through the woods, unconsciously placing her feet so as to move quietly, only her thumbs outside the tight pockets of her shorts. She wore her favorite Hunting outfit, adjusted herself to allow for her growth. Faith paced by her side. Spring buds adorned every leafy branch, and the sun beamed down, spearing shafts of brilliance through the shaded green paths.

It should have cheered her.

She'd left her child's bow and arrows behind. *That had been just another lie.* They weren't magic, and she must've looked stupid walking around with the toy. Had he used to laugh at her?

"I'm *seventeen* now, but he won't buy me a proper bow and arrows! What's with that? Doesn't he *want* me to hunt?"

Faith looked up at her, a worried expression on her face, and she bent down and hugged her, tight, relishing the warmth and the mix of doggy and electricity smells.

Everything was all messed up and stupid. Like, everyone knew the attack on Godsson this year was going to be the worst one ever, but she was still banned! "I can't believe they won't even let us watch with Mr Shanahan, now, either. What're they gonna do if *She* gets past Godsson?"

It still made her angry that they'd even disbanded 'Team Sara.' Sure, there'd been no *obvious* problem the first year of her ban, but last summer....

They'd wanted to lock her in her room, too, at first. But maybe her uncle *read* her determination- *Oops*. She reflexively corrected the thought. Maybe her uncle had *guessed* her determination to smash her way out if they'd tried.

So the closest that she and Faith had been allowed during Her attack on Godsson last year, was outside by the front steps. All they could do was wait, watching for the participants to emerge. Expecting disaster.

And at midnight it became clear that things had gone very wrong indeed. Some of the soldiers had suddenly started setting up an awning and getting out first aid stuff while others had charged inside.

Of course they'd stopped her and Faith from going with them. She'd wanted to just dive past: but she could tell they weren't fooling, and she didn't want to do anything so they could say how it *proved* she couldn't be trusted.

Nor did she want to get Faith in trouble.

Besides, she knew it hadn't been a complete disaster. It just hadn't had that feeling.

Less than a minute later, the front doors had slid open, soldiers charging down the front steps carrying stretchers with moaning bodies. In the *field hospital,* they started removing bullets. That it was only bullets, though, proved *She* hadn't got properly loose.

It'd actually been pretty cool watching them sew people together and bandage them up. None of them died, either, which was nice: good guys shouldn't die.

She heard a little bit of the conversation among the soldiers. Apparently one of the agents had 'just happened' to have a breakdown, from the stress of listening, and attacked some of his friends.

In other words, *She* had played Her usual tricks.

Then everybody just continued waiting. Eventually, though, they'd let her go inside as far as the foyer, to wait for them all to come out.

In the light of the exit sign, her uncle had been the first to emerge, looking exhausted. Probably on his way to heal up the agents.

When she stepped forward into the light, he'd jumped before seeing it was only her.

She'd stared at him. Knowing it was his fault. She could have helped, if he'd let her be there. Instead of convincing everybody to ban her.

He hadn't said anything, just frowned at her – like she cared about *that* anymore – before brushing past her.

It helped, discussing it with Faith. Unlike certain other people, Faith didn't mind how often they talked about it, either. "I just *know* the attack this year's gonna be the worst one ever." Faith looked up at her, agreeing.

She had a feeling *no one* knew what to expect this time.

And now, that attack was only a few months away.

"I'm *seventeen*, now. That's practically an adult. Don't you reckon?" Faith did. "So I've started, *again,*" she added, rolling her eyes, "trying to persuade Uncle to get them to un-ban me. Even if it only helps Godsson 'emotionally.' As if." She snorted, and Faith tilted her head quizzically. "I still can't believe how dumb Grups can be.

D'ya think *I'll* get dumb when I get old?"

She looked at Faith, but Faith just grinned at her. "Nah, you're right. But I still need to work out how to convince Keepie to let Godsson teach me how to fight Her."

Just the thought of having *that* conversation made her heart sink.

Faith's tail dipped low. *Rats*. Now she'd made Faith depressed, too. "Oh, come on, it won't be that bad. Keepie's not as bad as most Grups. And getting Godsson to teach me magic-fighting makes sense, right? *Heaps* of sense."

But Faith just looked worried.

For some time now, they'd been steadily moving up into the foothills behind the Institute. Not too far ahead was the rocky outcrop that still had the impact crater from where Faith's lasers had just missed her, all those years ago. She smiled despite herself. Keepie had never found out about that.

"Come on, I'll race you to the top!"

She sprinted forward, before Faith powered ahead along the trail, curving up. She, though, could take the short cut, since she could climb.

But Faith still beat her to the top, looking very pleased with herself as she sat back on her haunches. From the heat still radiating from her turbine pods, though, Sara knew she'd only *just* gotten there first.

Together, then, they sat and looked down on the Institute below. Faith snuggled next to her, almost bumping her off the massive slab of rock, but licked her face to apologize.

She giggled, cheered a little by the distraction, then continued the conversation.

"The funny thing, or maybe the worrying thing, is that instead of just saying 'No. You're banned'," she said, making her voice deep and gruff like her uncle's, which made Faith smile, "he just said 'We'll see,' this time. And I could tell he meant it."

Faith nudged her.

"Yeah, I know. I reckon it just shows how worried they all really are. 'specially since he knows I still need to go inside Godsson's cell if we're ever gonna defeat Her once and for all."

Faith looked sideways at her, worried again.

She shrugged. "I decided not to try to hide *that* any-more: that way he doesn't look too hard for other stuff."

It was sad that she couldn't trust Keepie anymore. She missed him. But she had to keep her distance. Anything else would've made it *impossible* to keep her secrets, instead of just incredibly hard.

Maybe if she raced Faith back down to the Institute, it'd cheer her up?

Things just weren't fun any more.

CHAPTER 35

Harmon sat at his desk, developmental graphs hanging in the air before him, fighting off a dismaying sense of helplessness. Somehow, it was not working. Or rather, it had stopped working. Progress had stalled. She no longer seemed really *gripped* by the role he had prepared for her. Occasionally, she even attempted resistance to his guidance. And she still had not Unfolded.

The experiment itself was failing.

He needed a stronger link to the role he had chosen for her. He needed to tie her to her part, needed to get under her skin. Perhaps some sort of convincing ceremony. Something primitive, to sound forth a responsive chord from the collective unconscious. Blood, perhaps? Yes.

A real bow and arrow would be too obviously lethal, too dangerous. He knew Sara's behavior was only barely tolerated as things stood. He smiled, recalling Professor Sanders's reaction on seeing her in her 'Leather Goddess' outfit. Practically apoplectic. Good thing he'd been there to smooth things over – it would never do to have the Director begin to question the project. So: no real bow and arrow, despite her many requests. And needless to say, a gun was out of the question. Far too easy. Hmm. What about a slingshot? Superficially childish, so he could claim he thought it was 'just a toy; but in the right hands, lethal. Yes. That would be perfect.

With a flick of his MetaStylus he brought up a shopping precinct window, sent off a search. For perhaps a minute then he studied the list of products, before deciding on the Ascorp PowerShot. It looked sleek and deadly, sure to appeal to her.

He clicked on 'accept' and transferred the funds.

Satisfied, he turned to the feed from the gym. He had taken to leaving it active, the holovid running with the sound muted so her music did not disturb him. Occasionally, she would be doing something odd, like standing on one leg with her eyes shut for minutes on end. Normally, though, she was very active.

He found it soothing to watch her stretching and straining, strutting and pirouetting on the balance beam, tumbling and flying around the uneven bars – or indeed, using them as balance beams! – or diving and spinning over the vaulting horse. While he constructed magical theories or designed subtle experiments to test them, he found that just having the small holo on in the background often centered his thoughts or sparked ideas.

Sara visited the place at odd hours, and he liked that touch of randomness, too. Sometimes he would cease working and just stare, like some god of Olympus following a mortal's enactment of the drama he was scripting. Most satisfying.

He returned once more to his struggle to design an experiment to detect the race consciousness directly. Lost in thought, a knock at the door made him jump. He glanced at the projection of the tiny gym, hovering in the air just above the corner of his desk. Sara was not there. And now was *not* the time for interruptions.

"Go away," he called, not looking up. Nevertheless, the door opened.

"Sara, when I say –"

"Hello, Harmon. Just dropped in for our usual little chat."

Oh no, Harmon thought, looking at the calendar. Yes, indeed: it was bimonthly report time. He resigned himself to a lengthy interruption, as Sanders enquired about his research.

After all, while a small government research grant assisted with many of his expenses for his experimental 'training program,' it was the Institute that provided food and board for his subject. And the Director liked to keep track of his people, liked to spend some time going over each researcher's work: both to see if he could offer helpful suggestions, and to keep an eye on how the Institute's money was being spent. At any rate, that was what happened when Sanders visited his colleagues, Simmons or Ramsin. *Had* visited Ramsin: the fellow had left, last year. Claimed his services were hardly needed any more. Yet his departure had occurred only weeks after asking whether Harmon thought there might not be something *real* behind Godsson's imaginary foes.

Ramsin had sidled into his office on some pretext one day, then begun babbling about hiking.

"Do you go for walks in the grounds, Dr Alex? Your young ward certainly spends a lot of time out there. Alone." He nodded, as if he'd just made a telling point.

"Did you know... I mean, do you think there might be something *real* out there?"

"Oh? Have you been seeing Sara's invisible-to-magic creatures in the grounds, too?" He had stared behind his colleague's shoulder, just to needle him further.

But Ramsin had *flinched* and jerked around, and begun scanning Imaginally for some ultra-stealthy predator right there in his office. As if he believed he was being pursued. Long seconds passed before he turned back around, and saw Harmon watching him, smiling.

The fool had made some excuse, then scurried off. And resigned the following week.

No doubt Sara had been the invisible stalker. But Ramsin's departure had been no loss.

Now was no time for reminiscence, though, with the Director standing at the other side of his desk. Once more attempting to pry into his ideas and review his spending.

So for the next hour, through a judicious blend of persuasion, misdirection, and extremely subtle magic, he would satisfy the Professor without really letting him learn a single solid fact about his work. Or, for that matter, revealing the true application of certain expenditures, like the holovid feed from the gym to his desk. Thanks to the privacy shield, the feed could only be viewed from Harmon's position. He casually redirected the projection out of sight to the floor at his feet, while appearing to casually place his MetaStylus on his desk.

At that moment, Sara entered the gym and crossed over to the vid set he had installed in there. He dragged his attention back to Sanders.

The Professor was basically a kindly man: it showed in the deep laughter lines round his eyes and mouth and in his often-mischievous expression. His own area of interest lay in the use of magic to heal the mind, and Harmon had to admit he was indeed good in that field. If the man had been more than marginally active magically, it would have made things impossibly difficult for Harmon.

The gentle battle of wits commenced.

Some time later, Harmon was momentarily distracted from his vague explanation of the long-term nature of his project when he noticed Sara had frozen, absolutely still, in front of the gym's vid screen. He couldn't see what she saw, but whatever it was had paralyzed her in mid-action.

And then she began to dance.

But what a dance! It was both wildly unlike her – he had never seen her do much more than sway or bounce in time to her music – and yet seemed to express the essence of what he sought to mold her into. It was at once a primitive hunting dance, a controlled explosion of pure action – and strangely erotic. He could only catch the most frustrating glimpses of the vid screen she was watching in the gym, as his feed tracked her while she stalked, spun, and tumbled before it. Intriguingly, she seemed to be watching a very old black and white, grainy, 2D image.

Suddenly, he realized he had been silent too long. He wrenched his gaze from the dancer, to see the Director looking at him curiously.

"What is it?" Sanders asked. "Something certainly seems to have caught your interest." He started to come round the desk.

Harmon thought quickly, glad of the holo's privacy shield. Canceling the gym input he called up a mandelbrot tour instead.

"Here, I'll show you. I use this as a sort of meditation aid, and sometimes it generates ideas." He blathered on, even as he inwardly cursed, consumed with curiosity as to what had so caught her interest.

At dinner that evening, Sara was quietly excited, but seemed to be trying to hide the fact. Intrigued, associating this with her dance, Harmon cast a mindmeld on his young charge. Her mind opened with the easy susceptibility he had come to expect. But as he penetrated her surface thoughts, they seemed to dart and scatter like a school of fish.

No doubt due to her unusual state of mind. He went deeper, taking her mind toward the gym earlier in the day, but her focus kept slipping – a trampoline session, a bout with the punching bag – she had recently become interested in fighting, and was trying to learn skills from holo trids, spending hours applying what she'd learned to the Wing Chun dummy that she and Shanahan had built. There was a strong sense of guilt, there, before her thoughts shifted and she was remembering a swim she'd taken the day before, in the lake at the back of the Institute, in the nude.... He wrenched the stream of thoughts back on course, but to no avail: they kept skittering away. Almost as if....

Sara had stopped eating. Was staring down at her food. Then he noticed the white knuckles of the hand holding her knife.

She's blocking me! The revelation staggered him. Not only did she have a secret from him; not only had she noticed the invasion of her thoughts; but she had successfully held him off! *No wonder progress has stalled.* How many other times had she held a secret from him?

Despite his shock he gave no outward sign of noticing anything unusual. The rest of the meal passed in silence.

He waited for some time before preparing to try again, shifting his senses to the Imaginal to monitor her emotions before recasting the spell. But he'd made no more than the first gesture to anchor himself in the pattern before her whole tone shifted to one of anger and defense. Instantly he aborted the attempt, and spoke to distract her. "What do you do, Sara, to challenge yourself these days?"

She sat tensely, expecting some other comment, he saw. He watched her defenses shift to counter the assumed new threat.

"I work on stuff," she said.

"Good," he smiled, carefully concealing his growing concern. "Good."

Sara stared down into her cereal bowl and took another spoonful, her whole attention really focused on her peripheral vision. Watching his fingers was best, she had learned. There was a special kind of dance of fingers that went with the spell he used to slide into her; before his spying presence crowded inside her head.

Sara took care to slump casually in her chair so he wouldn't know she was ready for him. She saw she'd clenched her fists, and relaxed them. Then, lightly alert, she waited with the memories of her swim, the day before, suppressing a smile. Those kinds of images worked best to distract him, to keep her true self private.

She couldn't keep him out, but she could control her own thoughts enough to ensure he mainly saw what she let him. It had been hard, learning how to 'plan out' thoughts in advance, lightly holding them ready to think when the need arose. She wondered if this was a test, some kind of training.

Whatever it was, Sara didn't like it. She found it creepy.

Harmon saw little of her the rest of the day. Was she actively avoiding him, or merely spending a lot of time outdoors? The former, he suspected, after monitoring her in the gym. He headed down there, only to find it empty, a climbing rope still gently swaying.

He didn't want to attempt the spell again as they ate together – he hardly wanted to condition her to be alert for such things at every mealtime – so instead, he requested a search for a list of music videos that had played between twelve and one the day before, and which were black and white. The list had about a hundred entries, but one stood out as being by far the most likely choice. A broadcast of a pre-Unfolding recording from some group called *The Troggs*, with a title that gave it away. He called up the lyrics and studied them. Some of the words were quite archaic.

Later that day, when Sara asked casually if he knew what the word 'groovy' meant, he was certain. He, equally casually, explained it was a very old word meaning something was 'right' – 'on track' or 'in the groove.' She had nodded and looked pleased.

A small victory for him, too, although he was unsure precisely how to use it.

He spent the next two days discovering it was remarkably difficult to sneak up on Sara. In growing desperation, he dug into the little published research on invisibility spell constructs. For the next two weeks he worked on the problem, exploring and creating the pattern for an appropriate and believable certainty he could use for such a spell. He soon came to realize it was an intrinsically difficult task, but pushed doggedly on. At the end of the period, though, when he tried the spell for the first time, his fears had been justified – the spell required so much concentration to maintain, that performing a simultaneous mindmeld of any worth would be impossible. Sara, meanwhile, had acquired a decidedly smug air.

Two weeks wasted.

And now, with those weeks passed, she had grown relaxed in his presence. Bordering on insolent, really. He chose an evening meal when she was tired from her physical activity of the day, clearly exhausted. Once more, he watched her without seeming to, slowly and carefully casting the mindmeld. With a rigidly controlled joy he completed the spell without her noticing it, and slipped into her thoughts. It had been so long, it was like rejoining an old friend, and he probed deeper. But suddenly the mental terrain shifted, altering in an instant from a warm autumn sunset to a glaring summer's day. He found himself trapped in canyons of inconsequence, stupid repetitive patterns of pointless activity and foolish thought. *She's blocking me again!*

Worse, her blocking was not the deceptive and fragile technique she'd used before, it was a confrontational and stubborn resistance. He could break through that resistance, he knew – but also knew without question that such a show of force would likely provoke her to respond with a direct confrontation.

He broke off, and without a word, stalked from the room. The Imaginal reverberations of her triumph felt like invisible lashes against his back.

Sitting on the edge of his bed one night soon after, he mused darkly. He'd been careless. Treating her almost with contempt, making little attempt to conceal what he did. He'd let her see too much, and now he was paying the price. Now, all his work teetered on the brink.

Not only had she become able to recognize the subtle physical signs of his spellcasting, not only had she taught herself to parry his mental examinations, but the longer this situation remained unresolved, the more it eroded his position of authority. He *had* to find a solution. *Think!* He had realized something was happening to her, something he hadn't planned, the day he'd seen her wild dancing when she thought herself alone in the gym. Rock and roll. That thought triggered another. What was the old saying? *Sex and drugs and rock and roll.*

Psychotropics!

At his desk, he paged through the information the net

so readily offered up. He needed something that would improve her suggestibility. It took hours of research to find the ideal candidate: di-hydro lysergic scopolamine. 'Scope.' Discovered only recently, but apparently already being used illicitly.

Illicitly. Hmm. Certainly, obtaining it that way would avoid awkward questions; and he could analyze it here easily enough, to ensure its purity.

Browsing around those areas turned up mentions of other street drugs, too: notably, 'beep' – a contraction of BP, from beta-phrodisia, presumably. Harmon remembered the excitement at the time, when Gunter Kerr published her breakthrough work on the chemical intermediaries of the sexual drive.

That would certainly distract Sara. He put the idea aside, however. 'Scope' was his main need.

So, in what sort of dives did one hunt this sort of thing? The rhythm of his tapping finger sped up. Yes, this could be quite educational.

He called a cab and an hour later was headed into the city with an annoyingly-chatty driver. A real pity that the Institute was considered a 'use-caution' destination.

The talkative driver was especially unwelcome tonight. How strange to be visiting clubs and bars at his age. The very thought made him uncomfortable. He had little idea what to expect.

Three bars later, he had found and mind-read a sleazy and very likely CID-less character by the ridiculous name of 'Quicksilver' to find, finally, a lead to obtaining the illicit substance he needed.

By the first bar, it had become clear he could not simply *ask* any of the denizens. For some reason, they assumed he was some kind of ham-fisted agent of the law.

By his fifth bar, he still could not help being somewhat fazed by the erotic gyrations of the girls on stage. He kept picturing his wild little Sara using her athletic talents the same way.... With an effort, he tore his gaze away and hunted for the man he'd been advised to seek out. From deeper in the gloom he caught the mirror glint he'd been searching for, and headed in that direction.

He forced himself to saunter over in a semi-slouch, trying not to look too out of place, yet he still had the uncomfortable feeling that half the patrons watched him with amusement.

The fellow was dressed in crushed black velvet, a barely-dressed woman draped against each side. Both women seemed entirely rapt by the man, who looked quite accustomed to such attention.

Harmon eyed the dark-haired girl on the left appreciatively, before looking back at his contact. Eyes chromed from some ocular modification gleamed steadily back at him. This was the one, certainly.

"Maestro?"

The head inclined slightly, and Harmon took it as an invitation to sit.

"I believe you can help me: 'Quicksilver' recommended you." Which was a small lie. However, Quicksilver's mind had been surprisingly easy to scan, and adjust, and the fellow would, if now asked, confirm Harmon's trustworthiness. A *most* useful spell, Suggestion. It would not be a wise move to try on this fellow, though, something told him.

"Speak."

Bristling at the terse air of command the man assumed, Harmon swallowed his natural response and answered instead with equal brevity.

"Scope."

The man nodded. "Quantity?"

He had determined his requirements. Had taken into account Sara's lower-than-adult mass, and the advisability of minimizing such forays as this one, as well as the desirability of a slow buildup. Fifty doses, he'd decided, to be on the safe side.

"Ten milligrams."

The man blinked. "Planning an Event, are we?"

Harmon only smiled.

"I can do that. And for a bulk order I guess I can give you a discount. Ten thousand creds."

Harmon avoided gulping – but only just.

"Meet me here, then, midnight."

Harmon nodded.

Later that night, carefully nursing a drink, Harmon followed the stage show as he waited. He pulled at his collar. The little vixen serving drinks winked at him before bending well forward as she served another patron his order, the deep cleavage of her formidable breasts outlined and lit by carefully-placed golden glow-cords.

She looked up, caught him staring, then saucily strutted past his table on her way to the bar, a heart-shaped glowing outline highlighting her swaying rear end as she smiled back at him.

As graceful as Sara, but using it for such *a different purpose.* Then he spotted Maestro approaching, this time with only a single woman. But the woman was naked, he belatedly realized. And desperate, too, for something. As they arrived at his table, Harmon noticed another thing: the woman was on a *leash*. Maestro sat, tugging the leash down.

"Heel."

Hardly believing his eyes, Harmon watched as the woman clutched at herself, obviously humiliated. But a feverish hunger seemed to underline her every gesture. Maestro reached out a finger and ran it up the inside of one bare thigh. The woman shuddered all over; her head arched back. When it ended, she slowly straightened up again; then sank to her knees on the floor.

"A demo for you: scope and beep. Two hundred of scope: one hundred beep. A good combo," Maestro gestured at the woman, noting Harmon's disbelieving stare.

"Micrograms?   And... this is the result?" Harmon wrenched his eyes from the woman's display. His earlier idea returned. The two in combination... "How much?" he asked.

Maestro smiled.

CHAPTER 36

At breakfast, although Sara complained about the taste of the Orange-o-Tang™, she drank it all the same. He had decided to start with a sub-therapeutic dose and build up. With only tens of micrograms, he expected to see no change.

However, about lunchtime, he glanced at the gym monitor and noticed her straddling the narrow beam, rocking gently forward and back.

"Well, well, well." He watched as the scene continued for a full fifteen minutes. "Who would have guessed you could be *so* responsive, little one." His rational, clinical side was pleased by the prospect of the smooth introduction of this new tool. On the other side, in a sort of pre-conscious mental maneuvering, a coil of desire wound itself one degree tighter, choking back the beginnings of shame.

But as the days passed and he gradually increased her dosage, he found *himself* being slowly gripped by the trap he had devised for her. It felt as if his own body was being gradually infiltrated by strands of sexual energies. She had long been proud of her body: aware of it. But under the influence of the drug, she had become actively interested in it – even fascinated by it. More and more, she touched herself – sometimes just lightly, gliding her fingers over her cheeks, then down her neck, appearing to revel in the feel of her own soft skin and the delicate touch of her fingertips. Sometimes she ran her hands down her sides, or clenched her legs... and he watched. He could not resist watching, as those fingers slid over that taut skin, dragging his eyes along with them.

Each touch seemed to reach inside *him*, winding his own tension tighter; each sensual gesture another weight piled on top of some invisible mass pressing in on him, so that at times he found himself physically straining, every muscle taut, and had to force himself to relax. It was almost as though he had been taking the drug too.

It was a good thing that most of the Institute's workforce was robotic, these days. Humans would have commented on the change in her behavior.

By the time he had increased her dose to a combined eighty micrograms, he knew neither of them could contain the building pressure. His work lay forgotten: as she spent more time 'exercising,' he became less able to concentrate on anything but her. Her dancing in the gym had become very like what he'd seen in the strobing lights of those dark dives where his eyes had been opened. Anticipation gripped him as each of her unconscious sexual signals dragged him deeper into the web of his own desires.

She had become his drug.

In a rare moment of lucidity he recalled with near-astonishment his original plan. The weapon. Blood. The ceremony. He'd been tidying the files in his private pocket of the net when he discovered he had even written himself a script. As he read his own notes from just ten days before, the enormity of the change struck him with a clarity so intense it was painful. These cool, detached words, this clinical air – only faint echoes remained.

He entertained the fancy that he *had*, in fact, been drugged; even ran exhaustive blood tests on himself. But no. Sara lay at its heart. He realized this the day he emerged from his lab to find her slinking down the corridor toward him. A hot wave flooded his mind and thought ceased. She wore only the briefest white bikini, startling against her sun-darkened skin. No time seemed to pass; she was simply there, pressed against him, hugging him, stroking his face....

Desperately, with a shudder, he drew the tattered remnants of his will together. Remembered his earlier plan. He disengaged from her arms, shakily.

"Come Sara, I have something for you. A present. For hunting."

This, in turn, awoke a spark of her old self.

"Hunting?"

"Yes. Come, I'll get it for you."

He walked ahead. He didn't think he could cope with the view if he walked behind her.

Neither spoke as they made their way to his office. As he opened the door and crossed the room, Sara followed silently behind. The door closed with a soft 'snick' behind them.

He crossed the room, and while his face and hands were shielded from her view, he prepared a mindmeld spell. As he moved behind his desk and caught sight of her again he subtly released it, and for the first time in months, she appeared not to notice as it settled over her. He kept an especially light touch.

«She watched him closely as he bent down, his fingertip unlocking the drawer. She herself scarcely knew how she felt. The burning emptiness seemed to grow by the moment. She bit gently at her lip as he slid the drawer open and placed the brown paper parcel in the middle of his desk.

«She approached slowly, the feel of her heated skin tight against her skull. She was confused: more than aroused. Like she was being stroked, all over.

«The edge of the desk bumped her thighs. She stopped moving, raising her eyes slowly from the parcel to his face. Slowly, she closed her eyes again, savoring the strange tight heat that twisted through her almost painfully.»

Her feelings were so intense that he himself felt an echo of them. It was such a peculiarly uncomfortable sensation he dropped the mindmeld. Yet, as if her reaction had spread to him somehow, he felt a surge of that same compelling heat. It was only with an enormous effort that he managed to drag his attention from her. Drawing a deep breath, he forced himself to concentrate on what he was doing. *Soon,* he promised himself. Soon.

She still stood facing him across his desk, eyes shut. He had the distinct impression that despite her enormous curiosity, the mystery of his gift was barely holding her attention. He noticed she was *not* standing still: slowly, subtly, she was shifting her limbs; gently rotating her hips, constantly bringing parts of her body in and out of contact with one another. A dreamy look came over her face, her eyes half-closed.

"Unwrap your parcel, Sara," he ordered, breathing hard.

She opened her eyes and reached for the parcel. With an ease that surprised him, she tore away the wrapping and cardboard to reveal the gleaming chrome and black slingshot. It had a pistol grip; a long steel spring. It looked sure and deadly, blunt power sketched in every line.

"It's called a 'PowerShot'," he told her.

The weapon snapped her out of her auto-erotic daze.

"Ohh," she breathed in wonder. "It's beautiful."

He watched her fingers tighten convulsively around the sculpted black hand-grip. With her other hand, she pulled the spring back – with less effort than he himself had needed when he'd tried it earlier. He suppressed a shiver. She gently released the tension, her expression now dramatically different. Practically carnivorous.

She laughed: almost a deep, coughing growl. He felt cold as her eyes fixed on his. Her other hand reached out, somehow guided surely to the small box of steel ball-bearings that were the device's ammunition. Abruptly, he wondered how he could possibly have watched the thing's demonstration, yet claim he had not understood he supplied her with a lethal weapon.

She was making him nervous. "Sara, I hope-" He shifted his perception to the Imaginal and his voice cracked. Her aura *boiled*. He'd never seen anything like it.

It was happening!

She was starting to Unfold, right here in the Institute. Following the archetype of the Huntress. With a lethal weapon in her hands.

With dismay, he realized he suddenly had no idea what she might do. "I hope I don't have to impress upon you how important it is not to use this weapon in or too near the Institute. It must be our secret."

In answer she only cocked her head to one side. "I'm going out hunting," she declared, and stalked silently from the room.

He slumped in a sudden release of tension: laughed, shakily. At any rate, he needn't have worried so much about her losing touch with the role for which he had prepared her. She had slipped back into it like a shark beneath water.

He eased back into his seat, eager to observe what promised to be her so long awaited Unfolding. Centering himself he slipped down inside, finally leaving his body. He would follow her Imaginally until she'd left the building, at least as far as the barriers – and make sure she wasn't going to attack any of the Institute personnel.

He wondered what she would kill.

CHAPTER 37

Outside, Sara stalked through her Jungle, but it was a jungle strangely changed. *She* felt strange, too. *So* strange. Her head ached; her mouth was dry; and the light was much too strong. The colors glowed so brightly they hurt her eyes. And the liquid ball of hot pressure was still building in her chest. It felt like something was squeezing the breath from her; like her skin was stretched too tightly over her body.

She didn't like it. She felt like she might explode.

The trees were filled with birds, somehow squawking and shrieking straight into her ears. It was unnatural, too much. She had only two anchor points in the cauldron broiling her: the cool, firm grip of the weapon in her hand, and the knowledge that she held the power to kill.

She held onto those two truths as the world beat upon her with such intensity she felt physically sick. At last, though, she held an adult's weapon. She clung to the thought.

The sound of the wind, of creaking branches and rustling leaves, all pressed in against her, so close that she spun around, suddenly sure that the forest had somehow come alive, stretched out and swallowed her.

She half-wished *She* would appear. She'd tear Her into little tiny pieces.

But the noise just kept pounding her, trying to drown her. She focused on the sounds from the tree she now stood beneath, a pigeon cooing in an absurdly booming voice. As if it had perched right against her ear. The volume of it frightened her a little. She couldn't get away from it. She scanned the branches to locate the source of the horribly loud sound. And as she did, it was like a holo contrast-control had just been turned all the way up – another shape suddenly resolved itself from the deeper darkness of the tree, hidden deep inside a bower of branches and leaves, that moments before had been darkly impenetrable. The weapon sat heavy in her hand. She raised it, sighted, her other hand slipping a ball bearing into its pouch and drawing the spring smoothly back. It was an owl she aimed at, she suddenly knew. Its eyes blinked open in the deep shade of its retreat.

She tasted its imminent death while color, sound, and smells seemed once more to pile up in waves against her.

She imagined her uncle's voice whispering to her: Kill! Kill! Yet somehow, the taste was wrong, the victim wrong. Too unsuspecting, perhaps? Too unaware? She didn't understand, but felt it would be an insult to... something... to make the owl her first victim. Deeply wrong.

She snarled in frustration.

A moment later, the cooing ceased in a painfully-loud thrashing of wings: the pigeon that had been tormenting her, scared into sudden flight. A fat bird, it hadn't even left the branches of the tree as she spun, sighted, and with a curious certainty that she could not miss – that her sling bullet *must* hit, or had already hit – loosed.

Its head literally exploded, and the bird's flight collapsed into a plunging fall. The sight of her success tore a cry of joy from her, shocking through her with a totally unexpected surge of relief, of *release*, her whole self shuddering with the missile's impact.

The small body plummeted to the ground, striking one branch after another on the way down in a series of sickening thuds, before thumping into a bush at the foot of the tree. To lie unmoving.

Sound and color drained abruptly back to their normal levels. Though she wanted to collapse to the ground as the sensation of release burned through every nerve, she locked her legs stiffly apart and struggled to contain the shocking pleasure, resisting as she strained to fight it down; panting with effort as she fought her own body for control. A part of her felt horror, dismayed that the death had felt so good. It shouldn't feel *good*. Not like *that*.

She would *not* give in to it.

For a full minute she stood trembling on the brink of some dreadful cliff before she felt able to trust her limbs again. At last, still shaky, she tucked the grip of her weapon into the waist of her shorts and moved over to her fallen prey, plucking it from the tangles of the shrub.

A fat gray pigeon, made both still and ugly by its violent death. It lay warm in her hands, blood still oozing from its neck. It looked pathetic. She felt sad, somehow. She had ended its life. That fact was dreadfully real; dreadfully final. Some distant part of her, some tiny spark, seemed to be trying to whisper to her, to warn her; but the whisper was silent: a mere breath. It made her think of an old man, for some reason. But the wisp of memory slid away.

She looked up, gazing past the small body, her unblinking eyes focused on infinity. Mentally she pictured a small soul winging its way Elsewhere, and offered it a silent acknowledgment.

Wetness on her cheeks brought her back to herself, and she brushed in surprise at the trickles of moisture.

She turned, crossing the lawn to head back to the Institute. But as she reached the edge of the gravel area, she hesitated, filled with a sudden reluctance – a feeling she should be outside, not in. Spinning on her heels, she ran into the woods.

-

Harmon's astral form circled the powerful Warding around the Institute's buildings.

He watched her sense her prey, and kill it. With a single shot. Saw her aura flare, Unfolding at last – only to watch her *fight it down*.

Furious, he watched her trudge toward the front steps, before turning back and racing out through the barrier, beyond his view.

What foolish game was this?

Long minutes later, the Institute's barrier flared in a Borealis display as she returned through the Ward. *What...?* The shimmering curtain closed up behind her almost like wings furling.

The Ward had reacted to Sara as if she were *almost* a threat.

The '*almost*'... it made no sense. None.

And he saw she had *felt* that interaction, too, as she stumbled at that instant, nearly dropping the dying ember cradled in her hands. He moved beside her to observe her as she stood, pushing one hand gingerly through the barrier, clearly puzzled.

Spinning around, she brushed past his spirit form.

And her touch *hurt*.

Impossible. Reflexively, he flashed backwards, to the front doors. On the lawn below, Sara moved now as if in the dark, one arm stretched out, trying to locate the thing she had brushed against. *Him*. Somehow she had touched his spirit. And *hurt* it.

That should not be possible. Not without both a focused effort of will, and full awareness of what she did. Not from a clearly accidental contact.

Had she Unfolded? If so, into *what?* He could not categorize the shape of her aura: not as that of a mage, nor as a shaman.

Her aura *had* changed, though. It looked... calmer. More self-contained.

Deeper.

Finally she turned, stalking up the stairs to the entry doors where he hovered. With a thought, he returned to his body.

When his office door opened he looked up, took in the plump little body she carried and her drained expression, and quickly shifted his perception back to the Imaginal. Her aura had settled into patterns so different from her usual that he barely recognized it. For one thing, the livid, charged tendrils he attributed to the influence of the beep and scope seemed shrunken. Somehow quiet. And the rest of it had altered in subtle ways. Simpler, clearer. Stronger, too. As though he were looking at some familiar bay's shore after a violent storm had reshaped its outlines.

She had approached, standing now before him with the bird held in both hands, the PowerShot poking from the waist of her tight shorts. Her eyes gazed steadily into his, waiting for him to acknowledge her kill. She was *not* offering it to him.

He rose and came around the desk, forcing aside distaste as he reached out and touched the bloody neck. "I see your first hunt was successful, Sara. I'm very proud of you."

He saw the unexpected praise warm her – softening her, a little, into vulnerability. She looked shyly down at the small body for a second, before gazing back up into his eyes.

Harmon felt he could almost *see* the shape of her future stretching ahead, and chose his words with care. His voice sank, low and solemn as he spoke in more formal tones.

"Up until now, little one, you have been playing children's games. But this is real, now. You have made your first kill."

She nodded her acceptance, eyes not leaving his. Remembering his script, he dabbed a finger into the creature's blood. With it, he marked her forehead, then each cheek. Her eyes shone.

As he anointed her, he spoke. "With this blood, I mark you and Name you."

He paused, and in more normal tones, explained. "Now that you are truly a hunter you have earned a new name: your adult name. I am sure you will like it," he Suggested.

Her eyes narrowed. She frowned, shaking her head, and he saw the spell shatter, broken by her unconscious resistance.

A minor victory for her, but it struck Harmon with all the shock of a slap in the face. She looked a little confused – hardly aware of this piece of psychic byplay. Mentally gritting his teeth, he focused his attention – indeed made it all but obvious what he was doing as he recast the spell. But he felt he needed more.

Reaching out to *her*, he laid his right hand gently on her arm. The physical contact, so rarely made, seemed to put her suddenly off-balance. Her eyes widened slightly as she looked up into his. He tried again.

"Yes, I am *sure* you will like your new name."

He held the Imaginal pattern of the spell inside himself, letting it swell as he channeled extra force into it before releasing it and directing it over her. It seemed to tear at him this time as it passed from him to her, and he panted with the effort of controlling the flow. This time, though, he felt the spell take root.

She nodded, fractionally.

"I name you *Leeth*!"

Her eyes closed as she accepted her new name.

He could almost read her thought – so *right*. She smiled.

With his hand still holding her arm, the silence lengthened. Suddenly, he was acutely conscious of the touch. Her body language told him she also was all too aware of the contact. He watched her aura, strands now pulsing and swelling. Sexual tension vibrated in the air between them. He mentally retreated once more to the safety of the script he had prepared all those days ago.

"Now we shall feast you."

She opened her eyes and grinned. *Leeth* grinned. Satisfaction and pride suddenly bubbled over into delight. In very much her old way, she whispered intensely, "Oh, yes, Keepie, yes! Let's feast!"

Together, they plucked it. He let *her* dress it, with a small but wickedly sharp knife, her eyes shining at the implied trust. Together, they prepared it. Cooked it, together. And together celebrated the Feast of Becoming.

Engrossed in their shared work, she didn't notice as he cast and slipped the mindmeld spell over her with exquisite delicacy.

Parts of the meal verged on the indigestible due to the cooks' lack of knowledge; but parts were wonderful – though he had to smile at her discovery that real flesh tended to stick between one's teeth, not at all like soyburger.

But as the meal progressed, the tension that had discharged earlier crept back and began to build. Her fever grew. He retreated further down the link as her senses began flooding her so strongly they started to overwhelm her. He had even allowed her a glass of red wine. He was quite pleased at her doubtful reaction. He sensed her appreciation of the full flavors, smooth and tart at the same time. He held his breath as she noted the unpleasantly bitter aftertaste. Relaxed as she thought nothing more of it.

She even drank it all, to please him.

He had dimmed the light earlier. As the small meal progressed, Sara's eyes – no, *Leeth's* eyes – seemed to grow larger and larger, until they were brimming dark pools. Desire seemed to move like some submarine behemoth beneath their surface. He shook himself mentally at the foolishness of the simile. Yet in a very real way, she made him nervous. The current he tapped, he suspected, ran very deep indeed.

After drinking all her wine, from the tall, slender glass he'd set out, she seemed unable to leave its stem alone, her fingers sliding up and down it. Harmon noted the flush of her cheeks. Her movements had slowed, smoothed. No longer bird-quick and jumpy. A feline sensuality instead surfaced, as she twirled the glass stem between thumb and finger. With her other hand, she ran a finger around the rim; stroked down the side; cupped the gently curved shape in the palm of her hand. She seemed to find the contact strangely intimate, strongly pleasurable. He continued his retreat, finally dropping the link lest her senses swamp him. Nor did he wish to risk reawakening her stubborn resistance at this critical juncture.

He watched as she shifted in her seat, crossing one subtly muscled, copper-bronzed leg over the other. Then slid it forward and back, purely for the pleasure of feeling one silkily curved calf whisper against the other, he knew.

Her eyes had half closed, he noted, the upper lids drooping down as she fell headlong into the enticement of her own senses. He watched, enraptured, as the drug took hold.

His intimate knowledge of her gestures and habits made him hypersensitive to her every action; made perfectly clear the meaning of each departure from her normal body language. So when the fingers of her right hand trailed casually up the smooth length of her forearm, he imagined it was his own hand generating the sensuous pleasure that triggered and then prolonged her self-caress. When she idly placed one hand on the underside of her breast, and then oh so slowly, let her fingers trail up over that curve and then down into the valley and up the other side, and her mouth opened in a small 'O', he knew she relished delicious sensations that flowed beneath her outwardly calm exterior.

He almost smiled. The drugs would make this so easy.

Mentally, he drew back, musing. Analyzing. A perceptive stranger would, at best, have thought she was flirting. A less observant stranger would have noticed nothing at all. Sara – no *Leeth*, dammit – Leeth herself was unaware of how clearly she was signaling to him. *She* assumed the slight movements caused by shifting her legs would pass unnoticed. Did not realize he drank it in and correctly interpreted it – knowing she relished the surreptitious nudging of thigh against thigh... and all the other, more subtle pressures and touches.

He smiled, amused. She thought she was arousing and pleasuring herself secretly. Right in front of him. For him, however, knowing her to be ignorant of his awareness, he had not only the thrill of watching her arouse herself, and the anticipation of what would come, but also the illicit thrill of the voyeur watching from the shadows, safe in his own secrecy.

And now for the next step.

He gestured at the music console across the room. Softly, the notes of his first selection seeped into the background of the room. He decided to skip the various interludes. Another gesture jumped it straight to the heart of the sequence – a shallow modern piece, but one with a pounding bass undercurrent and a primitive, even savage, rhythm.

Leeth's eyes slitted in pleasure, acknowledging it with the merest nod and a widening of her already wicked smile. On a whim, he shifted his senses to the Imaginal plane. What he saw was enough to reawaken his clinical interest: the thickly twining ribbons were noticeably tumescing, in driving pulses that matched the beat of the music. They twisted and throbbed suggestively, penetrating and threading the other parts of her aura. He found the movements engrossing: they *compelled* attention. He watched as the patterns and colors associated with the higher mental processes dimmed and diffused, while the simpler and more fundamental patterns became steadily more urgent and dominant.

At that moment, a contraction seemed to pass through the branches of her Imaginal form. Simultaneously, their intensity deepened. And now, the rest of the pattern seemed to be opening up. He watched, fascinated, struggling to formulate the concepts that would explain what he was seeing. It was as though parts of her aura were, were... *reaching out*.

With a start, he realized her aura was flowering, opening out toward him. He snapped out of his rapt daze. Leeth stretched, cat-like, and prepared to get up.

With the speed of desperation, he gestured at the console of the Yamaha CyberSound, jumping ahead right to the climax of the final piece he'd chosen. The music faded into stillness. In the charged pause before the new selection started, Leeth uncoiled from her seat and stood, staring at him hungrily. There was even a predatory gleam to her eyes, he fancied. A shock ran through him, as her movement triggered a proto-memory of a disturbing dream he'd once had.

And then, as one leg stretched sensuously out and she

began stalking toward him, the music rose and wrapped around her. He had found a more modern group, from her own playlist, who had a tribute to the almost one hundred year old song that had so inspired her, whose surging, driving bass would surely stir her blood.

It seemed to snare her, and she slowly turned, looking back at him over her shoulder. A look; a promise: *soon.*

Then the sudden, heavy beat caught her, crashing through her body like a breaking wave, and she turned and plunged wildly into the music.

> Wild Thing
> You make the light spring
> You make the world sing
>
> Wild Thing
> You make my eyes dim
> You make my soul dream
>
> ...

Her eyes flashed as she accepted the song as homage; took it into herself, and then expressed it in dance.

A primal, driving dance: her every movement a scribing of passion in the air. Each gesture declared her savagery, her desire. There was no restraint: she poured all her considerable strength, all her athlete's skills, and all her grace into the song.

She spun around him, whirling through the room. Twisting, weaving, tumbling through the air: stalking, grasping and killing, in mime. And every movement, every frozen pause, matched perfectly to the rhythm. It was a consummate exhibition. So much so, that lost in his appreciation of its sheer artistry, he did not at first see where it was headed; ignored the message being sent. Until, as her circling movements meshed and focused, drawing tight the net she wove around him with her body, his heart suddenly thudded as he realized: she came for *him.*

She tore her clothes from her body as the dance built to its climax: shredded them with an ease he found profoundly disturbing. The sight, together with her beautiful curves, beaded and glistening with sweat, flushed and urgent with passion, sank into him like knives, slicing away the last tatters of his reserve and detachment, awakening the power of his own libido. He was painfully aroused. But it was arousal laced with fear as she at last stood before him. He found himself on his feet.

"Sara, no, we shouldn't do this. I've changed my-"

"Who's *Sara?*" she demanded, cutting him off and pressing her naked, fevered body up against his. She guided his hands to her breasts, moaning in ecstasy at his touch.

Then her hands were clawing at his clothes, tearing and pulling, sliding and stroking, then forcing him down. She saw his eyes widen in surprise at her strength, and it pleased her. Together they fell to the floor, where she made a second blood-sacrifice in a moment of delicious pain.

In the smothering moment of pleasure, it felt to her as though she were tearing open in many ways: opening up on levels whose existence she could only dimly perceive.

She was Life. She was Death.

She was *Leeth*.

Later, by her side in her bed – and hadn't *that* been a strange thrill, darting naked from his office to her rooms? – Harmon lay awake, profoundly troubled. This was wrong, on so many levels. Immoral. Illegal. Any court in the land would see it for what it was: abuse, even rape. He wanted to blame *her*, but he knew the fault lay with him- self. *He* was not the one who had been drugged.

Should word of this leak out.... He would need to Sug- gest they keep this private moment private.

It must never happen again.

Couldn't I have found some other way? I should have stopped her; found someone her own age. But I didn't want that, did I? Even the *thought* of sharing her....

At least this way, she hadn't gone out and killed any- one. But now that the goal had been achieved – his theory, vindicated! – there was no need for any further indul- gences.

At least, not until she's a little older, eh Alex? a darker, still-hungry part of him whispered.

I should leave now. Return to my own bedroom. In-

stead, he lay propped up in the dim light, emotions and thoughts churning darkly within. He knew he should get up. Part of him urged the departure; but a part wanted to stay. In the warmth and comfort of her bed. He liked her, and suddenly it seemed possible to more than like her. She was almost beautiful; and so open and demonstrative....

He forced the weakness away, while he pondered. She had Unfolded, he was sure; yet there had been no display of magic at all. No spontaneous levitation; no uncontained outpouring of damaging energies; no uncontrolled astral excursion. Clearly, she still needed his supporting framework of psychic stresses to push her forward and onward to her full Unfolding.

Besides, he had the uncomfortable feeling that despite all his manipulation and preparation, despite the drugs and all the effort he'd expended on directing her to this point... in a way, at the very end *she* had seduced *him*. Had taken control at the key moment.

He had to stay strong. Had to remember she was so very self-centered, so very selfish – except when it pleased her.

So very appealing.

But wasn't that exactly the danger? He gazed at her clinically, finally seeing her beauty for the trap it was. A trap through which she would gain control, just as she'd tried so many times before. Always, it was a battle with her. Always, a contest of wills. But he was, after all, her creator. The architect of this whole experiment.

Yet see how easily she had overturned his detachment, how nearly she had ensnared him? How long had she been tempting him, after all, flaunting her body, her sexuality? *You* drugged *her; removed her inhibitions*, a small voice cried. Well, perhaps he had... but she *could* have resisted had she wanted. He knew, better than anyone, just how very well she could resist when she *wanted* to.

Indeed, had she not in fact engineered the entire situation exactly that way: by resisting, by making the experiment stall, by *forcing* him to resort to chemical intervention? Was Godsson right, seeing the shadow of the archetypal seductress, Lilith, in her?

He drew back, shakily. For a while, had she not even managed to confuse *him*, preying on his animal urges? As

if that could be enough to sway him for more than a moment! Well, he *had* fallen, yes. Had let his animal urges
take control. Had *let* her seduce him.

Should this get out, it *would* ruin his career. Ruin *him*.

But he would not allow that. The work was too important.

Well, if that was how she wished to play the game, it
would fit nicely with the next, necessary steps.

Perhaps she had even somehow sensed the ordeal she
must soon begin to suffer to reach her full potential. Now
that she had finally Unfolded, he could bring the experiment to a new level of intensity. She was stronger, now,
more resilient.

Yes.

Gently, he eased out of her bed. She made a small
sleepy sound of loss. For a moment, his resolve weakened
as he stared down at her. But then he straightened. He
had to stay in control. *She* was the one who would benefit
most from the experiment, after all.

He left the room.

CHAPTER 38

It was now five months after her seventeenth – and as usual, uncelebrated – birthday. Only a month until the summer solstice. But Harmon had decided it was time for her to start meeting people, interacting with strangers. The last time he'd taken her anywhere had been only their second expedition, what was it, two years – no, *three* years ago? Hmm. While it was far simpler to leave her here when he visited the city, perhaps that was a false convenience. Raising her almost entirely in isolation at the Institute could have untoward effects. Suppose she developed a fear of strangers, or crowds? So for today, he had decided they should again venture out into New Francisco. He had planned a steady escalation of contact with other people, culminating in dinner for the two of them at a nightclub.

They set off at 9 a.m for the Golden Gate Park: a gentle introduction. Parklands, much like those the Institute possessed – except this park was much larger, and populated. He himself had been surprised at just how populated it was, even when they first arrived at nine thirty. Joggers, picnickers, groups of people playing various ball games, couples strolling about. How different from even ten years before.

A fresh breeze brought the scent of recently-cut grass. In the distance, a compact robot mower traversed its area-filling path through the grassy areas, patiently stopping when a child ran up to it, before the mother dragged the boy away.

The park brimmed with trees, many of them quite old, surprisingly few freshly planted or transplanted. He pointed out the modern concrete paths, laid to replace those that had either been smashed during the Big One, or shattered by the ice of the Second World Storm at the end of '44. They'd been passing by Stow Lake at the time.

"This whole area remained underwater for five years, from the combined effects of the sea level rise back then and the deluge from the Storm. It would have been much worse, too, had not the Antarctic re-icing not been so well-advanced by then."

Sara giggled, but stopped the instant he frowned at her.

"Don't you mean the *Newtopian* re-icing, Uncle?" she asked, eyes wide.

"Bah! The fool politicians should have *at most* given them a ninety-nine year lease, not-"

At the pleased gleam in her eyes, he stopped himself, realizing she had been baiting him. He took a breath. "I suppose they did have other disasters on their hands, after the collapse of the net and the Second Storm."

"The *net* collapsed? For real? I didn't think it *could*. I thought it was indestructible!"

"We *have* covered this in your History lessons, Leeth."

"Did we? I don't think you ever..."

"Yes. We did. Apparently some Universal Constant wasn't."

She waited, then saw he'd stopped. "Wasn't what?"

"Constant. Something to do with quantum mechanics and how the Packed-light Effect simply stopped working."

He had lost her again, he saw. He also now recalled exactly the same glazed look the last time he had covered this topic. He had noticed that tendency before – her attention seemed much stronger if he could couch such information in dramatic terms: as a collapse, battle, or calamity.

Ah, well.

They continued on, simply enjoying the weather. Now noon, he slumped on a park-bench in the sun, resting.

He wasn't sure *how* it had happened – he'd planned to spend only half an hour or so here – but she'd dragged him backwards and forwards all through the park. It was her infectious enthusiasm, he supposed: her delight had been palpable. Somehow, she had sensed his decision that this was to be a special day for her. And so they had traversed kilometers of the park. She had invented a game of sprinting up to joggers, running alongside or just behind them for a while and then sprinting back to him. He had to smile: somehow the picture of a sheepdog herding sheep was irresistibly summoned to mind each time she did this. The men, for the most part, didn't seem to mind but the female joggers clearly did. Sara – *Leeth*, dammit! – Leeth seemed to enjoy both reactions.

Then she'd spent ten minutes hunting ducks *in* the duck-pond. The docile ducks were disturbed by the unusual occurrence of a human wading amongst them. By the time he had caught up to her, she had already caught one bare-handed and was gleefully on her way out to present it to him. She was quite cross when he made her put it back into the pond. It took wing instantly, of course. Leeth had looked at him reproachfully as it flew away.

After that, she'd wanted to find a swimming pool to rid herself of the smell of the slimy pond water. Fortunately, she was wearing only a thin halter and a pleated miniskirt, all in black. Luckily too, the pond had only been thigh-deep.

Harmon checked his map, and sighed. The pool of course was beyond the other end of the park.

He sighed, as she looked entreatingly at him. Besides, he could hardly take her to the restaurant he had planned if she smelled of duck pond.

-

Disten suspected there was a magical component to the Call. It had taken two years to slowly, uncertainly, identify the New Francisco or Oaklands area as the place where the solution would be found. For a year, now, he had lived quietly in a suburban backwater. Waiting.

And today, at 09:01:13 precisely, interrupting his study of research into means of altering mental states, awareness of the other had flared into awareness.

It had brought him to the northern boundary of the Golden Gate Recreation Center.

Disten's car parked itself. She was in there. Close.

Outside the car, the sunlight was very bright. *Narrow the eyes.* So many things to remember: eyes were easily damaged if exposed too long to too much light. A cost of having total control of the autonomic nervous system.

The car finished locking and Disten moved to enter the park.

"Excuse me, sir. This your vehicle?"

Disten turned. Two officers, one inside and one outside the police vehicle.

This again.

"Yes."

"And your name is?"

"Marc Disten. The registered owner. You have already checked the license and know this. You wonder why the expensive vehicle has suffered damage to its paintwork which has not been repaired.

"The damage is cosmetic. Repairs would take time,

and waste money since a pristine finish merely attracts further assaults. Is there anything else?"

"Well, yes, sir, we *have* had a complaint about this vehicle."

Disten waited.

"Offensive language and indecency."

"That is incorrect. When was the complaint made?"

"Ten minutes ago. Are you claiming you are unaware of the message on the back of your vehicle, Mr Disten?"

"There are numerous scratches on the rear. Has something new been added?" Walking to the rear of the vehicle, an inspection was made. Amongst the indecipherable gouges a new message had been added – 'Kill all Muties,' perhaps – as well as a new abstract diagram consisting mainly of large ellipses and circles.

He pointed to the fresh 'Muties' graffiti. "That is new, as is the diagram."

"Diagram, sir? You mean the enormous dick and pussy, sir?"

"Is it? Ah. This is the penis, yes? And this, the vulva." Disten considered the idea. "Yes. This would be seen as offensive."

"Well, yeah, clever of you to realize that, sir. And I might add, there are parts of the city where that anti-Mutie sentiment would get you into trouble, too. Serious trouble."

Disten thought about that. "Understood. You recommend removal. At the earliest convenience?"

"Well, yeah, Mr Disten, that might be a good idea."

"Do you have a permanent marker pen? Black?"

The officer who had remained in the police car had been shaking her head. At his question, though, she bent down out of sight, then sat up and flung a slim cylinder across the cruiser's roof toward her partner.

Disten caught it and turned, efficiently blacking out the deep score marks. He handed the marker to his interlocutor.

"That should suffice until spray paint can be applied. Is there anything else, officer?"

For long seconds the officer stared at him. Then turned back to his partner, whose expression Disten was unable to read, though she did shrug.

The man echoed that shrug, then turned back to Disten. "No, sir. You have a nice day."

How did the formula go? Ah, yes. "Thank you. You have a nice day also, officer."

Turning, he sensed which direction to proceed. A little further away, and now directly west. Instead of entering the park, he set out toward the path above the coast.

Tired from the long walk, Harmon had failed to tell Leeth she should use the shower facilities first. He hadn't realized his error until she had backed up three steps to jump the stone wall, plunging into the refurbished baths seconds later. He winced again, remembering the ring of detritus she'd left floating in the water, and the angry face of the female lifeguard as she stormed up.

He had had to apologize, pay a fee, and Leeth was still ejected from the pool, much to her disgust. They'd left quickly.

On the way back she had decided her clothes would dry faster, off, and somehow he had found himself wringing out her halter and skirt and carrying them while she soaked up the sun in just her bra and bikini bottom. She'd been fascinated by the rugged, dark coastline, and the surging waves, and for a while he let her explore as they made their way around the low cliffs before the terrain forced them to climb back up. With some relief, on his part: he would not want to be caught there when the tide came back in. It had only been a short walk directly south, to re-enter the park proper once more.

There, she had discovered a group playing baseball. Now dry, she had talked her way into the game; somehow even talked *him* into joining her. He'd had to prod her into donning her now-dry clothes first, though. That reverse striptease had certainly pleased the boys in the group.

He shut his eyes against the sun, smiling at the memory of her feral grin, her fiercely poised 'attack' on the first ball pitched to her. The young man, 'Skeet', had been clearly attracted to Leeth, much to the annoyance of his girlfriend. Knowing she was a novice, since he had just had to explain the basics to her, Skeet had pitched a gentle ball to her. The ball, Harmon recalled with delight, had almost taken the boy's head off. If he hadn't ducked....

Leeth had been fascinated by it all, especially the team-work. At that point, however, he had sensed potential trouble. He did *not* want his Huntress turning into just another team player. Besides, he was close to exhausted. So they had left, the sound of a developing argument fading behind them as they moved away.

Harmon let Leeth drag him right across the park before he decided she was far enough from the attraction of the group to allow him a short rest. They reached a quiet hollow with another pond, and together moved down the bank. Above, a willow draped its cool green shade across the ill-kept grass and algae-scummed water.

Completely exhausted, he sank down on a convenient, shaded park bench.

"I'm just going to catch my breath, Leeth. We'll hunt up some food shortly, so don't go wandering off." He closed his eyes in blissful relaxation.

CHAPTER 39

As Harmon and Leeth had receded into the distance, neither had been aware of the drama that played out soon after. Maybe if Skeet's eyes hadn't followed the departing figures so carefully; or maybe if the expression on his face hadn't been so obvious; or maybe if it just hadn't changed so completely when he turned and saw that his girlfriend had seen it, then it all would have been different and Skeet might have seen his next day.

But the blazing argument that followed broke up the game in seconds, their friends carefully fading away to leave the two lovers to it. Finally, Skeet's girlfriend stalked off.

He was still standing there, alone and scowling darkly across the park when a large stranger quietly approached.

The boy ripped his attention from his ex-girlfriend's departing back. "What the shunt you want, spamboy?" he blazed.

The man just stood there. Not moving. Then his expression altered, in a series of jerky changes that left his mouth stretched into a shape that didn't actually work as a smile. Like a robot might do. Skeet's hot anger disappeared like water sucked into parched ground. The youth shuddered and took a step back.

The man's head moved back and forth, as if scenting the air. Then the pale blue eyes focused back on Skeet, and the man opened his mouth to speak.

Then he paused, very deliberately swallowing and moistening his lips. As if preparing long-disused equipment.

Skeet watched, hypnotized, his own head shaking slowly from side to side, refusing to acknowledge an unconscious premonition of danger.

"The girl was with you?" the man asked.

Skeet took another step back, but with shocking suddenness the man was beside him, gripping his upper arm painfully. Face to face, Skeet's protests froze. Intuition screamed that some kind of human puppet now held him trapped with just one hand. His brain urged him to run, to get away, but his feet wouldn't move. Skeet felt cold, like he'd just jumped from summer to a chill mid-winter's day.

"The girl has tainted you. The taint can easily be cleansed."

Skeet moaned.

The fear irritated Disten. There was time: the girl had been in the area now for hours. One hand clasped around the boy's neck, silencing him.

-

"Skeet! Hey, Skeet! Where are you?"

Two of his friends, worried, were quartering the area they'd last seen him.

"I don't get it. Why wouldn't he answer his Link?"

"It's taking calls?"

"Look, I'm not stupid. I *can* tell the difference between a null link an' one that's just not being answered."

The two had now climbed the hill, scuffing through the occasional thin drift of leaves scattered between the tall trunks overlooking the ballpark. Somewhere nearby, the ethereal strains of *The Zombie Waltz* could be heard. The two exchanged a slow look.

"That's Skeet's Link."

"It's coming from those bushes over there."

"Skeet! Wake up, man, we've been looking for you!"

There was no answer. Then at last the *Waltz* stopped. Suddenly it seemed very quiet. The boy who'd called looked down at his wristcomm, which had finally rejected the address as not answering.

"It feel cold to you here?"

The other ignored him, moving with reluctant steps toward the bushes, and his friend watched tensely.

"Oh, Mother."

He stepped back a pace, then another, making futile shooing gestures behind him with one hand. He spun around, and his friend took a step back at the expression on the shocked white face. "Call the cops, Berry. Skeet's dead!"

"Are- are you sure? Maybe he's-"

"His head's on smekken backwards, man." His voice cracked. "Just call the smekken cops!"

CHAPTER 40

Sara watched Harmon settle himself down onto the bench seat in the sun and close his eyes. "I'm just going to catch my breath, Leeth. We'll hunt up some food shortly, so don't go wandering off."

"No, Uncle, I won't wander off." She never just *wandered*. She wondered why he wanted to rest. He wasn't *really* tired, was he? She cocked her head to one side as she watched him, thinking.

She was sure there was a reason he had decided they should spend a day 'out.' A test, maybe?

Just then, a jogger entered their clearing. Tall, healthy, tanned. His white teeth flashed in appreciation of her figure, and he whistled as he eyed her up and down. But there was a strange look in his eyes she didn't like. Like he was hungry. Like *she* was prey for *him!*

A weird prickle, a strange heat, flushed through her, ending in a fine trembling in her hands. Her fingertips felt weird.

The man powered past and up the low rise leading out, glancing back at her one last time like he wanted to eat her.

One last time.

She felt a surge of... heat? Turning, eyes tracking him as the idea hit her, the burn flared stronger. With a wolfish smile, Sara padded after him.

Hunting.

"Keepie." An urgent voice in his ear. "Keepie!"

The figure before him blurred with his dream... something prowling through a jungle? Something disturbing; familiar. He blinked.

"Keepie!"

He sat up, disoriented, rubbing his eyes.

"I have a surprise for you!"

He squinted at her silhouette, the sun blinding. But even so, what he saw looked wrong. He suddenly realized she was naked. And practically vibrating with suppressed excitement.

"Hold out your hand and shut your eyes, and I will give you a big surprise," she chanted the children's rhyme hoarsely.

Something was terribly wrong.

He held out his hand. Through the slits of his eyelids, a

moment before she dropped the repellently wet *thing* into it he recognized the organ. *Gods, it was* hot! His own heart stopped. No. She couldn't have...?

Just then, he heard a terrified scream in the distance. It went on and on. Leeth only grinned as she turned partly toward it. As his eyes adjusted to the light, he realized another thing that was wrong. Her front was *drenched* in blood. The screaming went on. His mind shut down. Leeth spun back to him, bursting with the anticipation of his joy. He looked down at the soft heavy thing he held in his hand. Somehow, he knew the heart was human.

Shit. Oh. Shit.

"I Hunted him, Keepie! I Followed, I Shadowed, I Pounced! He was strong, but I was stronger. I Killed him. Oh Keepie, it was *wonderful!*" She whooped with joy; did a sort of dance.

He stared at her in disbelief for long seconds. He looked down at the heart, frozen. She misinterpreted his gesture.

"Then, I realized you'd want me to bring you a trophy, like with my first Hunt.

"I thought of bringing you an easier bit to get off, but then I thought I should bring you back the proper thing, even if it *was* harder."

His mind struggled to cope. He had raised her, trained her, *striven* to mold her magically into the essence of the Huntress. Yet why was it only now that he understood the natural consequence of this? He had made her into a killer.

He looked at her with something not far from dread.

"I found a stick, and broke it to make a sharp edge."

She noticed, at last, his paralyzed reaction. She reached out and gently touched the heart. "I didn't hurt it, even though it wasn't easy to get out. I didn't know ribs would be so springy and hard to break. I didn't damage it, though, see," and she turned it over, reverently, wetly, in his hand.

His gorge rose, but he swallowed, forcing it down. Found his voice, with difficulty.

"Did anyone see you, Leeth?"

"No," she said scornfully. "Of course not."

The screaming had stopped, a strangely dissociated

part of his mind noted. They'd be searching for the killer, soon. He looked at her, looked at the grass around her, expecting to see a pool of blood. There was none. He looked closer at the ground. In fact, there wasn't any blood at all. He looked around, expecting to see a trail, and a body. Belatedly, he noticed the blood was *smeared* all over her face and upper body.

She wiped herself down, he thought numbly. *Afterward, she took the time to wipe herself down.*

She licked her fingers. With a horrified start he realized she was licking the blood from them. His stomach rose again. Suddenly, he remembered the thing he held. His hand shook as panic started to build. How would they get rid of it? For long seconds his thoughts spun in all directions. He took a grip on himself.

"Leeth, do you know what will happen now?"

"We'll have a Feast? I can collect firewood."

Mentally, he recoiled, stomach churning, and he barely held his gorge. But even as he did so, he noted the startling simplicity of her thought processes. He shook himself.

"No, Leeth. There won't be time."

She looked puzzled. Then disappointed. Then hurt.

"There won't be time because the police will be here shortly. They'll be looking for a killer. When they find her they'll arrest her. She'll be taken to jail-"

She started to protest, but he spoke over her.

"Taken to jail, before being *executed*." He wound down, panting as if from physical exertion. All those years, all his work. To be so foolishly wasted. He began to get angry.

"But why, Keepie? The police only arrest people who do bad things."

At first the sheer lunacy of the remark stunned him into silence. And then, he realized that from her point of view, all she had done was kill one of the gray people: one of the 'sheep.' That never, in all those years, had he let her be given the slightest clue that killing was wrong. Of course he hadn't. How could she embody the archetype if she thought that? He pressed his hands against his temples. *Think!*

"It's the Law, Leeth. There are rules that say you

mustn't-

"I mean, that if you kill anyone at all, the police have to find you, arrest you, and in the end, kill *you*."

"But...." She was silent a moment. "Even the *gray* people? Does the Law say you're not allowed to even kill the *gray* people?"

"Even them."

"But why? Why protect the sheep? What's the point?"

"Ahh." He wracked his brains for the correct answer for the Huntress. "It's not meant to be *easy*, Leeth. If it were easy, then hunting could be done by the soft, the slow, or the weak. So there are guards and obstacles, and you have to pit yourself in challenge against the protectors: the police."

Her eyes shone. "So they're hunting *me* now! And I have to prove I'm better!"

"That's right. You have to hide what you've done. Pretend you don't know about it. Get rid of any incriminating evidence."

She looked puzzled.

"Like being covered in blood," he pointed out. Then added, "or carrying a still-warm human heart. You need to wash. I think another visit to a pond is in order."

She grinned.

"And tell me, where are your clothes?"

"I took them off while I stalked him. They're not very far. About half way."

The heart, they buried.

Harmon's wish for no one to find them while she bathed and dressed appeared to have been granted. He now sat on the edge of another park bench while Leeth dressed in the sun, shaking her head about and rubbing her fingers through her hair to try to finish drying it.

Just as he decided it was enough, that they could leave, she stopped and jogged over to him.

"Two people coming. Big."

Damn, he thought. *It might look suspicious if we hurry off.* With an effort, he composed himself, waiting.

And waiting. Still no one came. Nor could he hear anyone, either. He looked at her, doubtfully.

"Are you sure?"

"Yeah. They'll be here real soon."

"How-" He stopped himself. Now was not the time to investigate.

"Remember," he Suggested, reiterating his advice, "You're just Sara. We're out in the park for some relaxation. You know nothing about anything unusual happening. You're a little worried by the scream."

He was surprised by just how well, how thoroughly, the spell affected her. In fact, he watched what transpired with something like shock. Even her aura changed! Noting her total unawareness of him, her inward focus, he quickly followed the first spell with a mindmeld.

Probing her mind, he saw what had happened, and gradually relaxed. He had framed her Unfolding as a marking of her transition to adulthood. For reasons that weren't clear to him, by giving her a new, adult name to signify that, it had changed her conception of herself in some fundamental way. His Suggestion just now had interacted with that. He watched as 'Leeth' was packed away and 'Sara' returned.

He felt a curious sense of loss; the return of the happy young child, Sara, made him realize *that* person was now lost to him. Lost through his own actions; slipping through his fingers as irrevocably as if she had fallen from a cliff.

With a shock, it dawned on him that he was reacting like a father who had just realized his little girl had grown up.

Yet despite reasoning that out, it still hurt.

He felt he hardly knew this new young woman, his feral creation. With *Sara* standing now beside him, he felt... at ease. A certain *tension* had dissipated.

Just how much had she changed? In her mind, he saw that Sara was still there: but Sara was a child. The person hidden now, beneath, was a woman.

He hoped-

Footsteps, trying to be silent, ended his introspection. He looked speculatively at the innocent young girl, Sara, as two men entered the clearing. Police. One, built like a professional football player. The other – built just plain *fat*. He shifted his perception to the Imaginal plane. Both men were tense, worried. Alert. Some dead sections in

Footballer's aura, typical of cyber augmentation. As their eyes fell on Sara he saw the increase in interest signaled by their auras. Then, with a mental start, he realized one of them was a mage. The fat one. Saw the shift in Imaginal pattern as the other realized that he himself was, too. Saw the fat one murmur to the big one as they approached.

"He says you're a mage, Uncle," Leeth – no, Sara – whispered to him. *How did she-? Could she* hear *them? How on Earth-?* The two citycops spread out a little, the big one drawing his gun. Harmon didn't have to fake anxiety as he spoke.

"Officers? What's the matter?" In inspiration, he put a worried expression on his face and looked around. Then back at them. "Are we in danger? Is there some creature loose in the park?"

The fat man's eyes narrowed. "Now, what makes you think *that*, sir?"

Sara spoke up. "We heard a woman screaming. Uncle cast a spell and could see her, off in the distance. There was a man on the ground, near her."

"A spell, sir?"

"A simple clairvoyance spell, officer."

The man had a truth spell running, Harmon realized, with a sinking feeling. At least, though, the faint trace of Suggestion he'd cast on Sara had been swallowed up inside her aura, as usual. Odd, really, now he thought about it. Could that signify the beginnings of some kind of resistance to it? No, inconceivable at this point, considering how often he'd used it on her and the Repetition Effect. Unless it was a consequence of her Unfolding? Had the change in her aura-

"You're a mage then, sir?"

He brought his attention back to the serious matter at hand. "Yes, officer. Dr Harmon."

"A doctor? And you saw a man's body, but made no attempt to go to him and heal him?"

"My doctorate is in Psychology I'm afraid, officer. I would have been of no use to the unfortunate fellow." Of course not – Leeth had taken his heart. He couldn't have healed him if he'd *wanted* to.

"Do you know anything about the murder, doctor?" the man asked, straight out.

Harmon had hoped the fellow would rely on the truth spell. He shrugged apologetically while mentally crossing his fingers.

"Again, I'm sorry. I was asleep at the time. I had dozed off in the sun. My ward here dragged me all over the park this morning, and I was quite exhausted." Which was all, quite literally, true.

The officer looked at him a moment longer then turned to Sara. Sized her up. Harmon could almost hear him thinking, 'No, no way this little chick could have done *that*.' The Sara persona, Harmon was pleased to note with a quick Imaginal scan, was well to the fore.

"And you, girl...?"

"Sara, sir."

"- Sara: do *you* know anything about this murder?"

Harmon suppressed an exhalation of relief. *Sara knew nothing. Leeth, on the other hand....*

"No, sir."

The mage-cop nodded. Just then his commlink buzzed, and he stepped away to take the call while his bigger and taller partner noted their Citizen IDs. Until then the fellow hadn't spoken a word, but the alertness in his eyes, the grimly-locked jaw, and his slightly-narrowed eyes whenever he looked at 'Sara' made Harmon suspect this one was the more dangerous of the two.

"You're fukken jokin'? *Another* one?" The fat mage listened a little longer, before turning back to them. He and his partner exchanged a look.

"You got their details?"

A nod, a few more hurried questions, a final warning they might be called on to give evidence, then they were off.

Harmon watched them go, letting out a heartfelt sigh of relief once they were out of sight.

"What did they mean, 'another one,' Leeth?"

She looked at him, confused. "Leeth? That- that's me, isn't it?"

His own experience certainly confirmed the Repetition Effect. The more often you successfully cast a spell on the same person, the easier it became; a fresh reason for the popular fear and distrust of mages. He casually removed the Suggestion, and she blinked and shook herself. He had to repeat the question.

She shrugged. "They just found another body in the park."

He winced. "Leeth, did you...?"

"No, I came straight back to you after my hunt." Suddenly her eyes widened in dismay. "Was I supposed to kill more than one, Keepie?"

He closed his eyes in relief, though a shiver ran through him at her question. "No, Leeth, one was more than I expected."

She grinned and took his hand. "What'll we do now?"

He gently disengaged. "I think it is time we returned home."

"Oh, no! Can't we just-"

Harmon guided her firmly, still arguing, toward the nearest exit.

-

Marc Disten did not arrive for over five minutes, then simply stood, head sweeping smoothly across the empty scene and then back again. She was heading swiftly north. So swiftly, she had to be in a vehicle. Unfortunately, her exit point was a considerable distance from the place where the Ferrari was parked. Even at a run, it would give her something like a ten minute head start. It was good that the sense of her location seemed little affected by distance. She would be found, no matter how fast she fled.

But cruising through the Sonoma Valley thirty three minutes later, the connection abruptly died. Disten pulled the battered Quattropotenza off onto the shoulder of the highway. Inside, expressionless, the large man sat thinking.

The abrupt cessation of the Call reinforced the new idea, that a magical effect was involved. If so, what had interfered? Living earth blocked magic: the world's stock exchanges were now kept underground, to prevent magical attacks that would halt trading. An underground dwelling, then? Or some other form of barrier?

Disten considered. In hindsight, spending the minutes it had required to try to Perfect the boy had been an error of judgment. That effort had failed and little had been learned.

She was very near now, though. There would be further opportunities. Time was irrelevant.

CHAPTER 41

Later that afternoon in the park, Detective Adam Garland stood to one side, giving his overweight partner space as they watched the specialist manifest the spirit of the Parklands. Garland noted Berlusconi's heavy jowls twist in distaste as the other practitioner got to work. He knew his partner distrusted shamans and their 'altered states of consciousness'; considered it a mere excuse to drug up and space out with magic.

Garland had had to break himself of the habit of referring to them all as mages, discovering it was the quickest way to send Berlusconi into a spitting rant. 'Mages work from theory. We construct consistent, reproducible spells. Not fukken hit-or-miss *artworks!*' Even now, Berlusconi's expression soured at the other practitioner's success as soil, grass, leaves and bark snaked together, weaving a framework for the patchwork thing that suddenly shivered with life.

But as it finished coalescing into visible sight, its inhuman shape made Garland's heart sink. Looked like the shaman's guess would be right.

Still, he had to try. He stepped forward as the city shaman turned to him and nodded. "It's ready. It'll hear you, and answer you. But try to keep it simple, okay?"

Garland nodded, turning his attention to the disturbingly-mobile form of the plant-thing swaying patiently before him. "Did you sense a murder this afternoon?"

The thing shifted confusedly. The shaman spoke, at the same time offering his thoughts to the spirit for inspection. "A killing of a human."

The disturbed motions settled. "A human died."

"Yes. A healthy man, jogging on the path that loops behind the picnic area."

Its form twisted and shifted further. "A human died, under today's sun. Under the shade of the oak..." the speech rustled out in words that faded into a dance of sweeping branches, somehow suggesting a sad struggle. Then it fell almost motionless, and he had the impression it could sense his effort to interpret its motions. It spoke again. "The oak of lightnings."

"Ah. Thank you, I'll confirm that later." Yes, that sounded like the first murder site. "Can you describe the killer?"

A long period of confused rustling followed. "A human," it offered, at last. "Very."

Very? What did that mean? He left that, for now.

"A man or a woman? Male, or female?"

It shifted uncomfortably. "It carried no small humans."

"Young, old?"

"Very new."

He frowned. "A child, you mean?"

Again, it shifted. "Fresh. New."

Garland sighed. This was getting them nowhere. But he persisted. "What did you mean, 'very'? A normal human?"

"Very human. Healthy."

Shit. So they were looking for someone who was very human, healthy, and 'new'? That narrowed it down to maybe half the city.

"Was it alone? I mean, just the victim and the killer?"

"No. Many were there. Much activity. Much noise."

He frowned, then realized even its sense of time wasn't the same as his. His eyes met those of the shaman. Maybe it *was* hopeless.

"What about the other human who died in your Park today, near the baseball pitch, between the sun when it was highest, and now: what can you tell me about that?"

The motion of the leaves slowed. "No other human died."

There was a long pause, and from the corner of his eye Garland saw his partner's face flush red, belying the deceptively friendly tone that he *started* with. "You really are a complete, one hundred percent nilspec waste of dirt, aren't you?" The spirit of course, seeing Berlusconi's aura, shrank back even as the shaman put out a restraining hand. At the look he received from the detective, the shaman lowered it just as quickly.

"Berlusconi." Garland stopped, hunting for words that wouldn't rile his partner further. "Quit scaring the spirit."

His partner bristled but clamped his mouth shut, and they went through the motions.

A weary hour later, a good distance away at the second crime scene, that of the murdered boy, the fresh invocation of the Park's spirit simply failed. They'd come here despite the shaman's protests that mere proximity to the scene of the second murder wouldn't tell them anything more. Strangely though, the magic hadn't worked at all.

Two uniformed officers stood now at the foot of the wooded hillside. Above them, shadows clawed down through the trees in the afternoon sunlight toward the three figures beyond the police marker tapes. Garland wasn't a Sensitive, but even he felt there was something wrong here. Not eerie, or creepy, though. Something somehow worse. As if something subtle but important had been stripped away. Hollowed out.

The three looked at one another. The corpse of the dead youth at their feet, the failure of the shaman's magic, the vague sense of winter: Garland saw it had them all on edge.

The shaman stared down the hill. "Let's move down lower, I want to try again."

Garland's large-bellied partner stared at the shaman while chewing his tobacco substitute, clearly trying to hold his temper. He spat on the ground. "Didn' you just say it didn' matter where in the park you did it, so long as you invoked your little dirt-buddy inside the Park's boundaries?"

But the shaman stubbornly stood his ground, and they trudged back down the hill.

Simply moving away from the murder site should have made no difference, Garland knew. So in a way it was even more disturbing when the spirit did at last appear. Though it looked somehow smaller. Smaller and *neater*.

From the expressions on their faces, none of this made sense to either the mage or the shaman. It was the *same spirit* – it had to be, it was the spirit of the Golden Gate Park; the shaman had summoned it with the same force; it was only an hour later. The spirit should not have changed so much. Garland saw the fear in the shaman's eyes. That would weaken and confuse him: not a good state in which to be invoking spirits. Garland's teeth felt on edge. This was all wrong.

And it only got worse when the questioning began.

"Did you see the murder of the man on the hill above us?"

They waited so long the shaman repeated his question.

"There is no hill."

Garland watched his partner-mage and the shaman exchange disbelieving looks.

"The hill right here. *Your* hill. With the dead human male a short way up it."

The spirit looked around vaguely.

It was too much for Berlusconi. "Up there, goddamn it!" he shouted, stabbing a finger up into the woods.

The fleshy mage's futile outburst visibly settled the shaman. "Up there," he repeated for the spirit. As the invoker, he was the one with an actual link to the entity. Still it seemed confused.

"Follow me, then," the shaman commanded. "I'll take you there." He began climbing the slope while it marched, rustling after him, the other two following along behind it. Part way up, some hint made the shaman turn to watch the spirit – just as it fell apart into a spiral of collapsing dirt and leaves.

Berlusconi, immediately behind the summoned spirit of the Park, nearly stumbled as he jumped aside to avoid treading in the stuff that had formed it, as if he thought the detritus might be poisonous. "What in the name of fuksake just happened?"

The shaman looked stunned. "It- Did you banish it?"

Berlusconi opened his mouth, then, with effort, took a grip on himself. "No. Because that would be stupid." He paused, and Garland watched as he visibly counted to ten. "It looked like it just fell apart. How about we try that again, more carefully, eh?"

The next time it fell apart even sooner.

The time after that, the shaman could not invoke it at all.

While his overweight colleague indulged his feelings in a long and creative stream of swearing, Garland turned to the uniformed men. "We're finished here. Go ahead and collect this body, too – we'll have to hope forensics can tell us something. Magic certainly isn't going to."

He moved off, deep in thought, his fleshy partner still inventing creative curses under his breath, while the shaman trailed numbly behind them.

For some reason, though, Garland's mind kept going back to the earlier two. Dr Alex Harmon and the girl, Sara.

Especially Sara.

Why had her hair been damp?

CHAPTER 42

That night, in the privacy of Harmon's rooms, they had another Feast. Finest cut prime fillet steak. He watched in wonder as she demolished hers. A large portion. Just as well he knew her appetite and had ordered accordingly.

"I don't know where all that food goes. If you're not careful you'll get fat."

She paused, a large chunk of very rare meat raised on her fork. She closed her mouth abruptly.

"Am I fat?" She put her fork down, looking suddenly distressed.

"No. I simply said if you're not careful you will get fat."

"So I *am* fat."

"No. Leeth, you are *not* fat. Your BMI was fine last month, and I'm sure it will be fine this month too. The weight seems to be muscle, not fat."

"You're saying I'm chunky, then."

"No! Muscle is denser and weighs more than fat. Your figure, in fact, is close to ideal for a girl your age."

"My breasts are too small."

He almost snorted his wine.

"Do you think they'll grow?"

He blinked, slowly, and at last said, "At the rate they have been growing over the last few years, I would say they might grow a little larger."

"Oh! You've noticed!"

He looked away, disturbed. He had noticed. He had noticed, indeed. But despite her continued provocations – conscious and unconscious – his resolve still held firm, however.

So far.

Certainly, it was not made any easier by the changes in her behavior. She had become more familiar, more physically affectionate since that night: often taking his arm, or stealing a quick hug before breaking free. Nor had he managed to harden his heart sufficiently to pour cold water on those small displays of affection. He found he almost welcomed them, strangely enough.

Leeth suddenly leaned forward. "Look, Keepie! Vid: mute off."

Both turned from the dining table, ignoring the remains of the repast as the projection enlarged and brightened, and the volume rose.

"... some new monster, roaming the idyllic Golden Gate Recreational Area? I'm now crossing live for a virtual meeting with metropolice spokesman David Burke, in a full-sense render of the actual murder scenes, provided for us by Tik Tek WorldWeave™. Whether you leave the world behind or weave a better one, you can always trust Tik Tek. Chief Inspector Burke, what can you tell MetroWatch about these shocking murders?"

The perky newscaster gestured around at the two dramatically mutilated corpses at their feet, labeled with translucent *'artist's impression'* lettering.

Leeth's face fell. "Which one is 'sposed to be mine, Keepie?"

"Be quiet. I would imagine it's the larger one, with the rib-cage artistically folded back."

Burke was middle-aged and jowly, and spared only a moment's disgusted look at the virtual corpses. "Frankly, Bobbi, there are some puzzling aspects to this afternoon's double murder. While both deaths were violent in the extreme, and the injuries were consistent with someone of great strength – and I don't want to single out any particular human subspecies – there are some strange differences.

"We've found traces of DNA from a female human on the first victim, along with fragments of wood – it appears a sharpened stake was used in the killing."

"That's my one, Keepie! But I didn't use the stick for-"

"Leeth, be quiet. This is important."

"We've also found traces of DNA from a male, Caucasian, who we believe applied the killing force to the second victim. Included amongst the other DNA contaminants on that victim, however, were some from the suspected female murderess."

"Fascinating, chief inspector. Sounds like they were working together. Presumably you have the identities of the killers?"

"Bobbi, we only have DNA samples from thirty-five percent of people who *have* CIDs-"

"What's sids, Keepie?"

"Citizen IDs. Hush."

"... and less than twenty percent from the CID-less scu- uh, from the *disenfranchised...*"

"What's dis-enFrench-?"

"Scum. Now *hush!*"

"... however, we do have one or two leads which we will be following up on shortly."

"Our artists have done a few sample renders of possible creatures, Chief. Would you care to...?"

Burke made his escape before the monster parade could begin, and Harmon ordered the volume down and frowned at her. "Leeth, I asked you if you had killed 'the other one' the police mentioned. You said you had not." He gestured at the vid. "But traces of your DNA were found on the second victim. How do you explain that?"

She shrugged. "I don't know."

"The truth, Leeth. Did you kill anyone else today?"

The words seemed surreal the moment he'd spoken them. Ignoring the feeling, he focused on her. On her aura.

"No." She frowned at him, puzzled. "Why did you ask me again? Why would I lie about it?"

Yes, why indeed? He began massaging his forehead. *What have I created?*

"Uncle? What's wrong?"

"Well, leaving aside the disturbing coincidence that your DNA was found on both murder victims, there is a much greater problem. Your DNA is now on record, linked to these killings. Apparently your own Citizen ID record doesn't contain a DNA sample, or you would now be in prison."

"Oh."

"Yes. 'Oh.' It also means that should your DNA be entered into the system at some future date, you will be linked to this killing and arrested."

"Oh. Can we change it?"

He wasn't sure which she meant − her DNA, or her records − but the answer was the same in either case. He sighed and shook his head, tiredly. "No, Leeth. No, we can't."

He felt, though, he was overlooking something. He drummed his fingers against the arm of the seat, chasing some horrible thought.

Oh, no.

The two police officers. Having to give their identities. They would come here and take a sample from Leeth, and that would be that. All over.

He sat staring dully into space. All his work ruined.

He was unsure how long he'd been sitting there before the decision filtered through to his consciousness. They would have to leave at once. Now, tonight.

His thoughts seemed to be moving in slow motion. *Shock*, he supposed, feeling disoriented. He forced himself to stand.

As he did, his comm link buzzed on the bench by the portable oven in his kitchenette. "Sanders here, Dr Harmon. Pick up. You have visitors who would like to talk to you. Police."

Harmon staggered, looking across in shock at Leeth.

She was grinning, excited. "Wow. This should be vish!"

"*Vish?*"

"Dr Harmon? Pick up, please."

He headed over to the Link.

"You know. Vicious." She screwed up her face in thought, then her eyes lit up. "We'll have to go on the run, Keepie! After I kill these ones they'll send more, won't they?" She clapped her hands together.

He stared at her in dismay, then gestured her to silence as he picked up the Link. "I heard you, Director." His mind seemed to start working again. "I imagine it's in relation to an incident today in the Golden Gate Park?" He nodded at the answer. "In which case I assume the gentlemen would also like to question Sara?"

He held up one hand to quell the outburst which his private use of her 'child name' always provoked.

"Your office? Certainly, we'll be up directly."

He cut the link, staring at Leeth who watched him, head cocked to one side.

"Do you have a plan, Keepie?"

"The Director will give us privacy if I request it. If the police have not sent a mage, I may be able to adjust their memories. Just don't kill anyone unless I say the word."

He stopped, barely believing the words that had just come from his own mouth. Leeth watched him closely, he saw, as she nodded with excited understanding.

His mind struggled through molasses as he desperately tried to think of a way out of the trap that had closed around them both. This was impossible, a nightmare. But all he said was, "Just remember you have to pretend to be Sara, Leeth. An innocent and harmless young girl."

But he dared not Suggest that – if worse came to worst, he would need Leeth, not Sara, at his side.

But not at his back. Never at his back.

CHAPTER 43

He very nearly ordered Leeth to attack, the moment he stepped into Sanders's room. The Director sat rigidly upright, but Harmon's attention had locked on his visitors.

The same two officers from the park. That could not be good.

The one he had thought looked like a footballer loomed even larger in the confines of the office – almost two meters tall. And studying the ribbons of deadness in his aura up close, he had been engineered with some combination of muscle augmentation, deep neural lacing, and sub-dermal armoring.

The other was the same fat mage who had questioned them in the park. Now though, the energized shapes of his aura snapped from one configuration to the next – but always folding hyperactively around a general pattern of readiness. Some kind of reflex-enhancement spell, presumably. The two also maintained a good separation, bracketing Leeth and himself.

There was no way Leeth could tackle the cybered officer, and somehow Harmon sensed the heavy mage had a whole range of combat magic at his fingertips. *We should have run*, he thought, sickly.

The man-mountain, *Detective Garland*, Harmon read from his badge, spoke. "Dr Harmon. Sara. I have been authorized to take a DNA sample for comparative evidence in a homicide inquiry." Perched on the Director's desk, testing the load-bearing strength of the composite material, the man indicated a diagnostic unit resting at his side.

Professor Sanders sat stiffly at his desk, the night pressing up black and hard against the large window behind him. His normally kind face looked almost coldly on them, his Imaginal form compressed in shapes of disappointment and emotional pain.

"Sara. Please press your fingertip to the sampler."

She held back, moving toward Garland while avoiding the unit, as if afraid it might leap up and bite her. Harmon saw the man subtly tense, certain he'd attack if she got too close – but in *her* aura he read simple excitement, fascination, and genuine attraction. Nor did he have to imagine the expression on her face – eyes wide, alight, lips parted. Presumably it was the reason the warrior allowed her so close, even allowed Leeth to place one hand flat on his chest, gently kneading the musculature while staring in fascinated dread at the diagnostic machine. Either that, or the man was that certain he could deal with her, despite suspecting her capabilities from the body in the Park.

He saw Leeth's arousal spike higher, and found his own teeth clench together for some reason as she moved still closer, nestling her small body up against Garland's muscled torso. "How can that little thing hold everybody's DNA?"

The man, clearly expecting her to explode into action, frowned down at her. Gently detaching her hand, he casually lifted her away, turning and setting her to face the unit. With her back now to him he looked suspiciously at Harmon. "It doesn't. It measures yours, and compares that to central records. Place your finger on the oval marking, Sara."

Harmon watched her half turn back toward the man, staring up into Garland's face, searching, before turning back to the device.

Harmon tried to force himself to relax as Leeth finally stepped forward, her aura coiling fluidly around her. Something in it reminded him of a cat slowly switching its tail from side to side.

Pressing her finger to the unit, she leaned sideways slightly toward the man. *No! She was going to attack!* The fat mage's aura sharpened, suggesting he'd just reached the same conclusion, even as the larger fellow tensed. Harmon tried to think frantically of a spell, some Suggestion that might help.

His desperate gaze passed over Professor Sanders, and for just a moment, he thought the man was smiling.

The DNA tester chimed a pleasant negative, and froze the room.

For seconds no one moved, or spoke.

The politely-red LED flashed once, twice, three times....

Caught in the moment before leaping, Leeth teetered, straightening only awkwardly. Beside her, the subliminal hum of the cybered officer abruptly stopped. Leeth turned around to Harmon, her expression almost comical as surprise fought carefully-crafted innocence.

He was just as confused as she, though. How in the name of all logic had *that* happened? Could the machine be faulty? He looked at Sanders, but the fellow now appeared simply oblivious to the high drama that had just played out right in front of him.

The desk groaned as the man-mountain twisted heavily around to stare at the unit. Its light flashed serenely on, off, on. He blinked, slowly. Across from him, the plump mage swore. "Goddamn," he breathed. "Negative match."

Harmon met Detective Garland's narrowed glare as the large man ostensibly spoke to Sara. "You won't mind if we run that test again. And take a blood sample back to the precinct for more careful testing."

The look he gave Harmon when the two finally left clearly said *this isn't over*.

CHAPTER 44

Tens of kilometers south, the youth watched with a smug air as his Ghost system signaled a second query against the centrally-altered datum. He opened a link to Eagle, who appeared to have been expecting the call.

"Done?"

"Sure. Incidentally, he did try it a second time, like you said."

"Good work, Nelson. Please shift her DNA key into your four hourly sweep set."

The boy grimaced. "I'd hav'ta drop something to do that. Those sweeps're already taking ninety percent of Ghost's idle capacity. And what's the point? I already changed the data for the police's sample. It'll never match."

"Checking only daily for her DNA being entered into the system leaves too large a window for... *other* problems to develop at present. Drop some other scheduled check and use that slot for hers. The hantavirus one, say. There's no real reason not to let the CDC act as first line of defense for that: it *is* their job, after all, not ours."

Nelson nodded. "So who is she, boss man?"

Eagle considered for several seconds, before deciding a careful answer could be beneficial. "Our records have data following her admission to an orphanage, her adoption, DNA samples, and so forth. On the public record you should find only her name and place of residence."

"So, what; you're saying you had somebody else erase her records?"

Eagle didn't reply.

Nelson snorted. "You should'a had me do it. Oh. Before my time, right? I betcha Ghost and I could dig up something."

"Even you, Nelson, would not be able to find anything," Eagle said.

The youth bristled. Which meant that now, it had become a personal challenge, as Eagle had known it would. "But do feel free to try, if it makes you feel any better. If you turn up something, let me know."

The boy thought for a while. "Why've you got DNA *samples* of her, though? Gonna grow some clones've her or something?"

"That would be expensive, Nelson. Not to mention untidy." Eagle smiled smoothly. "Keep all this to yourself please, for now. Need to know."

The boy grinned: another secret from *Mother* and *Father*. Chill. "What about the Institute? Who's this 'G' character that seems to be freaking everyone out? And what's it got to do with the *Dragon Emperor of China*, for fuck's sake?"

"Nelson. 'Need to know' applies equally to you."

"Why? It's not like I'm ever planning to leave: you give me better toys even than Asgard did! I'd have to be dragged kicking and screaming out of here. And if *that* ever happened it'd mean we'd been so fucked you'd have bigger worries than me. *Or* Ghost." He shrugged. "Besides, even if someone grabbed Ghost, they'd need a genius like me to figure out how to operate it. It's not like I've written a *user manual*." He giggled.

Eagle, of course, was unamused. "You should not know anything of the Institute, nor Lord Shen's... visit there."

Nelson ignored the note of exasperation. It's not like Eagle'd ever kick him out: he was their most valuable 'asset.' "I keep telling you, the more I know, the more connections me and Ghost can ferret out for you, yeah? If people don't want me to Ghost stuff, they should keep their computers off the network.

"F'r'instance, I took a look at the pattern behind those yearly 'attack' things."

Nelson noticed Eagle go still. He waited, but his boss said nothing. But from the look in his boss's eye, he had the man's complete attention. "And I can say that this year's one should be a doozy."

"Ah."

Damn. From Eagle's non-reaction, it looked like he already knew that.

Eagle raised one eyebrow. "Was Ghost able to correlate the secondary pattern to any stimulus?"

Nelson squirmed. "What secondary pattern?"

"Oh dear."

Oh dear? Shit, for Eagle, that was an explosion! But why? Because he now thought Nelson hadn't been smart enough to discover there *was* a secondary pattern? Or because he could tell he'd lied about not knowing there was one? Or, was it because Nelson hadn't been able to work out what lay behind the complex formula *even with Ghost's help*? But why would that matter so much?

"So, anyway, what happens if this G character ever gets loose, like 'Mr Smith' thinks is going to happen? The Dragon Lord'll teleport back in and zap him out of existence, or what?"

Nelson hadn't really expected his needling to draw any information from the older man, but studied his projected image carefully. "But you've thought about it, for sure. Probably got a Plan B, right? *And* plans C, and D, and E?"

Eagle almost smiled.

Nelson's eyes widened. "Shit! What? That means it's something freakin' awesome!"

"Just *don't*, Nelson. There are limits on what I will tolerate even from you. Nor should you be able to find anything about the girl. Though if you do," Eagle looked thoughtful, "I suggest you inform me as a matter of urgency. For all our sakes."

CHAPTER 45

Outside Harmon's office door, Leeth paused and checked her appearance, making sure she was nicely dressed. She wore her 'hunting outfit' – the brown doeskin with the lace-up front and fringed shorts that left her midriff nicely bare.

Nodding to herself, Leeth knocked at the door and carefully waited for the terse "Enter," before opening it to go inside.

Leeth watched Harmon's eyes travel up and down her body, and her lips curved happily. She slowed a little so he could take his time.

Smiling slightly, he gestured to the chair facing his desk. His visitor's chair was a discouraging piece of furniture – a heavy old carved wooden monstrosity, not really comfortable – but she effortlessly pulled it out and sat down, wriggling slightly to adjust to the seat's lumpy padding.

"To what do I owe this unexpected pleasure, Leeth?" Harmon asked.

The girl leaned forwards, suddenly very serious, genuinely unaware of the interesting things it did to her cleavage – for once. Harmon, with an effort, kept his eyes on her face. She still wasn't making his resolution any easier. Indeed, twice now he had had to put off her inappropriate advances with a 'when you're older,' rebuff.

Inside the security box, in the locked drawer of his desk, the illegal aphrodisiac drugs glowed like a distant lighthouse in his mental landscape. But he was uncertain whether it beckoned him *toward* metaphorical rocks, or warned him off. He should dispose of them. He would not use them again.

It was simply that they had cost a month's salary. Not to mention the risk he had taken to acquire them. Besides, he might find some legitimate use for them at some later date. Who knew what the future might hold, for them both? After all, once he published his results....

"Uncle? I *said,* you know how I'm learning Wing Chun?"

"Ah, your kung fu, yes," he said. Carefully.

"And you got me all those trids to study."

If she is telling herself that watching action trids is studying, *I may have a problem here*, he was thinking; but he let her continue.

"Well, I've watched them over and over, but I just can't see how they do lots of their stuff. Like in the *Fist of Death* trid, when there's the thing in the ceiling..." she got up from the chair, paused for a moment, then jumped, spinning in the air, one leg lashing upwards as she continued speaking, "...and he kicks it..."

She spun head over heels, Harmon's eyes widening in amazement as her foot brushed the ceiling before she tumbled out of sight below his desk, crashing to the floor with an impact that made his seat jump and him wince.

"Ow!" She climbed to her feet, frowning and kneading her hands. "You see?" I couldn't properly reach the roof, and it's hard to even land without hurting myself. But Nightshade kills it, *and* lands on his feet. I've tried and tried, and even played them slow, but it doesn't help. Sometimes they even cut out the important bits, just so you don't get to see how they do it!"

Leeth started pacing back and forth.

"And they're *all* like that. I think they're hiding something. Some kind of secret stuff. So I need a real teacher. Can I have a teacher? Please, Uncle?"

"Ah, Leeth – have you considered that perhaps these shows are just fantasy – that they may be faking these, er, maneuvers? Just as the 'thing' in the ceiling would itself have been faked?"

She frowned. "Sure. But I don't think so. Some things are obviously magic – like when they run through the air – but lots of other stuff I *know* I should be able to do, it's just there's some trick to it I don't get. Besides, there are lots of things everybody does – Nightshade, Joe Steel, Miss Bitch – that I can just about do, I'm sure I *could* do, if they just *showed* the whole thing from start to finish."

"You're sure."

"Well, yeah. Pretty sure."

Harmon tapped his stylus on the desk, staring off into space. She stopped pacing, forcing herself to stand still while he considered her request.

"And why do you want to know how to do these things?" he asked, just to be certain.

She cocked her head to one side, frowning. Tried to work out whether he was just teasing her. "Well, you know. To Hunt with."

"Mmm." Leeth noticed his faint smile as he asked, "and I take it you consider that knowing this sort of martial art is more important than more conventional hunting skills – guns, knives, that sort of thing?"

She shrugged. "I *suppose* they're important, too. But I want to be able to hunt just with... well, just myself." She reached out into the air between them. "I want to use my *hands*," she said, her voice suddenly throaty as her fists clenched shut on something invisible in the air. Then twisted. Harmon had to resist the impulse to shift backward in his chair.

"So can I? Have a teacher?"

Harmon considered. From the way she had framed her request, it appeared his mental blocks regarding Brian Shanahan were still firmly in place. As for the concept of having her prowling around with a gun or knife, practicing those skills – he winced at the mental picture. Bad enough she had her PowerShot. It would certainly be good for her to gain further martial skills, but the means would require careful planning. Perhaps in a year's time.

Aloud, he said, "That *is* a good idea. After the summer solstice, when things are back to normal. Of course, we will need to find the very *best* teacher for you."

Leeth beamed.

"But you must promise not to go killing people indiscriminately. I still don't understand how your DNA failed to match that found at the first scene. So if you want a teacher, you must swear not to kill anyone without my permission, first."

She rolled her eyes. "O-kay."

He wasn't sure which was more bizarre: his own statement, or the way she bounced from his office after agreeing to the condition.

Leaning back in his chair, he sighed. At least he had bought the necessary time. After the solstice, there would be ample opportunity to make appropriate plans – and to Adjust her expectations accordingly.

Provided they all survived this year's episode. With an effort, he forced the thought aside.

But later that night, Leeth thought how pleased Keepie

would be if she found a teacher all by herself. After all, she was practically an adult, now. It was nice he wanted the very best teacher for her, but that could take *weeks*.

A few minutes searching on the net turned up the *Red Fist Dojo*. It sounded *almost* perfect, and was real close, too.

He'd be so pleased! She giggled in delight, then carefully memorized the address. She should put on some fancy clothes, too. After all, she'd be going into the city.

And for the first time ever, she'd be going on her own! A little thrill ran through her at just the thought. This was going to be *so* cool.

CHAPTER 46

"Faith, *no*, I need space. And stop bumping my arm, you'll make me slip and then I'll get in trouble."

She pushed the dog to one side as she hammered the metal spike into the bitumen before taping the cosmetics-mirror to it. The next step took her ten minutes; first, checking that the angle of the mirror was roughly correct via her small laser pointer, then taping the laser onto the infrared emitter at the left side of the gate. Using it, she fine-tuned the position of the mirror, trotting back and forth as she adjusted its angle. It would have been *so* much easier if the infrared light wasn't coded: she could have just taped a light straight onto the photoreceptor. And Faith's persistent 'help' wasn't making things any easier.

It hadn't been too hard to learn about the non-magical security – it was amazing how much you could find out on the net if you knew the names or part-numbers of the actual equipment. After that, she'd just researched how to bypass 'coded infrared sensors.' She'd quickly decided it'd be much easier to reposition the one on the gate rather than any of the ones on top of the razor-wire wall. And she only needed to tilt the bottom one of the pair, since she only needed a little space to work in, to bend the bars enough to squeeze through. She had a car-jack in case she wasn't strong enough herself – though she was pretty sure she was, the bars weren't *that* thick – and also a rope and a metal rod so she could *un*bend the bars when she sneaked back in, later.

She giggled, then had to push Faith away again as she licked her upside the face. "Stop it, Faith! I'm spy-girling, this isn't play! Go and patrol or something!"

Faith, though, thought this was all far too interesting, and instead settled back on her haunches to watch.

"Well, all right. But you're not to tell Mr Shanahan when I go out, alright?"

Faith just grinned.

"Okay, this is the tricky part. Mr Shanahan said that a second of 'outage' is okay, so I gotta bend this around real quick. Here goes!"

She kept her eyes glued to the small white paper disk she'd put around the receiving-unit, then twisted the infrared emitter – with the laser-pointer now taped to it – toward the mirror until the red dot glowed back from the target. Fortunately, the infrared light wasn't a laser, so it had a broader beam.

Holding her breath, she waited for any alarms to start. Then with a grin stepped over the invisible beam and crouched down at the front gate.

"And *you* stay back there, like a good dog. Stay!"

Turning back to the gate, she gripped the bars and pulled with all her might; the car-jack ready just in case.

Leeth watched the car speed away into the darkness. *Well, that was weird.* She'd been getting on just great with the man. Alan. He was good-looking, healthy, *really* affectionate, and kind, too: stopping for her like that, to give her a ride all the way into the city. He'd seemed real honest and open, too, and judging by the way he'd stroked its material, he even seemed to appreciate the nice navy dress she'd chosen, even though she'd mainly picked it 'cause it left her legs free.

She frowned. Odd that his wife didn't understand him. He didn't seem all that complex.

On the other hand, he *had* behaved pretty strangely when she'd mentioned she'd just snuck out of the Institute for Paranormal Dysfunction. All at once, his whole attitude completely changed. He'd taken his hand off her thigh – where it had been doing interesting things – pulled over, and practically *made* her get out of the car.

Weird. Maybe he did that kind of stuff to his wife, too.

Shrugging, she looked around until she saw a street sign, then got out her reader and called up the city map. A minute later she'd slipped off her high heels and was laughing with delight as she flew down the hill, seeing how fast she could go, each foot coming close to skidding out from beneath her as she plunged down the roller-coaster hill toward the lights and activity of Union Square.

For some strange reason, the people at the bottom of that long hill were staring at her. Panting, she ignored them, spinning around so she could take it all in, laughing in delight. That made them *really* stare at her, she saw. Remembering her uncle's words about fitting in, she took a hold of herself. She had to blend in; look ordinary.

She put her heels back on. Then started threading her

way through the scintillating puzzle that was New Francisco by night.

The dojo had moved. She'd been surprised there'd been no sign displayed at the address she'd gotten from the net. But the guy who eventually answered the door had been real friendly. He seemed nice, especially the way he'd invited her in like that. She would have liked to stay, but she had to find the dojo and organize things, then get back to the Institute before Uncle missed her. She giggled as she thought how cross he'd be if he knew she was here. And how pleased he'd be that she'd found a teacher all by herself!

Two passersby glanced suspiciously at her, then hurried on. She laughed out loud. Her uncle was right about people – they really *did* seem timid. Even the guy, Alan, that she'd hitched a ride with.

She tilted her head, considering Hunting one of them. But then remembered her promise to Keepie. Besides, she wasn't here to *play*.

Actually, she was glad the Red Fist Dojo had moved. It gave her a chance to dive into the hurrying streams of people that flowed into and around the brilliant façades of the city's nightspots. Though, admittedly, the streams were thinning as her route took her away from the bright lights and into quieter, darker parts.

The fluoro-etchings of the street-signs on the buildings at the next corner had cracked and peeled away, but it didn't seem strange to her that she could read them, even so. She'd finally worked out why the horror-trids she sometimes watched always made everything go so black when they got to the good bits, so you could only see vague shapes and outlines. When she was younger, the nights *had* been like that. Dark and obscuring, like a heavy black cloak. Like the trids. And then she'd realized – that's what it was like for most people. Even Uncle – she'd watched him fumble around in her room at night, not seeing her, his hands stretched out in front of him. She giggled again at the memory of creeping up round behind him, as if *she* were the invisible monster.

Anyway, this was Folsom and Eighth, so the Red Fist Dojo shouldn't be far. She wondered why they'd moved.

Maybe they didn't like all the bright lights of Downtown? They probably got better people in this part of the city – people who weren't scared of the dark.

The sound of her high heels echoed and re-echoed down the now-deserted street. Her feet ached. Maybe she shouldn't have dressed up so much. But she wanted to look good when she met her teacher for the first time. And the clingy navy dress showed off her body nicely, without really restricting her movements, since it was quite short. She'd just slip off her shoes if she had time for a quick lesson tonight.

Something moved, in a doorway up ahead, and she stopped abruptly. It was low, on the ground, like an enormous grub....

Someone in a *sleeping bag?* She looked around, puzzled. Why would anyone get into a sleeping bag on the street?

Maybe it wasn't a some*one*. She moved closer, frowning, trying to stay quiet despite her high-heels.

Dark hair, middle-aged, dark complexion, and – "Whew!" she muttered, taking a step away – a very strong masculine smell. She blinked. Considered walking on. But it was just too strange to ignore.

"Hello!" she called, loudly enough to wake him.

"Unh? Wa's d'n?"

She blinked again. Did he just ask what she was doing? "Are you all right?"

He sat up, one hand reaching into his jacket and pulling out a battered-looking cashstick which he held up to her.

"Dum' a few creds?"

"Huh?"

"Slot me some change, miz?" he elaborated, waving the cashstick more determinedly in her face.

"Oh. You want some money?"

He rolled his eyes. "Yeah, gratz."

The 'stick waved stolidly in the air before her. She knew cashsticks were like credsticks, except you didn't need a CID. She also knew you used your thumbprint somehow, and touched it to the other person's 'stick. But she didn't actually know how to operate one herself. *Or* why he wanted her to give him credits.

A thought made her suddenly a little unsure of herself: should *she* have a 'stick? How did you even get them? Would she have trouble getting back to the Institute later, without money, if it got too late to hitch?

It'd take *hours* if she had to *run* back!

He was still waving his greasy cashstick at her. "Uh, I don't have a cashstick on me," she apologized.

He muttered something that sounded like 'flashin' null bim' as he rummaged about, the 'stick vanishing. He held up a plastifoam cup, rattled it.

"Tokens, then, Lady?"

She looked at the cup in confusion for a moment. Did he just call her a bimbo, then expect her to give him *money*?

"Look, I just stopped to see if you were all right. I don't have any money, I just wondered why you were sleeping in this doorway." She thought it better not to say that part of her, the childish part, had really kind of hoped he was some sort of giant larval mutant.

He stared at her a moment, then the cup slowly lowered. His enunciation suddenly became much clearer.

"Well, frick. Guess it just got too hot in my room at the Hilton. Came out here for some fresh air."

He stretched back out on the ground and awkwardly humped over onto his side, muttering as he pulled the grubby sleeping bag up around him again. "Frickin' dumb bim. No-money, no-brain. Wake a man 'a see if he's 'sleep. Dumb sliv null...."

Leeth scowled, spun round, and stalked off. She didn't know what a 'sliv' was, but she was pretty sure it was insulting. *And* she still didn't know why he was sleeping there.

She strode on quickly, angry now, her good mood evaporated. She had half a mind to go back there and shove his sleeping bag down his throat. If it wasn't for the smell. Maybe he was some new type of mutant, one that was allergic to *water*.

She stomped on, not quite muttering to herself. Then halted, startled, when a figure stepped from a recessed doorway to stand directly in front of her.

"Slow *down*, badette!"

Still cross, she'd almost walked into him. Khaki jacket,

black sweatshirt, black jeans. Very thin. She looked him up and down, grimacing, before stepping round him and continuing on.

"*Mean* little minx," she heard him mutter from behind, then noted his footsteps as he started following her. Up ahead, sprawled against a burnt-out Electrikar rammed diagonally up on the pavement, three more men watched her approach with interest. Her nose wrinkled in disgust as she saw that the one on the trunk was an ogre. It looked mis-grown, over-sized – bony brows sticking out too far, teeth and jaws too big. Piggy little eyes. Completely hairless too, with dead-looking whitish skin. It stood and approached from her right. She moved a little left to give it a wide berth. Uncle had never really made it clear exactly how infectious they were, but she didn't want to take any chances.

"Hey, sliv, what's the race? Grab a break."

The speaker, a human, leaned forward off the car, dusting down his vacated place on the front fender and bowing low as he offered it to her. When he straightened up, light gleamed off the bands of the healthy, muscled abs visible under his unfastened denim shirt and the biceps revealed by the torn-off sleeves. Mmm. He was pretty good-looking. And the way *he* said it, 'sliv' didn't sound like an insult.

She stopped. "What does 'sliv' mean?"

He smiled a wolfish smile that made her like him a little bit more. "Means 'sliver'." At her confused look, he waved up and down her body. "Just means ya young." He eyed her up and done, speculatively. "How age, enway?"

She lifted her chin. "Eighteen," she lied. "Almost nineteen."

His eyes narrowed in an interesting kind of way and she heard the thin one moving quietly up behind her for some reason. *If he got too close...* She smiled innocently. "I'm trying to find the Red Fist Dojo, actually. One-oh-two-oh on Seventh Street, isn't it?"

His eyebrows raised and he grinned. *Nice teeth, too,* she thought.

"Yeah, that's true. Meeting someone there? Or you taking self-defense classes?"

The others laughed.

"Self-defense?" She frowned. "Maybe. Sort of, I guess."

"Good idea," growled a deep voice to her right. As the ogre approached, she turned and backed away a little, making sure it couldn't touch her.

"Dainty little sliv like you, alone in these dark alleys – could get tasty cruel, eh?"

"I'm not a dainty little sliv, and I can take care of myself." She spun around to her left as the thin man now came almost within arm's reach, and she jabbed a finger at him. "And don't *you* come any closer if you know what's good for you!" He stopped, then moved back a little, smiling like he knew something she didn't.

She returned her attention to the grinning ogre. "And I wasn't talking to you," she added, before turning back to the handsome one.

For just a moment, she shivered, cold, and looked around. That had felt kind of like... was *Robo* around? *Here?* She did her not-looking, but didn't *see* him. In fact, it'd been a long time since she'd seen Robo. Not since the cold attack that one night. Years ago. *Could* he be out here, in the city?

The third man laughed. "Rufe, it does appear the lady is conversing with Randy," he mocked. "Seems like good looks win again, eh?"

She glanced at the new speaker. Registered a pretty, almost feminine face: fine features and skin, large eyes.

"Oh! You're Altered!" She took a step away from him, turned a little to 'Randy.' "You hang around with *mutants*? Aren't you worried you'll get infected too?"

Randy's chin came up, and suddenly he wasn't smiling. "Hey, they're not infected. They're just different. Where'd you get this 'infected' smek from, bim?"

The other two were scowling now as well. "Well, they are, aren't they? The Melt virus infected *him* and he mutated," she said, pointing to the ugly hairless ogre, "and this guy has all sorts of weird viruses re-writing his DNA. They're not really human any more, are they?"

"You dumb little sliv," growled the ogre, from her right. He reached out and grabbed her shoulder, spun her round to face him. "I think it's time someone-"

She'd hesitated almost too long, not happy about having to touch him even now that his hand rested on her bare shoulder.

Grimacing as she turned, she stepped in toward him. All the force of her disgust went into the blow that exploded into his stomach. She felt something rupture: his eyes glazed and his hand slipped from her shoulder as he bent over. With a scowl of distaste, she hammered her bare knee up solidly into his descending chin.

There was an unpleasant cracking sound, then he fell heavily to the pavement. Leeth backed away in revulsion, dusting her knee clean.

The Altered ran to his prone friend. Knelt down to take his pulse, then looked up, disbelief morphing the elegant planes of his face into an angry mask of hatred. "She killed him! The dirty little racist *sluk* killed Rufe!" Something appeared in his hand as he got to his feet, a blade flicking out with an ominous snick.

"Hey, guys, no, wait." From the corner of her eye she saw the thin one back further away. "We don't need more heat."

The pretty-faced one stepped forward, his knife weaving competently back and forth. She felt light-headed for a moment as the reality of her situation sank in. Suddenly everything was happening in slow motion. The Altered moved in, his blade slashing across, and she grabbed his wrist and hooked a leg behind him, intending to throw him down, like she'd seen Nightshade do on the trid a dozen times.

But he twisted, grabbing her, and they fell in a tangle, the knife slamming point first into the bitumen. His hand, now gripped by hers, slid down roughly off the hilt and onto the blade. He cried out in pain as it cut him, but thrust his other arm across her throat even as his weight descended on her, forcing her breath out in a rush.

She couldn't breathe. She tried to knee him, but the angle was wrong. Chest heaving, she tried vainly to draw in air, tried to pull his arm from her throat against the full weight of his upper body.

She struck at him, but he ignored her blows like they had no strength. She didn't understand. He seemed to be getting stronger. She struck again, and somehow he tore his other hand, bleeding and knife-less, from her grasp and brought it, too, to her throat.

I might lose, she realized, staring up into the Altered's livid face. The thought brought a flood of shame that scourged like flame. *No!* she swore to herself. *Never.* Deep inside, something took fire, spread up her arms. Snarling low in her throat she raked both hands crosswise across his stomach; felt them slice deeply into him: and rejoiced. Wet heat flooded over her as the Altered's triumphant glare drained into disbelief.

"No!" he whispered, face suddenly ashen. He fell off her.

She rolled to one side, sucking in huge breaths.

"You little bitch!" Randy snarled as he moved closer. She looked up as he kicked the abandoned knife away, well out of her reach. He was gazing down at his dying friend, his handsome face a mask of anger and grief.

"With his own blade!" His voice shook with rage.

With her breathing returning to normal, the strange weakness fading, she gathered herself to leap.

And saw he had a gun.

Her heart sank. Then a surge of anger burned the feeling away. All she'd wanted to do was go to the Red Fist Dojo! She looked up from the gun, and saw his eyes now on hers.

"That's right, bitch! Look at me!" He raised the weapon till the barrel pinned her with its ugly dead stare like a shark's black eye.

Thought abruptly vanished. She dived forwards, launching herself desperately up at him; registered the look of surprise on his face as he fell back a step. Her hand lashed out as the gun sounded like a thunderclap and something smashed into her.

Then her hand ripped through his throat and he flew backwards. She fell slowly, fighting the darkness swimming up from all around, swallowing her. She didn't even feel the impact when she hit the ground.

CHAPTER 47

In the New Francisco soup kitchen, Marc Disten froze, ladle poised just above the troll's large and very empty food bowl, head turning from side to side slowly, unseeing. *The Call.*

The old troll standing eagerly before the mouth-watering tureen of Irish stew, his limbs twisted by gargantuan rheumatism, stared down at the suddenly-unmoving man holding the brimming ladle, then looked across to the manager. Maisie, though, had her hands full with some gangers who'd sauntered in, looking for fun.

Abruptly, the ladle went back into the drum of soup and the man's eyes focused. "It is time to leave. There is important work to do."

The troll watched his server untie his apron and then cross the room, heading for the street while Maisie and the other volunteers called out angrily. They started after him, demanding to know what he was doing, where he was going?

The troll looked around shiftily, then picked up the entire drum of soup and began gulping it down swiftly, before anyone noticed.

Disten dropped the apron on the ground, oblivious to the angry shouts from the drafty room behind him. She was here. Back in the city. The pull was strong.

Trotting north along Potrero, he covered ground swiftly. But slowed, passing the remnants of the old General Hospital. The sense of anguished confusion from the many people inside flooded out, calling.

Their pain could be stilled; their confusion ended. In contrast, the call of the girl was fainter, less appealing.

For long seconds Disten stood, considering.

Moments later he was running north again. Gaining access to the closely monitored patients in the hospital would not be as easy as isolating derelicts from the soup kitchen, to bring to clarity. That much had been learned from those deaths. So much that could now be shown to the girl; to unlock what she in turn would reveal.

Not far, now. Disten jogged on.

The female was very close. Yet though the ugly disturbance she caused was stronger, it started to diffuse, making it harder to locate her.

Now was not the time to rush. Instead, more care was needed, to follow the dwindling Pull. Staring around the deserted, derelict streets, Disten paused, narrowing focus to just the pain of the chaos she radiated.

She was close. Why was the sensation fading, weakening?

Stepping around the corner, the answer became clear.

Soon he stood amidst the dead and dying. The opportunity had been spoiled. Disten's gaze swept back and forth. Wasted deaths.

The barbs of emotion that radiated from her, plucking and pricking, continued fading. In the wristcomm's harsh light the girl's skin looked unnaturally pallid. Bending down, Disten checked the pulse, felt it flutter weakly, then stop. Instantly, blissfully, the ugly chaos was gone, smoothed out into the simple regular patterns of sanity. The girl lay dead.

Yet moments later, chaos flared like migraine lightning across the whole scene. There was a presence nearby, wild with disorder.

Disten stood and turned, sensing it, feeling it draw toward him. Something about it felt... linked to the girl? Affected by the girl?

As he approached, it stilled, then drifted closer, before suddenly flaring again, jerking away; then, it too was gone. Fled?

Disten stood unmoving for a minute, considering the bodies. Useless. The... spirit? Had it been the spirit of the girl? It had felt very different, however. Far more ordered. Would it return?

The bodies were checked; searching for CIDs, clues.... Nothing.

Distant sirens wailed their ever-present cries through the night sky. Wind plucked at the jacket.

There was nothing more to be found, or done, here.

At last, Disten walked back along the route traversed earlier. The hospital should still be able to provide at least one useful subject.

CHAPTER 48

Leeth had disappeared soon after dinner. Now Harmon sought her out, though he wasn't entirely sure why, himself. He did want to talk to her. But more than that, a faint unease prickled at him. Something about her distracted air during dinner....

Carefully Percepting while he opened the door to her bedroom – he'd learned the importance of quickly locating her in the dark – Harmon looked about cautiously.

Strange. She wasn't in sight. He stepped back a little and fully opened his mind's eye to the flooding input of the Imaginal realm, twisting the well-learned detection pattern into existence to cast the spell.

Still no result. Odd. She must be shielded. No doubt outside, beyond the inner Barrier, prowling the grounds in the dark.

The thought of going out there to look for her was... unappealing, somehow.

A horrible thought sent him racing back to his office, but tapping into the video feed from Godsson's cell showed the inmate simply muttering and pacing. Alone. Of course.

He even *visited* Godsson, but the man was no help. If anything, he was worse than usual, rubbing his hands together and nodding as if he knew the answers to Harmon's question about where she was.

"Sara will be in my service soon enough, Alex," he had smiled, beatifically. "Although you and She have tempted her, when she is Perfect, she will be free. All will be freed."

There was something unnerving about those words. Hurrying from the cells, he resumed his search in earnest.

In the cold outside, glad of his long coat, he stood just beyond the Institute's inner Barrier. But recasting the simple detection spell still produced no result. As if she no longer existed. Now he was truly worried. That implied she was neither within the inner barrier, nor within the outer. She must be shielded.

She couldn't have left the Institute – she would have been unable to get out undetected past the cameras and other sensors, he told himself.

Had she fallen, knocked herself unconscious, perhaps? No: the detection spell would still have given him a distance and direction. She had to be shielded from the magic somehow. *Oh, hell. Had she been digging a tunnel, and the earth collapsed on top of her?* Magic could not penetrate the earth. And digging a tunnel was just the sort of bizarrely stupid escapade she would dream up.

She could be trapped, suffocating to death.

Lights from the Institute cast a wan illumination across the cold and dewy lawn as he flung himself free of his body. If the earth had collapsed, he should be able to sense *that* disturbance from the Imaginal.

Beside him, the brain-hurting Barrier englobed and hid the main building. His spirit darted away, scouring the ground.

But *still* he failed to locate her.

Hours had passed now since their evening meal. He could do a full Sending, of course, but he would need an hour just to refresh the ritual circle for the location spell. He called the security officer.

"Shanahan, have you seen Sara? I can't seem to find her. Is she out wandering in the grounds again?"

"No, Doc. Everybody's inside. Here, I'll check."

Harmon tried to stay unconcerned as his co-worker queried his network.

"No. She went outside earlier, but came back about an hour and a half ago." He could hear the grimace in Shanahan's voice. "Though she's given the system the slip once or twice. You want me to run a full search?"

"No. It's probably easier for me. No need to activate all the systems," *and file a report tomorrow.*

Shanahan didn't sound concerned. "Okay. But ping me if you change your mind, Doc."

"Certainly."

Annoyed by the cold of his now-damp coat, he strode through the dark to the little-used Rituals block. The small circle there, set up for clairvoyance, should be adequate. Abruptly he stopped and reversed his path. First, he'd need something of Leeth's. Hair from her hairbrush.

He was cursing under his breath by the time he finally returned to the rituals area with the necessary material. Damn the girl. It would be after midnight before he'd locate her, now.

The ritual ceremony was tediously complex, and required his full attention, despite his chafing certainty that something had happened to her.

Finally, Harmon felt the Imaginal link form, the initial surge of relief followed by a wave of shock as he sensed it snake far away into the night. Far beyond the walls enclosing the grounds. *How had she gotten out? And undetected?* Shaking his head, he cast the clairvoyance spell down the connection.

But at the distant scene of menace the spell revealed, his breath hissed out in dismay.

Hands clenching and unclenching, wishing he could hear what was being said, he watched the two youths and the mutants closing around her. *Couldn't she see what they planned?*

It wasn't clear what started the fight, but he groaned in dismay as the bad situation worsened. He watched with shocked pleasure as she disposed of the ogre threatening her. But that joy vanished as he saw the speed of her second attacker, armed with a knife. In the half-dark, he watched in confusion as her attacker toppled sideways off her body, clutching his stomach, while Leeth rolled the other way, onto her hands and knees. He saw her breathe in, great racking breaths. What had she done?

Where was *she?*

Abruptly, another figure moved forwards into the range of his spell. The youth held a *gun!* He caught a glimpse of the boy's face, twisted in an ugly snarl of rage as he spat angry words at her.

In cold dismay, he watched Leeth suddenly explode forward as the boy's arm lifted and the gun fired.

He cursed vividly as the two collided – and both went down. Leeth, on the ground, moved feebly, then stilled. Cold dread shot down his spine.

"No!" He screamed, nearly losing control of his spell. "Sara! Get up!" he shouted futilely. "Leeth! You *stupid* girl!"

He forced himself to breathe slowly. Forced himself to calm.

Clearly, she was in New Francisco. And if he could find her within sixty minutes, he could probably heal her. That was the time limit. Cell death could be reversed up until one hour had elapsed. So he had read.

But where was *she?* He couldn't shift the clairvoyance spell, since it was focused on *her.* Try to track her Imaginally? It would be confusing, but probably his best chance.

His attention snagged on a new figure, thin, who edged shakily forward, fearfully checking each of the bodies. Hadn't one of the youths fled, when the fight started? It straightened up and stood hugging itself for a few seconds, then darted forwards, grabbed up something from the ground, the gun perhaps, before scrabbling around for something else a little distance away. Finally, the thin youth ran off out of the range of his spell, into the night.

Harmon let out his breath.

With an effort, he manipulated his viewpoint until he was looking upwards toward the New Francisco skyline. Then cursed himself for stupidity as he realized that, of course, any landmarks would be much too far away to be inside the limited sphere of vision provided by the clairvoyance spell.

The Institute did have a vehicle. But the laser rangefinder unit had developed a fault months ago, so he couldn't trust its auto-drive. Nor could he manually drive and follow an astral link at the same time. Sweating from the effort required to maintain concentration on his spells, he ordered a cab, maximum priority. At this point, cost didn't matter.

The Sending had served its purpose, allowing him to link a clairvoyance spell to her. But already that linkage was fading. He knew what that meant.

Stepping delicately through the ritual circle, he carefully released the Sending while holding the link from the spell. One less thing to concentrate on.

From outside the barrier of the circle, he lay down on the cold floor. Now would come the hardest part: holding just enough awareness of his body to keep the clairvoyance running, while setting his spirit free. He had never tried to do this before. But it should, theoretically, be possible.

He eased his spirit from his body.

For a moment he felt the magic slipping from his grasp, but the image of Leeth's unmoving body seemed to focus his concentration wonderfully. Then he was racing through the night, his astral form following the tenuous thread of his spell.

Seconds later, he hovered Imaginally over Leeth's still figure: she was dying. *If only it were possible to cast spells while astrally projecting!* Or to link anything more substantial than sensory input to a Sending. *Like a healing spell.* He had to fight down a wave of desperation, then began furiously searching for any clue to her location. Only to stop abruptly as a curtain of vast space descended on him. Something on the physical plane approached her, its aura cold, hard, and utterly dark.

It seemed to be bipedal. An android? Something about it seemed robotic.

Its aura both repelled and fascinated him, radiating a sense of order as compelling as the gravitational pull of a black hole. But strangely hard to 'see.' There were no twining, shifting patterns of desire and potential. No flares of hunger or emotion. Just the impression of readiness, like some complex coiled trap.

He looked at Leeth's body, surprised by how calmly he could observe it now. He had drifted toward the unsettling presence, he noted, feeling a strong desire to be closer. *What an elegant simplicity it had!* His Imaginal surroundings seemed to be fading in a curious way, though. Becoming harder to sense, losing their meaning.

It was the thing. *Its structure is* infectious, he suddenly realized! The knowledge simply appeared in his mind. He glided backwards, abruptly certain that in spirit form he was dreadfully exposed, vulnerable. He dare not come into contact. He backed further away.

It simply stood, and he had the impression that the head moved, examining the small scene of slaughter. Only seconds had passed since its arrival. It stilled; Leeth's blood continued to drain onto the street of the slum.

A muffled, distant panic brushed against him.

The thing approached Leeth's prone body, and Harmon could only watch. The figure bent down, and he guessed it had made light.

Seeing it and Leeth together made a horrible kind of symmetry, like seeing a positive and negative image of the same thing. He was suddenly intensely aware of Leeth as a flesh and blood animal. Himself, too.

Was it a machine? But it couldn't be: only the living held auras.

Backing further away, his surroundings snapped back into normality, the feeling like emerging from a dark and frozen cave. But the relief was short-lived, as panic slammed into him again with full force.

He sensed the strange construct lose interest in Leeth and at that instant become aware of him, aware of his Imaginal form. But Harmon was already leaving, scanning for landmarks and cursing his way back to his body. He hoped the cab was on its way.

It was going to be close.

Harmon jumped from the cab, the driver obviously glad to see the last of him – clearly spooked once he'd realized his fare was a mage who was slipping in and out of his body as he located the thing he searched for.

He was still cursing quietly as he stalked down the street, hoping he had correctly pinpointed her location. The grubby, depressing but wide alley certainly echoed what he had seen from his astral scouting; and the chain-link fence looked familiar from the clairvoyance. Fortunately, the road was deserted. The moon had risen, now, above the buildings. By its light, plastic bags pressed like white faces against the mesh of the fence, wind fluttering their edges and curling coldly under his still-damp coat.

He came to the scene of carnage at last, although the bodies had been disturbed from how he'd last seen them. Each now lay on their backs, jackets opened and pockets emptied. Apparently scavengers had already picked the bodies clean, yet none had felt inclined to call the city-cops. He spared only a second or two scanning for the strange figure he'd sensed earlier.

Whatever it had been, it was gone now.

He ran toward Sara, his shoes sticky against the ground as he reached her. There seemed to be blood everywhere. *Just like last time.*

Awkwardly, he crouched down to avoid soiling his overcoat, and reached out to touch her still body. No pulse, and already her skin was cooling. He felt his hands shaking; his heart hammering so hard it was a physical pain. Desperately, he shaped the healing spell and wove it through the small, bloodied form.

The seconds ticked away, one by grudging one. Had it

been too long? For a moment he had the peculiar sensation that the *spell* resisted being cast. He sharpened his concentration, focusing the strange effort of will necessary in any spell-casting, forcing the panic away. Thoughts rolled through his mind in a curiously detached way, making him feel like an observer in his own head. He stared blankly north toward the distant streetlights, where background traffic rushed back and forth, oblivious to the small drama.

He knew of one person brought back to life an hour after dying. *The Journal of Metaphysical Practice*, June, '46. But there had been a strong emotional attachment in that case. He had no such attachment to Leeth. Merely a certain fondness.

The seconds crawled past. In the dark, he couldn't see whether the gunshot wound was healing.

Live, damn you!

Suddenly, he felt the flow of willed-*change* shatter some intangible barrier, and seconds later a shiver ran through her. Then nothing, for long, long seconds, until finally she convulsed. He felt her heart start. Still he poured the healing into her. Suddenly her chest struggled, rose, a tortured wheeze as she clawed in air, breathing again. He continued infusing her with the pattern of her own health, felt cells awaken and tissue start knitting together. Her eyes flickered open. Focused on his. For some reason, his eyes began to water.

"Keepie," she sighed. Then closed her eyes, smiling, as if soaking in a warm glow spreading from his touch. The surge of relief that flooded over him almost broke his concentration.

From that moment, the healing was scarcely harder than normal, though it took far longer. Mere minutes later, uninjured, she sat up. Turning on the light in his wristcomm, by its wan glow he saw that her head hung down, not looking at him.

"Sometimes, Wild Thing, I don't know *what* to do with you!"

Still she didn't look up.

He reached out, lifted her chin. "Sara, what on Earth were you doing?"

Her eyes reluctantly met his. She was scowling, with

that expression that made her look so young.

"Who's 'Sara'?" she demanded.

He blinked.

"Sara," he began, "is a young lady who runs off without telling anyone where she's going, and then very nearly gets herself killed!" Her mouth opened to reply. "And it's only by sheer *luck* I found you soon enough to be able to heal you!"

"I...." She looked down again.

"Yes? I can see I've been sadly mistaken about how much you've really grown up. Obviously I've been giving you more responsibility than you can deal with." He was breathing hard.

Her mouth tightening in a stubborn line, she wrenched herself from his grip and stood, turning her back on him. Suddenly, though, the tension drained from her stance and she trotted over to one of the bodies, squatting down to study it.

His jaw worked in disbelieving fury. *I save her life, and she turns her back on me and walks away?*

He watched her. Reaching out a hand to the body, she gently pushed the head to one side then stood, staring down.

"Uncle." Her voice sounded strange. "How did I do *that*?"

He scowled, but moved over to join her. Squinting in the dark, he aimed the small square of illumination of his wristcomm where she was pointing, then drew in his breath.

The man's throat was slashed across. Four deep parallel wounds, half severing the neck.

Mentally playing back what he had seen of the fight, he examined the other bodies. In the dim light, the stomach of the Altered had similar deep parallel slash wounds.

"I don't know," he answered slowly. Shifting his senses to the Imaginal, he studied her, carefully; took her hands and examined them closely. Especially her fingernails and fingertips. But in the end he was no wiser. "All I know is that somehow, you did indeed do this." He had the impression she was smiling.

"I did pretty good, Keepie, didn't I?"

"Yes, Leeth. You *almost* survived on your own, without

my help," he said, with enough sarcasm for even her to detect.

There was a pregnant silence.

"That's why I need lessons."

"I will be happy to teach you, Leeth. Though I warn you, the study of magic is difficult and slow, and you will need-"

But she had started giggling, even putting out one shaky hand, begging him to stop. "Why-ever did you think I meant *magic*, Keepie? I meant kung fu!"

He stared at her, nonplussed, dazed by the depth of her unawareness. It appeared she was unconscious of the fact that, whatever she had done here tonight, it had involved magic. *Somehow.*

He frowned, staring at her in the dark, across the two bodies. *Surely he had told her she had Unfolded. Hadn't he?* Wind gusted around them and he saw her shiver, then at last look away. Rolling her shoulders, she plucked at her dress. "Yuk! It's all sticky."

He said nothing at her attempt to change the subject.

"I think I got blood all over it. Lucky I chose a dark color." She stripped it off, over her head, and stood there unselfconsciously. "Boy, I bet I look a *mess*." She stretched her arms out in front of her in the dark. "Yep. I'm going to have to wash up, somewhere. And I guess I better not let anyone see me either, till I do."

He wiped a hand wearily over his face. He really shouldn't expect self-analysis from the child.

"Oh." She put one hand on his arm. "Keepie? What about my blood, here? Can you magic it away, so the police won't find my DNA like they did last time?"

"No, Leeth, I can't." He checked the weather forecast on his wristcomm. Heavy rain expected tonight. Nor was it likely the bodies would be soon discovered in this part of town.

He considered the three corpses. They looked CID-less, and given the area, they likely were. Even should the police investigate, the natural assumption would simply be that an argument had turned deadly. But he was not prepared to take that chance. He resigned himself to having to steal cleaning supplies from the nearest 24-7. Which was a long walk from here.

For the blood on herself and her dress, an invisibility casting and a public toilet should do the trick. Somehow he didn't think Leeth would be too troubled by the prospect of joining him in the Men's.

At least his painstakingly-learned invisibility spell would not have been an entirely wasted effort. But for the rest....

The more he thought about what they needed to do, the more useful the invisibility spell looked.

Twenty minutes later, they returned, Harmon still maintaining the complex pattern of the invisibility. Leeth seemed to be managing the heavy weight of both the bulky containers of bleach *and* the water with surprising ease. Scanning the alley, he dropped the spell with some relief when he saw it was still empty.

In the diffuse light of the electric lantern he'd obtained, Harmon looked in mild dismay at the scene of slaughter.

"Wow, there sure is a lot of blood, isn't there, Keepie!"

Harmon exhaled. "Yes. I hope you're not intending to develop it as a trademark."

Leeth grinned impishly. "Will you hold my clothes? I don't wanna get bleach on them." Casually stripping off completely, she handed him her recently-rinsed dress and underwear, then danced over to the bodies and began splashing bleach liberally around. She set to work with a will, singing happily, as if this was a wonderful adventure.

He shook his head. Stuffing her damp clothes into his coat pocket, he took up one of the brooms and began sweeping bleach and blood toward the gutter.

The cab ride home was awkward. After their successful in-visible heist of their crime scene cleaning equipment, and a full half hour washing away the evidence, they'd left the bodies and walked to Ninth. From there they caught the Muni as far as Pine. In icy silence they got off the tram to finally trudge up toward Russian Hill to muddy their trail. Outside a restaurant there, he called a cab.

Leeth shifted on the back seat, trying not to let the driver notice her dress was wet. Or the bullet hole in the chest.

CHAPTER 49

As the two ate breakfast the next day, Leeth insisted on having the trid on. She kept switching channels, watching the morning news reports, pausing as Nina Summers finished the corporation round-up.

"Thanks, Bart. I guess we'll all have to just wait and see how Mitsubishi reacts to *that* info. Do you want to make a prediction?"

"It's too early, Nina, though I'd just like to remind everyone the megacorp has always shown great restraint when reacting to this sort of provocation in the past. I think we can assume they'll do what's best for everyone."

Bart faded out, to be replaced by Nina's waif-like figure, now hovering high in the air over New Francisco. Letters of fire appeared in the air behind her, spelling out the legend, 'Breakfast from the Dumps,' and beneath it a holopad appeared, glowing enticingly with the 'Bodycount Bingo' logo. Harmon gestured, canceling the interactive pad that accompanied the picture. The ground rushed up as Nina's urchin-cropped blonde head expanded to fill the view, pouting seriously. Leeth copied the pout.

"A slight change of venue for our regular segment now, as gang violence last night reached out from the Dumps practically into the heart of downtown New Francisco." The view panned back, leaving Nina looking incongruously neat in the middle of a scene of slaughter.

"Keepie, look! That's mine!"

Leeth forgot her game of copying the newscaster's expressions as Nina turned, now appearing to stroll through the carnage, her gestures carefully pointing out the dead and how they died, while the camera obliged with graphic close-ups.

"I'm standing on the corner of Heron and Eighth, just five minutes from Union Square when the traffic is light. Joining me now virtually is city security officer, Craig Walters."

A tall, good-looking man in PeaceCorp security armor materialized beside her.

"Good morning Craig, and thanks for joining me here. What can you tell our viewers about the situation?" He looked around and the camera's view obligingly panned once more over gaping wounds, washed even cleaner by heavy overnight rain.

Somehow that made the memory of all their hard work scrubbing the crime scene doubly irritating.

On the trid, the private security officer was talking. "Statistically speaking, Nina, we have to expect these occasional random spill-overs of violence from the Dumps. Of course, we'll increase our patrols in this area to monitor the situation for a while."

"And how sure are you, Craig, this was just gang violence?"

The security officer shrugged. "Hell, all three are CID-less."

"Thanks Craig, and thank you PeaceCorp. Next, the shocking death last night in the old San Francisco General Hospital of its senior administrator in suspicious circumstances in the psycho-trauma ward. What *was* he doing with the possibly-naked female mental patient, and was it the witnessing of his murder that destroyed her very mind?

"But first, we'll cross live to Lacey Steel, on the set of her latest thriller, *Orbitzone* -

Harmon gestured the device off and turned to Leeth. She met his eye, looking suddenly apologetic. "I didn't do real good, did I? They only attacked me one at a time, but...." She sighed. "*That's* why I was on my way to the dojo."

Harmon shook his head. "No, Leeth. Last night's little episode has made me realize one thing at least. There is no way you would fit into a dojo."

"But-"

"No. Remember: they're *sheep*, Leeth. They think human life is sacred. If those people had had Citizen IDs, there would have been a real investigation. Perhaps they might even have invoked a street-spirit to see if it had witnessed the incident. I don't want your face on the register of people with martial arts skills. Or even known to that community."

"But-"

"What we will do, is organize proper vids for you to watch. Training vids. Vids of real bouts. We can even attend some live fights."

She considered this. "We'd probably have to go and see lots of them, wouldn't we?"

He sighed, and suppressed a smile. "Yes, Leeth. I suppose we would."

Her eyes lit up. "Did you know the Shaolin Wudang Association is practically just across the Golden Gate Bridge? It's in a place called Fort Mason. I found it last night, after we got back home. And it didn't get damaged even one bit by the Big Quake thing! It *was* underwater, but the whole school worked to fix the buildings up once the sea went back down. It's been there forever, it's older than *you* are, Keepie! And it looks even more perfect than the Red Fist Dojo!"

Leeth faltered to a stop at the look he gave her: correctly guessing that he wondered why she hadn't chosen the Wudang Association instead of the Red Fist Dojo, last night.

She probably shouldn't have used 'killer' as one of her search terms, the first time, but Leeth wasn't going to admit *that* out loud. Half to distract Harmon, she leaped to her feet. "Vid: search Shaolin Wudang Association, special events."

A soothing female voice began reading the scheduled bouts and exhibitions from the calendar of events which the screen now displayed. But Leeth had already darted over, excitedly pointing out the very first entry and talking over the synthesized voice. "This one, Keepie! That's *Siouxsie Cheng!*" She turned excitedly to him. "She's properly fast, like Bruce Lee was. She'll be fighting Maxxon Caine: she'll *destroy* him!"

Then she paused, and her shoulders slumped, and turned back to him, distressed. "But it's not for *six weeks!*"

Harmon blinked. Dare he hope it would distract her from Godsson's upcoming episode?

He shook himself. What was he thinking?

"Perhaps in the meantime you should monitor the news reports to see if there is further investigation of your escapade last night. We do not want another visit from Detective Garland and his overweight colleague."

Harmon considered the matter of her broken promise, but knew what she would say: the killings had not been *indiscriminate.*

Yet now she had manifested new and even more deadly abilities. Nor had he been able to determine how she had caused the injuries he had seen last night. Harmon wondered if she could briefly have grown *claws*?

He watched her as she munched happily on her final piece of wholegrain toast, with a dawning sense of the havoc she might wreak should she slip from his control.

As she finished her toast, he noticed she was watching him very carefully.

"Um."

He looked a question at her. But instead of speaking up, her eyes slid away. Frowning, Harmon tried to remember the last time she had hesitated to ask a question. *What on Earth...?*

"Uh, Keepie, you know the summer solstice is coming up?"

Oh, dear stars above: this was going to be bad.

"Well, you know how Godsson's the only one, besides me, who can fight Her...?"

"No. Whatever you're about to ask, the answer is no!"

"No, wait! I just want him to Teach me how to fight Her, better."

Was she insane? "No! You saw the video, Leeth. There is no way I will ever allow you into Godsson's cell!"

"What if I didn't have to go inside for him to Teach me?"

Harmon blinked at her. "And how do you imagine that would work?"

Leeth looked away. "Well, maybe he could magic up some more, uh," she waved a hand and darted a glance at him, "I mean, when I say *more,* I mean *especially* magic invisible creatures, for me to practice fighting. He could even coach me while I fought, you know? Like, call out instructions on what to do?"

Was she... was she hinting that Godsson had summoned a creature before, *for her to fight? No. Inconceivable.*

The Dragon's Barrier enclosed him. No. No spirit below the level of a so-called 'god' could penetrate that. Nor any magic except, perhaps, the Dragon's utmost.

But Leeth was still nodding, earnestly entreating him. "You could come with me, Keepie. That way you could keep me safe."

She's seventeen, he had to remind himself. Yet in many

ways, she seemed still only ten.

Leaning forward, she grasped both his hands. "We could even go right now. Come on, it'll be fun!"

Abruptly, Harmon withdrew his hands and got to his feet. "Yes, why *don't* we sort this out right now? Come."

The system went into lock-down the moment Leeth followed him through the first security door, while Brian Shanahan's voice shouted from his sequestered wristcomm a moment later.

"Doc! She's gotten into-." Silence. Then: "What the *divil?* Doc, are you all right? What's going on? I'm seeing *you* on the monitors with Sara."

"My apologies, Brian. I assumed that Sara would be permitted entry if accompanied by me."

"Sorry, Doc. No exceptions."

Harmon fumed, there on the upper landing of the stairs to the basement with Leeth. Who looked well pleased at being considered such a threat. It took several minutes of three-way communication between him, Professor Sanders, and Shanahan before Harmon and Leeth could proceed with their joint visit.

Harmon's mood was not improved by Godsson's reaction. Standing close to the narrow, thick window, he eyed Sara up and down.

"My, Sara, haven't *you* grown. I see your taste in clothing has not changed. And now you have seduced your Father into bringing you to attend me, I see."

Sara just frowned; Harmon, however, *flinched*. It took him a second or two to recover. "Sara is my ward, not my adopted daughter, Godsson. As you well know.

"What's this about you invoking spirits for Sara to fight?"

Sara started, gawping at her uncle. "What? I didn't... All I said was it'd be cool if he *could* magic up some especially magical invisible creatures like *Her*, so I could practice fighting them!"

She looked back to Godsson who now stared at her, eyes narrowed. She realized *he* now thought she'd broken her promise not to tell her uncle! She stared angrily back, microscopically shaking her head and thrusting her chin forward. "I just asked Uncle if I could get you to be my teacher, so I could help you fight Her better, this time! So stop being so mean!"

Godsson gaped at her. "You expect me to teach you, in a few weeks, a portion of what it required me *two thousand years* to learn?"

"Stop making stuff up, Godsson. This is serious. You're the only one who can teach me to fight Her." She shrugged, like she didn't care either way. "If you don't, fine. I'll just learn it on my own. But it'll be faster if you teach me."

Harmon felt the conversation slipping away from his control, onto paths he had not agreed to explore. "That is not the issue. The question is, have you been summoning some kind of creatures from the Imaginal, for Sara to fight? Some third kind of Incorporeal Being, such as you keep claiming exists."

"Oh, Alex, have I not been telling you for thirteen years now, that some *thing* followed me back from the Deeps? But, no, no creature which I could summon to me could penetrate these barriers to spirit and magic. Nor have I been summoning creatures for Sara to fight." He had only *attracted* one: to *frighten* her. And one more: to Perfect her. "That I swear, by my Father's Name."

He turned back to Sara. "I cannot teach you to fight Her as I do, girl. At most I could teach you how to hold her – you seem good at that."

Harmon allowed him to proceed. Either the simple 'instructions' would help reduce Godsson's delusional fears, or they were real techniques which would help Leeth resist a real threat.

Godsson continued. "Do not try to rip her apart, however – you must pin Her. Sheathe your claws."

Harmon started. *How...?* Had that been just a guess?

"Nor react with such fear. Just hold. Do you think you can do that? If you can hold onto Her here in physical reality long enough, I can destroy Her. Can you do that?"

Sara nodded. Eager, her eyes alight.

But for some reason, watching, alert for some trick or trap from Godsson, watching too on the Imaginal for any impossible magic leaking through the Wards, Harmon felt something terrible had just been done. There was too much eagerness in Godsson's body language.

Leeth of course couldn't see it. He watched her lap up the 'teaching.'

And what had Godsson meant by his talk of Leeth reacting with fear? He didn't recall ever seeing her react with *fear* during any of Godsson's episodes. It was as if Godsson referred to some experience the two had shared previously. Could he have been referring to the incident where she'd scored her own arms? All those years ago?

He had a bad feeling about this 'lesson.' "I think that's enough. Come, Sara."

But why did he feel the damage had already been done?

PART IV

(One week later)

CHAPTER 50

In the end, there had been no surprise visit from the police following Leeth's multiple murders in the city. Which was just as well, since as the summer days passed, the upcoming problem of the 'king tide' solstice soon absorbed all Harmon's attention.

He was not alone. This year, the event was being treated as if there would be significant danger. They would have more personnel present to offer support. Already, the area outside Godsson's cell had been remodeled accordingly.

The Director had even written to the Dragon Lord, politely seeking his attendance. The Chinese Embassy had equally politely declined. Though there had been a short, impeccably-executed addendum in *Han* characters which the FBI's experts said translated as either 'Kill the mage, finish the threat' or 'Kill the mage, make the threat real.' That ambiguity was deliberate, they said.

That postscript had killed any support for Mr Smith's preferred course of action. It also meant the hydrogen cyanide delivery system connected to Godsson's cell, a secret Brian Shanahan had very nearly blurted out to Leeth one day long ago, had become absolutely their last resort.

But when Harmon had made *that* comment aloud, a disturbing expression had passed across Professor Sanders's face. Apparently there was a further defensive measure of which even he, Godsson's primary carer, was unaware.

As final proof of the level of concern, Harmon's suggestion that Sara should once more attend had been approved. When he had informed her, though, rather than jumping for joy, Leeth had looked worried. Determined, but worried.

Harmon had a very bad feeling about all this.

But so, apparently, did everyone else.

They had all begun behaving as if Godsson's delusion were real. Had the madman affected them all? Had Sara's support for his delusion drawn them all into it? Or was it more like the old problem of climate change – people denying what they didn't want to believe until a tipping point came which forced acceptance?

He felt they would find out, one way or the other. Tonight.

Leeth paused by the rose bed at the edge of what she used to call the Jungle when she was little, watching as another truck swept up the long final curve leading to the forecourt. This one had soldiers in it, one hanging outside for some reason, and he did a kind of double-take when he saw her and Faith, and whistled, two long notes, one high, one low.

She looked down at Faith, wondering if he'd been trying to call the dog over. But Faith was better trained than that and knew not to go to a stranger. She turned, continuing her walk along the edge of the forest, only half-aware of the khaki-colored truck squeezing in alongside the black SUVs already there and the long black, and longer white, limousines.

She was talking things over with her friend. "I *should* be ready to join Godsson inside his room, Faith, if he needs me. I know it's not him doing it. It's Her. And I know I hurt Her before, twice. So I know I can help him, if I can just get into his cell. He's even told me *how* to help: I just have to hold Her long enough for him to blow Her up! And I think this time he'll *really* need me.

"But what if She gets inside *me*? Like she did to those two friends of Keepie's when he was young? What if she turns *me* into a monster? I wish Godsson could've taught me how to block Her out, too, not just *hold* her."

She bent down to Faith, who agreed it was a worry, but nuzzled her nose in against Leeth to reassure her it would be okay. Leeth burrowed her face into the thick fur, smelling Faith's unique mix of dog, leaves, earth, ozone and machine oil.

She sat back on her heels. "I don't mind fighting something real, something dangerous, that might hurt me or kill me. After all, Keepie could probably heal me up afterward." She shrugged. "Unless it was *real* bad.

"But Keepie can't fix me if I turn into a monster. And I... I don't think I could bear not being me. Let alone some disgusting *thing* with pulsing tentacles!"

She shuddered.

"I like the way I look. I really, truly, like my body. Except maybe it'd be nice to have bigger breasts and a slimmer waist. Well, just a bit."

Faith was looking at her like she was crazy, clearly

pointing out "Your breasts are way bigger than mine." She *whuffed,* quietly, which obviously meant "What you need is fur. You're practically bald."

"I am *not.* Humans aren't s'posed to have fur!" She laughed, and Faith grinned back, letting her tongue loll out goofily, trying to cheer her up even more.

But the humor quickly faded, and Leeth stood, the two continuing their circuit.

She waved her hands. "I mean, it's part of who I am. It's important, to me. Real important. And I like the look on people's faces when they see me. It's nice. I feel good. Even if Godsson says I dress like a, well, I looked it up. Like someone who has sex for money. But I don't!"

Faith looked up at her sideways.

"I *don't* look like them! I looked at pictures. They're all showing their breasts, and they have these sheer stockings and-

"Anyway, I don't. But Godsson thinks I do, and Keepie says that's a problem, 'cause Godsson thinks I'm bad. But he doesn't *really* think that. We're friends! He just gets cross. And it's because he's mad."

She looked down at Faith, who tilted her head sideways to catch her eye. "Oh, don't worry, I wouldn't say that to *Godsson.* That'd be mean. But he is. Just not as mad as everyone says.

"Anyway, I've dressed in something like Godsson says I should, you know, that covers everything up. So this should be fine, right?"

She gestured down at her clothing, the black cat-suit clinging to her body and covering everything completely from her shoulder-blades down. The black made it a little hard to see all her muscles and everything, unless the angle was just right, but still. She was kind of glad she hadn't ordered the one with the tail, though, in the end. That would have looked kind of silly.

"It even has built-in support up here so I don't need a bra!"

They continued on in companionable silence, crossing the road and continuing around the tree line. Behind them, yet another car drove up the road, but seconds later they both spun around at a strange sound, to see the car fishtailing across the grassy lawn before gaining traction and bumping back onto the road.

"That was weird: he drove right off the road!" She giggled. "I guess everyone's a little nervous about tonight." She checked her watch. "I better go inside. We're all getting a special 'briefing' this time. Do you think that cute shaman will be there again this year? The one I had to rescue, three years ago? I think he sometimes comes in the bad years."

She looked down at Faith, pretending she wasn't still thinking about turning into a monster. She didn't want to worry her. Finally she bent down to give Faith a last hug, and some more advice. "Anyway, you patrol out here tonight. And be careful. Especially if new-Robo is around. If you feel funny, just dodge away and run, like I taught you, okay?

"Come on, let's practice! Ready?"

She smooshed her hands in a mean-Robo kind of way down over Faith's head, flattening her ears, then they zigged and zagged, twisting and somersaulting, dodging across the lawn, till Leeth had to go inside. Bending down, she gave Faith one more, final hug just to encourage her and keep her spirits up, then put her shoulders back and went up the front steps four at a time.

Her uncle was striding toward the front doors as she pushed through, and he stopped and stared. "What are you wearing!"

She looked down at herself. Was that some kind of trick question? It was perfectly clear what she was wearing.

"No bra? And are you even wearing underwear?" He frowned. "Is that cloth, or have you just *painted* yourself black? I told you to... cover up... for...."

He ran down to a stop. "So you covered up."

"I did. I'm covered up, just like you said, Keepie. Specially for Godsson. What's wrong?"

"Leeth, your nipples are clearly outlined. As is your..."

"What's wrong with my nipples? Or my... what?" She followed his eyes downward. "My *vagina*?" she asked, spreading her legs as best she could, to check for herself.

Her uncle took a breath, but then just stood there. She straightened up and waited, hands on hips, beginning to get cross.

"Nothing is wrong with either, but you need to not just *cover* them, but to *conceal* them."

"Why? That's just stupid. He'll still know they're there."

"Because they send sexual signals. Men find them distracting."

She was sure he must be exaggerating, then suddenly remembered something.

"How distracting? Like it might make someone drive off the road?"

"It's possible. Yes."

"So I have to *hide* them."

"Yes."

"What about my face? Do I need to put a bag over that, too?"

"*Leeth.*"

"Fine."

"And hurry. The briefing starts in five minutes."

"I know. I'm not a child. That's why I came in."

"So go and put on some underwear. *Including* a bra."

At the look on her face, he felt it necessary to add: "And then put your... suit back on. Unless you *want* to appear unprofessional in front of all these men?"

And women, she mentally added for him, as she turned and stalked off.

Why hadn't he added 'and women?' And why hadn't he ever told her about nipples and stuff being distracting, till today? Why was it only *now*, when there were all these other *men* around? Though there were a lot more women amongst the influx of strangers this year. Probably she wasn't the only one who thought that maybe the thing affected men more strongly than women.

But Keepie had only mentioned the men. Was he *jealous?*

She danced up the stairs. He was! Keepie was jealous!

Surprisingly cheered by the thought, she ran to her room.

-

"Sara."

It was going to be awful, waiting so long. Two hours! Why did they have to go in so early? *She* never attacked Godsson till sunset. Usually.

"Sara!"

She looked up, to find pretty much everyone in the briefing room looking at her.

"Huh? What?"

All her life she'd known 'Sara' wasn't her real name. Why couldn't she tell anyone her *real* name, now that they'd found it? Why did *Leeth* have to be a secret name?

She saw some of the agents near her exchange looks, and focused on her uncle. "Sorry, Dr Harmon," she said, very *professionally.*

It felt so weird to call him 'Dr Harmon' that she almost lost her train of thought. "Could you repeat what you just said, please? I was mentally preparing myself."

She heard someone behind her snicker, and felt her hands clench. She sat up straighter, and *that* made several of the men seated in the chairs alongside her turn slightly more toward her. She felt her cheeks flush.

This was *horrid.* They were making her feel like a child.

"I wanted you to confirm that you had heard Commander Stone's order. She said, should anyone feel the need to take action, call out 'Target acquired' very clearly before engaging. So that it will be clear that you are taking conscious action, of your own volition."

Oh. She thought about that. *She* would probably take a while to learn all the secrets inside a person and discover they were supposed to call out the code phrase, first. "That might work," she finally agreed.

Commander Stone, who was only a little bit taller than Leeth but still somehow looked like she could take down *anyone* in the room, pursed her lips as several people around Leeth sniggered like she'd just said something funny.

But Commander Stone only said, "I'm pleased that you agree."

More people sniggered, and Leeth felt her blush grow stronger.

Several of the female agents looked across at her, one or two even shaking their heads. Like they disapproved of her. No doubt because she wasn't a trained agent.

Leeth just stared, hard, at Commander Stone. Kind of thankful for the anger that was beginning to build. At least it was a distraction from what lay ahead. She had a bad feeling there wouldn't be much more laughter tonight.

Commander Stone's eyes narrowed in turn, staring right back at her for long seconds, before she spoke again. "No, seriously, I am pleased. You are on the spot, and although every indication is that all this planning is merely an exercise in paranoia, the reason for all these support operations is the *possibility* that something we don't understand is happening. You have been included to help cover such possibilities. In that unlikely event, your intuitions could be valid."

Leeth blinked, astonished as she worked out that the Commander was actually taking her seriously. Sort of.

"All the same, having a non-magical, untrained civilian on the scene makes me extremely uncomfortable."

Leeth wanted to snap back that she *had* Unfolded, that Keepie had *made* her magical, but even from the corner of her eye his stare practically scorched her with its intensity, and she bit down on the words.

"Especially a seventeen-year-old girl," the Commander continued. "This is not a game." Her intense green eyes flicked down and up Leeth's body as if making some kind of point about her choice of clothes, or maybe her bare feet. Which just showed how Commander Stone didn't know *everything*. This was practically identical to what Ninja Swift wore in *Dark Hunters*.

"If in my opinion you begin behaving erratically or disruptively, I will have you removed, Sara. Is that understood?"

That would be bad.

"Yes, Commander. Understood."

Wow. That had actually sounded very grown up! She sat up straighter, pleased with herself.

"Very well. Let's move, people."

By 'eighteen thirty,' a full two hours and five minutes before sunset, everyone was in place, waiting.

They'd only been there ten minutes before Leeth started fidgeting. The waiting was going to drive her nuts, if she didn't do something.

No one else seemed to be twitchy; from Mr Smith scowling to one side, his hair starting to gray, now; to the male and female FBI agents; to her uncle – who was the only one smart enough to bring a chair to sit on; to the three shamans. *I wonder why they always send three*, she wondered? Was three a magic number, or something? No tall, cute shaman this year, though. This time, all three were women.

Why did that make her think one of them should have long, white hair down to her waist, and milky eyes? She chased the memory, but it vanished.

This waiting was already making her nuts!

"Commander, permission to pace?"

"No." Finally, though, when Leeth didn't argue, she seemed to unbend slightly. "I don't want you moving around, complicating the tactical situation."

"But I need to be able to check everyone, and there are lots more people this year. And it's not like they can shoot *Her*." From the way the agents' expressions shifted, most of them seemed to think they had *two* mad people to worry about: one contained in his cell and the other one outside it, with them. "So that must mean you're really here in case *Godsson* somehow gets free, right?" she continued, first checking that the light on the intercom showed it was just monitoring, not in two-way mode.

The Commander looked at her as if she'd managed to surprise her.

"But I look at all these people and kinda wonder, what if it just gives Her more targets to choose from? She's real sneaky."

"Come here."

She went, expecting the Commander was about to really let loose on her, but instead the woman just inclined her head, indicating she should take up a position alongside her. And there the two of them just stood, side by side at the place where the 'T' junction used to be, watching the room full of tense men and women.

It was kinda nice.

After a while, the Commander spoke, so quietly that only the very closest agents would have been able to hear. Well, and Leeth, of course, even if she'd been upstairs. Not that the Commander could know that.

"All the magician types say they can't see anything when 'she's' around. Even with that 'Imaginal sight' of theirs. So how do *you* see it, Sara?"

"I... it's hard to explain. It's a pattern. *She* looks like a pattern, I mean. It's almost like imagining. You see things line up and make edges that show some of Her outlines. Curvy outlines. It's a little bit like when you see shapes in clouds. Have you ever done that?"

At the Commander's nod, she continued. "But it's not the same. I've looked, but I've never seen Her in clouds. Or anywhere except in the J-, uh, in the woods, outside.

"The way the branches bend, or the ferns, or the flower stems. And always moving, and flowing, and always kind of... female curves. Sexy."

"It sounds very like just your own imagination, Sara."

Leeth looked sideways at the Commander. But the way she'd said it, she wasn't being mean. Just asking a serious question. Like she was still willing to consider the possibility that it wasn't just 'Sara's' imagination. And it was a good question, actually. She'd wondered the same thing, herself. She tried her best to answer.

"It is, actually," she admitted. "Quite like that. But when the shape moves – the *pattern* – slipping from one branch to the next, or swooping down to sort of undulate – you know, like a snake – in the grass, or dance in the ferns...."

"That still sounds like imagination."

"Except it goes on too long. For everything to move just right, for so long, so you could imagine it... That doesn't happen except when She's around."

She looked up: the Commander still looked unconvinced.

Reluctantly, she continued, and her own voice dropped lower, a bit embarrassed now by what she was going to have to share. "Yeah, but she also makes the *spirits* do mean stuff, sometimes. If they don't run away in time."

"The spirits. What spirits?" The Commander's voice had gone flat. Clipped.

"Well, I don't know, exactly. I can't *See* them, like magic people can. It's more like how I can see Her." She almost added, 'or not-Robo,' but thought that might be one step too far. She thought maybe the Commander was already beginning to doubt her.

"By how they move. Sometimes, the wind does funny

things. It'll twirl among the flowers, then swoop across a puddle and spin back, then swirl around some fronds, playing with them, you know, just kind of dancing around. Not like wind just blowing. Actually *playing*. You can tell, by the way it hangs around, swirling and diving and circling and swooping. Just having fun.

"Sometimes I'd dance with them." She smiled, remembering. "At first it surprised them, then they kind of seemed to like it." She didn't add that since she'd Unfolded she could even feel them, when she touched them. But she had to be careful to be gentle, or else she hurt them.

The Commander was looking at her strangely. *Commander Amanda*. Her name had almost made Leeth giggle until she'd looked into her eyes the first time. Leeth figured no one laughed at Commander Amanda Stone's name twice.

"But sometimes," Leeth said, "*She* would be there, and sometimes a spirit didn't realise and run away fast enough. Then, She'd make them do bad stuff." Noting the Commander's expression, she added, "like puffing leaves right into the middle of a huge web that'd taken a spider a whole evening to do. Or just gusting, or blowing sticks right through it, to tear it. I saw her make two spirits fight, once. That was awful."

Commander Stone just looked at her, for a long time.

"How about if you moved just slowly through my people? You think you could see 'her' if she gets out of that cell?"

For several seconds Leeth just blinked at her, shocked at not being ignored by a grown up. And an important one. Then nodded, definitely. "Yeah!"

She didn't think, though, it'd be a good idea to point out that She didn't really come *out* of the cell.

"All right. But keep out of my people's sight lines to the cell. Understand? And try to do it *lightly,* if you know what I mean? Don't be putting them off."

Leeth thought she did. She nodded.

"Okay, people," the Commander said, turning and raising her voice, "listen up. Just in case Sara *can* sense this thing, she's going to be moving around. Looking at everything. Don't shoot her, okay?"

Leeth grinned, and nodded her thanks for the trust. She decided she liked the Commander. She hoped the older woman would survive the night.

CHAPTER 51

For the first time ever, Leeth thought she sensed it before Godsson did.

It was still an hour till sunset, and she realized everyone had sort of hunched-in on themselves. Slowly, the room outside Godsson's cell had become somehow creepy. Like they were all actors in some scary movie, waiting for the monster to appear and kill the guy who least expected it.

In the new, open area, the narrow oblong window of Godsson's cell peered out at them like a gateway they were all expecting monsters to pour through. Looking around carefully, though, eyes unfocused, between the fifteen men and women spaced out, she could see no trace of Her.

But as the seconds piled slowly and patiently one on top of the other, like weights pressing down harder and harder, Leeth grew certain She was there. The creepy-movie feeling was the sort of mean trick She enjoyed. She caught the Commander's eye and nodded, once.

The Commander didn't *say* anything at all, but a moment later all her men and women seemed to snap more erect, coming to full alert. Several of them caught Leeth's eye, and she nodded to them to be ready, just as she had to the Commander.

And then Godsson cried out, golden light blazing through the small aperture looking into his room. She saw the intercom light flip into two-way mode, and Leeth, about to dart across and look in, paused to check first with the Commander. Who inclined her head, and then her agents stepped aside, making a clear path to the cell.

Godsson cried out again, a note of dismay Leeth had never heard before, and then she was squinting in against the glare.

He staggered, tearing at his hair, at his cheeks; then the golden glare winked out.

There was nothing in the room with him. Nothing to see. *But I wouldn't be able to see* Her *even if she was in there right now!* Leeth realized: *there was nothing to see her* with. Then Godsson's flesh started glowing as if lit from within, brighter and brighter. His skin shifted from red to golden as he *screamed*. Then light flared out from every inch of him, snapping back out into the usual thick golden dome, and he shouted in triumph.

For just a moment, Leeth thought she'd seen *curves* thrust out on the expanding surface of the spell. Then she felt Keepie's hand on her shoulder, pulling her away as he and then the shamans arrived to peer inside, their eyes already with that strange unfocused sort of glaze to them.

She let herself be moved back, even as Godsson began grunting with effort, the tone of dismay gone, but already a note of desperation that usually only crept in right near the end. In the bad years.

Something was Wrong. Something had already gone wrong.

There were too many people.

Since they'd gotten the new-generation service bots, the only people in the Institute normally, apart from the patients, were her and Keepie, Faith and Mr Shanahan, dopey Dr Simmons, and Professor Sanders.

Godsson's cries and shouts continued, and she forced herself to look, at all the men and women here, *certain* that something had gone badly wrong.

Her uncle and the three female shamans were stepping away from the small window with slight head shakes, but still somehow like they too knew that something was different this year.

Then she heard it – under Godsson's cries, the sound of gunfire. From above. Then machine guns. Then the dull roar of a truck engine. The soldiers, up above, outside!

But the Commander's head had tilted up, and then she and several of her men and women began swearing. "Lewis. Ferguson. Warne." She said. "Take a team and get up there. Take down anyone using lethal weaponry. Stay in contact."

Without a word, seven people sprinted across the room and down the corridor to the stairs. *She only said that aloud for our benefit,* Leeth realized. She was about to explain to the puzzled magicians about Her making the soldiers shoot each other, when the Commander herself spoke.

"It appears that several soldiers have just attacked their comrades. It's not clear if it's a terrorist action, or if something else is at work."

Leeth felt her heart sink strangely, as if the whole room was a lift that had just started falling.

Godsson's cries intensified.

Then she saw it. Saw Her. Everywhere, in every twist and curve in the shape of a sleeve, the sweep of a ponytail, the angle of an arm. The arc of a nasty smile. Lily was *all through the room*; coiled around *everyone!*

Godsson's hoarse cries grew frantic.

Leeth felt a whisper around her, a seductive shiver up her spine, a desire, a pressure. *Let me in.*

"Target acquired, *target acquired!*" she screamed, and threw herself onto the nearest person with the Wrongness twisted around her, scarcely absorbing the fact that it was a woman. She felt her fingertips tingle, a fierce surge of defiance flaring through every nerve, and she felt it, felt Her, like strands of ghostly nerves mockingly extended out from within the woman as if they were invisible control wires looping in and out of the agent's brain, hijacking her nervous system and twisting thoughts like puppet strings that pulled and pushed at the real woman.

Leeth *grabbed*, wrapping her hands around them and *wrenching*, tearing them loose, snatching at the unseen mass as it whipped free, now lashing at *her*, pricking and slicing as the threads tried to force their way in, even as she felt half of them flood toward the man nearest the Commander.

"Target acquired!" she screamed, hands already dropping from the confused woman to throw herself across the room at the male agent beside Commander Stone, who had already begun turning toward her in puzzlement, as if seeing someone other than his superior there.

Godsson's shouts grew louder, more urgent, and behind her she heard several struggles break out.

The man by the Commander was unbuckling his trousers – at least, until her hand shot up to slam into his chin. His eyes rolled up in his head and he collapsed like a discarded bath-towel. Leeth slammed to a halt and spun around. She looked away, unfocusing; looking *between*, not *at*. And glimpsed tendrils gathering, withdrawing from him. She leaped forward, her fingers sweeping criss-cross through the empty air and felt *something* invisibly part. Godsson cried out with a happy note, as if his opponent had just fallen back.

Mr Smith, she saw, was looking around in a kind of

outraged confusion, but Leeth thought he looked safe. Across the room, her uncle had gone white, his eyes fastened to her as if he'd just had some awful revelation. But she had no time for that as she dove, shouting, toward her next target. All around her, the agents now fought and struggled against their own teammates.

"Stand down, people, *stand down!*" the Commander ordered, striding amongst her men and women, reinforcing her silent commands with spoken words. Her eyes met Leeth's, demanding she *do something*.

Leeth paused, looking at the spaces between the people. All across the room, tendrils looped and coiled, clear to her eyes as a few of the agents tried to follow their orders, only to be forced to fight back as their friends tore at their clothes – or their flesh.

She saw the three shamans start to cast some big spell, and something about the unnatural calm that infused the hurried gestures told her they intended to send everyone in the room to sleep.

Which would free Her to concentrate all Her efforts on Godsson, instead of giving Leeth the chance-

"No, *don't-*"

But they were ignoring her, and it was all she could do to fling herself back and dive around the corner of the side corridor, hoping the magicians needed line of sight to their targets for their spells to take effect.

No! Why does no one *ever listen to me?* She could've woven a dance of destruction through the creature that had wrapped itself around all those men and women, tearing and shredding until there'd been nothing left except the part inside Godsson's cell, fighting him!

She heard bodies fall, slumping to the floor, and the sound of struggle cease; and then, within a second, Godsson cried out in horror, as if he suddenly faced overwhelming odds.

At least the stupid spell hadn't affected *her*. She jumped to her feet, to see Commander Stone back at the ex-'T' junction, sagging weakly against the wwall, blinking and dazed, as if she'd been drugged and was forcing herself to stay conscious by sheer willpower alone.

Godsson screamed, and she ran back into the other room and threw herself up against the small window, ignoring the area behind her now full of slumped figures, some bleeding, some half naked. Her uncle and the shamans followed her, crowding her out of the way, but she'd already seen enough.

Godsson's skin had been rippling, just like those two men all those years before. Despite his golden glowing protective circle.

"Let me in there – She's getting him!"

"No, Sara, it's him, not her-"

"Don't be stupid, Keepie! Did he do all this, too? And upstairs? I *saw* Her, Uncle. It's not him, it's Her!"

"Perhaps it is time for the cyanide?" one of the female shamans asked.

Leeth heard the door two floors above open, and steps hurriedly descending. Commander Stone staggered over to the woman, shaking her head. "Fifty-fifty. Remember the dragon's warning."

Leeth had no idea what they were talking about, but in his cell, Godsson shouted defiance, and the light changed from gold to green. She forced her way back there, beside two of the shamans who still stared in, pushing the women aside so hard they almost fell.

Godsson's flesh had stopped rippling, and she shouted encouragement. "Yes! Yes, Godsson, you can do it! You can beat-"

Then the whole surface of his now green and gold dome *undulated,* seeming to slip just a fraction, shrinking.

She was all over it, pressing down, sliding in. *She* was enormous. Gathered all together. Somehow Leeth knew She filled the room.

She spun back to her uncle. "Let me go in! It's wrapped all around his magic. If you let me in, I can kill Her once and for all!"

Her uncle stared. "Are you mad? You *saw* what happens to people who try to help!" He stepped forward, one hand gripping her shoulder. "No. No, Leeth. I forbid it. No!"

His voice almost broke, then, and he blinked, rapidly, and she saw *tears* in Keepie's eyes. In *Keepie's* eyes!

"I have to, Uncle. It's why I'm here, isn't it? I have to try."

The footsteps down the stairs turned into steps along

the corridor, and she recognized the sound of Professor Sanders's breathing before he appeared around the corner.

Godsson *keened*, and his light suddenly dimmed. When she turned back she saw his expression changing, alternating between desperate horror and vicious glee. Parts of his dome had holes, stretching out in curving tendrils which she knew were parts of Her.

"You have to let me in! There's no time left. Look for yourself!"

She stepped back.

Her uncle stepped forward, freezing as he took in the scene. "No."

Professor Sanders moved past him. Looked. Began punching the code himself as she watched. Her uncle grabbed his arm, pulling him away, and the older man looked past him. "Restrain him."

Commander Stone slid up behind her uncle, wove her arms through his, and effortlessly tugged him away, though she staggered slightly as she did so.

"Sanders! *No!*" her uncle shouted.

But Professor Sanders was already finishing entering the code, she saw. "I have to lock this behind you, Sara, you understand?"

Their eyes met for a moment. Then the door swung out and Leeth charged in.

CHAPTER 52

The moment she stepped inside, she realized it had all just been a trap. She was too small. Completely insignificant.

Several slender tendrils of *Her* withdrew from Godsson to envelop her, coiling around her as they sought entrance. They flowed over her; *through* her. Dwarfing her. Toying with her.

I've been tricked.

It was going to end for her now, too. *I should give up.* She'd be turned into a monster, alongside Godsson, and together the two of them would rage, and ravage, and take their revenge-

No.

Just that one small word.

No.

Those weren't my *thoughts.* And with that understanding, Leeth surged into furious motion. She threw herself into the enveloping strands, spinning around until they cocooned her. Then with a savage energy that came from herself, purely from her, she cut and clawed through invisible threads. Through the threads she sensed startled pain and dismay, and retreat. Again she threw herself forwards, *gripping* before it could flee-

But as she felt something twist and slide inside her, she knew it wasn't going to be that easy. She'd been a fool to have ever thought it could be that easy. The energy kept pouring in, filling her as it burned so liquidly; a terrible, joyous energy that spoke to every cell, to something deeper than the cells, something that intertwined and looped inside like paired snakes.

She'd been supposed to grab Her; grab Lily. Instead Lily had grabbed *her.* But could that work out the same way? Could Godsson still do what he needed to?

But Godsson was too busy struggling against the larger part of Lily which he fought. And, yeah, her entrance had eased the pressure on him a little. But somehow she knew that was only temporary, while Lily changed *her* into something monstrous to attack *him.* Attacking her friend, using her. If it even *was* Lily. It seemed... different. Bigger. *Developed.*

So instead of just *holding*, she clawed and shredded the outer creature, while she tried to work out how to fight the terrible thing she could feel gathering momentum deep inside her. Across the small room, Godsson cried out, light and *energy* surging from him, while she panted and whirled and spun and tore. But she wasn't enough. Godsson wasn't enough. They needed something more, something else.

The flesh beneath her skin *rippled*.

And in the dismay that shocked through her at that awful sight, inspiration struck.

She lifted her head. At the small window, her uncle's horrified face peered in, his white face pressed up to the thick glass.

"Keepie! Your invisible monster. You didn't believe me, but it's really real. It hates Her! It fights Her! We need it here. Can you call it?"

For an awful, endless second as she registered his puzzled expression, she thought he was just going to shake his head 'sorry.' But then his mouth opened, and he nodded, and she turned back to her own battle.

She cried her defiance, while Godsson fought his own war within his tattered protective dome. But as much as she fought, as fiercely as she tore and shredded parts of Lily, as they recoiled from her and she pursued, she could find no way to fight the change she felt building inside her, deep within her cells.

Even as she fought, the sounds from outside died, and she knew they'd turned the intercom off. Why would they do that? She strained, listening through the soundproof glass, pushing aside the sound of Godsson's gasps and cries.

"*Can you heal her from death by cyanide, Harmon?*"

"*Of course not. Unbinding cyanide molecules from the enzyme within mitochondria is no part of any human healing mechanism. And would you really risk a fifty percent chance of calamity? Now shut up. I'm busy.*"

She had no spare attention for anything except her own struggle, no matter the talk of cyanide. If she got turned into a monster, it was good to know they had a plan.

But time was up, she sensed. She turned despairing eyes to the man suffering similar tortures alongside her.

He'd stopped the rippling of his own flesh from within, before!

"Godsson! Help! Burn it out of me! Burn it out of me

like you did for yourself, before!"

Their eyes met, but he hesitated, looking shocked by her request for some reason, before a strange expression came over him, something cruel and gleeful, and he seemed to seize on that. One swift, complex gesture, and in the next instant she was burning alive, stunned silent by an agony that slammed into her like a solid wall, scorching through her, an expanding series of bubbles that scoured outwards from the deepest core of her, spiraling and un-raveling up and out, into cells, into nerve and muscle, and the screams exploded from her until she was nothing but shrieking torture made manifest, excruciated far beyond any word to describe pain.

Better than becoming a monster, was her last con-scious thought, and she welcomed the cleansing fire; hop-ing it might burn through *Her*, too.

It burned.

And it burned.

And it burned.

Forever.

And she endured.

Thought returned only slowly. Her next thought *wasn't* a thought. Just a sensation. Bliss.

No pain.

But a cry from Godsson shocked her mind back into ac-tion, and she shook herself, rolling to her side. She was free, for the moment, but he was still wrapped up tight, more holes than glow now in his warped and collapsing protective circle.

She forced herself to her feet, leg muscles spasming like they were still in shock, and tottered over toward him. She half fell, half dove through the largest gap in his shield, tumbling up to grab onto him, as much to pull herself up-right as to tear at those invisible threads.

She realized that he, too, was somehow holding onto Her, hurting Her, and she had to grin as she felt the sharp energy surge through her fingers to flare out past her nails, tearing into Her as Godsson fought alongside her.

It felt good.

She twisted one hand around Her and *held*, like Gods-son did; like Godsson had told her to do; but with her other hand she *shredded*.

But as the two of them leaned against one another; she dodging and writhing and Holding with her left while her right hand struck and clawed and stabbed, furling and slicing, defending and attacking, over and over... as the two fought, and fought, and fought... she gradually saw it still wasn't enough. As if She was just one end of a hose, connected to some endless reservoir of Awful.

Keepie's voice shouted from the intercom.

"Now, Leeth! Call the Institute monster to you now!"

She closed her eyes, wrapping her hands tightly in the invisible coils and then just holding on grimly as she imagined first Robo, then the far-more-scary non-Robo that he had become. Remembered herself teasing it, shooting it with her arrows, dancing away when it pursued. Called to it. Thought furiously, «She *is here for you!*»

And it came.

She opened her eyes as she felt its Wrongness, its Cold, and looked up into Godsson's face to see his eyes go as round as ping pong balls when non-Robo's chill presence suddenly flooded into the room, for some reason pouring out of Godsson himself, right there inside his protective dome. Despite herself, despite her resolve to stay, to hold Her, something about non-Robo so scared her that her resolve shattered and she cringed away.

Non-Robo swelled bigger, and she sensed frantic flailing movement around Godsson, saw his muscles tighten as she felt the strands twist in her own fingers, struggling.

Non-Robo swelled more-

She jumped away, crying.

She had to. She jumped away, even while part of her told her not to be such a coward, to go back. But her legs simply refused to obey her.

And non-Robo met Her, enveloped Her, and with a silent explosion, the two shrank, or were somehow pulled inside Godsson and sucked away.

Then the door was opening, her uncle and Commander Stone were hauling her out of the room, and the door slammed shut behind her.

She twisted around in their grips.

Inside, Godsson tottered over to lean up against the window, no longer surrounded by glowing domes or twined about with invisible tendrils.

"It's gone, Sara. It's finally gone!"

He stared at her. But there was something desperate in his eyes. Like he was telling her something else. Something about what their victory meant.

She sagged, tried to stand, failed, held up solely by the Commander's strong arms. She looked up into the woman's face. Who, she knew, could communicate with her people above. She put one hand on the Commander's arm. Gripped.

"Is Faith-?"

And then collapsed.

CHAPTER 53

For some time, she sat half-dazed at a table by the doorway of the cafeteria, vaguely aware of slightly-injured FBI agents and soldiers sitting around in various stages of shock or excitement, their clothing torn, gun-shot, and blood-stained. She gathered that the dead and injured had been carried into the gym, and Keepie was there now, trying to heal them all.

The word 'Faith' brought her up out of... sleep...? and she listened more closely.

"Damn, Coop, I tell you I've never seen anything like it. She's like, twelve years old, I'd say, a model *three*, which is, what, from ten years ago, but I've never seen any cyber mutt *think* like that! She must've taken down five guys on her own, and none of them could get weapon-lock her! Who trained her?"

Faith was all right. She smiled, and let exhaustion reclaim her.

When next she struggled awake, it was because she'd grown too hot – and found someone had covered her with a blanket. *Weird. Why would anyone do that, in midsummer?* A distant, heavy mechanical tread was drawing nearer. Tossing aside the blanket, she stretched, enjoying the arching of her back and the play of muscle and tendons, all the way to her fingertips, as she spread her arms wide, and back, and then stood up. She smelled food.

The men and women in the cafeteria fell silent, both those with the FBI armbands and name badges, and the soldiers in their khaki and camouflage. They were all looking at her.

The food smells strengthened, and the heavy steps came right up into the doorway, and she realized that they weren't looking at her, of course, they'd just been smelling the food. A heavily-cybered old soldier in a full exoskeleton stomped in, carrying a whole bunch of big white plastifoam boxes with delicious aromas flooding from them.

The talking started up again and everyone leaped into action, off-loading cartons from the old soldier and passing the food around, steam visibly rising from piping-hot serving containers.

It was so weird seeing the eating area full, with people at every table and more chairs dragged in. The food smelled delicious, like nothing she'd scented before. Her stomach rumbled, and she really wanted to stay, but finding Faith was more important. And Keepie, too. And Mr Shanahan.

She wriggled her bare feet on the floor, enjoying the cold of the tiles. Unnoticed, then, she headed out to find her friends.

It was fully night now, but Faith was waiting at the edge of the lawn. She sprang to her feet the moment Leeth emerged, racing across the stretch of gravel. Leeth plunged down the front steps, leaping to grab Faith in mid-air as they threw themselves toward one another.

Spinning, they tumbled together down onto and over the gravel, laughing and yipping, nuzzling and hugging. "Ouch, wait! *You've* got thick fur, but I don't!" She felt cuts and grazes on her elbows and back as she disentangled herself from her companion. *Maybe that hadn't been the best place for a reunion?*

Torchlight flashed past, then locked onto them both, making her wince and blink as pounding boot-steps skidded to a halt beside her.

"Stand down, K9, stand down! Are you all right, miss?"

She looked up from the offered hand to an earnest and youthful face. "Sure. Just a few scratches. I'll get my uncle to heal them, later." The man had angled his light away, and it took her a moment of blinking before she could see properly again. She looked at her lovely black cat suit and winced at the rips and tears. He wouldn't be able to heal *those*. Rats.

"Never mind, Faith." She nuzzled her again, taking several excited licks to the side of her face, laughing. "I heard you did real well: neutralized five soldiers all by yourself! Good girl!"

"Uh, miss, are you supposed to... are *you* Sara? Wow, you're...."

She reluctantly let go of Faith and stood up, reaching out to shake his hand like you were supposed to. "*Sara*," she snorted, before remembering. "Oh. Um, I mean, I guess so. I mean, sure, yeah, of course I'm 'Sara.' Pleased to meet you, um, corporal...?"

For some reason he blushed. "Uh, just Private, ma'am.

Private Washington, ma'am. *Jomo* Washington."

He had nice brown eyes, and a kind smile, though his eyes looked a little twitchy, like he'd been through a tough time. His khaki shirt was sopping wet – like he'd *washed* it! After a *battle*? He must be- Then she noticed the neat holes punched through that shirt to the dark skin beneath. Oh.

She stepped closer, smiling to show she was friendly.

Reaching out a finger, she touched the smooth bare flesh highlighted by the white of the undershirt visible through the hole. But at her touch, he flinched back.

What was the matter with him? "Gosh. Did, uh, did doctor Harmon heal you up from being dead? Do you know where he is?"

Jomo moved, splashing his light up.... She grabbed his wrist, stopping him almost before he'd started; before he could blind her again. For some reason he cried out and tried to jump back. She tugged him forward to stop him: she didn't want him shining his stupid torch in her eyes! But in the dark, she saw his eyes go wide. Somehow she'd scared him. A moment later, she even had to grab his other hand when it shot down toward his sidearm. She im-mobilized that, too.

That seemed to make him *really* scared: if Faith hadn't growled a deep warning from right behind him then, she wasn't sure what might have happened. He was moaning – "no, no" – as she gripped him, and she could feel him trembling.

What was wrong with him? He seemed terrified.

Oh.

He'd been attacked a little while ago by Her, maybe been shot by one of his own friends who'd gone crazy. And *he* couldn't see in the dark like she could. Probably he'd just wanted some light so he could see her face. And now some tricksy female thing had grabbed him in the dark.

How to reassure him?

"That was mean of them, making you go out alone in the dark," she told him. "But it's okay, you're not alone now." She did the only other thing she could think of, then, and moved forwards, drawing his arms around her before releasing him and hugging him.

He actually started trembling.

"I'm sorry, Jomo. I thought you were going to shine your flashlight in my face. I didn't mean to scare you."

For some reason, her words seemed to make him tremble even more, and she felt his hands start pushing at her, desperately trying to get away.

She felt helpless. What did you do when even a *hug* didn't work?

At that moment, she heard the front doors of the Institute swing open behind her, and footsteps. A broad torch beam swung over and spotlit the two of them. She let him go and Jomo jumped back and out of her arms.

A second passed before her uncle's voice rang out. "What are you doing, Sara?"

He sounded strangely unhappy. "Uh, Jomo, he was, I...."

She didn't want to say she'd scared him, she knew that'd be awfully embarrassing. "I was just asking Private Jomo where you were, Uncle."

She heard his steps approaching, the torchlight wobbling, and she turned around, looking down so she could shield her eyes.

"He was whispering it in your ear, I suppose. I see you've recently torn your clothes, too. All part of finding me, no doubt?"

"Faith and I kind of... rolled around on the gravel."

"Of course. Of course you would."

He was right next to them, now, and he looked Jomo straight in the eye. "I think you've helped my ward 'find me,' Private." He paused, and drew in his breath sharply. "My healing worked splendidly, I see. Even feeling frisky, I take it? But perhaps you should be continuing your patrol, if that is what you are supposed to be doing?"

"Sir, yes, sir!" the man said, snapping erect and saluting. Then practically fled into the darkness.

"Oh, Keepie, don't be so horrid. I grabbed him, in the dark, and he got scared. So I hugged him to try to calm him down, but that only seemed to scare him even more. I think he thought I was *Her*."

She looked up into her uncle's eyes, his face all scowly and angry, but gradually his expression softened, and he shook his head. "Were it anyone other than you, little one, I'd think you were lying. Really, 'Pouncing' on soldiers in the dark after they've just experienced a very frightening and disturbing attack? That wasn't the wisest course of action, now, was it?"

She wanted to explain it hadn't been like that, but he seemed to have calmed down, and that was the main thing, after all. She took his hand, and examined him more closely. He looked exhausted. Faith looked at her questioningly, but she gave the hand signal that meant she was okay, and Faith trotted off into the darkness.

She put one arm around her uncle as they reached the front steps, leaning into him, and he took the hint and let her help him climb the steps, his feet plonking down on the ground real heavily.

"How many soldiers did you heal up from being dead tonight, Keepie? It looked like Jomo had been shot through the heart and lungs."

"He had. But he was not augmented; and he was one of the early cases, so his healing went quite smoothly. The same wasn't true for all the others. Six, I could save. Three I couldn't. Fourteen others I was able to mend from relatively simple gunshot wounds, and two from being run over by a truck."

"Could you mend my scratches from the gravel, Keepie? Or do you need to go to bed?"

Her uncle looked at her a little strangely as they went deeper into the building.

"Perhaps after the debriefing. Come."

The debriefing wasn't as exciting as she'd hoped. The shamans kept looking at her the whole time, their eyes often doing the Imaginal-looky thing. It kind of creeped her out after a while. They'd whisper amongst themselves – which would have been great, because she could hear them quite clearly – except she couldn't understand the language they spoke in.

It made her want to shake them. But the moment she thought *that*, it seemed to set the three off on a fresh new round of urgent whispering.

Commander Stone was the opposite, and even made sure to sit next to her. Several times she smiled warmly, and spoke up for her more than once.

Keepie was furious with Professor Sanders, she could

tell, just because the Professor had let her go in to help Godsson.

No one would explain about the cyanide, though, when she asked. They just pretended not to even know what she was talking about.

But after that, it got real boring. Several times she'd even nodded off. But then an unfamiliar voice was saying something about a Dragon, and pennies finally dropping, and long games. She missed most of it, though. She was sitting where she could see Mr Smith's face, and only woke up properly when it gradually dawned on her that he looked like someone had poked a titanium rod up his spine *and* shown him pictures of his father turning into a were-wolf, or something.

The strange voice was a man's, but artificial. Even disguised, though, it carried an air of utter confidence. It was coming from the speaker in Professor Sanders's desk.

"At least we know now why he didn't want Godsson in his own country. Dr Harmon: three things. First, if you recall anything more about what the Dragon said regarding Feyborn, respond to the secure message I have sent you. Your information is likely to have strategic value for our nation.

"Second, if these incidents indicate the existence of a new kind of incorporeal entity, that too has strategic national value. Do *not* publish any research on this topic for now, however. You may discuss it amongst the personnel you deem fit at the Institute, naturally. You may also send reports on the topic to me via the same secure communication channel. Do *not* interpret that as a request for you to begin experimentation in the area. I doubt that any of us understands the risks involved."

"And the third thing?" her uncle asked. Looking a little off-balance, she thought.

"A suggestion regarding your ward. Now that she is awake."

Leeth tensed. *How did he even know I'd been asleep? Was he* watching? She looked around for a camera. The trouble was, they could be tiny.

"Make sure she understands that the Dragon is the head of state of a foreign superpower in competition with our own nation."

"Why do you care what *I* think about Lord Lao Pi Shen? Who are you, anyway? And why are you using a fake voice?"

Everyone went still: *all* looking at her now. Like she'd just said something stupid, or shocking. Except Keepie: he just looked a bit lost.

"Because you have befriended Godsson, Sara," the voice answered her, sharply. "And while none of us know why the Dragon chose to dump him in our country, it is certain it was to hurt us rather than help us."

"Godsson wouldn't hurt us! He's fighting Her for us!"

"I am in fact more concerned by the Dragon than by Godsson."

She wanted to ask more questions, but caught Commander Stone's eye: who shook her head, telling her to stop arguing.

"I'd like to keep the combined force on site for a day, then re-evaluate the situation," the Commander said.

"Very good. I leave that in your hands, Commander."

And then the unknown person got them all to agree to cover up the real cause. For the three foreign shamans, Leeth noticed he mostly did it by asking *questions;* for the other people there, including Mr Smith, he simply *ordered* them.

They had to cover it all up because apparently everyone in the whole world would get real scared. Other countries would say Godsson either had to be killed, or moved to some place where he could be watched by the international community. And while no one seemed real happy about having poor Godsson *here*, they all agreed *that'd* be a bigger mistake.

After he'd arranged that, the mysterious person handed the meeting over to the others, and 'signed off.'

Somehow, the debriefing was about to finish without anyone answering the most important question!

"So can Godsson be released now that we killed the thing that's been attacking him?"

This time everyone stared at her like she'd just grown a second head or something! Even Commander Stone kind of leaned away from her.

Didn't *anyone* understand?

But every single person in the room – even Uncle, this

time – was watching her like *she* might be dangerous; like maybe they should be locking *her* up alongside Godsson! It made her want to scream at them, but she knew that'd only make it much worse. So all she could do in the end was shut her mouth and kind of smile and wince; like '*Oh, yeah, of course, sorry, that'd be a* dumb *idea, wouldn't it? Ha ha. Whatever was I thinking?*' Dumb Grups.

Then they all started talking at once, about the 'possibility of infection,' and 're-hosting,' while the shamans all looked and looked at her, their eyes all funny. But in the end the oldest of the three shaman women said it seemed okay. Whatever *it* was. But all three kept Looking at her.

Soon after that, the meeting ended, to everyone's relief, and they all dispersed to their quarters.

And Keepie *did* heal her cuts and grazes from her tumble with Faith, before staggering back to his own room.

CHAPTER 54

She wasn't sure about the soldiers. The agents had been nicer: treated her more seriously.

It'd felt real good when Commander Stone had shaken her hand, in both of hers, and actually *thanked* her. 'Give me a call when you're a bit older, if you think you might like a career in the FBI. You've got potential, kiddo.'

Leeth had blushed down to the tips of her toes. Though she'd noticed her uncle hadn't looked too pleased.

But the soldiers had been strange. Some of them looked kind of sideways at her; some of them looked nervous, as if maybe Jomo had said something weird; and others kind of joked about her when they thought she couldn't hear them, about how they'd like to 'tap that ass,' as if she was just some kind of toy.

She memorized those ones, and began planning a Hunt.... But they left the next day, and things went back to normal.

Except they wouldn't let her go and talk to Godsson anymore. She tried all her sneaking techniques, but none had worked, and Mr Shanahan and Keepie got real cross with her for trying.

But she'd learned her lesson during the debriefing. *She* knew they'd killed Her, and so they could let Godsson go, now.

She'd even worked out that that was what that last look he'd given her had meant.

She just had to work out *how* to rescue him.

She also wondered about what would happen *after* she rescued Godsson: would Uncle want to join their team? That'd make it just perfect: then it'd be her, and Godsson, and Faith, *and* Keepie. But the way he'd looked at her in the debriefing when she'd suggested letting Godsson free, she was pretty sure he wouldn't want to.

Right now, inside Professor Sanders's office, the Director and her uncle were arguing again. She sat outside, slumped down against the door, pretending to be annoyed and bored and waiting for her uncle, in case the new security cameras were watching.

With the back of her head pressed against the door, though, it was super easy to hear everything.

Which was how she learned that everyone was still scared by Melisande d'Artelle, even though she was dead.

She also learned that the Dragon Lord Lao Pi Shen had *personally* brought Godsson here, years and years ago. And he'd warned them then about a 'fractally replicating pattern' of her death.

That was what Keepie thought had attacked them.

She wasn't sure what 'fractally' meant, but it sounded cool. She'd look it up, later.

There was also stuff about magic theory she didn't understand; and stuff about how apparently some people had begun to think Godsson was teaching her uncle things. Other countries even wanted to send 'observers' during Godsson's battles. Though Prof Sanders and her uncle called them 'episodes,' like it was some kind of trid drama, not a real heroic fight. And the other countries also wanted to send people to help 'treat' him. But she gathered the Emperor of China didn't want anyone except Keepie or the Institute to look after Godsson, and was quite fierce about that.

She also learned about the cyanide. It turned out they could flood Godsson's room with hydrogen cyanide – which was a poisonous *gas* – at any time they wanted, which would kill him in seconds.

She couldn't believe Professor Sanders could be so horrid.

She also learned what 'fifty-fifty' meant: the Dragon Lord had warned them, before the attack, that killing Godsson was just as likely to set Her free in the world as to block Her from getting here. Which was the reason they hadn't tried that during the big battle. 'Her' was a much better name than 'fractal death thing,' in her opinion. But it didn't matter anymore, since She was dead. Killed by Godsson and her, together!

They'd make a great team. She wondered if Godsson knew a flying spell? If he could cast it on her, then it'd *really* be like she was HyperGirl! If she could learn to shoot laser beams from her fingers.

At least everyone involved pretty much agreed now it had all been real. They no longer said it was just Godsson hurting himself each year as 'penance.' Which she'd look up the meaning of when she got back to her room. Unless it was one of those words that she had to ask Keepie about, that didn't have definitions on the net.

But since they knew it wasn't Godsson just hurting himself, it made it harder to understand why they wouldn't set him free. It seemed like partly they weren't sure they'd really ended Her, and partly because they were simply scared of Godsson himself. Professor Sanders and her uncle, even though it was pretty clear they weren't friends anymore, both agreed he was insane and a danger to himself and others.

Which just showed how much *they* knew. Sure, Godsson was a bit strange, but he wasn't *crazy*. Lots of people thought *she* was strange, too!

Really, he was nice, and wouldn't hurt anyone unless they attacked him. He was always saying stuff like 'Let he who is without the first sin cast a stone,' and 'turn the other cheek.' She giggled and had to cover her mouth, when she remembered *that* little misunderstanding. Godsson had been *so* cross.

It was funny you could find out the meaning of most words – like 'mooning' – on the net, but not others – like 'heaven,' or 'sin,' or 'angel.'

What *was* a bit worrying, though, was that Uncle thought Godsson didn't like *her* anymore. And just because she was growing up and becoming a woman, and sexy, from what she could gather.

She knew Godsson was a bit weird about not seeing too much skin, but she'd learned now what she had to cover up so she still looked good, but he wouldn't get all upset. So that'd be okay.

Probably the best thing to do, though, would be to sit down with Godsson and have a 'heart to heart' talk to make him understand. Maybe they could even cuddle? He *was* kinda cute. And if she did it straight after she'd rescued him....

She smiled as she pictured it, hugging herself and gnawing at her bottom lip.

The still-arguing voices snapped her back to the subject. She winced as she considered what Keepie would say after she'd rescued Godsson. But once he saw Godsson wasn't hurting anybody, he'd have to admit she'd been right. Again. Like she'd been about practically *everything*.

The second biggest thing she'd learned was that no one knew exactly what kind of magician Melisande had been –

shaman or mage – but that some people called her an Infection Shaman. Which sounded pretty awful.

But the biggest and the *scariest* thing she'd learned was that a lot of people thought Melisande's magic might have got inside *her,* and infected her.

'She' *had* kind of gotten inside, too, it was true; but Godsson had burned Her all out. She shuddered just at the memory of that... agony. She wasn't sure she'd be brave enough to ask him to do that, ever again, not now she knew what it felt like. Luckily though, because they'd killed Her, that wouldn't be necessary. She was pretty sure she wasn't infected. Besides, even when She'd gotten inside, it had been Her magic, anyway, not Her herself, with that slippery voice. Maybe that was what She'd meant all those times when she'd asked if she could have a ride?

She considered herself, then, seriously. Had she changed? *Was* she infected?

She sure didn't feel any different. She hadn't had any sneaky whispers in her head. She hadn't even had any strange thoughts that pretended to be hers, but weren't. Especially, she didn't feel mean or want to hurt things or mess things up.

But she'd keep alert just in case, she decided.

She just had two questions left, after all that listening. What to call their super team, her and Faith and Godsson? And how to actually rescue Godsson. Fortunately, she'd watched carefully when Professor Sanders had entered the code. Though there was all sorts of extra security, now.

In the end, she decided Mr Shanahan could help.

She'd visited him after dinner, even though she hadn't worked out the exact details. To start with, she just pretended to be a bit sad that all their visitors had gone and that everything was all quiet and boring now. He'd let her in, and of course they'd started talking about this year's battle.

Then she'd wondered what *she'd* looked like during the attack, and when he said 'Amazing', at first she'd just smiled, then asked how he knew, then discovered that his security cameras had recorded the whole thing!

Of course, she'd begged him to show her, not that it took much convincing. Each year, as she got older and wiser, she'd noticed Mr S got easier to convince.

But this time, with Keepie's new information about nipples and men and stuff, she wondered if *that* was part of it, too. Which had led to her Grand Idea.

So to start with, she'd acted all excited, and jumped on his lap to watch.

At first, he'd tried to say she should get off, but she distracted him simply by ignoring him and pointing to interesting-looking thumbnails on his screen and asking him to play 'that one,' then another, and another. And kind of pointing her nipples at him while she did it.

For a while, though, she'd gotten distracted by the video itself. It was weird looking at herself; especially when the attack started. Chills prickled down her spine when she heard herself shouting out 'Target acquired!' Though she hadn't thought her voice was that squeaky in real life.

She moved well though, she decided, studying herself. It even looked a bit like a movie, except that after she 'attacked' people – it kind of *looked* like she was attacking them, except *she* knew she'd been slicing at pieces of Her – instead of falling down, her 'victims' sort of shook themselves and woke up.

Watching it was fun. But at last she remembered her Idea, and began making sure to 'accidentally' bump her breasts into his chest as she exclaimed and wriggled about in his lap. Every now and then she'd turn to look at him before letting herself get absorbed again by the action on screen, squealing about how exciting it all was.

Seeing the *hunger* in his eyes, and feeling the hardness pressing up under her thighs, felt good: made her feel powerful. And it was then that she knew her plan to find out what she needed to know was going to work. *She* had become the one in charge, not Mr S. It was like she had a superpower that could bend men to her will.

Just like *She* had said she could show her how to do. For a little while, she even worried that maybe She was still inside, and tricking her. But there was nothing sneaky or tricky about it. It was more like their bodies were both real hungry.

It was a very short distance from there, to wondering what Mr S would be like with his clothes off, with him *in-*

side her. She'd kissed him, first. He tried to pull away, to say they shouldn't. But when she unzipped her suit and pulled his large hand onto her breast, he didn't stop her. She snaked her other hand under her, between his thighs, and worked at his zipper. After that, it was all she could do to wrap her legs around his waist as he stood up and carried them both deeper than she'd ever been in his thickly-walled little house; through the small kitchen and down the narrow hallway past his toilet, and finally into his bedroom. And onto his bed.

She hadn't gone easy on him. He'd wanted to stop after the first time, but by then she'd worked out her plan, and used some of the new tricks and skills he'd just taught her, to make him go a second time. For the third time, she'd gotten on top, riding him like she was a cowgirl, and he really seemed to enjoy that, especially when she leaned forward so he could reach her breasts.

Best of all, though, had been snuggling up together, afterward.

Mr S had gotten real worried, though, saying they shouldn't have, and that they mustn't do it again. She'd just smiled, and soothed him, and said it was okay; that sure, they wouldn't do it again. Not unless he wanted to!

It was weird: both Mr S and Keepie saying they shouldn't do it again. She wondered if all men were like that?

And then, just like men were supposed to, a little while later he fell asleep. She wiped herself clean, zipped herself back into her clothes, and crept back to his computer. The password for his screen-unlocking was 'ck9 space space Faith apostrophe 48': two times, he hadn't been careful enough while she'd been with him, and she'd watched from the corner of her eye.

She started going through his system, quickly gaining confidence. She'd expected it to be much harder to operate than it looked. But it really was just a lot of touching and gesturing, like she'd seen him do heaps of times. There were lots more security cameras than she'd seen before, including ones that were heat or motion triggered.

As she checked it out more and more, though, the more impossible it looked to sneak past all the security precautions, to get to Godsson. She found the cameras for Godsson, and then found the search function, and checked to see what things were keeping him locked in. She discovered there were *lots* of warnings and alerts that would go off, for all different sorts of reasons, even if the access code was entered.

But up at the very top level of the whole system, there was just a slider that could be used to take everything down for 'preventative maintenance or system reload.' She slid it down, and it asked for a reason, so she typed in 'preventative maintenance.' Then it asked how long for, so she clicked on 'one hour,' and an 'Are you sure?' box popped up, waiting for her to click on it.

She hadn't actually meant to rescue Godsson *tonight*. But she probably wouldn't ever get a better chance.

She reached for the button, then hesitated.

What about Keepie?

Her fingertip hovered, just over the red 'Yes' button.

Keepie wouldn't want to come. He thought Godsson was mad and would hurt people. She was sure he wouldn't even give Godsson a *chance* to prove he wouldn't.

Her finger hovered.

But she couldn't just run away. Keepie would feel *awful*. He'd feel like she'd abandoned him. Like everyone had always abandoned her.

Until Keepie.

Keepie had never abandoned her.

In front of her, the screen and her fingertip suddenly swam underwater. She squeezed her eyes shut, and shook it away. *Stop it! You're not a baby. You're practically eighteen.* Her fingertip slid to the right, over the green 'No' button.

Her hand felt heavy, dragging down. Somehow, she felt that resting it, sitting back, would be cheating.

Decide.

She couldn't abandon Keepie.

But she didn't have to *stay* away. She and Faith and Godsson could run away *temporarily*. They'd do lots of rescues and save people and stuff, to prove to Keepie that Godsson was good. Then she'd sneak them all back in one night, and surprise him.

She imagined his shock, and how it would turn to delight. He'd smile, and race forward, and hug her till she was afraid he'd squash her chest! And then they'd *all* escape, together!

Through a sea of swimming pixels, her finger swung back to the left, back to the red blob, and she touched the screen.

All the indicator icons went from green to red.

Even with the system turned off, she still needed to enter the right codes at each door. Tiptoeing down the stairs, she could still hardly believe that all kinds of alarms wouldn't start blaring out, any moment. She knew it was silly to tiptoe, but she couldn't help doing it anyway.

Down the corridor from the stairs, glaring up at the new security camera, with its red light off... oh. If anyone woke up, and noticed the lights were off, they'd realise what was happening.

Well, we'd just better be gone before then.

The intercom light on Godsson's door showed it was off, and she hadn't figured out how to turn it on. The day of the attack, it had just happened by itself. Probably there was a remote control.

She rapped on the window, and Godsson spun around. When he saw her, he raised one eyebrow, then made his greeting gesture, which she knew now was a spell.

"Sara. This is unexpected. To what do I owe the pleasure of your visit?"

She touched her fingertips to the glass, which was as thick as the door itself, and felt the vibrations as he spoke.

"Uncle says you don't like me anymore. That you think She infected me."

He looked at her, like he was sizing her up. "And what do you think, yourself?"

"I think it'd be pretty stupid to let you out if I was."

And punched in the code.

CHAPTER 55

Godsson looked surprised, then wary, but at least he didn't instantly englobe himself in his golden protective circle against her. *That* had to be a good sign.

"Come on, we have to be quick. I turned off all the security."

He stepped to the doorway of his room, looking at her strangely, then stared up at the security camera with its light not glowing red, before dropping his eyes back to her. "So, no one can see what we do down here?"

"That's right."

His gaze went distant, like he was looking somewhere else. Had his hands just twitched? Had he just done another spell?

"What's the matter? Can't you get past the Dragon's Barrier spell on your room?"

Godsson shook his head, still not looking at her. "No. The Ward blocks only magic." He frowned. "How much of the security did you turn off?"

"Well, all of it. Everything."

"Really? You claim you have taken down the barrier wall?"

"Uh, I'm not sure what you mean. Do you mean the big circle around the buildings? I don't think so."

Godsson shook his head, while his eyes continued scanning some distant vision.

"Look, come on! I turned off all the *electronic* security. If there's magic barriers, I don't know what to do about them. But Uncle and I go into New Francisco sometimes, and I've never seen him do any magic to go out. Or in, either. And I snuck out once, too, on my own, and there was no magic barrier."

His eyes came back to her, and he seemed to notice her clothes. He actually winced – winced! – but didn't say anything. He was *so* weird about clothing.

He *finally* stepped out of his cell, then took her hand. Turning it over, he examined it, then stared deep into her eyes for a long time, like he was looking right into her. Then his eyes went weird, like she'd seen her uncle and those shamans do, but Godsson's gaze kind of prickled, then burned, deep inside her.

She smacked his chest. "Stop that. It kind of hurts. Plus we don't have much time. Faith is coming too."

That caught his attention.

"It'll just be the three of us. We can team up and travel the country fighting evil. I decided we can be called, uh, *'The Godsson Squadron'*." She looked up at him, suddenly feeling shy. "Do you like it?"

He just blinked at her, like she'd confused him somehow.

"Come on! Don't stand there like a dummy! I'm not sure how long till Mr Shanahan wakes up."

He let himself be led, staring around almost in wonder at the new room, and the corridor leading to the stairs. "Did you knock him out?"

She flushed. Something told her he wouldn't approve of her seducing Mr S to trick him. "Uh, kinda, yeah. Now come *on!*"

The rescue, after that, went surprisingly easily. With all the security turned off, they just walked up the stairs from the basement and out, using the door codes. It was actually kind of helpful how they'd tied all the security together into one big system, that Mr Shanahan – or someone using his computer – could just turn off.

Faith was waiting, just like she'd told her to, and trotted forward as they came down the stairs. Godsson wasn't paying any attention at all, though. Instead, he was just spreading his arms wide and drawing in great deep breaths; staring up into the starry bright sky, slowly turning around like he could suck it all in.

It was a lovely night for an escape: warm with hardly any wind.

"Godsson, this is Faith. Faith, this is, um, should I say *Mr* Godsson, or just Godsson?"

Godsson looked around, like he couldn't see her properly, and then waved his hand gently and a small globe of soft light appeared. Then he turned his head slightly from side to side, his eyes going more sideways, and then he started looking worried and his eyes fixed fiercely on hers. His mouth opened.

She pointed down, quickly. "Uh, *that's* Faith, Godsson."

His eyes dropped, and Faith gave a small growl as their eyes met.

"Stop it, Faith." She dropped to her haunches to give her a quick hug, and a talking-to. "He's a friend. You can trust Godsson."

Faith still watched Godsson, her tail quite still.

"Faith is a *dog?*"

Leeth bristled, and glared up at him. "Yeah, a *cyber*-dog. And she's real brave, and smart, too. She subdued five soldiers on the day that She attacked. All by herself."

"God's Son, a girl, and a dog," he muttered, turning away from them, once more taking in the night sky.

She stood up. "Yeah, it's just the three of us."

He turned back to her, studying her carefully. She tried to smile, putting aside thoughts of Keepie. Left behind.

For now.

"Oh, what troubles you, Sara? Do you feel regret, at turning your back on your Father? Abandoning him?"

"We'll come back! I'm *not* abandoning him." But it *felt* like she was. She knew what it felt like to be abandoned. "Yeah, I know what that's like," she whispered to herself.

He must have heard her.

"Really?" he asked, innocently. "Who abandoned you, Sara?"

"Everyone! Except K-, except Uncle."

Now he looked curious. "Oh? Everyone? Who?"

"Yeah. Everyone. Like my... before...." *What?* She tried again. "They... I was only..." But... she'd always been at the Institute. Except... she *had* to have a mother, didn't she?

For a moment, she saw a long curtain of silky black hair hanging over her face; remembered reaching up to grab it...

The image vanished, leaving a ringing *absence* in its wake.

Godsson stepped up, wrapping his arms around her. "I'm sorry, Sara. I didn't mean to distress you." One hand brushed her hair back from her face, and she looked up into his gentle smile, lit by the soft golden light he'd summoned earlier. "A question to ask your uncle one day, perhaps. No doubt he can explain what he... what happened to you. He must know."

She shivered, an odd feeling running through her, and she clung to him. It was nice to be held.

He suddenly looked embarrassed, and pulled away. And studied her, thoughtfully, in the golden glow. With a frown, he turned and walked away.

"Um, maybe you should put out your light? In case someone wakes up and looks out? I think Dr Simmons and Professor Sanders's rooms face this way."

He turned back, pausing, and smiled at her like she'd said something silly. "I don't think we need to worry about them finding me and taking me back inside now, Sara."

That was something else she should tell him, too, she thought. Her real name. For a moment, she thought his eyes narrowed dangerously, but he turned away too fast. He headed for the drive, crunching across the gravel like he was the one leading the way. *And* he hadn't turned his light off. She glared at his back through the sloppy gray material of his track suit, and suddenly noticed he was wearing slippers. She giggled, and she thought his shoulders tensed slightly when she did, which made her giggle again.

Good. It looked like he was still a *little* bit jumpy about her. She didn't like being taken for granted. Faith nudged her side, and she bent down to give her a quick scratch behind the ears.

They crossed the short stretch of grassy lawn – still torn up a bit by all the cars and trucks of the last few days – and then they were on the sealed bitumen drive, heading toward the woodlands. On their way to the front gates.

One thing she wasn't sure of was how bright his light would look to *other* people. To her, even from this distance, it made the nearby trees, their trunks and branches, glow in a big circle all around them. Like a sign saying 'here we are, come and get us.' And they hadn't even reached the trees yet.

"I really think you should put out your light, Godsson. You can hold my hand, if you can't see."

He stopped, and turned, and looked at her strangely. "Why do you wish me to walk in darkness with you, Sara? If that is even your name. It isn't, is it?"

How did he know that? "Uh, well, no, I was going to-"

"Very well. Let us end this, now. Come, Melisande, do your worst."

"What?" Leeth made frantic *stop* gestures, shaking her

head.

But Godsson wasn't looking at her anymore. His gaze had gone distant again, here on the last slightly-raised piece of ground before the road dipped and swooped through the woods. He turned, gesturing in a sweeping circle.

And the whole night sky over their heads blossomed in a kind of wispy rainbow-streaked dome, a wash of utterly beautiful translucent colors: vivid emerald, amethyst, ruby, yellow, blue.

"Ohhh." She'd seen pictures like this. The aurora. But this one was much closer, much lower, arcing right over them, filling the sky and following the contours of the wall that snaked all around the Institute.

"Oh, Father, they fear me so much they have set barriers of blood and bone for all the wall. How many died, to lock the Deeps inside?"

He lowered his arms, and the glorious light above dimmed and faded.

"Godsson, that was lovely. Do it again?"

She unbent her neck, seeing Godsson staring fiercely at her once more.

"Come, Melisande. Quit your pretense. We are still locked away from the world, I see. Here is as good a place as any I am likely to find. Show yourself. I Call you."

"Stop, Godsson, no!" She leapt on him, tried to stop his hands from moving. He was preparing some kind of spell against her. Faith growled as Godsson tried to throw her off, but she was both strong and desperate. She felt his hands move, his fingers, and remembered Mr Shanahan's footage of Keepie's friends, burned to a crisp in a few seconds.

Frantically lacing her fingers through his, she pinned them. She knew the finger-wriggles were important, and had to hope that stopping them would stop his spell-casting. His face, inches above hers, suddenly looked scared. From off to their right, Faith growled, low and threatening.

"Stop it, stop it, I'm not Melisande, I'm Leeth! My real name is *Leeth*!"

"L'ith." He went still, and after a moment, she loosened the grip of her legs around his thighs. Neither of them moved, for long seconds.

Then he bent, slightly, letting her put her feet back on the road. His eyes went spooky again, then even stranger, more intense, like before. Again she felt that unpleasant prickling and then burning, down to her bones.

"Would you *please* stop that?"

Gradually, she felt his tension ease, and she risked letting go of his fingers.

"Alexander called you that, didn't he? 'L'ith.' Oh dear. You don't even know."

"Oh dear? *Oh dear*? What does that mean? Know *what?*"

Behind Godsson, the night sky lit up briefly with a flare of angry red, a briefly-curving arc of light like Godsson had done, but on a smaller scale, and only from a single point, near the front gates.

She felt an awful feeling, swelling all around her. The woods had gotten creepy all of a sudden. Like the three of them were alone in some Eerie Woods. Like they'd just been transported into some horror story. She felt that same strange feeling of her heart sinking, like they were all dropping down in a lift.

"No, *Godsson*, you didn't...."

All around them, above them, dark, sharp edges danced in the tree branches grasping for them.

"But we *killed* Her, Godsson! How can She be back? You big stupid *dummy!*"

She wanted to thump him, but instead she backed up to him, ready to defend him, feeling the familiar tingle charge through her fingers. "Faith! Here, girl, quick!"

Faith joined them just as his golden dome burst into life all around him, only this time she was inside it, with Godsson and Faith. Bigger than in his cell, much bigger, it touched the tree branches, bending them away as it sprang out. The branches made a pattern of curving evil edges all over the outside.

"She's bigger. How can She be even *bigger*, Godsson?"

And then the edges were inside, all around her, as if there had been no barrier at all, no protective magic circle. Godsson cried out, grabbed Faith's collar, and jumped back. His golden dome shrank inwards and something *pushed,* throwing Leeth clear. Ejected from the circle, invisible threads wrapped around her.

She tore, and thrashed, and felt them part, felt them writhe in pain and whip and slap at her, but *she* was the target this time, no one else. As fast as she tore and cut, more wrapped around her.

"Godsson!" she shrieked. "*Help* me!"

"That's it, L'ith, hold Her!" Godsson began working some kind of magic, grunting with effort, and she felt its impact through the mass still building around her. The weight against her eased slightly, pressed by his attack. It shifted and warped, losing ground. She fought harder, but no longer clawing and slicing, just *holding*, like he'd shown her, though every instinct screamed at her to stab, and cut, and tear.

But the longer she fought, the more She seemed different. No whispered words. No sense of subtlety. Just an answering anger, building to rage. They *had* done something to Her, inside. Killed a part of Her. But not all. It continued building to a cresting wave, towering over her, as deep as the night. Beautiful lights blossomed above her, arcing again to cover the sky. But the more Leeth grabbed, and wrapped around her, and resisted, the greater the force grew, like she was feeding it. Like it was wrapping tight around her, becoming inescapable. Like she was binding it *to* her.

Godsson redoubled his own efforts, and as seconds stretched into minutes, her own heartbeat began to dominate her senses. Sweat ran down her face, stinging her eyes, and gradually she grew aware that they were no longer alone. Keepie was there. Professor Sanders. Mr Shanahan.

The aurora was back, too, the light even brighter than before, lighting the whole sky.

Her eyes met Godsson's, and she saw dreadful sorrow, and regret, and he did *something,* and gold and green light as bright as the sun slammed into her, through her.

And she felt it, then. A tug in her belly, like her umbilical cord had grown back, but *inside,* and connected somewhere *else:* and as Godsson's light burned into her she felt it flare into savage joy, but it wasn't hers, not *her* joy, as the brutal beam splintered and shattered into a rainbow, arching and arcing around her like a peacock's tail made of light.

She knew, then, she'd been naïve. They hadn't killed it. It was some magical death pattern thing, and you couldn't kill a death pattern. Not by *killing* it. That might even make it stronger. It'd just keep coming back, again and again, forever.

And it wanted revenge.

Suddenly Leeth knew what was needed; what the magic demanded. A new life, here, right now, to give to Her; or a new death.

She was pretty good at *one* of those things.

It would've been all kinds of cool: Hunting bad guys with Godsson, or Commander Stone, and Faith. Her eyes started to swim. Angry, she shook the tears away.

One last time, she met Godsson's eyes, and nodded. Then stopped fighting, stopped resisting.

And let Her in.

Godsson saw what she had done, and his blast focused in on the center of her chest. Something like rainbow wings unfurled from her back, rooted in her beating center.

And when it was all inside, blossoming and about to unfold from her heart like a terrible angel, she made a spade of her right hand, and plunged it into her chest.

Staggered, *screamed*; then forced it in harder.

CHAPTER 56

Godsson felt it collapse; felt his spell blast through Sara at the instant she died. *They* died. The two, bonded together as one. His magic burned back through the blood link to where She had been birthed, and detonated.

The connection shriveled before Sara's body had begun to crumple to the ground.

"*No!*" Harmon shouted as Faith lifted her muzzle and howled.

Harmon threw himself forwards to heal her – only to be slammed sideways by an invisible force at a gesture from Godsson, thrown from the road to roll stunned and helpless down the small embankment.

Shanahan fired, again and again, and Godsson turned, trying to speak above the sound while bullets ricocheted in random directions from his golden globe. A single complex gesture knocked the security officer unconscious.

Godsson and Professor Sanders faced one another on the quiet stretch of black bitumen, the only light coming from Godsson's protective barrier. Harmon scrambled back up the bank and charged back to them.

Godsson turned to him. "My apologies, Alexander, but you were about to do something unfortunate."

Faith howled, again, then crept forward, belly scraping the ground to sniff Leeth's body, nudging her with her nose. Godsson looked down, then ignored them.

"Unfortunate! *Unfortunate?*" Harmon stared at the madman. "I can still heal her. I think. Just-"

"Heal her? Are you mad?"

The accusation stunned Harmon into silence.

"The threat is over. My sacrifice was not in vain."

"*Your* sacrifice-!"

Godsson shrugged. "Your ward's too. She failed, and gave herself up to the Enemy. Then found that loss of Self more than she could bear, and sinfully took her own life. In that moment, with the Enemy tied to one like herself, locked into our world and subject to our laws: *then* could I finally slay her."

"That's not what it looked like to... never mind. All right. Thank you. But the threat is ended, so now let me, let *us* both, together, try to heal her."

"I am sorry, Alexander, but only the Son of God may rise from the dead. Besides, should we raise her, the link may re-form. She is too like d'Artelle, in spirit."

"Sara is nothing like-"

"*Sara?* Have you yourself not named her 'L'ith?' Either way, your small Lilith was too like Melisande. And becoming more so. How long have you been shaping her, Alexander? How long has Sara been connected to the Deeps? How much of Sara was even left, at the end? You had been turning her into an animal. A predator, living on instinct. Unreasoning. What kind of Archetype have you been creating, Alexander? Did you even know what you were doing, playing with things you cannot possibly understand?"

With a visible effort, Harmon controlled himself. "She may seem a wild thing, but she is in fact remarkably disciplined. As shown by her actions these last few days, especially in helping end the threat which *you* endured for thirteen years. She is *nothing* like d'Artelle. Nothing.

"And I will heal her. Or die trying."

"My dear Alexander. I am the Son of God. I could literally squash you like an insect."

At a casual wave of Godsson's hand, Harmon found his weight increasing, multiplying. Slammed down sideways against the ground, he felt his shoulder crack. The weight continued to increase, grinding the bones together. Screaming, he pushed himself backwards, his back and head slamming into the road. Blackness swarmed into his vision; gasping, he fought it down. Each breath a desperate struggle.

Professor Sanders stepped forward, one hand falling from his ear, sweat beaded across his brow. "Godsson. Please. Return with me to your cell. You can't be certain, even now, that the threat of Melisande's death is truly ended. Wait a year. Just a year, to see that you have indeed defeated your Enemy. The Barriers are still secure. It's the safest place for you. If you are truly God's Son, is that small additional sacrifice too much to ask?"

Godsson seemed to consider the remarks seriously. But then he shook his head. "No. Were I not certain the threat was ended, then I would do as you suggest. But, no."

"I'm sorry, Godsson, but you can't leave."

Godsson smiled at Sanders. "I think you'll find I can,

Professor." He spared a glance for Harmon, still panting and struggling on the ground. "But I see you're determined to heal your daughter, Alexander, and we can't risk that. Yet am I a gentle God; I will not hurt you. I'll simply take her body with me. You can collect it for burial in, say, one hour? That would be fitting – after all her efforts, she deserves *some* recognition for them, misguided as they were."

Another gesture, and his muscles bulged slightly as he increased his physical strength, only a faint crease across his forehead giving any hint that balancing three spells required any concentration. He stepped toward her body, his protective shield staying fixed around him. In its golden glow Leeth's skin looked flushed and healthy.

"I'm sorry, Godsson, but you really can't leave." Sweat stood out plainly on Sanders's forehead, and he looked extremely nervous.

Godsson smiled as he bent down and slid his arms under Sara's small, limp body.

Sanders took a small step forwards. "You can't leave simply because the moment you come within a hundred meters of the outer wall, the Institute and every one and every thing inside it will be immolated by the nuclear bomb installed right here. All automated. There's nothing I can do – except choose to set it off earlier, if I wish."

Godsson, effortlessly lifting his burden, froze in shock. For just a moment, his concentration wavered as he read the truth in the older man's eyes.

For just a moment, his shield flickered. And Faith fired her rocket, snarling.

Godsson's shields were powerful: proof against magic; proof against physical attacks like bullets, even high-powered rounds or explosive shells.

Not so much against rockets.

Sanders was hurled backwards through the air by the blast. Harmon remained stuck like glue to the bitumen for just a moment, then suddenly the awful weight vanished and he, too, tumbled over in the wake of the explosion.

Godsson, globe and all, flew backwards through the air, Sara falling from his arms to smash on the ground, and Faith leaped forwards, crouching low over her body to protect her as she fired her second rocket, now from near point-blank range.

The blast threw the dog into the air, one sharp *yip* torn from her lungs, as Godsson's golden glow winked out. Harmon staggered to his feet and charged forward, desperate to reach the madman before he could gather his wits. Grabbing the stunned mage, he began pounding his head into the bitumen of the road.

Let's see how good your powers of concentration really are, you son of a bitch!

CHAPTER 57

He might have kept pounding his patient's head into the tarmac after Godsson fell unconscious – just to make sure he didn't come around before they could get him back in his cell – but Professor Sanders's limping arrival brought him back to himself. Flinging himself to his feet he raced across to where Leeth's body had fallen.

Surely, the laser-like blast must have bored a hole through her heart? But her chest looked mostly intact, and fortunately, she had been inside Godsson's protective globe for the dog's first rocket.

There was almost no blood, and his spirits soared, only to crash as he looked closer. He needed more light.

"Hello? Are you all right?"

That was Simmons, late to the party as ever, up on the Institute's front steps. Harmon heard Sanders answer, but he had already seen Shanahan's flashlight shining from the rose bed. Ignoring the other two, he ran over to get it, then raced back to shine it over Leeth's chest. *Into* her chest.

Sweet, buttered hell.

The stretchy material of her skin-tight top had pulled back, revealing the injury: exactly as wide as her hand. The wound angled slightly up, straight through her left breast. Gingerly, torch tucked awkwardly under his chin, he pulled the edges of the cut further apart.

Sweet buttered hell on rye.

She'd stabbed her hand sideways, slipping between the fourth and fifth ribs, angling up through the middle of her heart, he guessed. Sliding *between* the ribs. He couldn't see how deeply she'd stabbed, but it had been deep enough to stop her heart instantly.

The chest wound was ghastly, yet not as bad as he'd feared: whatever spell Godsson had blasted through her, it appeared not to have done any physical damage. *Why was there so little blood?* Had the light vaporized it?

He shook his head. He should be able to do this. Thanks to the Repetition Effect.

Off to one side, he heard Simmons gasp. "Good Lord, what- Oh! Fuck! Godsson! *Godsson's out of his cell!* Professor Sanders!"

Harmon's icy tones slapped into the man's panic. "Yes, *Doctor* Simmons, we had in fact noticed that ourselves. Perhaps you could make yourself useful by holding this flashlight for me, rather than screaming like a girl?"

"B-but G- G- Godsson-"

Professor Sanders's cool voice broke in, his tones gentle and reassuring. "Yes, Simmons, I'm just trying to bring Brian around. He and I will then take Godsson back into his cell. Would you prefer to help me with that, or to hold the torch for Alex?"

Sanders approached. "I'm dreadfully sorry, Alex. So young... Wait. Alex, what are you doing? You're not going to try to heal her, surely? What about what Godsson said? How can we-"

Harmon locked eyes on him. Sanders was old; almost frail...

Perhaps his thoughts showed on his face, since Sanders backed away, one hand going to his ear. Harmon had no idea who he might be calling, but it didn't matter.

He tuned them all out, summoning the energies, the will; calling up the healing pattern as he sank his senses into the cleanly-severed heart. Quite remarkably sharply severed. *Her magic*, of course. Of course she'd used her own magic against herself.

She'd clipped the lower edge of her lung, too, he sensed, as well as cutting cleanly through both left and right ventricles of her heart. The wound, a hand's width, was fully fifteen centimeters long. She'd gone wrist-deep into her own chest.

But healing required blood, and Godsson's laser-like spell had *vaporized* it. If she had been magically exsanguinated.... But her dramatic self-injury must have stopped her heart instantly; before it could pump all her blood through the destructive beam. A remarkable stroke of luck.

Micro-organisms already swarmed and reproduced, but he burned them away. Gathering the strands of her flesh together, he felt her cells respond. So far, so good. *This was going to work!*

Senses focused totally within her chest, he wasn't even aware when Simmons plucked the flashlight from under his chin and shone it down over his psychic surgery.

At last, the healing slowed, stopping. He watched her chest rising and falling, waiting for her eyes to open.

And waited.

Keeping the healing active, he concentrated, wove his mindmeld, and entered... to find nothing. Just quiet emptiness: silent rooms and vacant halls of memory. The air moved with a calm tiredness, fading eddies drifting toward sleep. That long, last sleep.

She slipped from him, and the pain of that loss struck him with stunning force. In empty halls, he turned, a wordless cry of anguish, and called out to her.

For just a moment, a shiver ran through the empty stillness. Hesitant; doubting.... He cried out, again, calling her back.

And a wave of warmth crested, plunged through him, and Sara's eyes blinked open.

"Keepie?"

He was shocked to feel his eyes swimming. But instead of breaking his concentration, or making the spell falter, instead the healing seemed to surge more strongly than ever. She made a small sound of pleasure, her eyes falling shut once again as the cells of her breast knitted together.

Then he felt her tense, felt her own eyes on his, and he shifted his senses from within to without.

"Keepie! How come I'm alive? Didn't it work?"

"It worked, Leeth. You did it."

"And then you saved me. You *do* love me, don't you, Keepie?"

He tried to shake his head, no, but found he couldn't move the muscles of his neck for some reason.

Despite his silence, she smiled, a small but very satisfied smile, and let her eyes drift shut again.

Again, he felt water swim into his vision. Blinked it away, and sighed, the healing *flooding* from him.

Finally he felt the last stretch of flesh stitch together, taking extra care with the alignment of the edges of the skin at her breast. He sank back, arms across his knees, then let himself fall fully backward.

Just smiling up at the wash of stars splashed across the night above. Feeling satisfied. Though there would no doubt be hell to pay for this latest escapade. His heart sank at the thought. She had gone too far this time, he suspected. But he was too wrung out to process that concern right now.

In front of him, a sudden gasp of indrawn breath signaled that Leeth was 'back.'

"She was inside me, Keepie. I trapped her in my heart, and then I stabbed her. I killed myself to kill her, 'cause she needed a death. 'Cause she'd been born from a death."

"I thought it was something like that. Godsson believes his own magic helped."

She crawled up to sit cross-legged beside him.

What a strange place to be having a deep magical-philosophical discussion, he thought.

"I think maybe it did. I think it was locked in my blood. Godsson's light *burned*. I felt it burn *through* me. Beyond me, to somewhere Else."

"Ah. That makes sense."

"But if it needed my death to end it, to end the *Her*-pattern, what does it mean if I'm back alive? What if it means She'll come back?"

"That's a risk I'm prepared to take, Leeth."

She smiled, and looked away.

He heaved himself up, then stood. "Come on, Wild Thing, can you walk, or do you need me to carry you back inside?"

It was rather amusing to watch her expression, as outrage at being considered weak fought her desire to be held. The healing should hold, but there was always the sense that one should let the cells 'remember' they were back together where they should be, before stressing them unduly.

She got to her feet, with not quite the bounce she normally evidenced. She looked around, frowning.

"Um. Where's Godsson?"

"The others carried him back inside. Into his cell. He can heal himself when he wakes up."

"Oh." She frowned. "Why will he need to heal himself? What happened after I, after I stabbed Her?"

"Leeth. You understand that I am a trained psychologist? Even though I rather hope Godsson's annual 'attacks' will cease thanks to tonight's events, Godsson is *clinically insane*. He's also one of the most powerful mages on Earth. He cannot be allowed out."

"But what happened?"

Stars above, she still doesn't believe me! But he didn't need to convince her immediately. He just hoped they would be given the time.

"What *happened*?"

He smiled. "Professor Sanders distracted him, then Faith blew him up with her rockets. Both of them."

"Wow! I wish I'd seen that! Where's Faith? Did Mr...."

Leeth looked around, surveying the destruction. Her gaze stopped on a strange sack, off to one side. Furry, with... legs? No. *No!*

She hurtled over, knees sliding through the churned up grass and dirt as her worst fear was confirmed. *"Faith!"*

The sight didn't make sense to her: Faith was bigger than this, this broken, still lump of scorched flesh and metallic components.

"Faith!"

Harmon watched; saddened. The dog had been dangerous. In more ways than one. *This would be a valuable lesson for her to learn*, he told himself: that people die. Even good people. That she herself might die. Perhaps the death of her friend would temper her own rashness; might even save her own life, one day.

"Keepie, quick, heal her! Before it's too late!"

He walked slowly over. "I'm not even sure I could. I don't know whether my healing spell works on animals. And even if the spell might work, all that cyberware would interfere. Block the magic." He had learned *that* lesson deeply, the last few days. "I'm sorry, Leeth. You need to accept that Faith-"

"*Heal* her, Keepie!" she practically screamed at him. "I *know* you can do it! We're all animals, you said so. Your magic will work!"

Her fingers, he saw, clutched and worked at the fur of the dead dog as she stared up at him, tears streaming, pleading with him.

Her face twisted in grief and desperation as she begged him. "Just heal her! I'll do anything if you just *heal* her!"

She would never forgive me if I didn't at least try, he saw.

"Please, Keepie." Her voice had sunk to a whisper.

Harmon saw a kind of horror awaken as she saw that indeed he *might* refuse her this. For some reason, the expression that dawned on her face made him feel like she'd stabbed *him* in the heart.

"I'll do anything," she whispered. "*Anything*, I promise. If you just Heal her." Begging.

As she gripped the dead dog, oblivious to the seeping machine oil mixing with the blood and internal fluids in which she knelt, he found reasons to try. *Perhaps it would be good for her to think that sheer determination can be enough.* That willing something hard enough could make it so. A good attribute for his Huntress archetype to possess.

He knelt down opposite her, his knees nudging her recent defender's furred body. "I'll try, although I don't know if the healing magic will even work on a dog. But I want you to promise to be obedient, in future. To stop arguing and protesting every simple request."

"I'll try, Keepie. I will." Then her expression hardened. "But only if you Heal her. Not if you just *try*."

Even now, she bargains. He had to admire her spirit.

But that very intransigence sparked a steely determination in himself, in turn. He would not just try to heal the creature, he would succeed. *And* take what she had freely offered, in payment.

Her face stared up into his, and her expression softened once again. Knowing now that he would try. Believing that he could do the impossible.

"Please, Keepie. I know you can do it if you try. I *know*."

Harmon's heart did not melt. Not quite.

As he laid his hands on the animal, the joy that instantly suffused Leeth, making her arms and legs tremble in excited hope, seemed to bathe him in a curious warmth.

Positioning both hands against the worst injury, then, where the forward weapons pod on the left shoulder appeared to have been partially torn from its seamless meld with the animal's flesh, he moved his perception to the Imaginal and cast the spell.

This was going to be difficult....

Half an hour later, Harmon slumped back, exhausted, against the cold lawn. When he'd finally turned the tide and the dog's heart and lungs had started pumping once more, it had whimpered, in dreadful pain. Leeth had simply stared at him from across the body of her friend, her eyes saying it all. Leeth had stretched out, pressing herself carefully alongside her friend, whispering words in her ear.

She didn't let him finish until Faith could stand under her own power.

"Call Mr Shanahan, Faith. Call him, go on."

A red light began blinking on her collar. Thirty seconds later, they heard Brian Shanahan in the distance running and shouting. "Faith! Can ye hear me, girl? *Faith!* I'm coming! I'm coming, girl, hang in there!"

"It's okay, Mr Shanahan," Leeth called out to him, restraining Faith before she could re-injure herself as she fought to go to him. "Uncle saved her! She's okay!"

Shanahan's knees plowed into the lawn as he slid to a stop beside them, and soon the three of them were a laughing, crying, *licking* bundle of three-way joy.

Harmon, lying beside them watching, had to smile despite himself. Then Leeth flung herself onto him, hugging him too. "Oh, Keepie, Keepie, you did it. You're wonderful! I love you so much!"

Shanahan and Leeth together carried the cyber dog back to his security out-building, Leeth explaining to her the whole way that Mr Shanahan had a supply cabinet full of spare parts waiting, saved specially for her. Harmon staggered along in the rear.

He quite welcomed Leeth's support when they left to make their own way back inside, together.

Surely, she had no more surprises for him. Surely, now, they could all rest?

CHAPTER 58

As Disten rounded the next bend, ahead on the winding country lane, a pair of iron gates swung into view, glowing brightly under the vehicle's headlights.

The girl awaited, through those gates. Behind the wall from which the borealis display had lit the night sky, not five minutes before.

Getting out of the vehicle, Disten read the sign:

> Institute for Paranormal Dysfunction
> DANGER – KEEP OUT
> Authorized personnel only

Looking left and then right, there was no intercom system; no means to call to request entry.

No matter. The bars on the gate would be no obstacle.

The instant the barrier was touched, however, a massive flare of red auroral light flashed up in a huge arc lacing into the night sky.

Disten blinked.

It was dark. Hard bitumen pressed from below. Some unknown portion of time appeared to have passed.

Disten sat up, feeling dampness in the hair at the back of the head. Ahead, the vehicle idled, blocking the view of the wall. Puzzled, feeling oddly disoriented while standing back upright, the fingers were examined in the wash from the headlights. Blood.

Disten moved up to the car, vision shifting strangely.

Concussion.

The pull, a savage hook through the spine, was gone. Ahead, through the gates and past the wooded area, bright light flared, the rumble of an explosion following a moment later.

Disten approached the gate once again, then turned back from there, to where consciousness had been regained. Calculated a trajectory, that crossed over the vehicle.

Behind, another flash of light followed by the sound of another explosion.

The girl was gone. Again.

Disten climbed back into the car, considering the head wound. Medical treatment would be wise. As would removal of evidence.

Reversing the car around, Disten got out with a bottle of water, eyeing the blood on the road, illuminated in the powerful headlights. Poured the water. Then re-entered the vehicle and set the destination to New Francisco.

The Institute for Paranormal Dysfunction. The girl, or spirit, appeared to be connected to it. It would bear future investigation.

And the girl. Whose body had been examined, as she lay dead in an alley. Gone again, now. But death did not appear to stop her.

That was good. She would come again.

And when next she emerged, she would be taken, and Perfected. Together, they would communicate that Perfection to all humanity.

CHAPTER 59

At 7:55am the next day, Leeth stood grimacing as her uncle ripped through her wardrobe, finding something 'more suitable' for her to wear for their meeting with the Director.

She finished adjusting her bra and picked up the ultra-thin black clothing he'd gone red at when he'd opened her door.

"But I spent, like, half an hour cutting parts away so the holes look deliberate! What about now that I've put on underwear? Can't I just-"

Her uncle turned, thrusting black denim jeans and a white blouse with collar and buttons into her hands, removing the remnants of her ninja suit and tossing it behind him. "No. And we now have less than five minutes. Get. Dressed."

He continued lecturing her as she quickly shrugged into the top and wriggled into the jeans. She got it that she was in trouble; but she *shouldn't* be. *They* were the ones who were wrong, not her. "And I wasn't trying to seduce Professor Sanders! I was just trying to look good."

She heard her uncle's teeth grinding.

"Well, why didn't you tell me before, that men liked seeing-"

He pushed her toward the door. "Yes, Leeth, I see now I should have, but let's leave that discussion for some other time."

In the end, they arrived right on time anyway, so he hadn't needed to make such a fuss.

Though Professor Sanders's 'Come in' didn't sound as welcoming as usual. Maybe she *had* better be careful.

"Sara." For long seconds, the Director just looked at her. "What are we going to do with you?"

She bristled, but kept waiting. They didn't need to *do* anything with her. They *needed* to let Godsson free!

"Do you understand that what you did was wrong? *Very* wrong?"

For a moment, she considered lying, but that wouldn't help Godsson.

"Why? What's he ever done wrong? Except save everybody?"

At her side, her uncle made a small noise, and Professor Sanders sat back, his bushy white eyebrows flashing upward. "Dear me." He looked from her to her uncle, then back to her. "He did kill two people. I thought you had been shown the footage?"

"No, *She* turned two people into monsters to kill *him*, and *he* killed the monsters!"

His mouth opened, then shut. She wanted to press her attack, but sometimes it was best to let your opponents make mistakes.

Professor Sanders looked from her, to her uncle. "You know, in light of what we've learned, she does have a point, Alex."

Yes! For a moment, she thought she'd convinced Professor Sanders. Until his next words. Frowning, he turned back to her.

"But Godsson is criminally insane, Sara. He has harmed other carers who entered his cell for a routine health check, before we learned the necessity to avoid that. He believes he is a Son of God, two thousand years old, and that he has some mission to 'save' humanity from itself. He is one of the most powerful mages in the world today, and he is *completely delusional.*"

Sara frowned. "Well, yeah, sometimes-"

"So he is powerful, insane, and certainly a great danger to those around him. Even when he is alone, there is one monster in that cell. He acts on whims, triggered by thought processes that make little sense to us... and for those reasons he is being legally held here. Do you understand what *that* means?"

"Well, yeah, it means he needs friends, so he can show everybody he's *not* dangerous."

Professor Sanders stared at her like she'd just said something stupid. She looked at her uncle, but he had his eyes scrinched shut and was squeezing the bridge of his nose.

"No, Sara." She looked back at the Director, who was looking sorry. "It means that breaking him out of his cell was a criminal act. It was against the law. Do you understand? Even if you disagree with the law, you can't simply ignore it. That's not how it works. Has your uncle not taught you that?"

If he thinks that about just letting Godsson out, what would he think about killing sheep? I definitely better lie, this time! "Well, yeah, of course."

She heard her uncle breathe in, only then realizing he'd been holding his breath. *Huh? He'd been worried I was about to say how it was just there to protect the sheep? Why would he be worried by that? Unless... was the Professor a sheep? Whoa!* What would *that* mean...?

But aloud, all she said was, "I just thought, well, if we just *showed* everybody that Godsson was nice, and wouldn't hurt them, then they'd have to change their minds."

"That's irrelevant. What you did is called a prison break, Sara. It's illegal. You broke the law. Now, it appears that you hadn't realized that; nor do we wish to advertise what almost happened here." Professor Sanders looked regretful. "But the facts are that you entered a secure cell and freed an insanely dangerous lunatic. Your rash actions could easily have proven utterly catastrophic. It would still cause a major political incident if news ever leaks out."

"So you *need* me not to tell anyone!"

Professor Sanders suddenly didn't look either kindly or harmless, at all.

"Don't try that route, Sara. Seriously. The stakes in this game are far higher than you understand. And if you did speak out, the consequences for yourself, for Godsson, for this country and even the world could be terrible. Do not dream of threatening to do that.

"Let me speak clearly: if you try again to release Godsson, you will go to jail and you will stay there. For a very, very long time. I am not joking."

She'd never seen Director Sanders like this. He looked a completely different person. His eyes bored into hers, but she refused to look away.

"Do you see? Do you understand now? Regardless of whether you think it's fair or unfair, Godsson must remain here. Only if the courts one day decide he should be released, would that ever be permitted."

Still he stared.

"Is that clear enough?"

"Yes."

"Good. But I also want your promise. I want you to promise me you won't attempt to release Godsson again."

He clearly wanted her to agree. But she thought carefully about what he'd just said, and had to shake her head. "Uh-uh. I can't promise that. If I promised that, I couldn't even try just to *convince* people they should let Godsson free."

Sanders blinked. Then smiled. "Very well. I don't wish to stop you advocating on his behalf, to those few who know he is here. Promise me this, instead: that you will only attempt to seek Godsson's release through legal means."

She thought about that. Then took a deep breath and let it gust out. "All right."

The Director just looked at her like he knew that hadn't been a promise, and she scowled. "Oh, all right: I promise I'll only try to get Godsson freed *legally*. Okay?"

The Director sighed. "Yes. Let's shake on that." He stood up.

It was strange, shaking the Director's hand. He had a nice grip. Firm. They let go, and she stepped back. Feeling somehow more grown up.

"Very well, Sara, that will be all for now. Please leave us, while I discuss things with your uncle."

The two men watched her leave the room, closing the door carefully behind her. Harmon went to speak, but Sanders put up a finger to stop him, and looked at the display projected up from his desk, shaking his head. "*Intercom*: Sara, I'd prefer you to wait elsewhere for your uncle."

He waited, then looked at Harmon. "She has Unfolded, Alex, hasn't she? Into what? What are her abilities?"

Harmon considered denying it. "I think she has *begun* to Unfold, yes. I believe she has further potential." Sanders waited for him to continue. "To be honest, I'm not sure *what* she is."

Sanders considered that. "Well, it must still be very pleasing for you. Your theories vindicated, at long last. Especially given the circumstances. I assume you plan to publish, eventually? Will you let me review your paper?"

Harmon inclined his head, just a little stiffly, and Sanders sighed. "So. To business. Your position here-"

Harmon interrupted. "What of Sara? What's going to happen to her?"

Professor Sanders looked regretful. "I don't know,

Alex."

Harmon started to respond. "But surely, she's only seventeen, we can-"

"Seventeen? Yes, I can see the headlines now."

Harmon fumed but could hardly deny the point.

"All I can say at present is that the investigation is still underway and no decision has yet been made. I doubt she will be allowed to stay, however. And I dare say your own position here, especially as Godsson's therapist, is probably no longer tenable. Bashing one's patient unconscious is likely to have that consequence, you know."

Harmon waved a dismissive hand. "With his shields temporarily down, disrupting his concentration and knocking him unconscious was our only hope."

"I agree with you, Alex. I even predict the investigators will come to the same conclusion. The key issue, however, is that your ward broke into a secure-" At Harmon's reaction, he held up his hand. "Very well, she didn't break in, but she illegally operated Shanahan's equipment. For the purpose of releasing *Godsson*. That is the issue: she freed *Godsson*. You remember, she in fact suggested we should do so during the debrief. And then was expressly forbidden from doing so. You recall the moment?"

Harmon's look said he very clearly did.

"And in your professional opinion would you say it was at that moment she made up her mind to break him free?"

Harmon pursed his lips, not wanting to answer, but he himself had already come to that conclusion some time ago. In hindsight, he should have realized what her question had meant. "Yes."

"Look, Alex, she *is* only seventeen so I imagine, especially considering the fact that no one wishes this incident to become public, she's likely to get away with a short custodial sentence. It may not even go through the court system – unless you wish to push for that? No, I didn't think so."

Harmon could see where this was headed, however, and he cut to the chase. "You want us to leave." It was a statement, not a question.

But for the second time this morning, Sanders surprised him.

"Not immediately.

"I sincerely believe Sara is unlikely to attempt a second 'rescue' in the *near* future. Nor do I think Brian, assuming he is allowed to retain his position, is likely to fall for the same trick twice, hmm?"

Sanders watched Harmon, wondering how he'd felt at discovering his ward had seduced Shanahan, and winced inwardly at the reaction he read. Nor did he relish what he had to say next.

"As for your own position: you do know Godsson best – better than anyone alive. In addition, the whole magical aspect to this latest adventure your young ward has just put us all through *is* rather baffling. So I think, although I may be jumping the gun here, that you should begin going through your notes and preparing for a handover to a successor. That will be my recommendation to the Investigating Committee. But let me be quite clear, Alex: I have already begun looking for a suitable candidate for your replacement. It will take some months, however. My *belief* is that you will apply your best professional efforts to assist us in that transition. And my *hope* is that you will be willing to do so.

"There are big changes ahead for you, and especially for Sara. I'm sure the remaining time will be useful for you and her both."

Harmon nodded, numb. He had expected it, but still the words shocked.

Sanders spread his hands. "I'm sorry, Alex. That's the best I can do."

"I understand. Is there anything else?"

"Ah, there is one small thing. Yes. Sara mentioned seeing a red flare at the outer Barrier, before she and Godsson were attacked. Any thoughts?"

"A *red* flare? Hmm. A monochrome reaction suggests a very narrow span of 'interests' in whatever was probing." He frowned at the Director. "I assume it *was* merely a probe? Nothing actually penetrated, did it?"

"A physical breach? You know as well as I, the Ward's reaction would have been quite different. But all the same, we've checked what we could. An extensive search of the grounds has found nothing. No sign of disturbance; no tracks. Nor outside. Although from what Sara said, the 'testing' of our defenses would have been near the front gate, possibly on the road itself. So we wouldn't expect to find tracks."

What a change in attitude, Harmon thought. *He's taken Leeth's solitary report seriously enough to have the entire grounds searched.* But aloud, he simply said "I could ask Godsson if he noticed it; if he has any suggestion." Knowing Godsson however, he was just as likely to nod knowingly and look pleased. "Though in the circumstances, it may be better for *you* to ask him than me."

Sanders nodded wryly.

"If that's all?" Harmon asked. But at the door he paused, and turned back. "When Godsson was preparing to take Sara... you were just bluffing about the nuclear device, weren't you?"

"Of course, Alex. Of course. I just needed to say *something*, to break his concentration."

Harmon stared at the kindly professor for long seconds. It was all the answer he was going to get, though, he saw.

At least now he knew what lay ahead. There would be no more surprises.

CHAPTER 60

Harmon, Sara and Shanahan's first meal together following her latest escapade should have been more than awkward: given that she had very nearly managed to kill both herself and Shanahan's beloved Faith; *after* first seducing Shanahan to set the whole disaster in motion.

Harmon had almost felt sorry for the man: knowing he'd been *used* like that. The hurt which Shanahan felt, showed clearly on his face. Harmon could only imagine what Shanahan must be feeling: guilt, shame, betrayal, chagrin.

It only slowly dawned on Harmon that he didn't *need* to imagine how Shanahan felt.

It was Leeth who spoke first, in the end. As if scarcely aware of anything wrong. She'd simply gone straight to Shanahan, hugged him around the shoulders and squeezed in beside him on the bench seat. "Sorry for tricking you," she said, patting him on the thigh.

Shanahan looked panicked, his eyes fixed on her guardian, clearly fully aware that Harmon, or Sara, could choose to bring criminal charges. With that thought, Harmon realized he too was once again in exactly the same position.

And it would take only one careless remark from Leeth to expose that fact.

"*Tricking?* Sure, and that's one word for it." He looked at a loss as to how to proceed, even meeting Harmon's eye as if asking for help. "What you did was very wrong."

"But you enjoyed it! And so did I. And it was the only way I could think of to rescue Godsson."

Both Shanahan and Harmon froze, then shared a look. But it was Harmon who responded. "And do you think he *still* needs rescuing, Sara?"

Her chin thrust out. "I promised Professor Sanders I wouldn't try to rescue Godsson again."

"Because you know now that he was quite happy to kill you, and even tried to stop me reviving you. Yes?"

She waved the comment away. "But Godsson was right! *She* might have come back when you healed me. But since she didn't, and me and Godsson really truly killed Her properly this time, *now* we could let him free. Why can't we? What laws has he broken, anyway?"

"Dear sweet Mary Mother of God," breathed Shanahan

in horror. "Sara girl, yeh can't be serious!"

She rounded on him. "*Why? Why* are we keeping him locked away in that tiny little cell? He's saved everybody in the whole world, *twice* now, and we keep him locked up! That's horrid, and cruel!"

The two men just stared at her.

"And all you can all say is, it's 'coz he's mad and he'll hurt people!"

Her uncle made a noise. "Sara: he killed you!"

She turned back to him. "'Coz he *had to!* But now he doesn't have to, so we should let him out!"

"Jesus, Mary, and Joseph." Shanahan clutched his forehead.

"You *promised*, Sara."

She slammed back in her chair. "Yeah."

"And you intend to keep that promise, don't you?" Harmon leaned forward, not even trying to disguise his casting of the mindmeld this time.

"Yes." She scowled furiously back at him, while Shanahan continued his quiet stream of praying and swearing.

At least the awkwardness regarding her seduction of Shanahan had fallen into its correct perspective.

But as days passed and it seemed Sara truly did plan to honor her promise, things somehow settled back into a semblance of normality.

Though Harmon knew the sands were running out.

Tonight, Leeth sat opposite Harmon in the cafeteria, waiting impatiently for the others to enter and join them for the evening meal.

For his part, Harmon was musing on the recent events, and on how strange it was that it had brought them all closer together. *Perhaps we're all feeling a little vulnerable and uncertain*, he thought. *With one exception, naturally.*

For once, though, Leeth was not explaining why Gods-son should be released. Instead, she was trying, again, to enlist her uncle's support in convincing the security officer that Faith needed some serious attention for her cybernetic systems. She was so wrapped up in her earnest exposition she was unaware that Harmon had stopped listening.

But he looked up when she fell silent mid-sentence, tilting her head and slowly pivoting around in her chair to face the entryway. "That's not Dr Simmons *or* Professor Sanders's footsteps with Mr Shanahan!"

So Harmon had a few seconds of warning when Brian Shanahan entered the cafeteria with a stranger in tow.

"Ooh, he's cute, Keepie!" Leeth half-whispered. The newcomer was tall, she saw, taller than her uncle or Mr Shanahan, and looked very fit. Broad shoulders, deep brown eyes and strong, dark eyebrows that lifted appreciatively as he spied her in turn. A strong jaw, stubbled with a five o'clock shadow. His hands looked large and strong and firm, too. "Who's *he*, Uncle?"

From Keepie to Uncle in two seconds, Harmon thought. "I don't know, Sara."

She spun back around, and he recognized her annoyed frown as acceptance of the need to use her 'baby' name. Harmon was no longer quite sure what lay ahead for them both. Leeth had thrown her huge spanner into the intricate gears of all his plans, but they had both intuited that it might well involve some... fluidity of official identity.

"Alex, Sara," the security officer said. "This is Jackson Stark, mechatronics specialist. Jackson, this is Dr Alex Harmon, and his ward, Sara."

Jackson shook hands with them both before casually seating himself beside Sara. *Fast worker*, Harmon thought.

"Mechatronics? Can *you* fix Faith?" Leeth asked, grasping the newcomer's forearm excitedly.

And we see her increased demonstrativeness is not reserved solely for me. For some reason, Harmon felt a mild irritation. As if he were jealous. But Leeth was still chattering.

"Jackson Stark. That's a cool name: you sound like a secret agent! Or a trid star – you're good-looking enough to do action movies. Do you know martial arts? I have a Wing Chun-"

"Sara. Perhaps limit yourself to three questions at a time for the poor fellow?"

Jackson chuckled and placed one large hand over Sara's two, which still gripped his forearm. He patted them reassuringly, but then left his hand covering hers.

"That's all right, I don't mind. I guess you don't get that many visitors, eh? But to answer your first question,

Sara, yeah, fixing Faith is within my skill set. I'm a bit of a dogsbody, to tell the truth."

Sara pulled her hands free suddenly, leaning away. "Oh." She looked uncomfortable. "Um, you don't look- uh, I mean, really? What, um, parts...?"

Harmon took pity on her before she could embarrass herself further. "He means he's a jack-of-all-trades, Sara, not that he's altered his DNA. That is true, I assume, Mr Stark?"

"Yup, I'm one hundred percent human," he grinned down at Sara as he thumped his chest.

He literally *thumped his chest*. It made Harmon want to hurt him.

"Oh. So will you be doing anything besides healing Faith's robot parts while you're here, um, Mr Stark?" she asked.

"Call me Jax, Sara. Yeah, the Director wants me to give the whole place a going-over. I gather you've had a fair bit of drama recently. I hear there was some security breach for which I'm apparently not allowed to know the details."

Leeth suddenly looked uncomfortable.

"Judging from the crater on the drive," he continued, "and the damage to Faith herself, it's pretty obvious you've all lived through some interesting times recently?"

If you only knew, Harmon thought.

"So, um, what other stuff besides Faith will you be fixing, um, Jax?"

He smiled down at her, wolfishly. "Well, before I even got in through the front gates, I noticed some of the bars were just slightly askew. And the photocell on the inside was loose, almost ready to break off. Bits of adhesive on the emitter unit, too. Weird."

Harmon had not even been aware that there *were* sensors there.

For once, Sara had nothing to say, and turned back toward her uncle, a 'help me!' expression on her face.

"Am I missing something?" Shanahan asked, looking at Stark, before his head swiveled like a tracking missile to fix on Sara. "Shit, girl, you're worse than a pack of bloody gremlins!"

"Gremlins are *real?*"

"No, they're not real!" Shanahan waved a finger accusingly at her. "And don't be playin' your games with me, young Sara. I know perfectly well you know I was speaking metaphorically."

Sara's eyes went very wide. "What's *metaphorically*, Mr Shanahan?"

Shanahan growled; Stark just laughed.

The evening meal turned into quite a jolly affair, despite the uninspiring food. Jackson Stark was good company. A smooth talker, but knowledgeable on a broad range of topics.

Leeth noticed that her uncle had become quieter as they ate, though. Once or twice she even intercepted a strangely-thoughtful expression when he looked at Jax.

Harmon, for his part, had begun to see new possibilities. So much had changed, with Leeth and Godsson's defeat of *Her*. Shocking, but fascinating. Unfortunately, Godsson was proving unhelpful: he now 'knew' Melisande d'Artelle had been Lilith reborn, and that Leeth had been infected by 'spores.' He also now refused to speak at all of the mysterious 'deep realms' below the Imaginal.

And Harmon needed to find a new stressor to progress Leeth's Unfolding. He had not expected her development to follow normal paths – that was, after all, one of the two key points of his experiment – yet he had expected something more than acute hearing. And a curious talent for slaughter.

Her Unfolding had also 'reset' her resistance to his Suggestion spell. Re-establishing that control would be essential while he helped her adjust to living amongst normal society. Amongst the 'sheep.' He winced. Yet how could he have foreseen this outcome?

All too soon, now, she would be eighteen, and his official period of custody would end. Perhaps he could use her own willfulness, somehow.

Leeth had turned to Jackson and almost leaned into him now, both her hands casually gripping the man's thigh as she made some point, so blatant in her interest that for the first time, the newcomer had begun to look uncomfortable.

"Ah, tell me, Sara, just how old are you?"

She pulled back. "I'm... nearly eighteen."

"Oh."

"Why? What does that mean: 'oh'? How old are you?"

"I'm thirty two."

But having received her answer, it was clear she didn't know how to capitalize on it. "Well. Okay. What? Why are you looking like that?"

At first, Stark looked surprised. Then just smiled and settled back in his chair, his eyes never leaving hers.

Leeth smiled back.

Harmon wasn't entirely sure he was comfortable with her rapidly-developing infatuation with the man. Especially if the fellow was prepared to ignore her age. Yet this new situation certainly put him in a rather awkward position. How did he explain to her she was under-age, given his own error in that regard last year? Not to mention his wish for his Huntress to be untrammeled with mundane notions of 'proper behavior'?

And all the while, Leeth stared up into Stark's eyes.

-

It took 'Jackson' two days to fit and adjust Faith's replacement parts to his satisfaction. Followed by a further day of Leeth's cajoling and goading to convince him of a problem in the right lateral rotator cuff, even though it had not been injured in the incident.

A rocket blast, Jackson learned.

Faith couldn't complain, naturally, and indeed had seemed quite happy following his initial repairs. But after watching Sara race and tussle with the dog, and joining them on their afternoon 'patrol' of the grounds, she had apparently impressed him sufficiently to order an upgrade to match the replacements he'd used in repairing the CK9's injured side.

Everyone had been shocked to discover Sara could match the cyborg animal's pace. But it wasn't until that evening's meal that Harmon began to suspect the truth about Leeth's Unfolding.

Stark had spent several periods in the gymnasium, tightening and adjusting various fittings and ordering and replacing others, while Sara demonstrated some of her balance and gymnastic routines. At dinner that night he recounted Sara's feats to Shanahan and Harmon.

"Her balance is uncanny: she uses the uneven bars like balance beams! Her routines on those are spell-binding!"

He draped his arm around Sara's shoulders, and she happily nestled against him, smiling in pleasure. "And I could watch her trampoline work for hours."

I'll bet you could, thought Harmon, sourly. The body language between Stark and Leeth had changed. He scarcely needed to work a feather-light mindmeld to know there had already been some mild sexual play between the two.

"And on the rings – god, her upper-body strength! Seriously, I reckon your girl's routines are almost Olympic standard. Unorthodox as hell, so there'd be a fair bit of work to adapt them so the judges wouldn't mark her down just on technicalities."

Leeth glowed under the praise, and Stark suggested that Harmon should order some high-jump equipment – he was of the opinion she might already be able to break the world record.

It appeared that Leeth's magic had been directed inward, affecting her body and senses.

CHAPTER 61

The next day, Jackson was supposed to begin his checking and upgrading of the Institute's security systems.

Leeth had raced through her morning routine in the gym, and the night before, borrowed a ladder from Mr Shanahan after dinner. He'd been suspicious, and insisted on helping her. So she'd had to pretend she wanted the ring bolt high over the door into the gym so she could hang Christmas decorations later in the year.

For some reason that had made him look sad. But he also hadn't looked convinced, and had been careful to take the ladder away afterward, too.

Leeth waited by the door now, her eyes shut while she listened. Finally, she heard Jax's quiet footsteps descending the stairs. She jumped and grabbed the rope now threaded through the ring bolt, shimmying up it till her toes reached the mantle.

Then waited, listening.

What if he didn't visit her, this morning?

But his footsteps approached, coming right up to the double doors – then stopped.

Come on, come on, step in!

The doors swung open, and looking down through the narrow gap between her and the wall, she saw Jackson cautiously enter. All the better. She turned her head, to make sure he was fully in, then jumped gently back, turning.

"Rarrr!"

He spun, starting to jump away, but the deadly cheetah had already Pounced her prey, overbearing him and hugging him tight as she rode him to the floor before the giggles took her. For a moment he thrashed, eyes wide before realizing it was just her. She kissed him in delight.

She was on top, just the way she liked it. She watched his eyes soak her up, as if he wanted to lick her all over.

"Do you have to check the security today?" she asked. "There's always tomorrow. I could show you around the Institute, all my favorite places."

He looked tempted, but in the end sighed and lifted her off him, moving her to one side. His large hands around her waist made her bite her lip. Suddenly she wanted him. *Now.*

But Jackson just laughed, insisting on doing his job.

"Why don't you tag along with me, Sara? Maybe we should check the whole perimeter, make a day of it? We could grab some food and drink before we head out."

He took her hand and sprang to his feet, which made her smile, and she let herself be led out.

But she was frowning as they walked down the road to the front gates. She noticed him look down at the hole in the bitumen, where she'd hammered the spike for the mirror; but he didn't stop there, just raised an eyebrow as he headed straight for the IR emitter.

"Huh. Look at that: the mounting's loose. No wonder Shanahan's getting so many false alarms."

She had to unclench her fist when he turned back toward her as he opened his toolbox. And then just stand there as he pulled out the old one and connected a new one; bonding it to the stone surface this time, after replacing the far sensor with a simple mirror and checking the alignment.

"There! That shouldn't work free, and it's now only a single active system." He checked the top one, too, and even though that was fine, insisted on replacing it as well.

They followed the wall around, with him using a telescoping mirror-sensor thing to check the top, and marking a whole bunch of entire trees for removal because they'd gotten too close.

When they got to the first of her... swings, she'd taken his arm and started trying to distract him, but he caught sight of the rope anyway, and pulled himself free.

"Hang on, what's that?" He moved around the trunk, his head craning up, and she saw him spot the end of the rope tied to the branch over his head. "Here, give me a boost."

He had to explain about linking her fingers together, and she seriously considered flipping him on his head to knock him out. Instead, she had to just grit her teeth and help him reach up to *her* rope, and then watch as he used it to climb right up to where she'd tied it to the sturdy branch that stretched well out from the leaning tree.

It took her the whole time he spent untying it and climbing back down to get her temper and her expression back under control.

This wasn't turning out at all like she'd imagined. Jax

was a lot smarter than Mr Shanahan. She narrowed her eyes, watching his every move, asking how everything worked. It was clear, though, it'd be much harder to get around his new stuff than Mr Shanahan's old stuff.

By the time they returned to the Institute, and he started wandering around outside and checking all the security cameras on the building itself, she was having trouble acting happy. He kept turning around each time he heard her knuckles cracking.

That night at dinner, Jackson described how it appeared that in several sections of the ceilings of every floor, some cameras had been re-positioned and thermal sensors tampered with – that, or unusually clever squirrels had wrapped them in layers of insulation material. As Stark's report continued, Mr Shanahan had gotten paler and paler, staring at her in dismay. Worse, it quickly became obvious that they all knew it was her who'd been behind it all.

In one day, Jackson Stark had undone years and years of her work.

Of course his stupid alert eyes had found the tunnel under the wall in the south-western region of the grounds, too, and the other two trees she'd attached ropes to, that had branches near the walls. He'd even spotted the lengths of fine fishing-line on several of the outdoor security cameras; and of course then he'd found the eye-patch arrangements she'd crafted.

"None of the software systems had been tampered with – guess your gremlins aren't into computers."

All three men had looked at Sara.

"Bejeesus, girl, d'you have no conception how dangerous...? If any of our inmates... Oh, gods."

Mr Shanahan covered his face with both hands, groaning. He looked up and across the small table at Jax. "Have you- you'll have to report all this to the Director, won't ye?" His soft accent had become just a little broader all of a sudden.

"I'm afraid so. On the positive side, none of the breaches were accessible from outside. Except the tunnel. And *that* had a kind of padlock arrangement behind the camouflage at the far end."

"Oh, Jesus, I'm going to lose my job," moaned Shanahan. He looked accusingly at her uncle. "This is your fault! You let her run wild! Oh, god."

She put her hand on his arm, but he shook her off. "But the inmates hardly ever go out into the grounds, Mr Shanahan," she reminded him. "And Faith or I would keep an eye on them if they did. I promise."

Mr Shanahan just groaned.

She looked across at Keepie. He had a funny expression on his face. She thought he'd be cross with her; or maybe, secretly amused. But instead, he just looked kind of sad.

"What's wrong, uncle?"

But he wouldn't say.

CHAPTER 62

At the knock on his office door that evening, Harmon had been unsure which of the two to expect: Leeth or Jackson. In the event, it turned out to be his ward.

She stomped in and flung herself angrily into the heavy chair across from him. He didn't have to wait long.

"Jax won't let me have sex with him!"

Harmon blinked.

"And *you* won't, either! Jax says I'm too young – like you always do. He even thought I was a virgin!"

Harmon pictured his career crashing down around his ears.

"Don't worry, Keepie, I kept it a secret like you said, even though he wanted to know *who* I'd sexed with, here.

"Why does everyone say I'm too *young?* That doesn't make any sense. Obviously I'm not too young. Jax and I do lots of *other* neat stuff, but as soon as I try to put his-"

"Leeth, stop. I don't need the details."

She looked annoyed. "But why do you all say I'm 'too young'? Look at me, I'm a grown woman, you said so yourself." She jumped up from the seat, throwing her arms wide before beginning to pace angrily. "And *you* keep saying we have to wait. For what? What's so special about being eighteen?"

Harmon had been expecting this. Unfortunately for Leeth, he could see only one route to safety for them all.

"Leeth, I don't know exactly what was happening to you the night you Unfolded. I gather you felt an unbearable pressure, as if you were ready to explode."

Because I drugged you. And *why* had he done that? The 'Scope' – yes, that had been necessary to break through her uncanny resistance to his Suggestions. But the 'Beep'? *There had been no real excuse for that.*

But he could let none of that show. "Is that correct?"

"Oh, *yeah!* Massively."

"And you didn't give me much choice in what followed, either, did you?" Her aggression had taken him by surprise; and fortunately should allow him now to make her think *she* were the one who had been at fault. Part of him cringed; part of him stood back and sneered: *this is the altruistic researcher, is it? Pedophile!* But it was this, or see his career destroyed; his stunning breakthrough rejected, even lost.

And heaven help Leeth without his understanding of her, now, when she would soon need it the most. At least now he could start undoing some of the damage he had unwittingly done her. Besides, it *was* true: she hadn't given him much choice.

"Well, no, but I knew you-"

"In a sense, Leeth, you raped me," Harmon declared, somehow keeping a perfectly solemn expression on his face – even, perhaps, managing to convey disappointment at his ward's unfair behavior.

"That's.... But... but you *wanted* to, Keepie! I know you did!"

"True, Leeth. True. You are a very attractive young woman. Practically irresistible. That is not the issue, however. The problem is that what we did was illegal."

"Huh? Why? I know people sex each other! Half the net is full of it. Well, maybe a quarter. There *are* a lot of cats, too."

"It's your age that makes it illegal, Leeth. Nothing else. You are under-age. I could be sent to jail because you raped me."

Oh yes, very clever, Alex. But one day she'll learn the truth, and there will be hell to pay. He struggled to let none of his inner shame show. If only he dared erase her memory of it. Perhaps one day. When she was older...

"But I didn't- and anyway, even if I did, why would they send *you* to prison instead of *me?*"

She was so upset she didn't even notice him delicately drape the Suggestion spell over her mind.

"*Because* you are under-age, Leeth. The Law – which protects the sheep, the gray people – sees you as a child, irresponsible. In need of protection and not answerable for your actions. I, on the other hand, am considered an adult by the Law and have no such legal trickery to protect me."

"But that's not *fair* – I made you do it, Keepie!"

Her eyes were watering, and that on top of what he was doing now, made him feel physically sick. How was this different to drugging her? But it was necessary, until he could adjust her to fit into normal society.

"True, but no one would ever believe that, Leeth. They would say I tricked you, or coerced you. Especially as I'm a trained psychologist. They would say I had 'groomed you' to make you act that way."

"That's stupid!"

"Yes, Leeth. It is. But that is what would happen."

She was silent for a long time, then, clearly thinking; while inside, his shame burned the brighter. At the misuse of her trust; at the abuse of her naivety. But at the same time, he felt a sick relief. Shame warred with self-interest. *But were we separated, who would understand her as I do?* he asked himself. Who else could hope to control her?

"So that's what Jax meant?"

"Yes. I gather you have been pushing him, as you did me?"

"Yeah. And I *almost* convinced him, too."

Harmon shook his head portentously. "That's very bad. If you did, and it became known, he would be sent to jail. Likely, then, it would come out about our own love-making last year, too, and I also would be sent to prison. And Brian Shanahan, too."

Leeth looked stricken.

"Although... perhaps...?" He trailed off.

"Perhaps what, Keepie?"

"Perhaps I could devise some exercises for you, in self-restraint? I dare say I could design some mental training which would strengthen your willpower; enable you to control your sexual urges so you would be less of a danger to those closest to you."

Now, parts of him were screaming. This next step was too far. But stress was a necessity. She was the steel he forged: he was the blacksmith; her pain the fire and hammer; her spirit the anvil.

"Would you like me to prepare a mental strengthening regime for you?"

"Oh, Keepie, yes! Would you?"

"Very well. But I must warn you, it won't be easy. You may have to suffer. Are you prepared to endure real hardships, just to improve your strength of will, to protect those who care about you?"

"Of course. It sounds ultra!"

He felt sick. This was wrong. So very wrong.

But a darker part of him whispered: *it's for her own good. Who knows what further talents she might develop?* He would just have to be careful. Remain clinical.

"Hmm. Do I gather from your body language that you are feeling quite worked up, even aroused, right now?"

She nodded, chewing her lip.

"Well, perhaps we could begin tonight. Let me think... Ah, I have it! A simple exercise, to start with: get up on my desk, Leeth. On all fours. Your task will simply be to stay still. Do you think you can do that?"

"Sure!"

She nimbly hopped up onto his desk.

Deep in her psyche, Harmon found the worn and abraded links that connected her fears to her stress systems, and began unlinking and re-linking those systems to different parts of her psyche. Yes, this looked an excellent source of pressure to advance her Unfolding.

And given that her magic seemed to be directed entirely inward, into her own physical and mental abilities.... *Yes, this should work well.*

He would just have to be careful.

CHAPTER 63

She *hated* the new lessons. They were horrible and confusing and at the end she always felt like she was about to explode. She was never quite sure whether she wanted to sex her uncle, or hurt him. *But that was the point*, he'd say: *she had to learn to control herself.*

She flinched, but otherwise held herself still as the cane struck again.

But kneeling on his bed in the horrid 'schoolgirl outfit,' with her hands tied, she heard his outer office door slowly open and then several pairs of feet quietly entering. They paused, then moved stealthily toward his bedroom. She craned her neck around to her uncle, her head frantically nodding toward the doorway.

The footsteps stopped just outside the door, then she heard a faint tap as something pressed against it.

"What do you hear?" her uncle asked.

She spat out the ball gag. "There's a whole bunch of people right outside!"

Before her uncle could react, the door leading to his bedroom burst open and men with guns poured in. Not just men: Jax was there, and those two cops who hated her: the fat one and the huge one. As well as three other men with guns. From the speed with which the huge one darted across the room to cover her and her uncle, she didn't even need to hear the ultrasonics of his cyborg muscles to know he was in full combat mode.

The fat one – the mage – was the one she'd have to deal with first, though. Mages were always the trickiest. But why was Jax here? And why did he have a gun? And why wouldn't he meet her eyes?

All six men were staring at her, then their gazes went to Uncle standing behind her with the cane.

Oh, no, this must look really bad for poor Keepie! She felt her face blush bright red. She wanted to slice through the ropes and explain, but it was already too late.

The huge cyborg spoke. "Detective Adam Garland, New Francisco metro police. I would advise you against resisting arrest, Dr Harmon."

She heard her uncle's in-drawn breath, and the sound as he fell back into the chair by his bedside. She saw one of the other men move to her left, to keep him covered.

Jax stood in the doorway, as if expecting them to run;

and then the fat cop, the mage, moved up to her and flipped open a small blade and began cutting her free. She got ready to make her move.

She heard her uncle gasp and straighten; heard him whisper, just for her: "Leeth, don't-"

The man to her left shot Keepie.

For a moment she froze, disbelieving. '*Leeth, don't-*'

Don't what? *Don't let them take me*, of course!

She heard his breath sigh out. She twisted in the fat cop's arms as he continued to cut the ropes around her knees. And saw her uncle on the floor.

Unmoving.

She felt her heart stop. *They'd* killed *Keepie!*

It only took a moment to break the mage's neck, and at the loud *crack* they all looked at her. Now what? *Oh! They'll have read the reports about the attacks, and Her!* Maybe she could *trick* them?

As the fat mage collapsed at her feet, she screamed, staring into the doorway and pointing to where Jax stood. She visualised *Her* there, sliding into the room, coiling around Jax. It wasn't hard to remember the fear she'd felt back in Godsson's cell. Still staring in terror at Jax in the doorway, she scrambled off the bed and to her left. Working her way closer to the man who'd killed her Keepie.

"Stop it, keep it away," she begged as she moved toward him, as if she thought he could protect her. He just stared from her, to the doorway, then back to her, confused.

Good.

One of the other police turned, gun aiming down at the floor as he scanned the doorway, trying to see whatever she was seeing, sidling around to put himself between her and Jax in the doorway, backing toward her to cover her.

Now.

"No!" she screamed out, staring in horror at Jax and throwing up her hands as if *he'd* just done something. The man angling back toward her got close enough: as fast and as hard as she could, she punched him *once, twice* in the kidneys, feeling things rupture.

Backing away from that man, now toppling in front of her, brought her to her next target: the man who'd killed Keepie. Feeling behind her, her hand made contact, and she clutched at his clothes as if in fear, pressing back against his front.

But the others were no longer fooled. She saw their guns already tracking toward her. Bracing her shoulders, her back still pressed up against the front of the man behind her, she *jumped*. Just a small jump, but she felt her head strike his chin as he now half-held her. Heard the *crack* from his neck.

The big cyborg fired, but she was already spinning around behind her latest sagging enemy, grabbing him around the stomach to take his weight as he slumped against her, using him as a shield. The other cop came too close – a cobra-fast throat punch took him out, from behind her human shield.

She had to take down the cyborg next. It was just him and Jax left. After Jax, she'd make Dr Simmons heal Keepie.

Something stung her shin, then another in the arm she had around the man she was holding up, and suddenly the room wavered into darkness.

She didn't even have time for a last thought.

CHAPTER 64

Detective Garland, watching at the rear of the gurney they'd handcuffed the girl to, saw her stir, saw her eyelids flutter.

Her lips moved. "Keep-y."

She blinked, her head falling to one side. Her pupils were dilated, and he saw her hunch forwards and her cheeks puff out as if she was about to heave. *She shouldn't be coming around yet!*

"Move it," Garland ordered the PI, Jackson Stark, as he lowered his end from the foot of the stairwell.

They'd entered the final length of corridor leading to the front doors. From outside, flashing lights splashed red and blue through the glass doors.

The girl seemed to recognize the ceiling above her, and he saw her wrists and ankles jerk against the metal cuffs.

Then she froze, her eyes going wide, and she lunged upwards, all four chains snapping taut. He heard metal groaning, saw one hand dragging impossibly up as the metal rod it was fastened to *bent*, the chain biting into her wrist – but he was already drawing his gun. She lunged sideways, spoiling his shot and forcing him to grab the trolley, fighting to stop it tipping all the way over. Stark cried out, going for his weapon.

Garland fired, but she twisted again, the trolley partly shielding her, and he heard the tranq *spang* against its metal. She cried out, the same weird thing – "Keepy" – as she tore at her unyielding metal bonds, trying to tug the trolley over her for protection, still wrenching at the cuffs. He saw a link start to part.

What the fuck?

Crouching down, aiming carefully, he shot again. This time it struck, and a second later she slumped unconscious again.

Stark began wrestling the gurney back upright, the dead weight of the girl making it difficult. "*Jesus!* I thought she was about to get free!"

Garland said nothing, just watched to make sure she wasn't playing possum. Finally, holstering his tranq pistol, he stepped up to the end of the gurney and flipped it upright, dragging the girl cuffed to it by her wrists and ankles back into view. She flopped limply.

"You said you put two darts into her, up there, Garland."

"I did, *Stark*."

"Jesus, look at her wrists. She's bleeding pretty badly."

"Yeah, well, she should've thought of that before she tried to snap the cuffs. Stupid bitch. There's a first-aid kit in the lock-up. We'll spray her with quick-seal." He motioned Stark forward and began pushing the trolley again. "What'd she mean by 'Keepy'? What's that?"

"I think that's what she sometimes called her uncle. Dr Harmon." Stark paced ahead and to one side, his own sleeper pistol now out and ready. He kept one eye on Sara as if he expected her to start lunging up again like a wild animal. "Oh. Shit: she thinks we *killed* him." Stark's eyes met Garland's. "*That's* why she went crazy. Back in his office, and again just now. You think that might be considered extenuating-?"

Detective Garland snorted. "I don't even know she's *human*. Who knows what kind of crazy shit goes on here? I still have her pegged as the perp for two killings a year ago at the Golden Gate Park, bugger what the DNA evidence says. I reckon her shithead Uncle altered the DNA magically. I'm gonna test her again."

He moved to the side, examining the chains on the cuffs. *Jesus.* One wrist was torn down to the bone, but she'd bent the cuff, and one of the links had indeed opened. He shook his head in disbelief. *Freak.*

He gestured Stark ahead. "You get the door. And keep your pistol out. Maybe next time we won't get a warning as she comes round." He frowned. She should've been out for another fifteen, thirty minutes, easy.

They reached the front doors and Jackson Stark, 'Private Investigator,' undercover as a mechatronics engineer, keyed them open. Stark again took the front of the trolley, lifting, while Garland took the back, muttering. "Extenuating circumstances? Jesus." He shook his head in disbelief. Stark must be an idiot.

Stark went first, backing carefully down the wide stone stairs in the evening light. One police van still waited, lights flashing: the other, carrying Harmon and the recently-healed members of Garland's team, already gone.

Two days earlier, Stark had found the drugs in the locked drawer in Harmon's office. They'd still been there tonight, Harmon's fingerprints all over the container.

Stark bet the blood tests would show they were both dosed up on them, too. Sara had been practically in heat. Remembering, he passed the evidence bag over to Garland, who took one quick, experienced look.

"Shit." Garland recognized them before his imaging unit had scanned and counted them. "Scope *and* Beep. Twenty seven doses. Dirty bastard."

At least Harmon had healed the two guys the girl had killed, before they'd locked him up and driven him off. Including Garland's partner, Berlusconi. *Who'd be mad as… oh,* fuck! "Stark."

Garland had frozen, staring now into the darkness past Stark to the front drive.

Behind Stark, a long, low growl rumbled, growing angrier by the moment. The next sound was one Stark had never wanted to hear again; *thought* he'd never hear again, after the Eco War down South: the soft hum then the *snick* of a rocket pod locking open in the Armed position. He winced. One of the two rocket pods he himself had checked and made certain was fully working, only days before.

It would blow both of them to smithereens. He heard a second soft hum and *snick,* and his eyes shut, briefly. Gently then, using his body to cover the movement, he pulled out his Colt Terminator .44.

Garland had carefully lowered the gurney, angled as it was still halfway down the steps, and slowly locked the brake on with one foot.

"Easy, boy, easy."

The growling deepened.

"That's a fucking cyborg dog, Stark. Why is there a fucking cyborg war dog aiming two mini-rockets at us?"

"That's Faith. An Asgard Model 3 CK9, with maximum weaponry fit-out. They have… a dangerous inmate here. And she's, ah, in good working order."

"Why is it aiming its rockets at us, Stark?"

"Because it loves Sara. Move closer to her: Faith is also a real smart dog. She won't fire if Sara's close to you. Oh. And she has lasers, too. Built into her optics. I wonder why she hasn't used them to take us out?"

Garland began moving his hand slowly toward the holster with his Nemesys Sleeper, but the dog's angry snarl stopped the movement. That, and the red dot of a laser sight on his hand. "I see what you mean."

As he moved his hand away from the holster the snarling settled back to the low growl.

"She can't understand us, though, can she?"

"She's still only a dog, Garland. Neural implants don't let her understand *language*. But... I think she does know some words, yeah."

Garland's voice suddenly got a lot friendlier. "That's a good girl, Faith. Good dog. Guarding Sara, yeah?" He continued in the same friendly tone, but catching Stark's eye he glanced at the man's weapon. Stark had drawn it carefully, and his body still shielded it from the war dog's view. "She's about six meters back from you, aren't you, girl," he continued in the same friendly tone, "and maybe two meters to your right. What would you rate your chance of taking her out with a head s.h.o.t, there's a good girl?"

Stark understood. "I'm an excellent s.h.o.t and very fast; but I'd say, only about a ten percent chance. She's that fast."

"Shit."

"What about you? Could you...?"

"If she'd let me draw my g.u.n, maybe."

Pounding footsteps came around the side of the building, Brian Shanahan scrambling to a sudden stop on the loose gravel.

Faith's growl rose again. There was another short hum and a heavier click from behind Stark. He recognized the sound; and saw Garland's expression sour further. "That's her rear machine-pistol. She can independently target that," Stark explained, helpfully.

Shanahan was staring in dismay. "Faith! Stand down, girl! What're you doing, lass?"

Faith just growled. And refused to stand down.

"I just love this fucking place," said Garland.

CHAPTER 65

This time when she came around, she was outside. Jax was talking to her. Softly, gently. Reassuring. She smiled, briefly, before she remembered how he'd betrayed her, betrayed Keepie- *Keepie!*

Then Jackson's words penetrated the mush in her brain. "Your Uncle is alive, Sara. Tranquilized. Sara, your Uncle is fine, he's not dead. Sara, your-"

Keepie was alive? Keepie was alive*!*

"But we have a little problem, Sara."

She heard Faith growling, and turned her head to see.

The small motion made the gorge rise in her throat, and she had to struggle not to throw up. Her head swam, her tongue felt thick, and she had an awful pain in her head. And wrists. They felt wet. Why were her wrists wet?

She was strapped to a trolley, angled down the front steps of the Institute, her pulse pounding in her head.

"Your Uncle is fine, Sara, he's not dead, just tranq-"

"Okay, I get it, I'm not stupid. Faith? What's the matter, girl?"

Faith's growling suddenly stopped. There was a short, hopeful whine.

"Yeah, I'm okay. Sorta." She turned her head, more slowly, and saw Faith at the edge of the dark. "Oh, wow! Your new rockets are so pretty! Oh! You've got a *machine pistol*, too. That is *so cool!* I didn't know you had a machine pistol."

From the top of the steps, Professor Sanders's voice came. "Sara, it appears that Faith objects to you being arrested. I need you to-"

She snorted. "Well, I guess you'd better not arrest me, then. Arrest me for what, anyway? I didn't do anything!"

The huge detective loomed forward slightly; Faith growled. He growled back. "You assaulted four police officers and killed two, and say you did nothing wrong?"

"You attacked *us* first! You shot K- You shot my uncle." Though she had, maybe, killed a few of *them*. And Jax said Keepie wasn't dead. Keepie was alive! The trouble was, her thoughts felt like they were struggling through molasses. *Why was it so hard to think? Oh. Yeah. Tranquilizers.* But Keepie was alive!

Professor Sanders was speaking again. "Sara. Faith can't get you free. She can't fire her rockets, or she'll kill you. And even if she uses her lasers to take us out, you'll still be cuffed to the gurney. There is also a stealth-chopper delivering a sniper to the area as we speak. She'll be here in perhaps ten minutes. I don't know where she will set up, but unless you convince your friend to stand down and disarm her weapons, I'm afraid Faith will be shot. And she is only acting out of misguided loyalty to you. We still need her here at the Institute. Don't make your friend sacrifice herself."

Leeth felt tears well up in her eyes. Could the Director be bluffing? But listening for it now, she could hear a *whuff-whuff-whuff* of some kind of silenced helicopter passing nearby. For a moment she saw a dark oval shape cross the night sky from the same direction.

"Where's Keep- Where's Uncle? Is he really all right? Let me see him."

Professor Sanders came down the front steps. Faith growled, and he stopped. "Your Uncle has been arrested, Sara. He's already been taken away."

"I don't understand! Everything had just gotten to be *perfect*!" She and Godsson had killed Her; Jax was real sexy; she was learning how to control herself; and then...

"Sara! Please. Faith is running out of time."

She heard the *whuffing-shushing* noise slow; stop.

"Let me free."

"Sara, we can't-"

"Faith won't believe me unless I'm free." It was true; she knew it instinctively. "I promise I won't hurt anyone." She felt suddenly tired. So tired. "Or try to escape."

She'd only been trying to do good.

"Please."

"Look, I saw what she did back inside," Garland began, but Professor Sanders interrupted him.

"She's not lying, Garland. I'll take full responsibility. Unlock her, and do it quickly. The sniper is moving into position. And Faith really is rather exceptional."

Leeth stared up at the huge cyborged cop, saw his frustrated anger. She looked him in the eye. "Please. I'm sorry. I thought you'd killed my uncle."

For several seconds he said nothing.

"And if Faith gets shot because you didn't unlock me in time, I swear I will *hunt you down and kill you.*"

Strangely, at that, he smiled. "Okay. That I believe."

"Quickly!"

"All right, all right!

"Faith," she called out. "It's okay. They're letting me free, see?"

Faith growled, then whined.

But Garland already had her ankles loose, and she started sliding sideways off the trolley.

A few seconds later, with her wrists free, she stumbled gracelessly down the steps and across the gravel to her best friend in the whole world. Faith prowled forward, stiff-legged, her rockets still aimed toward the steps and her rear gun tracking Mr Shanahan.

Then Leeth's arms went around her friend, and she collapsed next to her. "There, girl, stand down, Faith. Put your weapons away. I just need to go away for a while. You need to stay here, and keep... keep everything safe while I'm gone. I'll be back, I promise.

"Oh Faith, I *promise* I'll come back as soon as I can."

CHAPTER 66

Later that evening, Professor Sanders, acting on a strong intuition, entered the cafeteria. Sitting alone and hunched over a coffee cup, Brian Shanahan looked up with an eager expression of hope that faded the instant he saw who had come in.

"Not happy to see me, Brian?"

"No, it's not that, sir, it's just..." he gestured vaguely.

"You were hoping that a certain someone was going to surprise you one last time, eh?"

Shanahan looked embarrassed, but nodded. "Yeah. Dumb, huh?"

Poor fellow, thought Sanders. *In some ways he's been through the worst of the wringer. Never even knew he was being played. Used.* "And how is her faithful companion?"

"Jesus. You'd think she'd just had a litter of pups taken from her. She spends all her time sitting at the front gates, waiting for Sara to come back."

"And how about you, Brian? How do you feel?"

"Like shit. Sorry! Jesus... I don't know." Shanahan wrung his hands.

"This relates to her latest escapade, I take it? You were a little... sketchy on the details as to how she gained such complete access to your security system."

Shanahan looked up, startled; even blushing slightly.

"I'm sorry, Brian, I haven't been as forthcoming as you probably deserved. I do notice these things, you know. I'm rather good at it, in fact."

Shanahan stared at him as if the Professor had begun doing a striptease.

"I was ordered not to change the access codes on Godsson's cell, Brian, after this year's Solstice attack." He met his security officer's eyes squarely, waiting for him to process that information.

Shanahan gawped. "But that's insane. I mean, *Godsson!* Ordered? What do ye mean, *ordered*? Who gives *you* orders? Sir?"

Shanahan looked even more lost now than he had before the Director joined him.

"Here, give me your coffee."

Shanahan dazedly handed it over, a strange feeling growing as he watched the Director warm it briefly in the microwave, then top it up. Even through his daze, he noted the professor knew his preferred settings: when had the Director taken the time to learn *that?* Then at the drinks dispenser he used his privileges to add a very generous dash of Irish whiskey, before returning to the table and passing it back across to him.

"I think you'll need this," the Director offered.

Shanahan found himself shaking his head.

"Drink up," Sanders urged him, not unkindly. He even looked faintly embarrassed.

Shanahan took a deep gulp, preparing for bad news, feeling the coffee and whiskey burn as it went down. Despite himself, he relaxed. Braced for the worst, but somehow ready. "Go on. I'm already sitting down, after all."

Sanders's embarrassment appeared to deepen at the small attempt at humor.

"I'm afraid you've been rather set up, Brian. Quite a long time ago, actually. By a very... important person for the well-being of our country."

Shanahan just stared at him.

"Jackson Stark – he wasn't a private investigator I hired. And like you, I'm sorry to say he too was set up. For him, I was ordered to simply say I had become suspicious of Alex's relationship with his under-age ward, and ask him to investigate. The maintenance work was just his cover story. But I was ordered *not* to brief him properly. Then to stand back, as it were, and let things happen. Just as I was instructed not to have you change the passcode on Godsson's cell."

Shanahan took another large gulp of his Irish coffee. "But *why*, by all that's Holy? And who has the authority to take risks like that with *Godsson?* That's- that's beyond insane! It's bloody madness, is what it is!"

"Well, no. Faith's rocket-intervention that night pre-empted a sniper in the hills out the back. By approximately zero point three seconds, I was told."

Shanahan blinked, rapidly. "But- but even a sniper- those shields-"

Professor Sanders sighed. Reaching inside his jacket he withdrew a heavy black case from his pocket and from it took a strange metal projectile: as long as his hand, yet as slender as a drinking straw, with twists of gold, silver, and black coiling through it. It seemed to jump down onto the table, rather than fall. Nor did it bounce; or roll, despite the slight tilt of the table surface; but sat heavily in place. *Squatting.*

"Jesus! What's that?" Shanahan found himself instinctively drawing back from it.

"A special load for a Barrett AM16: a rather unique alloy with magic-piercing properties, I'm told. Each one of these rounds costs approximately 8,000 credits, apparently. This is a refinement of the design they had ready for d'Artelle just before she vanished. Though this one is far smaller, designed to stun through hydrostatic shock rather than fragment and kill. The plan was not to injure our patient so badly he could not have been healed."

Shanahan paled. "But... but even so, what about that damned *thing* that 'followed' him, that everyone said was the *real* threat?"

At that, even Sanders looked bemused. "Apparently, a key part of the whole exercise was the slender hope that Godsson and Sara together would deal with it, once and for all."

"But how could *anyone* know they would succeed in that? What kind of loonies made *that* decision? How did they even know it was possible *to* do that?"

Sanders's expression reflected the same surprise. "I asked the same question. He said he has access to unusual information sources; that it was an outcome he'd been *hoping* for. I rather gather, though, those hopes had not been high."

Shanahan breathed out, not exactly in disbelief. "And you say this feller is 'very important for our country'? Why? Who is he?"

"I'm sorry, Brian, that's Need To Know. But he did have a message he asked me to deliver especially to you."

"To *me?*"

"Yes. He said he is pleased with your role over the years – 'your contributions toward a successful outcome' – but would encourage you to be a little less trusting in future. But the key point he asked me to impress upon you was this: you are not to speak of Dr Harmon's and Sara's time here at the Institute to anyone, apart from myself – ever. He asked me to emphasize the 'ever'. Do you understand?"

Shanahan stared at the Director, stared down at the disturbingly-deadly looking round on the table between them, then gulped the last of his coffee.

"I reckon I do, Professor. By Jesus, I reckon I do. A bit of a long planner, is he, your boss? I reckon I wouldn't want to be working against *him*."

Director Sanders nodded emphatically. "Quite, Mr Shanahan. Quite."

For a while, then, they sat together in a surprisingly companionable silence; especially after Sanders picked up the disturbing munition and carefully put it away. "Oh, there's one other thing I wanted to mention, too."

Shanahan leaned back, wishing he hadn't finished his coffee already, and braced himself afresh.

"It's simply that with our major threat dealt with, the Institute is to return to its original purpose. More patients, more personnel. And because many of the victims will not be dangerous to others, there's even been talk of a companion-animal programme."

Shanahan blinked, looking suddenly hopeful.

"That's right. As well as some additional CK9 units for guard duties – and I rather hope Faith will prove able to pass on some of her unique training to a younger generation – there will also be other animals of a less-militarized nature brought in."

Sanders pretended not to notice the moisture that suddenly appeared in his security officer's eyes. "I'll run the plans past you. You may wish to have a hand in the selection and introduction of Faith's new 'pack,' eh?"

Sanders left the cafeteria. It was nice to be able to give someone some good news, for a change.

CHAPTER 67

Alex Harmon, and his ward, Sara, had never reached the metro police holding cells. Instead, each had been transferred to a more secure facility. Separately. At the order of the head of the Bureau for Internal Development.

'Eagle' had Harmon brought in first. The mage wore electronic goggles; his hands locked into rigid gloves. He would be casting no spells.

From the instruments built into his desk, Eagle noted the mage-psychologist's elevated heart rate and cortisol levels, despite the air of calm confidence he projected. The MEG readings only reinforced that assessment.

Eagle allowed the silence to grow.

Harmon forced himself to relax. Settling back as best he could against the straight-backed chair, he looked at his bound hands; then began counting the elements designed to induce tension and fear. His eyebrows raised slightly as the count steadily mounted, and he smiled into his interrogator's now-frowning face. *Just who were these people?* Every indication suggested government, but was that genuine, or a deception? "You're not the police," he said at last. "Yet you are able to command the police force."

There was no reply.

"I have not been charged, and my requests to see my ward have been denied. You do have Sara, I assume?"

Again, Eagle said nothing; although he did nod.

"So Sara and I may be of use to your organization," Harmon mused aloud. "Which means you don't really wish to bring criminal charges against her. Which, by extension, would make it awkward for you to bring charges against *me*, wouldn't it?" Harmon took the man's continuing silence as agreement. "So perhaps you should explain what this is all about?"

Eagle laced his fingers together and smiled. "Interesting reasoning, Doctor. Suppose I grant that our organization could allow certain murders to go unpunished; that your young killer would be an asset. But frankly, I don't see that I need *you*; and from what I've seen, your ward will be better off without you."

He leaned back in his chair, and watched Harmon's cortisol levels skyrocket. Wirelessly, he connected to Garland, who waited – impatient and furious, no doubt – in an adjacent room. *«Garland: bring the girl in. Thank you.»*

Behind Harmon, a door slid open. Half-turning in his chair, he heard a man's short curse, then running footsteps crossing the room.

"Keepie!" The impact almost knocked him from the chair. "You're really alive!"

Eagle ignored her. "Garland. Put the gun away. I have the situation under control. Please wait outside a little longer."

No one spoke as the heavy tread crossed the room, and the door slid open and shut once more.

"Take the seat beside your uncle, Sara."

"Who are *you?*"

"You may call me Eagle."

She sat down, turning to her uncle. Eagle noted Harmon's eyes dart down to the girl's unfettered legs, then nod fractionally to her. He suppressed a sigh. *Amateurs*, he thought.

Clearing his throat, he interrupted their silent communication. *These two would not appreciate subtlety.* "Have neither of you noticed the concealed laser cannons?"

A momentary silence.

Eagle inclined his head toward the vase of flowers on his desk. The briefest distortion in the air, the smell of ozone, and the flowers sizzled and collapsed into black ash that drifted down onto the desk.

The silence stretched out.

After a moment's tension, the two sank back into their chairs. Inwardly Eagle smiled. If any of his 'guests' over the years had realized that the enormously powerful laser was trained on that one spot only and *could not* be moved... then his error in judgment would indicate he was no longer fit for his position.

"I have some questions I wish to ask. Please do not attempt to lie or evade the truth – I have an impressive array of sensors at my disposal here, so I will know."

For Harmon, bound and constrained, the problem requiring solution was – who were these people? Presumably government, if 'Eagle' could order the detective around. Garland did not seem the type to be involved in anything more criminal than a drinking binge. He wished he could flip his senses to the Imaginal, but the damned eyepiece made that impossible.

"Let's start with some easy questions...."

To calibrate your equipment, Harmon thought.

"Your name," Eagle said, looking at Leeth, "is Sara, yes?"

"No," she said, lifting her chin defiantly.

Eagle glanced down casually at his desk. Frowned slightly. "Your proper name is Sara."

"No."

Eagle's words became slightly clipped. "Your given name is Sara."

"No." She shook her head. "It's Leeth," she said proudly.

Eagle looked down again, then regarded Harmon with a faintly accusing air.

Harmon shrugged. "If you have finished calibrating your instruments, perhaps we could proceed to the real questions. Why do you expect our co-operation?"

Eagle was surprised but pleased that Sara had been able to beat the equipment by lying about her own name – however she'd done it. That would be very useful, indeed. Perhaps this would work out as well as he'd hoped.

He shrugged. "If you prefer, I can have Detective Garland come back in and do as he has recommended? That will mean drug and abuse charges for you, Doctor, and of course the end of your career. For Sara, two charges of murder. Initially. By that I mean, two *in addition* to the two police your ward killed earlier this evening."

Harmon blanched. The girl, Eagle noted, smiled. He turned to her. "The two men are, of course, fully recovered."

Leeth looked surprised, then angry. She glared at him. "If there hadn't been six of-"

"Leeth!" Harmon interrupted, his visored face swinging to the girl.

Ahh, Eagle thought. That was better! So. It seemed his long, long patience was going to pay off. "You feel no remorse at the killings?"

For a moment she looked angry, but that gave way to what looked like genuine puzzlement.

"Huh?"

"Guilt for the murders. For taking human lives."

Leeth looked at Eagle blankly. "How *else* can you kill

people?"

Eagle snorted. Looked back to Harmon. "Well, Doctor. That *does* tell me a few things, doesn't it?" It looked as though, at last, wet operations could recommence for the 'Accounts Department.'

Eagle studied the girl. A *truly* conscienceless killer who was otherwise normal? Or merely a sociopath? If the latter, her applications would be more limited.

"What do you feel when you kill, Leeth?"

Leeth looked at him, slowly deciding he was genuinely interested. As she thought about it, a smile came to her face. "Proud, I guess."

Proud, Eagle mused.

"I'm a Hunter," she volunteered.

"Ahh." He thought for a moment. "Tell me, Leeth – how would you like to work for the government? Spying and such. How would you like me to make you a true Hunter of Men?" He wondered if either of the two – children of the modern age – knew whom he paraphrased. Probably not.

She thought about it briefly, then grinned. She looked at Harmon.

"I'm asking *you* Leeth." Her head snapped back to him. "What do *you* think?"

"I think that'd be *great!*"

Eagle allowed himself a smile. "So do I, Leeth, so do I."

They smiled at each other. *She really* is *quite charming*, he found himself thinking. Then blinked. For a second, the momentary lapse of concentration rankled, but then it gave him pause. He noted the way she leaned forward a little, the unconscious invitation in her body language. *Well, well, well.* Perhaps useful for other operations, too.

"One more thing, Leeth: what do you remember of your earlier life, before the Institute?"

She looked at him blankly. "I was always at the Institute."

Eagle looked at Harmon. *How very convenient*, he thought. *For us both.*

"I see. Well, I think that's all, for now. No doubt you would like to say farewell to your uncle?"

Her face froze, and she moved behind him, putting her

still-cuffed hands on his shoulder, and shook her head. "Nuh-uh. I'm not gonna work for you unless you take Keepie, too. I need him."

Eagle stared at the girl, but her amber-flecked eyes stared straight back into his, refusing to give an inch. Eagle concealed his smile. "Very well."

He turned back to Harmon. "Have you heard of the Bureau of Internal Development?"

"Ye-es. You're part of the FBI."

Eagle allowed himself a small smile. "That is indeed the impression we try to give the public: a small, innocuous part of a well-known larger agency. In fact the Bureau is an intelligence service, charged with nothing less than returning America to its position as the world's pre-eminent superpower."

Harmon blinked. "Challenging."

"Quite. And as low profile as the Bureau itself is, you will both be considerably lower profile. You will be inducted into a boutique agency concealed within the body of the Bureau itself – the Accounts Department."

"*Accounts?*" Harmon glanced at Leeth, but she merely looked intrigued. She clearly had no idea what an accountant did.

"Yes. While the general public is barely aware of the Bureau's existence, the same cannot be said of our international partners. Bluntly, the so-called Accounts Department undertakes surgically-precise dirty work. Entirely self-funded. No money trail to be uncovered by difficult questions from senate appropriations commissions. Its true purpose is not known even to the rest of the Bureau. Sara – perhaps I should say, Leeth – will be a definite asset, given her proclivities. The two of you will be given quarters here at the Department, in New Francisco. From now on, you will refer to your girl always as 'Leeth,' and she must always refer to you only as 'Doctor.' I am 'Eagle.' Consider yourselves probationary agents of the United States government."

"*Yes!*"

Leeth startled both men by leaping into the air, somersaulting, and landing on her feet. One fist punched up into the air.

"I'm gonna be a *super-spy!*"

She leaned forward, onto Eagle's desk. "Can I have a cyborg dog companion? Faith and me make a *great* team!"

Eagle looked at Harmon. Then back to Leeth. "No, Leeth, I have more subtle plans for your skill set. Besides, Faith is still needed at the Institute."

Another door opened and an armored drone gently buzzed into the room, to escort the two from the room, deeper inwards – Harmon in a daze, Leeth still exuberant, chattering excitedly.

Eagle turned away, gazing thoughtfully into the distance. He'd been right to maneuver those two together.

Now the second stage could begin.

AFTERWORD

And there we'll leave our characters until next time.

I hope you've enjoyed the start of Leeth's story, as much as I enjoyed writing it. If so, you may be pleased to know that the sequel, titled *Harsh Lessons*, is basically complete. I expect to publish it mid-2016.

If you enjoyed this, and would like to let others know that, please read on a little further while I rabbit on about 'the new publishing industry' and how you can help, if you wish. I think authors and readers could be on the cusp of a golden age, should they choose to take control....

PUBLISHING, 2015

Although my hopes are to the contrary, I rather suspect this book won't take the world by storm. So I think I can afford to offer to personally respond if you have questions or suggestions on my web site:

https://www.AToeInTheOceanOfBooks.com/

This book has been self-published, and I've decided to do something brave, or perhaps dopey: apart from doing what I can at a personal level, I'm basically leaving the marketing of the book to word of mouth. That means I'm leaving it up to you. If you liked it, please mention it – in conversation, or on Facebook, Instagram, Pinterest, Google+, Twitter... whatever you prefer. If you enjoyed it, that'd be a way to thank me which I'll much appreciate.

If you'd like a sneak peek of what's in store for Leeth, I've included an early chapter of the sequel, *Harsh Lessons*. How much more trouble can Leeth get into?

And please do tell people if you enjoyed this: I'm depending on you.

Thanks!

Eh? I didn't say anything about Publishing in 2015?

Surely.... Oh. I see. You're right. Okay. So, this book was self-published. In my view, the power of publication is in the process of being taken from the hands of the giant traditional publishing companies; also changing is the huge part that luck plays in finding a publisher's editor or Reader who shares the author's vision. Instead, I think all of that is being placed in the author's own hands.

The downside, however, is that the problem of discovering a new book in a genre you like has suddenly become harder; and the problem of separating the *good* books from the not-so-good, harder still. In the rapidly-evolving self-publishing 'industry,' much is written and much is theorized about how to solve these problems. Many gurus say you need lots of followers on Twitter, or that you must pay to have your book promoted to large groups of people; along with many other ideas.

My hope, though, is that the ideal solution may be quite straightforward, and lies in the hands of readers simply doing what comes naturally. If you like a book (this or any other), tell the people you think it might also appeal to. *Tweet* or *Like* it. I think that if you, the reader, does that, then truly good books will be discovered in exactly the measure they deserve.

I also think that taking this approach puts all the success of a book in the hands of just two groups, the *right* groups: readers, who decide both what they like *and* how much; and authors, who write the best books they can. No one else. No middle men, no advertisers, no outside arbiters of taste.

Oh. And reviews....

If you really want to go above and beyond, write a review. *https://www.goodreads.com/review/edit/28217372* is the link you'd use on Goodreads.

To the first 50 people who publish a substantive (say, 50 words or more) and honest review of *Wild Thing* – good or bad, I read them all – and the first 20 people to find a previously-undetected error in this book: email me at my address below to receive a free electronic copy of either the sequel when it's ready, or any of the earlier books, at your choice. I keep email addresses strictly private, and only use them to send the free ebook. (I also reserve the right to decide if something is a genuine error or my peculiar style!)

Without further ado, here's an early chapter of the *Wild Thing* sequel, which will be published in July 2016.

luke.kendall@gmail.com, Dec 2015. @LukeJKendall

Agent Emma Salt, her slim figure hugged by the white, zip-fastened cat-suit, followed the maze of underground corridors leading to the Department's private dojo and gymnasium. The new inductee would be there, having her first session with Paul Kawatsu. *A first session with Dojo in the dojo.* She shook her head. Why did Paul's unimaginative code name bother her so much? The wrongness of it was like an itch she couldn't quite reach. Maybe the *other* new inductee could tell her – he was a trained psychologist, Mother had said. She wondered what he'd be like. And the girl, too. Young, they'd said.

Gods! She was actually excited by the prospect of a new face. *I've been between missions too long.* She wished James were back. But a new face would do as well, for a while.

Of course, each person joined the Bureau with a clean slate and no obligation to discuss their past. *Thank god!* Although in practice – with sympathetic listeners who were sworn to secrecy – well, things came out in their own time. Meanwhile, though, there was the opportunity to penetrate a pleasant little mystery from whatever inadvertent clues were dropped.

Sometimes it wasn't hard, sometimes it was. Take Paul, for instance. With his Japanese background and knowledge of that country's criminal underground, it had suggested Yakuza membership – except for the lack of tattoos. The truth, in the end, had turned out to be stranger.

Of the new pair's history, she gathered even Father and Mother, the nominal Heads of the Department, knew little. Less, even, than Eagle normally passed along with one of his 'finds.' They'd told her the man, the girl's legal guardian, was a mage – *about time we had one again, too* – and a researcher in magical theory, which was impressive. He was to be called simply the Doctor. The girl's name was 'Leeth,' and apparently there was something strange about that, from the look Father and Mother had exchanged. Father had stressed her youth, and that she would receive special mental training from 'the Doctor' and intense martial arts training from Dojo. They'd also asked Emma to be friendly, but to avoid any philosophical discussions of the ethics of combat, or morals in general.

Emma considered those last points, recalling the look on Mother's face – she'd *not* been happy. Emma wasn't at all sure she herself liked the direction the clues were leading – martial arts training, immorality, and a strange name that suggested the word 'lethal.'

Most disquieting, though, were the final, casual instructions. "Oh, and in the interest of clear communication, use plain English with our new colleagues. We don't want to burden them with learning our technical jargon." *So they were disposables?* Perhaps that explained Mother's unhappiness. Perhaps.

Her mood lightened as she turned the corner into the final stretch of corridor, the overhead lighting tuned to match the leafy woodland scene displayed on the corridor walls. On her left, a swallow dipped low under a branch, reappearing on the wall to her right before disappearing in amongst the trees, heading deeper into the forest. Sometimes she wished she could step into that landscape and follow them. She sighed in appreciation. If they did have to spend so much of their time buried in these deep concrete corridors, at least the Department went to the trouble of brightening them up. She wondered what Checkbook had thought of the expense. No doubt Eagle had simply overridden his objections.

She was near the dojo now, and a thump from beyond the double swing doors recalled her own introduction to Paul's teaching techniques. She smiled wryly. It had been an ego-battering experience. She'd been glad James and Preacher had been there to share the suffering. Even Father had trained with Paul, bearing the punishment without complaint: the old man was tougher than you'd guess. She wondered how the new recruit would handle it, alone.

The sound of bare feet slapping the floor at a running pace met her as Emma reached the doors. Looking through the small perspex window into the room beyond, she was just in time to see a young woman's body arc gracefully into the air and land with a bone-jarring slam on the blue mats on the floor. Emma winced in sympathy, but watched with interest.

Paul, of course, looked completely fresh, and completely in control. The girl lay stunned, briefly, before rolling to one side and pushing herself up onto hands and knees, breathing hard.

"Never lose your temper," Paul admonished. "Head and heart must balance. When the animal dominates, judgment vanishes – strength undirected is easily deflected."

Ahh. They're at that *stage.* So 'Leeth' must have some degree of skill. And a temper, too, since this *was* her very first session.

The girl didn't respond, merely stayed on all fours, her sides heaving, drenched in sweat. Her hands were bunching up the material of the mat she crouched on. Emma frowned. From memory, that stuff was really quite tough, you couldn't-

The muscles of the girl's legs were subtly tightening, her weight shifting microscopically. Then she was up, flying toward Paul even as she spun into a flashing crescent kick. She was fast!

But Paul was ready, of course. Swaying aside, he pivoted then chopped down and back – a powerful elbow-strike into her side which the girl absorbed without a sound. Emma winced again, then more so as the girl landed hard, rolling, and struggled to come to her feet. She failed, clutching her side instead.

Emma replayed the engagement. *That had not been a very elegant attack.* She looked the girl over more carefully. Quite young, despite the womanly curves; and now huddled into herself, obviously in pain. Paul's blow must have been harder than it looked. Emma felt sorry for the girl as, head bowed, she rose clumsily to her feet, hugging herself to relieve the pain.

The tableau stretched out, neither person moving. And at last Emma realized something was wrong. Paul hadn't moved forward to assist her in any way: in fact, he kept his distance. Looking as if he expected another attack. And more than that: he seemed tense. Far more tense than she'd ever seen him.

The girl seemed to shrink slightly, a breath sobbing out. Still Paul didn't move – except for a minute rising and falling of his shoulders. *Wait – Paul's breathing hard?* Then Emma's eyes widened in surprise as the revelation hit her – the girl was trying to *lure him closer!*

What the devil was going on? This looked far too serious for a training session.

The girl seemed to realize her trap hadn't worked, slowly unwrapping her arms from her waist, raising her face to meet Paul's cold gaze. *He's angry.* And then she looked at the girl's face. *Quite pretty,* she started to think, just as it transformed into a mask of focused hatred.

Emma stood transfixed as the girl raised her hands before her in the Mantis position, and moved slowly toward Paul. *The Mantis position? Did she think this was some silly movie? Just who had trained her?*

Paul took a defensive posture. The girl, Leeth, moved determinedly closer. Emma watched, and saw that Paul had decided to let her try her attack, simply waiting.

Leeth feinted: Paul read it as such, counter-moved to take advantage of it, and parried the real strike that followed. Surprisingly, her blow nearly landed, *and* was forceful enough to jar Paul's counter strike off-line. And instead of moving away as his elbow hammered into her ribs, jolting her backwards with a gasp of expelled air, she turned in closer to lash out with her foot. Paul responded too fast for Emma to see properly, striking down at the leg, blocking another attack from a slashing arm and answering with a blow to the head before dancing back.

The sequence of attacks had been so fast they'd triggered Emma's own combat augmentations while she'd strained to follow the exchange.

The girl collapsed when her weight came down on the leg she'd just kicked with as she'd tried to follow him. Again, Emma winced. She saw Leeth press her hand, briefly, to her eye and cheek, where Dojo had struck. It'd turn into a *lovely* shiner, if she'd read it correctly. She frowned, though. There was something wrong here. Something wrong with the whole atmosphere. This should have been a simple sparring session, but instead it seemed like a serious fight.

Paul stared down at the girl – from a surprisingly-generous distance. In fact... *why* was Paul, of all people, standing so far back? Did he think she could *leap* at him from two meters away, on the ground? And though it was often hard to tell what he was really thinking, she sensed he was as mad as she'd ever seen him.

And cautious. He hadn't spared even a fraction of his attention to acknowledge her presence, outside the doors. Emma felt a shiver run through her.

What had the girl done? And something else, too. Emma herself had been on the receiving end of Paul's punishing blows, when things got hard and fast. And they *hurt*. Yet the girl had scarcely made a sound.

Paul was speaking again.

"I said you must not lose your temper. Yet you have. Very well. Now you must lose your *anger*. I cannot teach you if you will not think. And we are here so I may teach you."

The girl massaged feeling back into her left knee while he spoke. She didn't answer, though. Merely forced herself back to her feet. She looked tired, and hurt. But still angry, very angry.

Emma watched in disbelief as the girl moved in as the aggressor, *again*. Even Paul seemed surprised as he took the amateurish attack apart, this time with three perfectly-executed but intensely *painful* nerve strikes, Emma knew from experience. Apparently, Paul had decided to make a point.

Two lightning blows to the girl's radial nerves, briefly paralyzing both arms, and a powerful blow to her right leg's peroneal nerve, just above the knee. Emma saw the leg fail – but instead of collapsing, Leeth instantly shifted, somehow staying upright.

Still utterly silent, barely on her feet, and her head down. But not in submission, *that* much was obvious. Rather, so he couldn't see the look in her eyes.

In tones of disgust, he spoke again, words Emma had never heard him say.

"I cannot teach you. You refuse to learn." He pointed to the doors. "Go. You have failed."

The girl looked up, suddenly dismayed. She shook her head. Wordlessly. And then at last, spoke. "No!" Now, finally, at the point of tears.

Paul pointed to the doors, eyes never leaving the girl's face. Even now.

"No," she grated out, her jaw clenching tight. Her head went down slightly. Then she rolled it, very deliberately, from one side, to the other. Emma's eyes widened at the sound of the rippling crackle of muscles popping. Unbelievably, the girl flung herself through the air, attacking again.

For Paul, it was like being attacked by a whirlwind. One knee, and a second, smashed at his sides with astonishing force, barely deflectable; a palm strike simultaneously with an upward elbow blow, all while she was in mid-air. And the palm strike flowed into a hammer-blow from the following elbow. Twisting and bending just enough to parry the onslaught, as her hands crashed back down sooner than was possible, his eyes met Leeth's.

And there he read something strange. A look on her face as if she had something *more* in her arsenal, in reserve. Something which she held back.

As her feet touched the ground, relying on their contact to keep her upright and balanced, he swayed back, denying her that support, sliding around her. Efficiently, while positioning himself for his own attack.

They hammered at one another, then – Dojo, with minimal expenditure of energy; the girl, attacking with shocking speed and force. It continued far longer than Emma could believe, on and on; until finally the girl's head smashed back, Dojo's forearm a club, and Leeth flew from him unconscious, to the mats.

Emma watched, holding her breath.

Paul Kawatsu swayed, then folded forward, arms resting on thighs, his shoulders heaving as he sucked in breath after breath.

In a daze, Emma pushed through the swing doors. She stepped in and around Paul, who met her eyes. His blazed with anger – yet behind that, a strange delight. And the anger was not, she saw, at *Leeth*. He continued resting, his breathing now under control, and Emma waited. Finally, gathering his reserves, he stood, then crouched down and with an effort, lifted the girl.

Paul looked at Emma across the inert burden cradled in his arms. "You saw?"

"Yes, I saw." She shook her head. "I didn't understand, but I saw. How- what? What is she? Is she *augmented*?"

Paul shook his head. "No. Father and Mother say she is not. And it is so. She does not move in that way." He frowned. "I do not understand... all she did."

Emma opened the doors for him, and they moved off down the corridor, by unspoken agreement heading to the infirmary.

"What happens now?"

"I do not know. Her style is poor, but she is remarkably fast, and strong, and..." he grasped for the right word – "hard. She has great potential. But her spirit...." He grimaced.

"What do you mean? I thought she seemed *too* spirited, if anything. I couldn't believe *she* kept attacking *you*."

He shook his head. "We came very quickly to the barrier of her pride." He looked sideways at Emma. "Which is common. But there was more. It was as if she thought I attacked *her*. Her *self*, not her body. As if she thought I attacked her spirit."

They walked on in silence for a while.

"And that made a barrier to my teaching I could not penetrate."

"So what happens now?"

He shrugged slightly. "Something changed, at the end. She heard me. But though she had lost the fight, and she knew it, *still* she attacked. And despite her speed and ferocity, tired and injured as she was, her attacks were easy to counter. Except at the very end." He paused, clearly savoring the memory. "But in the field, or in battle, I fear for her. Were she wounded or outmatched, I think she would attack, ready to die foolishly rather than retreat, regroup and rethink." He shook his head again. "She needs much instruction."

He looked with distinct satisfaction down at Leeth then back to Emma, and nodded. "*Hai*, shame of failure will unlock this oyster." The delight returned to his expression. "This one, I will *teach*. I will speak to Father."

They walked on. "I do *not* wish to speak to her guardian."

Emma looked at the cold anger on his face; then down to the young, bruised girl in his arms. Bruises which in a way he had been *forced* to inflict.

An unpleasant shiver ran up her spine.

Dojo left Emma in the infirmary preparing the medical scanner, signaling to Father that he wished to report face to face. The carved wood-paneled door whisked aside at his approach.

"Dojo. How did the first training session go?" The man behind the desk sat with military correctness, brushing the holo-display out of existence with a curt gesture. Although in his fifties, he adhered to a sensible exercise regime. Blue eyes in an austere face focused alertly on him. Then narrowed, noting Dojo's sweat, and disheveled look.

"Ah, a little bit strange. She will be... a challenge to teach."

Father looked intrigued. "Why? She was extremely keen to be given martial arts training. What happened?"

"You informed her of my abilities in this area?"

Father frowned. "Yes. I stressed you were a true Master of the Art. Pre-eminent. She was, as I said, *very* keen for you to teach her. She literally bounced from the room, she was so eager." His voice hardened. "What *happened*, Dojo?"

"You warned me not to underestimate her." Dojo paused. "The warning was necessary. She is as dangerous as you say. And when I have finished teaching her...."

He bared his teeth, but in something darker than a smile, and for some reason Father felt the man was *warning* him. Dojo's gaze went distant, and hungry, as if a long-held promise lay now in reach. And his next words confirmed that.

"When I have finished teaching her, we may have the weapon we need against *him*."

Father blinked.

"But there is something... wrong with the girl," Dojo continued. "She may not be completely sane. She has some basic skill, and you told her what to expect. Yet still, *she* launched the first attack on *me*." Dojo shrugged. "Much spirit, not so much sense. And she is as fast as you said. Faster.

"So. At first she listened to my words, and improved. But soon grew frustrated when she could not penetrate my defenses. Her attacks became more determined. She lost her temper. I explained to her she should not. I showed her, anger was senseless. She regained control. From then until the end, she sought only to kill me. But at that end... it was *glorious*." Dojo's delight was palpable. "And what she did..." He shook his head. "She is wildly unpredictable. She controls her center of gravity. You understand? *Magic*. Finally, you bring me the student you promised."

"And Leeth herself?"

"She is now unconscious in the infirmary."

Father waited, but did not see the embarrassment he expected. "Yet you are not," he prodded.

Dojo, remembering the fleeting expression on the girl's face at the height of their battle, smiled. "Of course. Yet, she held something back."

Father looked surprised.

Dojo shrugged. "I do not know what, yet. But after I have taught her...."

His smile turned wolfish. "Today, it was as if I fought a wild animal. She did not reason, reacting purely on instinct. And I think maybe she is not a complete person – she cannot deal with failure, except by a direct attack on its source." The smile vanished. "As I said: maybe not so sane. She may be impossible to teach."

"Impossible? Or just very difficult?" Father asked. At Dojo's angled head, he continued. "An agent who can barely tolerate failure will be useful, you must agree. Stubbornness can be a desirable attribute."

For a while, both men thought, before Father spoke again. "Her training will not follow the same path you've used for your other students, will it?"

"Not so much."

"Very well. You and I both know that to master the Art, you must master yourself. You say she is incomplete? Complete her."

"Ah. So simple."

Father frowned, unaccustomed to sarcasm from the warrior. Then saw that the man's anger had returned.

"You said the mage, 'the Doctor,' had raised her. Her incompleteness is his work, then. Did he know what he did?"

Father's expression went a little cold. "He is a trained psychologist. Yes, I would say he knew what he was doing. I will review this incident with him, immediately." Father's eyes returned to Dojo. "Eagle says the Doctor has laid the groundwork for a most useful agent. He wants us to 'round her out.'

She is to become an assassin. She herself *wants* that."

Both men frowned at the implications. Dojo shook his head.

"You don't think she will make a good assassin?" Father asked.

"No," he responded without hesitation. "You will see when you review the session. Maybe she will be too good."

Father saw the hunger return to Dojo's expression. "But we can't let that long term goal ruin her *medium* term usefulness, Dojo. We need to be able to control her."

Dojo inclined his head. "Until we unleash her."

Both men shared a look, hoping Eagle knew what he was doing.